Salt Bride

LUCINDA BRANT BOOKS

— Alec Halsey Mysteries —

DEADLY ENGAGEMENT

DEADLY AFFAIR

DEADLY PERIL

ALEC HALSEY MYSTERIES: BOOKS 1–3

— Salt Hendon Books —

SALT BRIDE

SALT REDUX

SALT HENDON COLLECTION

—The Roxton Family Saga —

NOBLE SATYR

MIDNIGHT MARRIAGE

AUTUMN DUCHESS

DAIR DEVIL

PROUD MARY

SATYR'S SON

ETERNALLY YOURS

FOREVER REMAIN

Salt Bride

A GEORGIAN HISTORICAL ROMANCE

LUCINDA BRANT

A Sprigleaf Book
Published by Sprigleaf Pty Ltd

Salt Bride: A Georgian Historical Romance
Copyright © 2010 Lucinda Brant
All rights reserved
Editing: Martha Stites, Cathie Maud Cabot & Rob Van De Laak
Cover art and photography: Larry Rostant
Cover model: Amanda T.
Design: Sprigleaf

Typeset in Adobe Garamond Pro.

Also available in ebook, audiobook, and foreign language editions.

ISBN 978-0-9872430-0-3

10 9 8 7 6 5 4 3 2 1 (i) A/I

for

Andrea
&
Cathy

PROLOGUE

WILTSHIRE, ENGLAND, 1759

THE GIRL in the narrow wooden bed was in agony. Curled up in a ball, legs drawn up to her small breasts and thin arms wrapped tightly about her knees, her whole body shuddered with excruciating contractions. She had no idea if she had been in pain for five hours or twenty. Exhausted and bathed in sweat, her cotton nightshift with its little lace cuffs and pearl buttons had become twisted and tangled with the bed sheet. Both were soaked with blood.

In the brief moments of reprieve between each painful cramp, she whimpered for the hurt to go away. Her big blue eyes stared imploringly at her nurse, as if a simple kiss from this most treasured servant would make everything better again as it always had with a childhood bruise. But no matter how tenderly the girl's feverish forehead was bathed or soothing words of comfort offered, the contractions continued unabated, the intervals becoming shorter and shorter until the girl lost all sense of time and space.

Tears coursed down the nurse's sallow cheeks. She pressed the wet cloth to her own mouth. It was all she could do to stop herself sobbing uncontrollably at the sight of her beautiful, sweet-tempered child in such torment.

"Have the girl drink this and tomorrow she won't be troubled," she had been ordered.

Obediently, Jane drank the bitter-tasting draught, on reassur-

ance that the medicinal would ease the nausea and restore her
appetite. She had then thrust the tumbler back at her nurse, laughingly accusing her of poisoning her.

Poison.

Yes, Nurse had poisoned her beautiful girl. She knew that now
as she bathed Jane's tortured forehead free of sweat. She would
pray to God for forgiveness for the rest of her days for not
protecting her girl, for trusting her betters to do what was right
and proper when all along they had planned for this to happen.
But she had poisoned Jane unwittingly. The same could not be
said of the other two occupants of the darkened and airless
bedchamber, or the girl's absent, unforgiving father. He had
disowned his only child for losing her virginity to a noble seducer
who lasciviously planted his seed then discarded Jane like a used,
worthless thing.

Murderers all.

Nurse dared not look over her shoulder. But she knew the
man and woman were there, in the shadows, waiting. Jane's cries
and her ministrations to help ease the pain did not make her deaf
or blind. She knew why they were there, why they suffered the
stench and the ignoble sounds of suffering; why they could not
avert their eyes from the offending sight of the waif-like creature
with the translucent skin and distraught gaze who convulsed,
sweated, and bled before them. They had to satisfy their own eyes
that the murderous deed was done. How else could they inform
her heartless father that his wishes had been satisfactorily
fulfilled?

Nurse hated them. But she reserved her greatest hatred for the
noble seducer. It gave her the strength and single-minded purpose
to fight to keep her precious, ill-used girl alive. It did not stop her
jumping with fright when a firm hand pressed her shoulder.

"The physician will be here soon," Jacob Allenby assured her.
"The recent snow fall must have delayed him."

"Yes, sir," Nurse replied docilely, continuing to rinse out the
soiled cloth in the porcelain bowl on the side table.

"Physician? Good God, what use is a painmerchant?" scoffed
the female over Jacob Allenby's shoulder. She came out of the
shadows to warm herself by the fire in the grate, her carefully

painted face devoid of emotion. "It is evident my medicinal is working to everyone's satisfaction. A physician will only interfere."

The merchant rounded on her. "Forgive me for not trusting the word of an angel of death!"

"Pon rep, Allenby, how dramatic you are," she drawled, a soft white hand to the heat. "Anyone would think by the creature's moans she is at death's door. She isn't. Syrup of Artemisia hasn't killed anyone of my acquaintance—*yet*." She glanced at the bed in thought. "Of course my apothecary on the Strand advises that the required dose be taken immediately a female suspects she is with child, usually the first month her courses are overdue," she mused matter-of-factly. "That this dolt waited four months before confessing to the fruits of her wickedness necessitated I increase the dosage to compensate for her sly stupidity. After all, one must be absolutely certain the monster is expelled."

Jacob Allenby ground his teeth. "You're a cold-blooded feline, my lady."

"No. I am a pragmatist, true to the patrician blood that flows in my veins," she said conversationally, preening at her upswept hair, adorned with pearls and ribbons, in the dim light cast on the oval looking glass above the mantel. "Blood connection is prized above all else. Bastard offspring of indeterminate lineage have no place amongst our kind." She glanced at the reflection of the middle-aged merchant, whose frowning gaze remained fixed on the suffering girl in the narrow bed. "Nor does mawkish sentimentality. Why you agreed to take her off Sir Felix's hands, I shall never fathom."

"Sir Felix Despard is a spineless drunkard who should have kept a better eye on his only child or she would not now be suffering. As for my actions, they're not for you to fathom."

"Indeed? As a Bristol Blue Glass manufacturer, you could do worse than take as mistress a nobleman's quick tawdry rut. She is the offspring of a baronet, when all is said and done. Used. Discarded. But still very beautiful."

"You'd know all about quick tawdry ruts, my lady."

"You rival Mr. Garrick, to be sure. This unholy alliance we've formed is so diverting. La! I do believe it's the best night's entertainment I've had since—"

"—since you went down on all fours at one of his lordship's orgies?"

"Shall I show you my technique?" she teased, tickling the end of Jacob Allenby's snub nose with the pleated tip of her delicate gouache fan. She pouted. "Tiresome little merchant moralists must dream of rutting titled ladies. In your dreams is the only place you're accorded the opportunity of *entering* society."

"I pity your offspring, my lady," the merchant stated with undisguised loathing and put space between them.

The lady's hazel eyes went dead. She stared coolly over Nurse's shoulder at the girl in the bed, who continued to hug her knees tightly and whimper in pain. Just turned eighteen and with no prospect of future happiness. Good, her ladyship gloated, and recalled how the squire's beautiful daughter had captivated society on her first public engagement.

It had been at the Salt Hunt Ball, and the girl's extraordinary beauty, coupled with a refreshing natural modesty, caused a sensation amongst lords and ladies alike. Unsullied and brimming with naïve optimism, charming to all and sickeningly self-effacing, by the end of the evening she had received three proposals of marriage and two declarations of undying love. Embraced by Society, it was expected she would marry title and wealth.

That very night her ladyship had found *them* together in the summerhouse down by the lake: The handsome nobleman in all his splendid, wide-backed nakedness and this beautiful eager virgin with her tumble of waist-length hair the color of midnight. They were blissfully riding to heaven together, as if they were the only two in the Garden of Eden. It had enraged her, but what had crushed her dreams and broken her heart was spying the ancestral betrothal necklace of the Earls of Salt Hendon around the girl's white throat.

The tragic consequences of the lovers' unbridled lust could not have made her happier. But when she least expected it, in those rare moments when she permitted herself to smugly believe she had regained absolute control of the future, the image of those two heavenly lovers joined as one haunted her waking hours and turned her dreams to nightmares.

"You, sir, have no idea to what lengths this mother has gone to secure her son's future," she stated dully and retreated into the shadows just as the girl let out one last guttural moan which filled the quiet of the airless bedchamber. "For God's sake! How much more pathetic whining must I endure?" she growled, and threw her fan at the wallpaper in a temper. She slumped down on the horsehair sofa in a billow of blue velvet petticoats. "Allenby, have the wench examine her. She must've expelled the brat by now."

Nurse began to sob openly.

"I wish there'd been another way, my dear," Jacob Allenby apologized with real remorse. "You must understand that this is the best outcome for her, with the least pain."

He patted Nurse's shoulder and then he, too, retreated into the shadows.

Understand? Least pain? Nurse wanted to scream. How did any female recover from the loss of a child, be it from miscarriage, still-birth, or from having been taken away at birth? And Sir Felix would have had every right to take it away. Sent to an orphanage, it would never know its mother, never have a father. Best if the child was taken now, barely formed and unknowing, because giving birth to a bastard child was a sin, a stain for life. Her poor suffering darling Jane didn't deserve such ignominy.

"Please. Please, *please*, God. Please let my darling live," Nurse whispered and buried her face in the bedclothes, squeezing the cloth so tightly that her fingernails dug into the flesh of her palm and drew blood. "Please, no more pain. No more suffering."

And as if in answer to her prayers, an eerie stillness descended upon the bedchamber. The girl ceased to move and finally lay quiet amongst the down pillows in the middle of the narrow bed, the agony of the contractions abating and giving way to relief, emptiness and loss.

Jane blinked at the guttering candle on the side table, tears staining her cheeks, knowing that it was not just sweat from her painful exertions that bathed her exhausted body in cool wetness but blood, her blood, and the blood of her unborn child; life extinguished. Quiet sobbing made her turn her head. She touched Nurse's lace cap, which instantly brought the woman's tear-stained face up with a jerk. Her voice was barely a whisper.

"Silly. Don't cry. There's nothing to cry for now."

ONE

LONDON, ENGLAND, 1763

"TOM, DO I HAVE A DOWRY?" Jane asked her stepbrother, turning away from a window being hit hard with rain.

Tom Allenby glanced uneasily at his mother, who was pouring him out a second dish of Bohea tea. "Dowry? Of course you have a dowry, Jane."

Jane wasn't so sure. When her father disowned her four years ago, he cut her off without a penny.

"What is the amount?"

Tom blinked. His discomfort increased. "Amount?"

"Ten thousand pounds," Lady Despard stated, a sulky glance at her stepdaughter. Annoyance showed itself in the rough way she handled the slices of seedy cake onto small blue-and-white Worcester porcelain plates. "Though why Tom feels the need to provide you with a dowry when you're marrying the richest man in Wiltshire, I'll never fathom. To a moneybags nobleman, ten thousand is but a drop in the Bristol River."

"*Mamma*," Tom said in an under voice, close-shaven cheeks burning with color. "I believe I can spare Jane ten thousand when I am to inherit ten times that amount." He regarded his stepsister with a hesitant smile. "It's a fair dowry, isn't it, Jane?"

But Lady Despard was right. Ten thousand pounds wasn't much of a dowry to bring to a marriage with a nobleman who reportedly had an income of thirty thousand pounds a year. Yet

Jane hated to see her stepbrother miserable. Poor Tom. The terms of Jacob Allenby's will had disturbed his well-ordered world.

"Of course it's a fair dowry, Tom. It is more than fair, it is *very* generous," she answered kindly.

She retreated once more to the window with its view of London's bleak winter skies and gray buildings and wished for the sun to show itself, if but briefly, to melt the hard January frost. Tom could then take her riding about the Green Park. Somehow, she had to escape the confines of this unfamiliar townhouse crawling with nameless soft-footed servants.

But there was no escaping tomorrow. Tomorrow she was to be married. Tomorrow she would be made a countess. Tomorrow she became *respectable*.

Tom followed her across the drawing room to the window seat that overlooked busy Arlington Street and sat beside her.

"Listen, Jane," he said gruffly. "You needn't rush into this marriage just for my benefit. Attorneys for Uncle's estate said there is still time…"

"It's perfectly all right, Tom," Jane assured him with a soft smile. "The sooner I'm married the sooner you inherit what is rightfully yours and can get on with your life. You have factories to run and workers who are relying on you to pay their long overdue wages. It was wrong of Mr. Allenby to leave his manufacturing concerns and his estate to you without any monies for their upkeep. You shouldn't be forced to foreclose, or to sell your birthright. Those poor souls who make your blue glass need to be paid so they can feed their families. Should they be made destitute, all because your uncle willed his capital to me? You are his only male relative, and you have an obligation to those who now work for you. We know why your uncle made you assets rich but cash poor, why he left his capital to me—because he hoped to force a union between us."

"Why not? Why not marry me, Jane?"

"Because despite being my brother *in law*, you've been my little brother since I can remember, and that will never change," Jane explained kindly. "I love you as a sister loves a brother, and that is why I cannot marry you."

"But what of Uncle's will?" Tom asked lamely, not forcing the argument because he knew she was right.

"We have been over this with Mr. Allenby's attorneys," Jane answered patiently. "The will does not specifically mention that I must marry you, Tom, and so we are not obligated to do so. That was an oversight on your uncle's part. The attorneys say that I may marry *any man,* and the one hundred thousand pounds will then be released in your favor."

"Any man?" Tom gave a huff of embarrassed anger. "But you are not marrying just *any man,* Jane. You are marrying the Earl of Salt Hendon! I cannot allow you to make such a sacrifice. It is not right. Surely something can be worked out. We just need time."

"Time? It has now been *three* months since Mr. Allenby died and you cannot keep putting off your creditors. How much do you owe, Tom? How long do you think you can go on before you must sell assets to meet your debts?" Jane forced herself to smile brightly. "Besides, is it such a sacrifice to be elevated from squire's daughter to wife of the Earl of Salt Hendon? I shall be a countess!"

"Wife of a nobleman who is marrying you because he gave his word to your dying father and feels honor-bound to do so," Tom grumbled. "Not because he wants or loves you... Oh, Jane! Forgive me," he apologized just as quickly, realizing his offence. "You know I didn't mean—"

"Don't apologize for the truth, Tom. Yes, I am marrying a man who does not care two figs for me, but in doing so my conscience is clear."

"Well, if you won't marry me, then marriage to a titled lothario is better than you remaining unmarried," her stepbrother said in an abrupt about-face that widened Jane's blue eyes. "Only a husband's protection will fend off lecherous dogs. Living unmarried in a cottage on the estate was all well and good while Uncle Jacob was alive to protect you. But even he was powerless the one and only time you ventured beyond the park. You became fair game for every depraved scoundrel riding the Salt Hunt." Tom squeezed her hand. "Uncle showed more restraint than I. I'd have shot those lascivious swine as let them take you for a harlot."

That humiliating incident had occurred two years ago but the memory remained painfully raw for Jane. What Tom did not know was that the lascivious swine of which he spoke were in truth the Earl of Salt Hendon and his friends. On the edge of the copse, with her basket of field mushrooms over her arm and dangling her bonnet by its silk ribbons, she had not immediately recognized the Earl astride his favorite hunter, with a full beard and his light chestnut hair tumbled about his shoulders.

He had brought his mount right up to her and stared down into her upturned face with something akin to mute stupefaction. Then, much to the delight of his boon companions, he exacted a landlord's privilege for her trespass by dismounting, pulling her into a tight embrace and roughly kissing her full on the mouth. She had tried in vain to push him off but his arm about her waist was vise-like, and he continued to crush her mouth under his, violating her with his tongue; he tasting of spirits and pepper. When he finally came up for air, his brown eyes searched her shocked face as if expecting some sort of revelation. It was only when she slapped his face hard that the spell was broken, and he was brought to a sense of his surroundings. He released her with one vicious whispered word in her ear and a low mocking bow.

Even now, two years on, remembering how pitilessly he had whispered that hateful word, Jane shuddered and swallowed. He could very well have stabbed her in the heart, such was the hurt that came with that one word: *Harlot.*

She smiled resignedly at her stepbrother, all of one-and-twenty years of age and with so much responsibility resting on his thin young shoulders.

"But what else were they to think, Tom? I, an unmarried girl cast out of her father's house, living under the protection of an old widower, they could not take me for anything less than a harlot."

"No! No, you're *not*! *Never* say so!" he commanded, a glance across the room at his mother, who was pouring out more tea into her dish. "You made one tiny error of judgment, that's all," he continued. "For that you must suffer the consequences for the rest of your life? I say, a thousand times, *no.*"

"Dearest Tom. You've always been my stalwart defender, though I don't deserve such devotion," she said in a rallying tone. "You cannot dismiss what I did as a *tiny* error of judgment. After all, that error caused my father to disown me and brand me a whore." When Tom made an impatient gesture and looked away, she smiled reassuringly and touched his flushed cheek. "I cannot —*I do not*—hide from that. If your uncle had not taken me in when my own father disowned me, I would have ended up in a Bristol poorhouse, or worse, dead in a ditch. I will always be grateful to Mr. Allenby for giving me shelter."

"I'd have looked after you, Jane. *Always.*"

"Yes, Tom. Of course."

But they both knew the unspoken truth of that lie. Jane's father, Sir Felix Despard, would never have permitted Tom to interfere in a father's justifiable punishment of a disobedient and disgraced daughter. The loss of her virtue and its tragic consequences had bestowed upon Sir Felix the right to cast her out of the family home, alone, friendless, and destitute. Jane had disgraced not only her good name but also her family's honor. She did not blame her father for her disgrace, but Jane would never forgive him for what he had ordered done to her.

Regardless of what others thought of her, she still believed in upholding the moral principles of fairness, honesty and taking responsibility for her actions. The predicament she had found herself in had not been of her father's making, it had been hers and hers alone. But Tom would never understand. He had been spared the whole sordid story, for which she was grateful. Tom was an earnest young man who saw the good in everyone. Jane hoped he always would.

"You're the best of brothers, Tom," she said sincerely, and swiftly kissed his cheek.

But Tom did not feel he had earned such praise. He grabbed Jane's hand.

"If you had accepted any man but Lord Salt!" he said fiercely. "He always has this look on his face—hard to describe—as if someone has dared break wind under his noble nose. The way his nostrils quiver, I just want to burst out laughing. You may giggle, Jane, but God help me to keep a straight face if the rest of the Sinclair family have the same noble nostrils!"

The butler chose that moment to interrupt.

"What is it, Springer?" Jane asked politely, bringing her features under control.

"Lord Salt and Mr. Ellis, ma'am," the butler intoned.

Stepbrother and sister exchanged a wide-eyed stare, as if caught out by the very object of their gossiping.

"What? *He* is here *now?*" Lady Despard blurted out rudely, and before the butler could confirm that indeed the Earl of Salt Hendon and his freckle-faced secretary waited downstairs, added with a trill of breathless anticipation, "What a high treat for us all! Shall I order up more tea?"

Jane informed the butler in a perfectly controlled voice that he was to show his lordship and Mr. Ellis up at once, and to bring a fresh pot of tea and clean dishes. But no sooner had the door closed on the servant's back than she sank onto the window seat, as if her knees were unable to support her waif-like frame. She was deaf to her stepmother's entreaties that she go at once to the looking glass and there tidy her hair and straighten the square neckline of her bodice. And she was blind to her stepbrother's frown of concern, thinking that if she'd brought her needlework to the drawing room she could at least pretend occupation and never need look the nobleman in the eye.

Coming face-to-face with the Earl of Salt Hendon, Jane lost the facility of speech.

MAGNUS VERNON TEMPLESTOWE SINCLAIR, ninth Baron Trevelyan, eighth Viscount Lacey, and fifth Earl of Salt Hendon, strode into the drawing room on the butler's announcement and immediately filled the space with his presence. The papered walls and ornate plastered ceiling shrunk inwards, or so it seemed to Jane, accustomed to the Allenbys, who were all short and narrow-shouldered. The Earl was neither. He was dressed in what Jane presumed to be the height of London elegance: A Venetian blue frock coat with elaborate chinoiserie embroidery on tight cuffs and short skirts; an oyster silk waistcoat that cut away to a pair of thigh-tight black silk breeches, rolled over the knees and secured with diamond knee buckles; white clocked stockings encased muscular calves; and enormous diamond-encrusted buckles sat in the tongues of a pair of low-heeled black leather shoes. Lace at wrists and throat completed this magnificent toilette. Yet, neither ruffled lace or expertly-cut cloth could hide the well-exercised muscle in the strong legs, or the depth of chest and width of shoulder. But he did not dominate by size alone. There was purpose in his stride, and when he took a quick commanding glance about the room, the intensity in his brown eyes demanded that those who fell under his gaze pay attention or suffer the consequences of his displeasure.

Lady Despard, standing near the fireplace, brought him up short. She dropped into a low curtsy, giving his lordship a spectacular view of her deep cleavage. When the Earl tore his gaze from her overripe bosom, it was to turn and regard Jane with a disdainful glare. A look, hard to read, passed across the nobleman's square face, and then it was as if he suddenly realized he was being less than polite. He bowed slightly as Lady Despard rose up and with her son crossed the carpet to greet him.

Formal introductions gave Jane time to find her composure. She stood frozen, awed by the sheer physicality of the man, unable to bend her stiff knees into the desired respectful curtsy. She appeared calm enough, but inwardly she felt sick to her stomach and relieved at the same time. She was glad that he barely looked at her. When he did, it was with tacit disapproval, and as if to make certain she was paying attention. This expression stayed with him when he spoke a few words with Tom. Jane saw it in the clench of his strong jaw and the way in which his lips pressed together in a thin line, giving his classical features a hard, uncompromising edge. Yet, no amount of cold disdain could diminish the fact he was a ruggedly handsome man.

Tom managed only a few words with the Earl before his mother interrupted. She looked up expectantly at the nobleman from under her darkened lashes and endeavored to engage his interest with a run of small talk; her inanities about the inclement weather, particularly the unusual severity of the frosts for the start to the new year, receiving polite but monosyllabic replies. Jane frowned and was embarrassed by her stepmother's blatant flirting with this jaded nobleman, who was obviously accustomed to and thoroughly bored by the wiles of women who constantly threw themselves at him.

When he turned his powdered head and stared straight at her, as if he were well aware she was taking full measure of his person, Jane was so startled to be caught out that she felt the heat rush up into her white throat. The fire burned more brightly in her cheeks when he had the bad manners to look her over, starting at her thick black braids caught up in a silver net at her shoulders, lingering on her breasts covered by a plain muslin bodice, before traveling down the length of her petticoats to her matching silk slippers. When he frowned, as if she did not meet his expectations, Jane dared to put up her chin and stare back at him before turning to the window in dismissal.

Her gaze remained steadfastly to the driving rain, despite being aware that her stepmother was now droning on at the freckle-faced secretary, Mr. Ellis, whom Jane had failed to notice standing a few steps behind his noble employer, and who was now doing his best to be polite and interested in Lady Despard's London sightseeing forays. Then, close at her back, she heard Tom's eager response to the Earl's invitation to take part in a game of Royal Tennis, being held at his lordship's private court at his Grosvenor Square mansion the day after next. Tom said he would be honored to be included in his lordship's tournament.

His lordship's tournament indeed, thought Jane, when only a few minutes earlier Tom had been poking fun of his lordship's noble nostrils!

The Earl drawled something banal about hoping this Arlington Street address—usually occupied by his lordship when Parliamentary sittings continued on through the night—was proving satisfactory accommodation for Tom and his mother. Tom thanked his lordship for the use of his townhouse, saying that as soon as it could be arranged, he and his mother would let a suitable residence of their own for a month or two, to enjoy what London had to offer before returning to Bristol. The Earl told him to take his time. There was no immediate rush for them to vacate. And then the room fell silent.

The silence went on for so long that curiosity made Jane turn away from the window. Had there been a chair close by she would have sat upon it from shock. Tom had deserted her, settling with his mother and the secretary, his friend from Oxford days, in the far corner of the drawing room, to take tea and talk over old times. They had left Jane to face Lord Salt alone.

His lordship stared over her head and out the window.

"Miss Despard, it is customary to permit me to bow over your hand," he drawled, with just that touch of insolence required to bring immediate obedience.

But Jane was too much affected by his closeness and his earlier unfavorable appraisal to be bothered with the niceties of a formal introduction, and her hands remained firmly clasped in front of her. She told herself she was being obstinately bad-mannered, but, for the first time in years, she allowed emotion to rule her tongue and spoke her thoughts.

"I am fully sensible to the honor you do me, my lord," she answered in a clear voice, gaze riveted to the engraved silver buttons of his waistcoat. "But I am not ignorant of the fact it was forced upon you in a most ungentlemanly manner. It is a circumstance I bitterly regret and wish I could alter."

There was the smallest of pauses before Salt said in his insolent way, "You've had ample opportunity to release me from such a damnable circumstance. You merely had to refuse the honor. Still, there are some eighteen hours before the ceremony…"

This blunt speech did tilt Jane's chin to his face, blue eyes wide with astonishment. He was offering her the opportunity to give him an eleventh hour reprieve; indeed his very manner suggested he expected her to do so there and then. That she wanted to release him from his forced obligation with all her heart was momentarily forgotten with the wound to her feminine pride. That he did not even have the good manners to disguise his abhorrence for a match that was of her father's making, not hers, angered her into giving an impudent reply.

"You cannot imagine, my lord, that I leapt at your backhanded offer of marriage," she stated with as much coldness in her voice as she could muster. "Doubtless there are dozens of females eager to take their place at your side as Countess of Salt Hendon. I wholeheartedly wish you'd offered for one of these ladies, for then this horrid situation would never have presented itself."

"I am not in the habit of making life-altering decisions merely to oblige others," he replied coldly, gaze remaining fixed to the wet windowpane. "Yet... Knowing you for a fickle female with no heart and even less brain, who has the barefaced cheek to accept a *backhanded* offer of marriage, I should indeed have married the next fresh-faced virgin who presented herself for mounting."

Jane staggered back a pace, mind reeling and hand out to the heavy brocade curtains for support at such crude speech. "How... How *dare* you speak to me in such a repulsive manner!" she whispered indignantly, a fervent glance at her tea-drinking relatives at the far end of the room. "I am not one of your whores who you can—"

This brought his hard gaze down to her beautiful face. "Come now, Miss Despard," he said with bored indifference. "Your show of offended sensibilities insults my intelligence. It is a bit late in the day to exhibit virginal outrage." He watched her throat constrict, and when she turned her fine nose to the window, giving him a view of her lovely profile, he smiled crookedly. How well she played the part of indignant female! As if she were the injured party. "By the way, I don't waste conversation on whores."

"If you hope to unsettle me with your-your—by *that,* then you are vastly mistaken in my—in my—" She stopped herself and bit her full lower lip, for how could she say the word *character* when she had none?

He seemed to read her mind, for he said so softly that she could only just hear him, "You were wise not to say it. You lost what little character you possessed when you thumbed your nose at constancy and decency to take up with a conscienceless old merchant. But as you are your father's daughter, I am inclined to believe Sir Felix never taught you the meaning of such words. Thus I will own that the fault lies with me for being taken in by your beautiful face."

Jane bravely met his gaze, and seeing the loathing in his eyes, a painful knot formed in her chest, making it difficult for her to breathe. She did not understand what she had done to deserve such hatred. He spoke of her not being constant or decent, and yet if there was one thing she had been in those days, weeks, and months after the night in the summerhouse, it was constant. Nor did she understand why he had such an intense dislike for Jacob Allenby, the only person to offer her sanctuary. She knew there was no point defending her own character with this male colossus of unreasonableness, but there was no reason for him to besmirch her protector. She forced herself to remain outwardly calm.

"Your vast experience of the type may give you some latitude to speak to me as you would any whore of your acquaintance," she said in a steady voice. "But it does not give you leave to besmirch Mr. Allenby's unblemished character. I have never heard an unkind word spoken about him. And despite the difficult circumstances in which I lived under his roof, I never had cause to—"

Salt goggled at her, appalled. "I won't stand here and listen to you praise—"

"—*slap* his face!"

There was a moment's heavy silence, then the Earl let out such a bark of genuine laughter that he startled those taking tea to momentary silence.

"My dear Miss Despard, pride still smarting?"

"I have no idea to what you are referring, my lord."

"Don't you?" he asked curiously, the anger gone from his deep voice. "I'd wager my best Hunter you were sorely disappointed when your merchant protector intervened that day on the Hunt. Truth be told, you had no need to lash out as you did. I wasn't about to offer you a second helping of my vast experience."

"What a *dull, hollow existence* you must lead to hold to the memory of such a trifling incident. I assure you I had not recalled it until now."

His smile was sardonic. "It was to your dull, hollow existence I was referring, madam. Your hand hasn't been the only one to have slapped this noble cheek."

"What a comfort to know there are females who have spurned Wiltshire's libertine lord!"

"No. I never said that. Every other slap invited pursuit; yours, I'd no desire to satisfy. Easy game doesn't interest me. No, don't turn your face away," he commanded in a low voice, pinching her small chin between thumb and forefinger and forcing her to look up at him. "Do we go before parson tomorrow or not?"

To her shame and embarrassment, Jane felt hot tears sting her eyelids and she swallowed hard, unable to give him an immediate response. He had exposed the raw nerve of her life under Jacob

Allenby's protection by stating the painfully obvious. The old Bristol merchant had kept her fed and clothed, and in return, whenever he visited the little thatched cottage that nestled in a grove between the Sinclair lands and the Allenby estate, she was at his beck and call. If it hadn't been for Tom's supervised quarterly visits, her life would've been unbearable. And now this arrogant nobleman dared to sneer at her and expect release from an obligation he had given in good faith.

It humiliated her to think that on his deathbed, her estranged father had forced Lord Salt to honor a promise made to her years earlier. Her father had fulfilled his life's ambition in bringing about her marriage to this arrogant nobleman by means of blackmail, with no thought to her feelings in the matter or the mortification she would endure as wife of a reluctant husband. It humiliated her further that Jacob Allenby had written up a despicable will, leaving her no choice but to accept the Earl's offer of marriage or watch her stepbrother face financial ruin. And as much as she wanted to release Lord Salt from his forced obligation, as much as she wanted to tell him why she must accept his backhanded offer of marriage, she could not; it was with an aching heart and a halting voice that she gave the Earl the answer she knew he did not in the least want to hear.

"There are factors—circumstances—Yes, my lord, we will go before parson tomorrow."

"You surprise me," he said with an ugly pull to his mouth. "But what female could resist the lure of a coronet? Be good enough to hold out your left hand."

Listlessly, Jane did as she was told, and was rewarded by having an old gold filigreed band set with sapphires and diamonds slipped over her ring finger. She did not look at it, nor was she aware the band was too large for her slender finger until the Earl mentioned he would have the ring resized once they were married. She thought her mortification complete until she was ordered to sit on a ribbon back chair placed in the center of the Turkey rug by the fire. It was only then that she realized she was alone in the drawing room with the Earl and his unobtrusive secretary.

Tom and his mother had abandoned her.

TWO

"You will sit, Miss Despard."

It was a command Jane ignored.

"Very well. Let that be your last act of defiance," Salt replied coldly, taking a turn about the room, circling her as a lion does its prey. "Tomorrow, once you and I have been up before parson, spiritually and legally we become one. Make no mistake, Miss Despard, I am that one. As that one, you, as my wife, will act in accordance with what is in my best interests. Never forget: Wherever you go, whomever you see, however you conduct yourself, it is I that society sees, not you."

Jane understood. He was intent on making her realize how thoroughly undeserving she was of the social position to which he was reluctantly elevating her. And yet, what she was thinking was how much he had altered since they had danced at the Salt Hunt Ball four years ago. It had been her eighteenth birthday that day, and her first proper social engagement—her coming out as a young lady.

During the hunting season, and later the Salt Hunt Ball, indeed during the whole of that wonderful autumn month preceding her eighteenth birthday, he had been an entirely different being from the one standing before her now. She remembered that behind those thin uncompromising lips there were beautiful white teeth, and that he possessed an infectious, good-humored laugh that made his brown eyes crinkle at the corners. And then there was the summerhouse…

Instantly, she mentally pulled herself up.

It didn't do to let her thoughts wander to the summerhouse by the lake and what had occurred there. The summerhouse made her acutely aware of the consequences of her impulsive actions, and that only brought forth darker, more unspeakable memories, memories she tried desperately to suppress. Nurse had told her not to dwell, she must go forward, not look back. That was the last piece of advice Nurse had given her before her death. She missed her nurse terribly. She wished with all her heart she was with her today. She needed her strength and her no-nonsense approach to life. Go forward, don't look back, child! Looking forward meant accepting the Earl of Salt Hendon as he was now, not as he had been during that fateful autumn.

"I will take your silence as assent and not stubborn disobedience," he stated, circling her once more. "You are not unintelligent, and thus you will see that if you play your part in public, if you adhere to the strict upbringing you had as the daughter of a country squire, society will, given time, come to accept you not only as my wife, but as the new Countess of Salt Hendon. As Lady Salt, you will soon be invited everywhere. As for Polite Society's private opinion of you, that is of supreme indifference to me." He signaled impatiently for his secretary to step forward. "But how you conduct yourself as my wife is very important to me and to my family. To this end, I have had a document drawn up which sets out the rules governing how you will live as Lady Salt. Ellis will read it aloud and you, Miss Despard, will sign it as evidence of your understanding of how your life will be conducted from this day forward."

"This document, my lord," asked Jane with studious enquiry, but unable to hide a sardonic dimple in her left cheek, "does it state terms by which you will conduct yourself as my husband?"

The choking sound came from Mr. Arthur Ellis.

Salt's lip curled. "Don't take me for a fool, Miss Despard. You will listen to Ellis, and when he's done, put your signature—"

"Oh, this is all very unnecessary!" Jane complained with an impatient sigh, annoyed beyond endurance by such insufferable arrogance. She sat upon the chair. "You said yourself, my lord, that once we are married we become one, and that you are that one. Then what is the purpose of my signature to a document that you could very well sign in my stead? You have made it perfectly clear that I cannot do or say anything without your permission. Is there not some wording in the marriage vows about obeying? That should suffice, surely? Besides, if you've no thought for me, then spare one for your secretary, who, as anyone with eyes can see, is as uncomfortable with this wretched business as I am!"

For the second time that morning, Salt goggled at her. Not only that but he could not speak.

Mr. Ellis, despite Jane's accurate observation and wishes, thought it best to begin reading aloud before his lordship burst a blood vessel. He had seen his employer angry, he had seen him furious, but never had he seen him so angry that he was lost for words. In the three years he had been employed in the Earl's household no one, not servant, retainer, friend or family member, had ever spoken so frankly to his lordship.

Looking at Jane over the parchment in his trembling hands, it was as if it were only yesterday that he had first gazed upon his friend's beautiful stepsister, and fallen under the spell of her loveliness on the spot. And so it was with the hint of a smile that Arthur began to read, though the smile soon disappeared when his concentration returned to the written word.

He had not given much thought to the Earl's strictures at the time of their dictation, except that they seemed just and necessary for the self-preservation of a great and wealthy nobleman about to marry a young woman who had lived unmarried with an old Bristol Blue Glass manufacturer. Yet, taking another glance over the sheaf of papers at the girl who sat ram-rod straight, hands clasped lightly in her lap, he felt acute discomfort to be reading out what was nothing less than a sentence of life imprisonment. Albeit the prison was a magnificent sprawling Jacobean mansion in the heart of Wiltshire, but it was a prison nonetheless.

"...As to the dowry Miss Jane Katherine Despard brings to the marriage, a dowry bequeathed to her by Jacob Allenby of Allenby Park, Wiltshire and Bristol, Lord Salt refuses to accept a guinea of the ten thousand pounds," Arthur Ellis continued after a short pause to clear his throat of nervousness. "Further, Lord Salt instructs Miss Despard to bring to the marriage only those possessions that were hers at the time she was denied the protection of the house of her father, Sir Felix Despard, Squire of Despard Park, Wiltshire. Thus, everything that was gifted to her by Jacob Allenby: Clothes, jewelry, money, writing instruments, china, linen, furniture, servants, horses, equipage, in fact anything at all that was purchased with Jacob Allenby's coin, will not form any part of her dower. The said articles are to be discarded and disposed of before marriage.

"Upon marriage, Lord Salt forbids Lady Salt to live in London, to visit Bath or its environs, or to visit Bristol and its environs. Lord Salt directs Lady Salt to live year-round at his seat in Wiltshire, Salt Hall. Lady Salt will be confined to Salt Hall, and may take exercise only in the immediate parkland surrounding the Hall's main buildings. Lady Salt is not to venture beyond the lake or the gardens without the express written permission of her husband. Lady Salt is not to take it upon herself to visit any of Lord Salt's tenants, the vicar and his good wife, or visit the local village of Salt Hendon.

"Lady Salt has her husband's permission to do with her apartments at the Hall as she so pleases. Her apartments will consist of a bedchamber and six adjoining rooms, plus a room and closet for her personal maid. But the remainder of the one hundred and sixty-seven rooms are to be left as she finds them; so too, the grounds; so too, the summerhouse by the lake, a place within the parkland expressly forbidden her ladyship. Once a year, when his lordship opens his house for the Salt Hunt, Lady Salt will confine herself to her apartments and the small rose garden and courtyard thereto attached. From time to time, Lady Salt may have visitors to Salt Hall, but Lord Salt must approve them in writing before their intended stay. None by the name of Allenby may trespass on Lord Salt's lands. Furthermore and finally—"

"No!" Jane interrupted, up off the chair. "I will endure much, my lord, but *that* I will not tolerate! You may strip me of every material possession given to me by Mr. Allenby, though that is no great loss, but you cannot strip me of my memories. You can lock me away in your hideous house and dictate my movements, but as

I am quite used to my own company, that will be no great depriva-
tion. But you *will not* take from me the only family I have." She
sniffed back tears; it was a prosaic action, yet it caused the secretary to drop his gaze from her lovely face. "Tom is my brother,"
she continued in a calmer voice, turning her head to look at the
Earl, who had not moved from his position by the window. "You
may argue that he is my brother *in law* only, but he is the only
brother, the only close relative, who has cared anything for me
since the death of my mother when I was not quite a year old.
And he was the only relative to continue to own me after I left my
father's house. I love him dearly. I will not allow you to banish
him. He may visit me whenever he chooses or-or-or—"

"—or what, Miss Despard?" Salt drawled to the rain-spattered
window. "You will stamp your pretty foot and refuse to go through
with the wedding? Please, say the word…"

Jane stared at the broad back for a good ten seconds, and then
sat down again in defeat. She shut her eyes hard to stop the tears
and dropped her head, hands clasped tightly in her lap.

The secretary felt his stomach turn over.

Finally, the Earl turned his back on the clearing sky and
propped himself on the sill.

"I beg your pardon, Miss Despard," he said quietly. "At the
time the document was drawn up, I was unaware that Mr. Thomas
Wilson had been required to take the name of Allenby under the
terms of his uncle's will. Ellis will correct the document to read 'no
Allenby but Mr. Thomas Wilson Allenby, her ladyship's brother,
etc. and so forth'."

"Thank you, my lord," Jane replied, unconsciously twisting the
unfamiliar oversized betrothal ring and audibly sighing with relief.

The Earl inclined his powdered head and turned again to the
window, but not before his secretary saw the crooked smile that
twisted his mouth. "Ellis? Have you lost the facility of speech?
Pray continue. You're forgetting I have a prior engagement which
requires I be elsewhere within the half hour."

"Yes, my lord, of course," the secretary mumbled, and
coughed, for he had been glancing at the next and final paragraph
to be read aloud, and wished himself anywhere but in this drawing
room, standing before this lovely young woman. Jane's impas-

sioned interruption had broken his flow of words and as such would only highlight this next stipulation all the more. "Furthermore, when his lordship is in residence at Salt Hall, Lady Salt will not seek to question, interfere, or acknowledge her husband's domestic arrangements—"

"You mean to bring your lovers to Salt Hall."

The secretary paused, but as the sentence was a statement and not a question he continued, though he couldn't stop the flush to his freckled cheeks.

"—This in no way negates Lady Salt from her responsibilities as a dutiful and obedient wife. Should his lordship desire to avail himself of his—of his conjugal rights, his wife will oblige with mute servility. This document dated this day, and so forth, etc., etc."

Mr. Ellis noisily reshuffled the pages to hide his embarrassment, not a glance at either party, and quickly crossed to the small walnut escritoire in the far corner of the room, where it had been placed by the undraped window to catch the muted rays of sunlight of a cold January day. He picked up the inkpot, but had not flicked open the silver lid when he was directly addressed by Jane. Such was his surprise that he jumped and would have spilled ink down the front of his fine linen waistcoat with its polished horn buttons, but for the fact his thumb remained poised over the lip of the closed lid.

"Mr. Ellis?" Jane enquired with a frown of puzzlement, as she slowly rose to her feet but did not move away from the chair. "This document makes no mention of any children of the marriage."

"Children?" the secretary repeated thinly, voice breaking on the word, a swift telling glance at his employer who remained inert. Slowly, he replaced the inkpot on the desk and picked up the quill. "My lady, I-I—Ma'am—um—Miss Despard, there is—there is no-no such paragraph dealing with such an-an eventuality. No provision has been made for children of the marriage."

Jane's frown deepened, more so because of the note of nervous apology in the young man's voice. "Mr. Ellis, that document is most frank, and therefore so must I be when I tell you that it stands to reason if a husband exercises his conjugal—"

"Ellis, be so good as to wait a moment in the passage," Salt ordered, a rough jerk of his head at the door. He watched his secretary hastily rearrange the sheets of parchment and quill and ink before scurrying from the room with a short bow. "Poor Arthur. You have disconcerted him, Miss Despard."

Jane was frowning at the closed door, but she turned at this and regarded the Earl openly. "Yes, I must have. I am sorry, for he is a nice young man. But I don't see why he should be so coy when one must assume that if a husband and wife share a bed—"

"Miss Despard, I am unable to father a child."

This statement was greeted with such an expression of horrified disbelief that the Earl let out a deep laugh of genuine good humor, finally allowing Jane to see his lovely white smile.

"My dear Miss Despard! Priceless! The look on your lovely face is—*priceless.* Dear me! I must own I'm glad you're not a virgin. Only a woman familiar with the carnal delights of the bedchamber could so misinterpret such a statement. Accept my apologies for disconcerting you." He made her a bow, smile vanishing as quickly as it had appeared. "I am still very much a man, Miss Despard. What I should have said, to make myself perfectly plain, is that while I am more than capable of the act, the physicians tell me I am unable to beget a woman with child."

"How is that possible?"

Salt glanced up from drawing on his fine kid gloves and saw it was an earnest enquiry, and not one designed to unsettle him. He had to grudgingly admit he preferred her direct approach to the timid dissimulation used by most females.

"Years ago, I fell off a horse in full flight over a fence. I landed very hard and awkwardly on a particularly cherished part of my anatomy. It was excruciating. My—er—*ballocks* swelled to the size of apples, turned black and went hard. To say I was extremely worried for my manhood would be a gross understatement. I was advised by the learned physicians who attended on me that although the swelling and bruising would subside I had in all likelihood suffered some internal injury that would leave me barren. Since my recovery, I have had the hollow satisfaction of rutting with impunity. Not one of a string of mistresses has presented me with a bastard which would seem to confirm the physicians' learned opinion."

"Years ago? How many years ago?"

"Ten."

"*Ten* years ago?" Jane blanched. She reached out for the ladder back of the chair to steady herself. If he believed himself infertile then… He did not know he had impregnated her that night in the summerhouse… Her note had never reached him… He had not chosen to ignore her… He remained ignorant after all these years… But surely… So many questions and possibilities swirled about her mind that she felt herself sway and thought it prudent to sink back onto the chair. She looked up at him. "My lord, what you say is not possible."

Embarrassed by her acute disappointment to this news, and annoyed that he should feel a stab of inadequacy at not being able to provide this heartless jezebel with a brood of brats, he snapped back impatiently, "Miss Despard, it is not only very possible, it is fact. Now you will excuse me. My carriage will collect you tomorrow at eleven and convey you to my house in Grosvenor Square, where a private ceremony will be conducted without pomp and circumstance. And, God willing," he muttered to himself as he crossed the Turkey rug, "with very few persons in attendance to witness my humiliation."

A blank-faced footman opened the door for the Earl.

The sheaf of parchment on the little escritoire awaiting Jane's signature fluttered, but was ignored.

Jane forced herself up off the chair and scurried after him, determined to say something, but her thoughts were such a jumble of mixed emotions that she had no idea where to begin or what to tell him. She certainly couldn't bring herself to inform him there and then that the physicians who had advised him he was barren had got it wrong. He would not believe her without proof. Jacob Allenby's constant sermons about the wanton wicked ways of the nobility had her convinced that the Earl was not the sort of nobleman to concern himself with the fruits of his couplings, and she had been given no reason to disbelieve him. But here was the Earl telling her that he was infertile and had believed himself to be so for the past ten years! Why then had Jacob Allenby lied to her? How then was she to disabuse the Earl of his conviction? And when?

Jane did not know what to say, or how to tell the Earl that he was as fertile as the next man, without breaking down into a flood of tears for the loss she had suffered. So she kept her mouth shut. When the right time presented itself, she would confess all to him, but that time was not now.

At the door, the Earl hesitated, turned on a low heel, and almost collided with Jane, who was close at his back. She managed to pull herself up only inches from falling into his arms, which he had instinctively thrust out to stop her falling forward. They were so close that her petticoats crumpled against his long muscular legs and she caught a hint of his masculine cologne. It was such an evocative scent that she was gripped with a sudden frisson of desire, and was so shocked by it that she quickly stepped away and hung her head.

Salt gently tilted up her chin with one gloved finger, forcing her to look him in the eyes. Wordlessly, he searched her beautiful face, a knot between his brows. Her liquid blue eyes stared back at him with such frankness that he could almost deceive himself she was without guile. The pouty curve to her lovely lips was so rosebud red and made for kissing that he wanted to crush her mouth under his until they were bruised and numb.

Bruised and numb…

That's how he felt, how he had been feeling for so many years now that he was drained of hope. He wanted to blame her and the false promises of love and devotion he had tasted in her kisses. Beauty such as she possessed was utterly beguiling, and yet so wretchedly deceptive. He reviled everything about this young woman who was to become his wife and countess and yet there was no mistaking her inherent allure. She had captivated him four years ago, trapped him, made him lose his head, forget all that he had been taught about being a gentleman and what he owed his name, and made him cast caution to the four winds.

He had allowed his heart to rule his head.

In a single night of passion he had ruined a gently-bred girl of good family, destroyed his honor, and given Jacob Allenby the means by which to have his revenge on him. He hated himself for what he had done to Jane, but he reviled her for not having the strength of character to believe in him; to wait for him; to be constant and true. She had not waited. Worse, she had not kept secret their night of passion as she had promised, and was rightly disowned by her humiliated father. Even more appalling, she had run to the protection of Jacob Allenby, a man he loathed and despised, a reprobate who masqueraded as a moralizing windbag.

With the passage of time and countless lovers, he convinced himself he was cured of Miss Jane Despard. And then, two years ago, while on the hunt, he had come across her gathering mushrooms in a field scattered with awakening wildflowers. With a sickening thud of realization, he knew he had been fooling himself. He was *not* cured. He festered with guilt for ruining her and for still wanting her. He sank lower still by giving his word to her dying father that he would indeed honor the pledge made to her in the summerhouse on her eighteenth birthday, and marry her.

Marriage, if it did nothing but expunge the burden of guilt and restore his sense of honor, was worth the humiliation of friends and family. He could at least get on with his life with a clear conscience of righting a serious wrong. That he still wanted her, desperately, he could easily cure. He would make her his wife, bed her, and then banish her to his estate, lust and honor both satisfied. Yet, the gentleman in him made one last futile attempt to force her to realize what sort of union she was entering into.

"Miss Despard, you are a young woman with many child-bearing years ahead of you. With your face and figure, you could easily ensnare yourself a wealthy husband capable of giving you children. Release this barren earl from his obligation."

Jane curtsied, but kept her gaze lowered, because her eyes were brimming with hot tears of shame. Real regret sounded in her voice. "I am sorry to disoblige you, my lord, but I must marry you."

There was the briefest of silences, and then the Earl was gone, the door slamming so hard that Jane jumped and took an involuntary step back, fearing it had come off its hinges. Alone, she crumpled to the floor in a billowing balloon of petticoats and gave in to her disordered emotions.

THREE

"*UST?*" SALT REPEATED at the end of the landing, still frowning.

"I beg your pardon, my lord?"

Startled to receive a response, the Earl brought his gaze down from the far wall of the stairwell void to find his secretary squashed up against the mahogany balustrade, trying to be inconspicuous. Poor Arthur, reading that document aloud had taken it out of him. Still, Salt couldn't help teasing his secretary.

"Well, Ellis, what do you make of the lovely Miss Despard?"

But Arthur Ellis had been long enough in the Earl's employ not to be surprised by anything that was asked of him. "I have no thoughts about Miss Despard, my lord," he said blandly, as he followed his noble employer down the stairs to the entrance foyer.

Salt put out a hand to the butler for his sword and sash, gaze firmly fixed on his secretary. "Very good, Arthur. Now tell me what you think."

"Miss Despard is little altered since last we met."

"Meaning?"

"She presents to the world the same well-bred young lady now as four years ago, my lord."

The Earl was shrugged into his heavy greatcoat by the butler.

"You ignore her intervening history, perhaps?"

"No, my lord. But you asked for my thoughts."

"What else?"

"My lord?" said the secretary, stepping out of the way as the Earl adjusted his ornately sheathed sword before buttoning his greatcoat.

"Don't be obtuse. You have eyes. You're still smitten by her beauty. Admit to it!"

The secretary's mouth slackened and he felt the heat in his face, not only at the bald statement put to him, but also because he happened to glance at Springer just then, who was standing at the Earl's shoulder and thus out of his master's line of sight, to find the butler smirking from ear to ear. Still, the secretary managed to bravely meet his noble employer's unblinking stare.

"To be completely truthful, my lord, Miss Despard remains the most beautiful young woman I have ever had the privilege to gaze upon."

"Yes, isn't she," Salt snarled, and with such bitterness that Arthur Ellis audibly gulped, and with the butler took an involuntarily step away. "A word of warning: Never permit sublime beauty to lull you into a false judgment of character."

"Yes, my lord."

There followed an awkward silence as the two men awaited their noble employer's pleasure, but as his lordship was momentarily preoccupied with some frowning thought, the secretary took the brave step of moving time on. He coughed into his fist.

"If your lordship has no need of me this afternoon I will offer my services to Miss Despard, as you requested. The transfer of Miss Despard's belongings to Grosvenor Square and arrangements for tomorrow's ceremony…"

"Yes. Yes," Salt murmured, coming out of his abstraction. "Go and play lapdog to your heart's content." And snapped his head around at the butler. "Offer Mr. Ellis whatever he requires, and ensure Miss Despard's maid is given every assistance."

"I am at Mr. Ellis's service, my lord," Springer replied, adding with a note of apology, but with eyes agog in anticipation of the Earl's explosive response, "but unfortunately, I am unable to assist with the latter part of your request, as Miss Despard has come up to London—I beg your lordship's pardon to mention it, but Mrs. Springer is most insistent that such a remission be rectified—

without a maid." When the Earl continued to stare at him as if he were speaking an unknown foreign tongue, the butler continued, a little less confident than before. "Mrs. Springer being told by Lady Despard's maid, a haughty creature with an inflated sense of self-worth, that Miss Despard has never possessed a lady's maid, other than a nurse who, most regrettably, died some years ago of a complaint of the lung. It is a mystery to the members of this household how Miss Despard copes without the services of a lady's maid."

The Earl closed his eyes for the briefest of moments, as if the domestic arrangements of his household were all too much for him, then looked to the plastered ceiling before saying very quietly to his secretary, "I regret I must add to the burden of your secretarial duties, Arthur. Be good enough to put your head together with the Springers to employ a suitable lady's maid for Miss Despard, this female personage to be installed at Grosvenor Square by tomorrow morning at the latest. And Springer—"

"Yes, my lord?" the butler said cheerfully, thinking his sensible third daughter, Anne, who was very unhappy in her present situation in the house of Lady St. John, would do very nicely as lady-in-waiting to the future Countess of Salt Hendon. He couldn't wait to tell the good news to his wife.

"—be discreet, or you'll find yourself mucking out my stables."

With that withering statement, Salt stepped out into the hustle and bustle of Arlington Street. Carriages, sedan chairs, and horse and rider competed for space with pedestrians in heavy coats, muffs and hats, and the more adventurous and needy cart sellers, although there were few of the latter and even fewer pedestrians because of the intense cold. Instead of turning right to walk the short distance to St. James's Street, to spend a few hours of quiet solitude at White's, the Earl reluctantly went left and hailed a hackney chair to take him to Half Moon Street. Here he was set down at a particular townhouse, where resided Elizabeth, Lady Outram. A voluptuous blond widow on the other side of thirty, she had buried two elderly husbands in quick succession and was in search of a third. In the meantime, she catered to the Earl of Salt Hendon's strong carnal appetites, and in return enjoyed his benefaction.

In Salt's pocket was a short, scrawled missive from Elizabeth Outram, requesting his presence in her drawing room without delay. The matter was urgent and could not wait. The note had arrived just as he and his secretary had set out for his interview with Jane Despard, and thus he had had no time to write her a reply. But he was not in the habit of going at the beck and call of his mistresses, and if he had not had a prior engagement he would have made Elizabeth Outram await his pleasure.

Still, he could not put off the inevitable. She would be offended and sulky and stamp her foot at him for being a neglectful lover, but it wouldn't take him many minutes to bring her to heel, and they would end up in bed. Bedding Lizzie would be a welcome change from the long hours spent on parliamentary business, and the bitter realization that tomorrow he was to be married to a young woman with the face of an angel and the heart of a conniving whore, who didn't have the wit or will to employ a lady's maid!

Why had she used the word *must?*

It was such an inoffensive little word, and yet it burned itself into his brain the moment she'd uttered it. How dare she pretend it was she who was entering into this marriage under sufferance.

His lofty parents must be turning in their graves!

Salt barely had a large well-shod foot inside the drawing room of the Half Moon Street townhouse when Elizabeth, Lady Outram, flew off the silk-striped chaise longue and into his embrace. She wrapped her arms about his strong neck, pressed her voluptuous curves to his tall, hard torso, and looked up at him with a doleful expression. The Earl mentally sighed and readied himself for the inevitable feline tantrum.

But Elizabeth surprised him. She let him go, stepped back, and coolly offered him a glass of burgundy. Her initial overexuberance was replaced with a tightly controlled façade which left him puzzled. He took the glass and watched her pour out a burgundy for herself. She hesitated, mentally preparing herself. She had been forewarned by her good friend, the Earl's cousin Diana, Lady St. John, that the Earl intended to cast her aside.

It was Diana St. John who had first brought her to the attention of the Earl, and it was Diana St. John who now informed her that her year was up and it was time for Elizabeth to find herself a new benefactor. If she had no one in mind, Diana could point her in the right direction. As if she needed pointing in any man's direction! She had known from the first that the Earl of Salt Hendon never kept a mistress for more than twelve months, and even then they never had his complete devotion. She had made plans for her future long ago and had several casual lovers who would drop to kiss her feet if she said the word. But it had not taken many days into her affair with the Earl to realize that none of her attentive suitors would ever measure up to the lusty nobleman now standing in the middle of her cozy drawing room.

She counted the Earl her most attractive and accomplished lover, and she would sorely miss their lovemaking. It rankled that she had not managed to outlast the tenure of his previous mistresses. She had boasted to Diana and others that she would easily keep Salt's interest for two, perhaps three years at least. When Diana's letter had arrived only last week, she had suffered a great blow to her self-esteem. She couldn't believe the Earl was finished with her and she aimed to prove it to Diana St. John, whatever her friend's warning about not making a fuss.

But there was another, more disturbing piece of news that, if true, would signal the death knell to their affair: The Earl of Salt Hendon was about to marry a young beautiful girl from the counties. Elizabeth knew she could not compete with such a winning combination as youth and beauty. It would explain his neglect of her over the past couple of months and why, even when he did bed her, he was distracted and detached.

She followed him to the fireplace, where he stood warming his hands, and placed her wine glass on the mantel, allowing her dressing gown to slide off one shoulder to expose a quantity of rounded breast, as if it were the most natural accident in the world. She made no attempt to cover herself and smiled with practiced coyness when the Earl's eyes strayed from her painted face.

She removed the half-empty glass from his hand and set it next to her own.

"You've neglected me these past few months, my lord," she purred, a glance up at him under her darkened lashes as she pretended to adjust her dressing gown, but allowing it to slip further off her shoulders to the floor, so that she stood before him in only corset and white stockings. "Do you not think I am owed an explanation for your blatant inattention?"

From habit he drew her to him.

"Neglect, Lizzie?" he murmured, unlacing her tight silk corset with practiced ease. "I should hate to think you've been neglected in my absence."

She ignored the veiled reference to her casual lovers and made a halfhearted attempt to squirm out of his embrace. But more than anything, she wanted him to make love to her. It would be a welcome change from the overeager lovemaking of Pascoe, Lord Church, and the inexpert fondling of Pascoe's penniless cousin Billy Church, whose worth resided in the fact he was the boon companion of the Earl's officious secretary. Billy was only too willing to share confidences about his friend's employer when roused to the point of no return by Elizabeth's expert tutelage.

When Salt pulled her corset free and dropped it to the floor, leaving her in all her glory, she gasped in a little breathless whisper, "Why, my lord, have a care! Do you forget we are in a drawing room? Someone might enter at any moment!"

"That someone being me," he quipped.

She tittered and melted against him at the thought of him deep inside her as he bent to kiss her throat, but wanting him to kiss her mouth, knowing he never would. Of all the places he had kissed and pleasured her, he had never kissed her mouth. Not that it disturbed her greatly. In all other respects his skill as a lover and the sheer size of him more than satisfied her. Yet, if he would just kiss her mouth, she knew he was hers and hers alone. She went for the buttons of his breeches, but he caught up her hands and put them behind her back as he stooped to kiss her breasts. She was taken aback by his ardency at this the beginning of their lovemaking. There was a hunger about him, as if he'd gone without a woman for some time, his want as great as that of a thirsty man in need of water. It thrilled her to think she had aroused this urgent craving in him, and she couldn't wait to impart this newfound power to her friend Diana St. John.

But her triumph was short-lived. Just as quickly as the spark was ignited, it was extinguished. The Earl pulled himself free of her embrace and set her aside. And when he blinked down at her as if she was a stranger, flushed and short of breath, Elizabeth was shrewd enough to realize that it was not she who had brought out the carnal urgency in him but the creature who occupied his thoughts when aroused. How right she was.

The moment he'd closed his eyes on Elizabeth Outram, into his mind's eye appeared a pale, ethereal beauty with big, questioning blue eyes that looked up at him with disconcerting frankness, and whose rosebud mouth invited plunder. That he wanted desperately to make love to this ethereal being was not in question. That she was none other than his future wife, whose mere apparition possessed the ability to affect his manhood, made him seriously question his virility.

Disgusted with himself, he quickly turned away and adjusted his clothing.

Unsatisfied, and her self-esteem in shreds, Elizabeth angrily scooped up her discarded dressing gown and made a drama of covering her nakedness, despite the Earl having his back to her.

"After a twelvemonth of my hospitality, I believe I have earned the right to know something of your plans, my lord."

"Have you?" he answered indifferently. "My plans I leave to my long-suffering secretary."

"And your letters to discarded mistresses?" she asked bitterly. "Do they require a woman's touch and so are left to be penned by Lady St. John?"

"Lady St. John? What are you blabbering on about, Lizzie?" Salt asked gruffly and turned to face her. "What letters?"

Elizabeth rummaged in a drawer of the mahogany bureau by the window, found the letter she was looking for, and presented it to the Earl with a flourish and a questioning lift of her perfectly plucked eyebrows. "My twelvemonth notice. Like your previous interests, Sarah Walpole and Maria Leveson-Gower, just to name the two ladies known to me personally. Lady St. John has provided us all with our notices to vacate."

Scowling, Salt opened out the single sheet of parchment with two fingers, stared at the familiar sloping handwriting, turned it over to inspect the broken seal, then folded it. "May I have this?"

Elizabeth shrugged a shoulder. "By all means. Is it news to you?"

When he did not respond but finished off his glass of burgundy, Elizabeth had her answer.

"Is selecting the Earl of Salt Hendon's Countess also part of Lady St. John's cousinly duties?"

He lowered the wine glass. "Such tedious details are of concern to no one but myself, my dear."

The edge to his voice made her wary, but she could not help herself. "So Diana doesn't know. Good. If she did, she'd not have been able to resist gloating the news to me. It's a secret, is it?"

"A word of advice, Lizzie. You are far more beautiful when you're not ruminating."

But Elizabeth wasn't listening. She was taking comfort in the fact that her friend had been kept in ignorance, and that she would suffer certain devastation when the news finally reached her that the Earl, the great infatuation of Diana's life, had secretly wed another. She hoped she was there to witness Diana's downfall. The great Lady St. John needed pulling down a rung or two, such was her smugness at being the mother of the Earl's heir and his closest female relative.

"I never thought you would marry," she confessed truthfully.

"Nor did I," he remarked, as he shrugged on his frock coat.

She rushed over to him then and threw her arms around his neck. "If it's a marriage of convenience," she asked hopefully, "then surely we need not end our liaison?"

He removed her hands and turned to the looking glass to adjust the folds of his cravat. "I apologize for Lady St. John's letter. It was not her place to bring our enjoyable connection to an end. But her letter coincidentally arrived at a most opportune moment."

Elizabeth pouted. "So you're going to let her get away with it?"

"I have enjoyed our times together, Lizzie," he replied smoothly.

That he used the past tense was not lost on her, and she tossed her blond curls with a huff. "Your little country bride will bore you within a week of marriage!" When this had no effect on him, she sighed tragically, a finger outlining the pattern of an embroidered flower on his waistcoat as he continued to fiddle with his cravat. She tried to cajole him. "In gaining a wife surely you need not forfeit your visits here…"

She made one last attempt to rekindle his interest, going up on tiptoe to kiss his mouth, her naked body under the thin silk dressing gown pressed against him, hand cupping his sizeable manhood. But he quickly turned his head away before her mouth touched his, removed her hand and put her away from him.

"My dear, may I suggest you give the latch key to Pascoe, the only Church I've ever come across who actively promotes promiscuity and vice in all its forms."

Elizabeth put up her nose and spoke as if she had no idea to what the Earl was alluding. "Lord Church? What is he to me? I have so many, many admirers."

At the door, Salt bowed to her with excessive politeness. "Ah. And I thought you had an eye to the main chance."

"DAMN HER!" SALT MUTTERED, thoughts still consumed with Jane's declaration that she must marry him. As soon as he returned home he would have his secretary get his hands on a copy of Jacob Allenby's will. He didn't put it past that merchant hellhound to add some odd codicil to his will, all to inflict a final humiliating revenge with his last dying breath.

Absently, he pressed his gloves on a blank-faced footman standing in the vestibule of his club in St. James's Street. He then presented his back to another to help him out of his heavy great coat, oblivious to the group of noblemen who had all turned to look at him on his muttered oath.

"You may damn as many females as you please, Salt," drawled a smooth-tongued, perfumed and beribboned nobleman up to his ear. This confection of lace and velvet regarded the Earl with quizzing glass plastered up to one eye and a bejeweled white hand holding aloft an enamel and gold snuffbox, and added with a snicker, "But we'll be damned if you're going to get leg-shackled without the commiserations of friends by your side."

Salt came out of his abstraction and eyed Pascoe, Lord

Church, with resentment, nodded to a group of bewigged nobles being divested of swords by attentive blank-faced footmen, and strode through a number of noisy card rooms to the sanctuary of the reading room. Here he took refuge in a comfortable wingback chair in the farthest corner and spread wide a copy of the *London Gazette*; indication enough he wished to be left alone. But Pascoe Church and Hilary Wraxton Esq. did not take the hint, and soon Salt found himself being scrutinized over the top of his newssheet by their powdered heads. He sighed, kept his eyes on the newsprint, and made no effort to offer the two gentlemen the vacant seats opposite.

"There's a rumor that you're getting married tomorrow," said Pascoe Church, and flicked a speck of snuff from his embroidered cuff, although his attention was firmly on the Earl's profile. "It says a great deal about our friendship when your nearest and dearest know less than the hired help! One would think you wanted such a momentous day to pass unnoticed."

"Yes, one would think that," Salt stated and turned over a page.

"Now we know, got to invite us! Don't he, Pascoe?" Hilary Wraxton assured the Earl with a confiding smile. "Got to be surrounded by friends and family. What!"

"Most certainly," agreed Pascoe Church, nonchalantly dangling his quizzing glass by its black riband. "But perhaps our dear friend has his reasons for not wanting his friends in attendance?"

Hilary Wraxton blew out his cheeks. "Reason? What reason? Not every day a man takes the great plunge, except Pascoe with your sister. Said next Sinclair to walk the matrimonial plank would be Lady Caroline. But if Salt wants to tie the knot before his sister, then so be it."

At this revelation Salt glanced up at Pascoe Church, a faint rise to his eyebrows.

"The Lady Caroline, walk the plank?" Lord Church said with a light laugh, clearly flustered and fighting hard to keep his cool façade under the Earl's haughty gaze. He tossed off the quizzing glass so that it fell against his silken chest with a thud. "I have no idea where you get such notions, Hilary."

"From you," Hilary Wraxton replied simply. "Last week, when sitting down to whist with Walpole, you said you'd almost got up the courage to approach Salt about—"

"*Courage?*" Pascoe Church snorted. "My dear Hilary, when the time comes for me to approach our dear friend here—"

"You are destined for disappointment," Salt interrupted softly, returning to peruse the newssheet.

Hilary Wraxton sighed deeply. "Guess that settles it, Pascoe. The Lady Caroline ain't walking any planks, matrimonial or otherwise, with *you*. When Salt says you'll be disappointed, you're bound to be."

"It settles nothing," Pascoe Church hissed in Hilary's ear, and to return the sting of his disappointment at being rejected as a suitable husband for the Lady Caroline Sinclair, said petulantly to the Earl, "Just so you are aware, Salt, the rumor in drawing rooms—"

"I can hazard a guess which drawing room," Salt interrupted dryly, with the flicker of a smile.

"Can you?" Hilary Wraxton asked in surprise, and viewed Pascoe Church through his quizzing glass with one hideously magnified eye. "But you said Salt hadn't the foggiest notion about your frolicking forays with Luscious Lizzie. You said—"

"Never mind that now!" Pascoe Church demanded, and tried to regain his composure and the cool venom to his voice. "This rumor, Salt, says that you're keen for a quiet wedding because the bride is either plain-faced and pudding-shaped with a pedigree worth a gilt frame, or—and this will amuse you greatly—the beautiful daughter of a drunkard merchant with upwards of a hundred thousand pounds to add to your coffers."

"But Salt don't need the blunt, Pascoe."

"What say you to that, Salt?" persisted Pascoe Church, ignoring his friend. "I'll hazard it's the latter. What a pity her great beauty and wealth will never be adequate perfume for the foul odor of trade that must forever linger about her person."

"And all the pudding-shaped heiresses are taken," added Hilary Wraxton with a firm nod.

"God help us when the divine Diana finds out," Pascoe

Church added with a sigh, for good spiteful measure. "What a social plummet for the House of Sinclair!"

"God help us indeed, Pas," agreed Hilary Wraxton with a sad shake of his powdered wig.

"God help you both if you don't scuttle off under the floor-boards from whence you came!" Salt growled as he shot up out of his chair to tower over the two men, and with such a look of suppressed fury that it did not need his hand about Pascoe Church's beautifully arranged cravat for that gentleman's throat to constrict alarmingly. But no sooner was Salt on his feet than he regretted his action, and was immediately angry with himself for allowing his sister's rejected suitor and his moronic comrade to prod the raw nerve of his upcoming marriage.

For want of something to cover the awkward moment, Hilary Wraxton made an elaborate display of checking the hour with his gold pocket watch before pronouncing that he was extremely late for an appointment with his wigmaker. Pascoe Church added that he too was needed elsewhere, although he did not offer up a name or direction. Salt wasn't sorry to see them depart, and watched the two noblemen waddle off in their high heels, huddled together as if in need of mutual propping up. And he was under no illusions about the thin-shouldered nobleman's ability to be vexatious. Pascoe, Lord Church, might have turned frigid with fright and lost his breath at Salt's angry outburst, but once recovered and at a safe distance, he would use his waspish tongue to good effect to ensure Polite Society was fully apprised of the Earl of Salt Hendon's upcoming marriage.

Cursing himself for such lack of restraint, Salt ordered a bottle of claret from a passing soft-footed waiter and resumed his seat, only to be on his feet within five minutes to warmly clasp the hand of his closest friend, the younger brother of Lady St. John, Sir Antony Templestowe.

A large handsome gentleman held in high regard by all who knew him, Sir Antony was considered by the Foreign Department, where he held a lucrative sinecure, to have a good head on his shoulders, and thus certain to rise to the rank of ambassador one day. No two siblings could be more opposite in temperament than the diffident Sir Antony and his social butterfly sister, the beautiful and gregarious Diana, Lady St. John.

"It's just as well Bedford could spare you from the Peace negotiations for a couple of weeks," Salt commented, looking Sir Antony up and down. "Paris has added inches to your girth."

"A couple of hours running about your tennis court should take care of M'sieur Chef's fine cream sauces and delectable *choux* pastries," Sir Antony replied good-naturedly as they both made themselves comfortable in wing chairs. He unbuttoned two silver buttons of his striped saffron silk waistcoat and accepted the glass of claret from a blank-faced waiter. "But I'm surprised the tournament is to go ahead. I thought it'd be left to Ellis to take your place on the court, what with you on your honeymoon—"

"There isn't going to be a honeymoon," stated Salt, taking out his gold snuffbox but not flicking open the enamel inlaid lid. "Parliament still sits, which means I've too much business to attend to here in London to go gallivanting about the countryside, this side of the Channel or that."

Sir Antony pulled his chin into his lace cravat and studied his friend a moment. "To say your letter informing me of your immediate intention to enter the matrimonial state knocked me off my chair would be an understatement, dear fellow. But I'm a diplomatist, so understatement is my forte. That you want to keep the occasion hush-hush is your affair, and I'll ask you no questions, if that is your wish, but surely I'm not the only one going to attend the ceremony to, as it were, prop up your elbow?"

Salt took snuff, frowning into the middle-distance. "The less fuss the better."

"What does Diana have to say about your sudden leap into the matrimonial fire?"

"I haven't told her.

Sir Antony hid his astonishment behind a frown. "Haven't told Diana?" he repeated mildly. "You're not getting leg-shackled without her approval, surely? God! She'll have a fit of the sullens that neither of us will manage very well. I wish I were still in Paris. You know what an interest she takes in you—"

"—and my earldom."

Sir Antony pursed his lips and counted to five. "Yes, you can be cynical if you choose," he commented. "But is it any wonder she takes an interest when she's the mother of your heir? Little Ron will one day succeed you. Up until four years ago, it was her husband who stood to inherit your earldom. St. John's untimely death affected her greatly, as it did all of us." Sir Antony shifted uncomfortably on the wingchair, adding flatly, "And you know as well as I that she married St. John in a fit of pique because you wouldn't ask her. And if you ask me, she still holds out a candle in hope that you might still get up the courage. Why do you suppose such a good-looking woman has remained a widow? It's not from lack of offers, I can tell you!"

Salt shifted his gaze to the dark red liquid in his wine glass, a heightened color in his lean cheeks. "Diana was the wife of my best friend and closest cousin, Tony. I have and always will hold her in the highest regard. But that's all I can—will ever—offer her."

"Granted. But Diana will never look on you as a brother," Sir Antony argued. "As long as you know that." He gave a halfhearted laugh. "No wonder you don't want me returning to Paris any day soon if Diana don't know your news. You'll need reinforcements when she's presented with your marriage as a fait accompli. And as for Caroline's reaction... If you haven't told your little sister she's about to gain a sister-in-law, I pray she isn't coming up to London, because we won't be able to contend with two grief-stricken females—"

"It's Jane Despard," Salt interrupted quietly.

Sir Antony's gaze never wavered from the Earl's handsome angular face, but his mouth hovered between an absurdly stupid grin and blank amazement, so that he looked stunned, as if someone or something had smacked him across the back of the head. Mute stupefaction made him drink his wine in one gulp, realizing now why his elder sister and the Lady Caroline had been kept in ignorance of the Earl's imminent marriage. The bride was so far off the social register—indeed being disowned by her father was as nothing when compared to her depraved lifestyle, living unmarried under the roof of an old Bristol merchant—that if the truth were ever revealed to family and friends, they would wonder at the Head of the Family's mental stability, and if it ever got out to the world, well, the Sinclair family would be forever ridiculed and thus socially ruined.

Not one to shirk responsibilities and being genuinely fond of Salt, Sir Antony was glad he had been recalled home early from the finalization of the Paris peace negotiations to stand shoulder to shoulder with the Earl at this difficult time.

"I thought—given the circumstances surrounding the offer—that she broke off the previous engagement..."

"Miss Despard informs me she must marry me."

Sir Antony's jaw swung open. "What? After thumbing her nose at your previous offer? The barefaced cheek of the little cat!" and then suddenly realized he was describing his friend's future wife. "I thought Miss Despard might have a shred of decency left and refuse you," he added, much subdued.

Salt's features were rigid and pale. It was an effort for him to speak. "God help me, Tony, so did I."

FOUR

W HEN ARTHUR ELLIS returned upstairs to the drawing room, he found Jane alone, seated by the fire, face turned to the flames as they crackled with new life amongst the blackened logs. For one heart-stopping moment, the secretary thought she had tossed into the fire the sheaf of papers he had labored over for hours, and his shoulders slumped at the thought of having to rewrite all four pages of closely-written script. But it said much about his own gentle nature that when he realized the Earl's betrothed had been crying, he was of the opinion that she really couldn't be blamed for destroying a document that clearly set out to humiliate and imprison her.

He offered her his plain white handkerchief, saying solemnly, "Should I call for Lady Despard?"

Jane shook her head and patted dry her cheeks before turning to the secretary with a bright smile. "No, Mr. Ellis. Thank you. I am quite all right. In fact I feel less apprehensive about tomorrow than I have in weeks. It was something he said… If he believes what the physicians advised, and that was ten years ago, then—it stands to reason the locket never reached him. And if the locket never reached him… He can't have known what happened to me… But forgive me, Mr. Ellis, you must think me cotton-headed. I am raving on at you about matters you cannot know the first thing about."

"Less apprehensive? You are not troubled by the contents of Lord Salt's document?" Uninvited, the secretary sat opposite Jane and unconsciously took back his handkerchief. "You feel better about tomorrow, Miss Despard?"

Jane smiled behind her hand at his look of total confusion.

"Mr. Ellis, I do believe your loyalty should be with his lordship and his sad predicament in being forced into a marriage he does not want in the least. Forgive me. I have disconcerted you again. Have you been ordered to collect that document with my signature upon it or face dire consequences? Oh! Mr. Ellis," she added when he glanced swiftly over at the little escritoire and a huge relief showed itself on his freckled face, "did you think I had burned it? For shame. When you have undoubtedly spent many hours deliberating over every word, and your handwriting so immaculate."

"I am only sorry that it was I who had to read it out loud," the secretary confessed, gaze riveted to her lovely face. "If there had been any other way, if it had not been necessary for me to be present, to save you the embarrassment, but unfortunately—"

Jane touched the young man's hand. "—Lord Salt cannot read the printed page without the aid of his eyeglasses. If he reads unaided for any length of time, particularly the newsprint, he suffers from the most unbearable megrims. He should wear his rims, but refuses to do so in public because his pride and vanity prevent him. Obstinate man. But I have said too much, and you are looking at me as if I have sprouted a second head!"

The secretary was so taken aback that the Earl's betrothed knew about his employer's debilitating eyesight that he nodded his agreement and stood when she rose from the chair. Very few people knew that it was an exceptional retentive memory that enabled the Earl to hide his disability upon most occasions, particularly when delivering speeches in the Lords or serving on committees where papers had been distributed beforehand. As for seeing his lordship wearing his gold-rimmed spectacles across the bridge of his long, bony nose, Arthur Ellis was quite certain the number of persons granted this privilege amounted to fewer than half a dozen. It was only when he was shut away in his bookroom, with only Arthur in attendance, that the Earl would sit hunched over a document, reading with the aid of his magnifying lenses. It begged the question how Miss Despard could know such an intimate detail about her future husband, but instead of asking he said diffidently,

"His lordship has instructed me to offer you my assistance with the sorting of your belongings; those which are to remain with the Allenbys, and those requiring removal to your new home in Grosvenor Square."

"Thank you for the offer, Mr. Ellis," Jane replied, picking up the document off the escritoire, "but I anticipated his lordship's directive and have only brought with me one portmanteau and two hat boxes. My petticoats and shoes, such as I had, I left in Wiltshire to be distributed amongst the wives and daughters of the parish poor." She handed the unsigned document to the secretary with an apologetic smile. "I'm afraid I have no intention of signing this hateful epistle, Mr. Ellis. I'm only sorry you must deliver the news to his lordship. Hopefully his misdirected wrath will be of a short duration, and he can bottle the rest until he has the opportunity to vent it on me."

Arthur Ellis gave an involuntary laugh and shook his head. He couldn't blame her, but he was surprised that this delicate beauty had the strength of character not to be frightened to stand her ground with his strong-willed employer. Arthur predicted interesting times ahead for the Earl once married to Miss Jane Despard.

The anticipation of the upcoming nuptials put a decided spring in his step as he went about his usual business the next day, despite an anteroom full of petitioners and the day's appointments already substantially delayed with the arrival of Lady St. John, her two children in tow.

The secretary did not approve of Lady St. John and her mischievous offspring, but it was not his place or right to say so. Nor did it surprise him that she always chose to visit on the only day in the week when the Earl received petitioners, and thus his busiest at-home day.

Tuesdays were open house day at Lord Salt's Grosvenor Square mansion, providing an opportunity to anyone who wished to put his case to the Earl of Salt Hendon, be it on a matter regarding a sinecure, patronage for a literary work or some such artistic endeavor, a hawker representing the wares of his manufacturer, or persons with some minor connection to the Sinclair family or the Earl's estates seeking assistance in some way.

Petitioners rarely managed to make it to interview on the first Tuesday of their petitioning, and therefore waited all day in the freezing, cavernous anteroom, with its marble floor and no fire in the grate. There were never enough chairs to go round and people stood for hours, only to be told to return the following Tuesday to wait all over again. The more persistent returned three or four Tuesdays in a row, all for the privilege of stating their case in the fifteen minutes allotted to them for an audience with the Earl.

None of this meant anything to Lady St. John. She sailed into the Earl's bookroom in a billow of exquisitely embroidered Italian olive velvet petticoats, her retinue behind her, and without a single glance at the nameless, silent and shivering crowd queued either side of the double doors, guarded over by two footmen in the Sinclair blue-and-gold livery.

Arthur tried to continue on with his work as if she were not there, but of course this was an impossible task when she immediately draped herself on a corner of the Earl's massive mahogany desk, with no regard for the piles of important papers her petticoats swept to the floor in the process. As for her two children, the boy and girl clambered up onto Uncle Salt's lap and demanded his attention. And of course Lady St. John's visits invariably required the involvement of most of the household staff to provide for her and her children's care and nourishment. The kitchen was sent into a whirlwind of activity to make and bake the little almond biscuits she liked so much and the particular Bohea tea at the strength her palate would approve. The butler was called upon to provide his undivided attention to her ladyship's whims, and at least four liveried footmen were dispatched to keep an eye on the children, to ensure there was minimal disturbance to carpets, leather-bound volumes lining the walls, mahogany furniture and soft furnishings. All this despite Lady St. John arriving with her own lady-in-waiting, the children's tutor, a governess and a Negro pageboy whose arduous task it was to go before her ladyship carrying a silk cushion, upon which rested her ladyship's fan.

Jane was set down at the door to the Earl's Palladian mansion in Grosvenor Square in the midst of this midmorning disruption. The under-butler sized her up: From her simply-dressed hair without powder, to her unseasonable silk gown of old gold, with light lace petticoats which lacked the requisite fashionable hoop. Over this was a wool cloak with frayed collar. The fact she had arrived without her maid in tow, put this haughty little man in two minds as to whether to close the door in her face.

Never mind the indisputable fact that she was the most breathtakingly beautiful female he had ever set eyes on. He had a job to do. It was all very well to admit grovelling petitioners on Tuesdays, but a beautiful female without her maid was another matter entirely. One which, Rufus Willis, under-butler in this noble household, wasn't too sure he wanted to tackle. Only the fact Jane had arrived in the Earl's carriage decided him that it was best to let her come in out of the intense cold. Perhaps she was the new maid Mr. Jenkins the butler had told him to be on the lookout for? But he hadn't expected the girl to use the front entrance. Without a bow and with a small wave of dismissal, Willis ordered Jane to follow a footman to the anteroom off the bookroom. She could wait with the rest of the needy masses vying for his lordship's attention and deep pockets until he had spoken with Mr. Jenkins to sort out what they were to do with her. Expect a long wait.

In the cavernous anteroom, Jane was deserted by the footman without so much as a bow of acknowledgement, which surely indicated to the waiting crowd, along with her shabby wool cloak, that she was no one of importance, and in all probability a newly-employed domestic. But in the midst of a crowd of half-frozen men, her beauty was a welcome distraction and she was immediately offered the rare commodity of a chair by several gentlemen who leapt to their heels, instantly captivated by such exquisite loveliness and effortless grace. A sprightly middle-aged gent with a Malacca cane won out, and Jane sat down beside this gentleman's wife.

It was not lost on Jane that as soon as she entered the anteroom every bewigged head turned to gaze directly at her. Bravely, she bestowed a kind smile on them all, as she had been advised to do by the soft-spoken stranger she and Tom had met while visiting the Tower Zoo. The stranger had in tow his nephew and niece and was showing them the lion enclosure, but every visitor was more interested in gazing on Jane, and she had no idea why. The sight of such majestic creatures so far from their homeland and kept in such a horrid space was quite depressingly sad, and perhaps this was why the tourists had turned their attention elsewhere? Yet this did not explain why every time she and Tom had ventured from Arlington Street in search of tourist spots, they had found themselves swamped by a veritable crowd of onlookers.

The soft-spoken stranger had enlightened them, saying that in this city it was perfectly acceptable for its citizens, gentlemen and ladies alike, to stare at a pretty young woman as a matter of course. No one thought it at all ill-mannered. In fact, it was considered an honor to be thus singled out, and so the object of everyone's admiration was expected to bestow a smile on all who admired her beauty.

How bored all these men are, Jane thought, as she finally dropped her gaze to her cold hands, and how icy it was in this massive room of marble and wood without adequate light and warmth. She wished she owned a muff such as the one the lady beside her possessed. She enquired of the lady and her husband why there was no fire in the grate of the large fireplace, at which the middle-aged man with the Malacca cane laughed and shook his bewigged head.

"If a fire were kept in here his lordship would have twice the number of petitioners waiting to see him."

"Yes, but as Lord Salt has only so many hours in the day, I doubt denying his petitioners some warmth is enough of a disincentive to keep people away, do you?" Jane replied mildly. "Providing a little comfort goes a long way in making people more agreeable, don't you think?"

The gentleman was momentarily taken aback by such a forthright speech from a wisp of a female, but his wife embraced Jane's maxim wholeheartedly.

"How right you are, my dear!" she agreed with a smile of

approval. "This is our third and last Tuesday waiting to see his lordship, and every one has been as cold as the last." She glanced around the imposing room, with its high ornate ceiling, wood paneling and marble floor, and at the long, tired faces, adding loudly, "I know his lordship can't make allowances for the frosts, and he labors long and hard on behalf of those who owe him their allegiance, but it wouldn't hurt to put a fire in the grate, and perhaps offer one or two more seats, or a bench."

"Hear, hear!" agreed an elderly man in an old-fashioned full-bottom wig.

Several other gentlemen nodded their powdered heads, and there was a general low rumble of assent. Even the attending liveried footmen, who were chilled to the bone, cast the woman a look of approval.

"Now, good wife, there ain't reason for us to complain about his lordship," the middle-aged gentleman reproved. "Not after all he's done for our boy."

The woman was immediately repentant and said confidentially to Jane, as if she were a friend of long-standing, "We have a great deal to be thankful for in his lordship's good offices. What with everything that's usually heaped on his lordship's plate, it was such a good kind act for Lord Salt to take Billy under his wing."

"Our son Billy is a very bright lad, and was up at Oxford with his lordship's secretary, Mr. Ellis," the husband added proudly. "He was determined to come to London to seek his fortune, little realizing the great hardship involved in securing gainful employment without the necessary good word of people of influence. We are well-connected people in our little corner of Wiltshire, make no mistake about that, miss, but the metropolis is cut from an altogether different cloth."

"And with five more children to launch into the world, it's not as if we could help Billy as much as we would've liked to," apologized the wife, an understanding smile up at her husband, who leaned in towards them with the aid of his Malacca cane to take the weight off his gouty toe, and to affectionately squeeze his wife's shoulder.

"But his lordship found a place for our Billy in the Foreign Department under the guidance of Sir Antony Templestowe," continued the husband, adding proudly for Jane's benefit, "Sir Antony is a most distinguished diplomatist, and Billy has every expectation of accompanying Sir Antony when next he embarks for foreign climes."

"Your son could do no better than have Lord Salt as his mentor," commented Jane, feeling that the couple was seeking her endorsement of their son's success. "And under Sir Antony's wing, I know Lord Salt's faith in him will be justly proved."

"Thank you, my dear," said the wife, taking her warm hand from her muff and placing it on Jane's cold fingers. "Goodness gracious! Your hands are as cold as the blocks of ice floating in the Thames! Should you like to borrow my muff for a few moments, child?"

Jane shook her head and thanked the woman, more than ever self-conscious in her worn cloak, a gift from her father at Christmastime when she was seventeen that she hadn't the heart to give up, not even when Mr. Allenby had presented her with a lovely new fur-lined velvet cloak with shiny silver buttons. She hid her cold hands in her lap under the cloak, the bitter cold from the marble floor seeping into her stockinged toes and up her thin ankles, and shivered, not from the cold but with apprehension of what was to come. It was the first time she had allowed herself to think about the consequences of going through with marriage to Lord Salt. The fact Tom was not with her increased her dread. He had gone to fetch his lawyer as witness, a stipulation of Jacob Allenby's will, and promised to be at Grosvenor Square not an hour after she was set down at the Earl's residence. The hour was almost up.

"What a pity his lordship can't find himself a wife as easily as he found our Billy employment," the husband announced good-naturedly, which brought Jane out of her abstraction to ask curiously,

"Why do you say so, sir?"

"What, miss? A nobleman with his wealth and looks and an ancient coronet to pass on to his descendants, why wouldn't Lord Salt want to marry? Stands to reason he's in need of a countess by his side, wouldn't you say so, wife?"

"Indeed he does, sir!" agreed the wife, a look about the room to ensure their conversation was being listened to by the rest of the frozen occupants. "Why, his lordship even favors children... Well, indeed he must, for the last two Tuesdays we've been here, he's always found an hour or two amongst his appointments to spend with Lady St. John's son and daughter."

"The young lad's his heir, wife," confided the husband with a knowing point to his nose. "And between you and me and those of the local gentry in our little corner of the world who regularly join the Salt Hunt, there is every reason to believe he has his eye on making the Lady St. John his Countess. And a more suited couple I ask you to name!"

At least a dozen powdered heads around the anteroom nodded in approval of this statement. There was a general rumble of consensus that the stately creature who had swept passed them with her retinue, without a look or a glance, had the noble bearing and condescending demeanor required in a Countess of Salt Hendon. A small number of petitioners were in silent dissent, glaring at the firmly shut double doors to the bookroom, all because they were being kept from their allotted appointment by the lady in question.

One gentleman in an absurdly tall toupee, stockinged legs that showcased padded calves, and an armful of rolled parchments, and who had arrived in the anteroom only minutes before, dared to voice this silent resentment, saying in a whining voice,

"I say! But if her ladyship becomes Countess none of us will ever see the inside of that bookroom. I, for one, won't. She don't like poetry. She don't like poetry at all."

Jane couldn't help a smile at this pronouncement, which was light relief amongst the general run of conversation about Lord Salt's need for a wife which had brought the heat into her pallid cheeks. The wife saw this and before her husband could launch into an attack against the young man in the absurdly tall toupee, said in a loud whisper,

"Husband, hush now about his lordship. We have put this young woman to the blush with all our talk about wives and children for Lord Salt, and we've no right, not if she has come to join his lordship's household. Oh, and look, the footmen are opening the doors!" She turned to Jane with a bright smile. "Mr. Ellis will soon be out with the list, so you won't have to suffer the cold for much longer."

"My good woman, pray don't raise the beauty's expectations," pronounced the gentleman in the absurdly tall toupee, who Jane noticed wore clothes cut from cloth befitting a gentleman. "Until Lady St. John makes her grand exit, there is little hope of a winter thaw anytime before spring."

He snorted so loudly at his own wit that a fine dusting of powder from his wig settled on his upper lip, causing him to sneeze and his armful of parchments tubes to fly up in the air before descending to scatter and roll away under chairs and across the marble floor. In panic did the gentleman-poet get down on all fours to scurry across cold marble with little thought to his rich attire, to retrieve his precious collection of poems, much to the delight and amusement of the petitioners.

Jane felt sorry for the young man. She immediately went to retrieve one of his cylinders which had come to rest in her corner of the anteroom behind the gentleman with the cane. She had to stoop to pick it up, had it in her hand and was about to rise, when a female voice, close, clear and authoritative spoke above a general commotion of leave-taking. Accompanying this voice was a heady feminine scent that, as if by sorcery, made Jane instantly nauseated, and she sank down on the cold marble. It was not that the perfume itself was offensive. It was sweet-smelling with hints of lavender and rose, and had it been used in moderation, no one could have called it offensive. But to Jane, it conjured up echoes of the past, and she was forced to put a hand over her small nose and breathe deeply through her mouth, telling herself that the wave of nausea would pass, that there was no reason to panic.

She remained sitting on the floor, waiting for the sickness to subside, the poet's rolled parchment in her lap, feeling foolish that a particular perfume had the power to create queasiness within her. It did not take above a minute to place where she had smelled such a distinctive perfume before, and the feminine voice that owned it. Recognition rode the waves of nausea that washed over her. She had not smelled it before or since the night her baby had willfully been taken from her before its time. Her father had condemned her as the most sordid and immoral creature alive and wanted nothing more to do with her for having lost her virginity so cheaply, but giving birth to the rotten bastardized fruit of her immorality, as her father had brutally branded her unborn baby, was never a choice.

Jane peered through a break in the row of ribbon-back chairs, hoping to put a face to the owner of the offending perfume. The lady was standing so close that had Jane stretched out an arm between two chairs, she could have laid a fingertip on the lady's wide-hooped petticoats of rich velvet. Two liveried footmen and a black pageboy in a bright green silk turban stood to one side of this magnificently dressed creature, who had to be none other than the Earl's majestic cousin, the Lady St. John.

Her ladyship fluttered a fan of delicate silk against her white bosom, upswept powdered hair draped with pearls, ribbons and feathers, and her beautiful face carefully made up with cosmetics. A mouche at the corner of hazel eyes completed her toilette. She neither looked left nor right at the crowd of petitioners, but straight down at the gentleman-poet groveling at the toes of her silk covered-mules.

Directly behind the dazzling Lady St. John was a tired-looking woman whose plain but well-made attire and small lace cap proclaimed her the lady's maid. And behind her, two children in rich silk costume, the girl dressed in a replica of her mother's attire, the boy younger and sickly, but quite the little gentleman in his matching silk breeches and waistcoat. Jane recognized them as the niece and nephew of the soft-spoken stranger she and Tom had met in front of the lion enclosure. Neither resembled the happy, laughing children at the Tower Zoo.

"My dear Mr. Wraxton! Why ever are you scuttling about on Lord Salt's floor?" Lady St. John wondered with a mischievous smile. She waved her bejeweled hand out in front of her. "No! Do not get up on my account. You look very well indeed down there. In fact, I do believe I have never seen a gentleman more suited to playing the part of devoted beagle hound. But with that interesting hairstyle you could be mistaken for a flamingo! Or perhaps it is as a pig snuffling for truffles that you snort about the floor thus?" She turned her beautifully-coiffured head left and right, as if it was a matter of course that the assembled company would find her wit diverting. "Yes, I do believe it is truffles you are after. Truffles of approval from Lord Salt for your little creative endeavors." When the gentleman-poet in the absurd toupee managed to scamper to his feet, clasping to his chest the salvaged bundle of rolled parchments with one hand, while the other kept his tall toupee from slipping into his eyes, she poked tentatively at the parchments with a long fingernail. "Why, are these *more* poems for Lord Salt's amusement?"

"A final selection of poems, dear Lady St. John," Hilary Wraxton announced proudly.

"If they're as absurd as the last lot, then they are bound to provide his lordship with an amusing diversion, however fleeting."

Hilary Wraxton beamed, Lady St. John's sarcasm completely passing him by, despite several bewigged heads in the anteroom openly sniggering at his expense. "Thank you, my lady. I am in expectation of Lord Salt's patronage, with a view to their publication."

Lady St. John lifted her arched brows and turned down her painted mouth in complete surprise. "So you think, Mr. Wraxton? Far be it from me to disillusion you, but if they are as ludicrously inane as your previous efforts, then you have wasted Lord Salt's time. I know just what view his lordship has in mind for them—up in flames in his fireplace." And with this cruel pronouncement and the appreciative laughs of several bored gentlemen sitting about the anteroom, Lady St. John swept out of the Grosvenor Square mansion with her retinue, leaving Mr. Hilary Wraxton to nurse his wounded pride and rolled parchments to his bosom as if they were under imminent threat of being turned to cinders.

"I do believe Lady St. John was in jest, sir," Jane told him kindly, handing the gentleman-poet the parchment she had retrieved. "But you need not take my word for it. Ask Mr. Ellis, who surely will confirm that your poems in Lord Salt's possession are unharmed."

"Miss Despard!" exclaimed the secretary, thick leather-bound appointment book hugged to his chest as he scurried down the long anteroom to Jane's side. He bowed to her. "Have you been kept waiting long? I had supposed Mr. Jenkins would've informed me of your arrival. I apologize for the delay. His lordship had some uninvited visitors…"

"Lady St. John and her two children?" asked Jane, with an understanding smile at his look of exasperation.

"Indeed," replied the secretary, unable to hide his displeasure. He quickly regained his smile and ushered Jane forward, "Please, come into the bookroom where there is a fire."

"I say, Ellis! Wait up!" Hilary Wraxton interrupted anxiously, wedging himself between Jane and the secretary. "Are my parchments safe, man? Has Lord Salt seen 'em yet? What does he think of 'em? He hasn't turned 'em to ash, has he?"

"I beg your pardon, Mr. Wraxton?" Arthur Ellis replied in shocked accents. "I cannot tell you if his lordship has read any of your poetry, sir, but I can say irrevocably that Lord Salt has done no such thing as put your poems to the flame. Now, if you will excuse us. Miss Despard…?"

Jane hesitated, a glance at Billy's parents who were smiling at her encouragingly, and touched the secretary's sleeve. "Mr. Ellis, Tom has not yet arrived, so we must wait. Perhaps, in the meantime, Lord Salt could see these good people, who have come three Tuesdays in a row?"

The secretary glanced at the couple, sensed Jane's nervousness and smiled reassuringly. "You would be more comfortable waiting for your brother in Lord Salt's bookroom, Miss Despard. I will see what can be done for the Churches."

With that he walked off, neither looking left nor right at the crowd of petitioners whom he knew all eagerly tried to catch his eye for some sign that they would be granted an interview with the Earl sometime soon. He had learned to be blind to the pleading, sometimes hostile, always expectant looks of the crowd who sought his noble employer's benefaction. Yet Jane could not help feeling, as she passed these silent bewigged gentlemen, that they must think she had jumped the queue, just as Lady St. John had done before her, all because she was a pretty female. Little could these sullen faces know she felt as if she were on her way to have a tooth pulled. No one could have the slightest idea she was about to be married to one of the wealthiest and most politically influential noblemen in the kingdom.

The feeling did not subside upon entering the Earl's bookroom, despite the long room possessing a fireplace at either end
with elaborate mahogany overmantels and blazing fires in each
grate which radiated comforting warmth. This hallowed inner-
sanctum was in such marked contrast to the sparseness of the
freezing anteroom that Jane blinked and could not help gazing in
wonderment. Everywhere candles burned brightly in elaborate
sconces, and two chandeliers filled the room with light. All was
comfort and ease, and yet on such a lavish scale that the visitor felt
anything but comfortable. Three walls were lined with floor-to-
ceiling shelves crammed with leather-bound tomes, the higher
shelves reached by climbing one of two mahogany ladders attached
to a polished railing which ran the entire length of the bookshelves. The fourth wall had long sash windows framed by heavy
curtains of gold and red velvet tied back with thick gold rope to
allow a view of the goings on in the elegant square below. Oriental
carpets scattered the polished wooden floor, and central to the
room was a massive two-sided mahogany desk with two wide
chairs drawn up to it on either side, the only other furniture being
an assortment of wingchairs and sofas arranged before the
fireplaces.

At one fireplace, three liveried footmen silently went about
straightening furniture and cleaning up what appeared to be the
remnants of a tea party, no doubt presided over by Lady St. John.
The secretary ignored this activity and went to the desk, and again
Jane followed. Mr. Ellis carefully placed the opened appointment
book amongst the neatly ordered piles of documents of differing
heights, along with a stack of scrolls, several books, and an elaborate Standish with quills and ink, seals and wafers. Jane noticed
that nowhere to be seen amongst this well-ordered clutter were the
Earl's gold-rimmed spectacles.

In fact, she did not see the Earl until it was too late. His
voice made her jump and spin about to face the second fireplace,
where he stood before the fire in the grate. He was dressed more
splendidly than he had been the day before, if that was possible,
except today he did not wear powder but his own shoulder-
length light chestnut-colored hair, simply tied with a black silk
ribbon at the nape. His waistcoat and breeches were of a rich

embroidered cream silk, which on closer inspection, revealed an intricate pattern of vines, fruits and small intricately-woven birds, all in the Chinese manner. An elaborately-tied cravat of delicate lace, diamond knee-buckles, white silk stockings and a pair of flat-heeled polished black shoes with enormous silver buckles encrusted with diamonds finished off this magnificent toilette. If Jane was self-conscious in her old wool cloak in the anteroom, here in the warmth and magnificence of the book-room, coming face-to-face with a thoroughly unapproachable bridegroom made her feel positively inadequate to the task ahead.

Still, when the secretary remained at the massive desk and she was beckoned forward to stand before the Earl alone, she managed to put up her chin and appear unruffled, even when Salt looked her over and ordered the butler, who had trod softly up the room behind her, to take her cloak and fetch her a glass of wine.

"I would prefer hot chocolate, my lord," Jane requested, shrugging out of her cloak and immediately spreading her frozen hands to the warmth of the fire. "I am sorry, but your anteroom could grow icicles." When no response was forthcoming, she glanced up and was not surprised that he was frowning down at her with mute disapproval. She presumed she would have to grow accustomed to such a look where she was concerned, so resigned herself to the fact and added without apology, "I disposed of the clothes given me by Mr. Allenby, which left only this gown and the wool cloak, all my father permitted me when he cast me from his house."

The Earl gave a huff of embarrassment and looked away into the flames. Inexplicably, her choice of words made him acutely uncomfortable, as did the gown she was wearing. He had last seen it when he had helped her out of it in the summerhouse.

"Sir Felix's twisted sense of humor, no doubt. By the way, that gown became you better four years ago."

Her surprise that he recognized her attire overshadowed his disparaging remark.

"I hardly think my father saw any humor in my humiliation, do you?" she said quietly, a lump forming in her throat as she studied his handsome profile. She wondered if within him there was a sliver of regret for what he'd done to her. It made her say spontaneously, "I never betrayed you to him."

At that, his head snapped round and he stared hard at her.

"*You* never betrayed *me?*" He scoffed. "Your kind doesn't know the meaning of the word!"

"What kind is that, my lord?" she asked curiously, shivering at the viciousness in his delivery.

He gritted his teeth. "Touché, Miss Despard. You and I know very well, so you needn't regard me as if I'm speaking an incomprehensible foreign tongue." He looked down at her and added with a sniff of disdain, as if reading her thoughts, "And you needn't imagine I carry the slightest remorse for what happened to you."

"Don't you?" Jane replied bravely, and shrugged, though his words stung more than she would ever let on. "No matter. I take responsibility for my actions, no one else."

Her simple response put him off-balance. "Very noble, Miss Despard, but your ignoble actions show you up for what you are."

She smiled sadly. "Sometimes actions mask what we truly feel. But I have never lied to give another false hope."

At that, Salt couldn't help himself. He was so angry he grabbed her about the upper arms and jerked her close, face thrust in hers. "How dare you feign to be the innocent party in this contemptible union!" he hissed. "How dare you pretend that you *must* marry me! Must? Ha! That's just a ploy, to justify to yourself why you're putting me through this—this *hell*. Have you no conscience that you're taking up my offer of a coronet under despicable circumstances? I wish to God I could lay the damn thing at your feet and walk away!"

Jane stared into his handsome face, distorted with pent-up rage, and willed herself to remain calm. How she wanted to fling his coronet at his sneering countenance and run away, never to see him again. But she knew this for a lie. She had thought about him so often in the past four years that it was surely unhealthy. At first she had blamed him for her predicament, but she was not a hateful person by nature and so the loathing quickly evaporated, leaving her with the sad dull ache of longing, and in the tragic knowledge that she still loved him. Not this incarnation that sneered down at her, but the man he was four years ago, who was kind and loving and honorable. This being she did not know at all and had no wish to marry, but she had to think of Tom, and ruining his future should she not go through with the wedding. She wished her stepbrother was with her now. She wanted the ceremony over with as much as this stranger who held her so tightly she was sure both her arms were bruised.

"My lord… My arms…"

Instantly, he let her go. She was so frail and had such slender limbs that he was sure he had hurt her. Remorseful and annoyed with himself for allowing anger to get the better of him, he turned back to the fire with a muttered apology.

"Forgive me, Miss Despard. It was not my intention to hurt you."

"Hurt me? Do you imagine this situation is less hellish for me, my lord?"

With a hand outstretched to the mantel, he looked over his shoulder and saw the tears in her blue eyes. "Only you can end the misery for us both before it begins."

Her full bottom lip trembled, and she dropped her gaze to quickly dry her eyes on the scrap of lace she called a handkerchief before bravely looking up at him. "I'm not about to cry off, my lord. I can't. I just hope you do not intend to do so again, because I—"

"I beg your pardon?" he interrupted, turning to confront her. "What do you mean *cry off*?"

"—I truly must marry and without delay," she concluded and watched in fascination as his face drained of all natural color. He looked ill. She took a step forward in alarm, only for him to back away, not wanting the nearness of her.

"Are you accusing me of breach of promise?" he asked in wonderment, feeling disorientated and slightly breathless, as if he had been struck between the shoulder blades with a heavy object.

"You may call it whatever name you choose, but it does not alter the truth, my lord."

"Truth?" Salt could hardly say the word. "What truth is that?"

Jane could well understand why he looked so ill for she had bravely voiced aloud what was indisputable. He might be a nobleman, but like all men of the nobility, the Earl prided himself on being first and foremost a gentleman; his word was his bond. But he had committed what the gentlemanly fraternity considered the deadliest of sins. He had broken his word—to her. He had called off their engagement two months after they had made love in his summerhouse the night of the Salt Hunt Ball, and cast her adrift on the world.

FIVE

OUR YEARS AGO, at the Salt Hunt Ball, after a month of
secret courtship, the Earl had proposed marriage to Jane
and she had accepted. A girl did not forget such a
momentous occasion. She remembered everything about such a
wonderful moment, down to the smallest detail. He had asked her
in his summerhouse, with its view out across the still blue lake to
an ancient stone bridge. The Palladian exterior of cold marble
columns and domed roof belied an opulent and exotic interior,
replica of the private apartments of an Ottoman prince, whose
guest the Earl had been while on the Grand Tour. The rooms were
decorated with beautifully-colored mosaic tiles and Turkish arti-
facts, rugs, silk hangings and embroidered cushions which glowed
under the soft, muted light cast by a hundred burning candles.

She had been wearing the gown she had on now, and he had
given her a gold locket set with sapphires and diamonds; a family
heirloom, he told her. The betrothal ring she now wore, with its
sapphire and diamonds inlaid in a gold band which was too large
for her finger, was fashioned in a similar style, and Jane reasoned it
must be part of a set to which the locket also belonged.

He had shown her the secret catch at the back of the locket
which opened to reveal a small space between the precious stone
and the gold-backing where could be placed a memento, a lock of
hair or a tiny note. He had made her promise that if ever she

found herself in difficulty, she was to send him a note in the secret compartment of the locket and he would come. He had made her promise this because he was leaving to return to London almost immediately and would be gone for at least a fortnight, perhaps a month. When he returned, their engagement would be officially announced, and they would be married without delay.

She had sent him the locket with a note when she realized she was pregnant. He did not come. A month later she received his letter, breaking off their engagement.

The day he had asked her to marry him had been the happiest day of her life and was etched in her memory forever. The day his letter arrived breaking off their engagement she had considered the worst day of her life, that she could sink no lower in despair and wretchedness, and then their baby had been taken from her.

She had kept his letter. She had wanted to burn it, to turn his horrid words of regret and mistake to ash, but her nurse, who could not read or write and so held the written word in reverence, had taken the letter and put it in a safe place, saying that there might come a day when the letter could prove useful. Jane wondered where that letter was now as she turned and regarded the Earl standing by the library window, hands behind his back, staring out into the square below, the latest petitioners dismissed with a view of his strong profile. She wondered if amongst his papers he had kept a copy of that fateful letter—perhaps not. He would not want his secretary coming across such a damning epistle.

Poor Arthur Ellis. Such a conscientious, hard-working young man could never have dreamed that, as part of his secretarial duties to a great nobleman, he would be required to deal with the more sordid details of his lordship's marriage. She wondered if he had had the courage to tell his employer that she refused to sign the edict of her imprisonment, and guessed that he had not, for surely the Earl would've shoved it under her nose as soon as she entered the bookroom.

Jane rose out of the wingchair as the secretary ushered in the next petitioners, the husband and wife with whom she had spent a cold hour in conversation in the anteroom. Mr. Church raised his cane and his wife smiled kindly in acknowledgement of her presence as they approached the Earl's desk. Jane waved back and watched Salt come away from the window and speak to the couple. She would have sat back down, but a large gentleman in powdered wig and sky-blue silk frock coat, who slipped through the double doors unseen, caught her eye.

He escaped the attention of Mr. Ellis, who had been included in the Earl's conversation with the couple, and made no attempt to approach the desk, but quietly tiptoed up the length of the library, keeping his back close to the bookshelves, as if not wanting to disturb the Earl.

Jane immediately recognized this large intruder as the very same soft-spoken gentleman whose acquaintance she and Tom had made at the Tower Zoo, and went to meet him. She was almost upon him before he saw her by one of the ladders, and he was so surprised and pleased to see her that he completely forgot he had entered the bookroom by stealth.

"By Jove! What a pleasant surprise," Sir Antony Templestowe announced, bowing over Jane's outstretched hand. "Now I may repair my remiss at the Tower. I did not introduce myself, nor did I catch your name, or that of the excellent young man in your company who I presume is your brother? You were both so good as to come to this bachelor's rescue and entertain my niece and nephew."

"Oh, but you were doing such a splendid job keeping their interest without our intervention, sir," Jane said encouragingly. "I gathered they were in high spirits because they had the freedom of their uncle's company, rather than under the stern tutelage of a somber-faced governess?"

"You figured all that out in what little time we spent in front of the lion enclosure? Splendid! By the way, my niece and nephew were just as taken with you as were the crowd of onlookers, and scolded me dreadfully for my lack of manners in not discovering your name and direction." He added with a confidential smile, "I trust you've taken my advice about the appreciative stares of Londoners?"

Jane nodded shyly. "I am doing my best, sir. But I must admit I don't think I will ever get used to such outrageous attention."

"Given time, you'll soon forget they are there," he assured her, and stuck out his hand to the Earl who had crossed the room to join them. "You really ought to put a fire in the grate out there, Salt," he said good-naturedly. "Is it any wonder nine out of ten of your petitioners can't cobble together two words in your presence, when they must be thawing out before your eyes. Of course, the other reason they're tongue-tied might have something to do with the fact you dazzle them with your magnificence. Have I seen that waistcoat before?"

He held the Earl's gaze and directed a significant sidelong glance at Jane, which Salt ignored. Sir Antony could have hit him for making him say it. "So won't you introduce me to your fair petitioner, who, I might add, because she is too modest to tell you of it herself, is London's newest beauty, and is mobbed wherever she goes." He smiled down at Jane who was blushing to the roots of her raven hair. "If I were you, ma'am, I'd ask for his lordship's protection under his sinecure as Keeper of Westminster Parks. I'm sure he can spare a dozen or so lieutenant-constables to protect you from an unruly mob of onlookers. What say you, Salt?"

Salt looked round from signaling for his secretary to approach with a gentleman in full-bottom wig.

"What would I say? That in less than an hour's time, Miss Despard, as my wife, will have at her disposal all the strong-armed protection she could desire to fend off the admiring hordes. Miss Despard, let me make known to you Sir Antony Templestowe, who, I might add, will one day rise to be an ambassador. Though from his stupid grin you would be quite within your rights to think him fit for Bedlam."

Sir Antony's silly grin remained fixed, and he had no idea where to direct his gaze, at the stern bridegroom or the blushing bride. He felt as foolish as he looked, and his sigh of relief was audible when a commotion at the double doors deflected attention away from his acute case of foot-in-mouth.

Arthur Ellis disappeared out into the anteroom and returned almost at once with Tom Allenby and his attorney in tow, both grim-faced. Two footmen were quick to close over the doors to the bookroom, as if denying entry to whoever was making demands out in the anteroom to be admitted without invitation to the Earl of Salt Hendon's inner sanctum.

"Apologies for the delay, my lord," Tom said without preamble, and made his attorney known to the Earl, adding brightly when he recognized Sir Antony, "Sir! What a pleasant reunion. Jane and I were lamenting only the other day not being forward enough to ask your name and direction. Weren't we, Jane?"

"You may all sit down to tea and cakes later," Salt bluntly interrupted. "Let's just get on with it, shall we? I'm glad you've brought your attorney, Mr. Allenby. Perhaps you would be good enough to furnish me with a copy of Jacob Allenby's will."

"That's hardly necessary, is it, my lord?" asked Jane, exchanging an anxious look with Tom.

Salt put up his brows. "But as you *must* marry me, Miss Despard, I think it *very* necessary, don't you?"

"I would be happy for your lordship to have a copy of my uncle's will," Tom agreed, a reassuring smile at Jane. "But that won't be possible until after my sister becomes Lady Salt, as my attorney did not bring a copy with him."

The Earl smiled thinly. "Oh, have no fear, Mr. Allenby, I mean to marry your sister, regardless of what is contained in Jacob Allenby's will. I merely wish to satisfy my curiosity. Now, shall we get this tiresome business over with? I have a full afternoon of appointments and am expected in the House after dinner."

The secretary and Tom Allenby exchanged a frowning look that did not go unnoticed by Jane. "What is it, Tom? Everything is in order, isn't it?" she asked fretfully, and looked to the attorney for an answer, but it was Tom who spoke, and to the Earl.

"My lord, I have asked her to wait in the anteroom until I've had a chance to explain matters to you, but my mother—"

"No, Mr. Allenby. Lady Despard is not welcome," Salt stated with extreme politeness, saying to his secretary in an under-voice, "Get her out. Be damned if I'll have that woman in here."

"Yes, my lord," agreed Arthur Ellis but remained where he was. "I will have Lady Despard escorted from the house at once."

"I'm afraid it's not that simple, my lord," the attorney apologized, clearing his throat, and bravely continued despite the Earl's hard stare upon him. "Under the terms of Jacob Allenby's will,

Lady Despard is required to stand as witness to the marriage of Jane Katherine Despard or—"

"I won't be dictated to by that merchant's wishes, dead or alive! That's an end to the matter. Parson, we're wasting time," Salt stated belligerently, and strode back to his desk to find the special license.

The little man in the full-bottom wig was quick to flick open his leather-bound bible at the place that held his notes, and then looked round expectantly at the assembled company.

"Jane, she must be in attendance," Tom whispered to Jane, a worried look directed at the scowling Earl, who was fossicking amongst the papers on his desk. "It's the penultimate condition of Uncle Jacob's will."

"Pardon my inquisitiveness, Mr. Allenby," enquired Sir Antony diffidently, "but if Lady Despard is not in attendance at your sister's marriage…?"

"Tom's inheritance will be delayed yet again. I cannot allow that to happen," Jane said simply and pressed her stepbrother's hand. "Don't worry, Tom. I'll speak to him."

"Perhaps you should allow me, Miss Despard?" suggested Sir Antony, with a smug smile of reassurance. "I have been known upon occasion to bring his lordship round to my way of thinking."

"Thank you, my lord. But I will make him see reason," Jane said firmly. "After all, he is just being stubborn for its own sake, and there is much more at stake here than any injury done to Lord Salt's pride."

Sir Antony bowed to her wishes and watched Jane approach the massive desk and its colossal owner, quizzing glass up to a magnified eye. "What an extraordinary young woman," he said with approval. "Tiny, but astonishingly tenacious."

"I do not understand why you will not grant Lady Despard admittance, when only yesterday you came face-to-face with her in your Arlington Street townhouse," Jane reasoned calmly. "It's for Tom's benefit that I ask you to acquiesce to the request. And it is the last occasion you need ever see her. Though why such a silly vain creature should bother you is beyond my comprehension. Unless—"

"Miss Despard, you don't know the first thing about—"

"—you don't wish to own a connection with her because you

took her to your bed and now wish to forget the liaison ever happened?"

Salt's mouth dropped open and he could barely speak above a whisper.

"Is that what—is that what that overripe tart told you?"

"Everyone knows casual liaisons are quite commonplace amongst your kind, so it's not as if you should be embarrassed in any way by her," Jane added conversationally, ignoring the Earl's angry blush. Jacob Allenby had made no secret of the Earl's sinful connection with his family and as her stepmother was known to have had affairs with several of Wiltshire's wealthy gentlemen, Jane had put two and two together. "She's not likely to say anything about sharing your bed because she would not want to embarrass Tom. If you would tell me what you are searching for, perhaps I could be of assistance?" she added in an abrupt change of subject. She watched him squint over the piles of documents he was moving and replacing in what seemed to Jane, no particular order, knowing he was blind to the print, and that this would only increase his agitation and likely negative response to the attorney's stipulation. When he glanced at her suspiciously, she added with a small, understanding smile, "Would it be such a burden for your noble nose to bear the weight of a pair of wire rimmed eyeglasses occasionally, my lord?"

"Special license," he muttered self-consciously, ignoring her question and stepping aside to allow her greater access to the desk. "Thank you," he murmured when she handed him a sheaf of parchment that had upon it the seal of the Archbishop of Canterbury. "Miss Despard, there are certain particulars concerning that woman that I will not discuss with you, or any other. It is a family matter, and one I refuse to allow Jacob Allenby to wreak his revenge from beyond the grave."

"Revenge?" Jane repeated, annoyed. "Is that all you can think about? I don't pretend to know the first thing about the feud between the Earls of Salt Hendon and the Allenbys, although you have confirmed by your prejudice that my stepmother is somehow involved in that dispute. What I do know is that if you don't permit her to stand as witness to my marriage, then my stepbrother, who is the innocent party in all of this, will have his future severely compromised, all because of some injury done your pride, and that I cannot allow."

"And what do you intend to do about it, Miss Despard?" the Earl drawled. When Jane opened her mouth then shut it again on a lame argument he added, "I'm surprised Allenby didn't take it upon himself to give you a one-sided explanation of the feud, as you like to call it, between the Allenbys and my family. Suffice it for me to say that you have hit the proverbial nail on its head. Your stepmother played her part well in that little melodrama." He held the special license under Jane's chin. "As for my pride... Where that family is concerned, I have none."

"If Jacob Allenby's will is not carried out to the letter, it is not only Tom's future which will be compromised, but the people who rely on him for their very existences," Jane argued. "Good, hardworking people who are employed in his factories. Surely you can relate to such a circumstance? There must be dozens of people who rely on you for their livelihoods, and if the numbers in your anteroom are anything to go by, there are dozens more waiting the opportunity to state their case in the hopes of gaining your patronage. I cannot believe that you, a gentleman, would willingly cause the ruin of a young man and those who depend upon him, and who has never done you a harm, all because of a feud you have with his mother's family, in which he played no part."

The Earl stared down at her flushed face and at the intensity in her blue eyes and had to concede that her impassioned argument was sound and surprisingly selfless. That he should feel a twinge of envy that she exhibited such passion on behalf of her stepbrother astonished and annoyed him. It made him say flippantly,

"Very well put, Miss Despard. When it suits your purpose you expect me to adhere to gentlemanly principles, and yet you have accused me of conduct unbecoming in a gentleman." He tickled her chin with the parchment. "Which is it to be?"

"I was not discussing your conduct towards me, my lord," she replied with quiet dignity, twisting the betrothal ring between her fingers at her back.

He lifted a mobile eyebrow. "Miss Despard, you speak with such injured confidence that I beg you to provide proof of the accusation of which I stand accused."

Jane's blue eyes held his gaze. "Certainly. At the appropriate time and place. But this is not it. You have a room full of onlookers awaiting us. The sooner the ceremony is performed, the sooner you can put this painful episode behind you and banish me to the backwater of your choosing. But you cannot do that, Tom cannot begin his life as an independent man of means, without Lady Despard's presence at my marriage, regrettable as the circumstance is for us both."

The Earl was laughingly skeptical. "So you are marrying me for Tom's sake?"

Jane nodded, all contrition, gaze dropped to the diamond buckle in the tongue of his polished leather shoe. He had such large feet. "If there was any other way, I would gladly take it, my lord."

He smiled, showing white teeth. "With that long face, I'm almost convinced," he quipped. "Then for Tom's sake, you must do three things and I will do what is required of me: Sign that document poor Arthur returned to me without your signature; provide me with the evidence that proves me less than a gentleman, and tell me why you are marrying me for Tom's sake."

Jane sighed her defeat and turned to the desk as one about to mount the chopping block, but the Earl grabbed her wrist and spun her back to face him. "After the ceremony will suffice for the document and the explanation. But I will know now why you must marry me."

Jane told him.

She wasn't sure how he would respond to the news that she was marrying him for no other reason than to allow her stepbrother to inherit what was rightfully his and thus free him up to pay his workers their long overdue wages, but she certainly never expected him to react in the way he did.

"You could marry *any man* and immediately forfeit the hundred thousand pounds that by rights should have gone to your stepbrother?" he said in disbelief. "By not stipulating Tom by name, that unscrupulous merchant was hoist by his own petard. How fitting!" He then burst into incredulous laughter, as if told a good joke.

If she had not been nonplussed by his reaction, Jane would

have delighted in his good humor because it stripped away his resentment, revealing the man she remembered and loved. She couldn't help smiling.

The rest of the party assembled in the library breathed easier at this turn of events, and the Earl remained in a surprisingly good humor throughout the ceremony, notwithstanding the presence of Lady Despard, who glowed with self-importance and had the satisfaction of knowing that the Earl had been forced to capitulate to her presence.

The ceremony concluded, the Earl bowed over his bride's hand, and as he straightened he winked at Jane, though there was nothing playful in his demeanor, and his gaze held a menacing intent.

"Now that Tom has his hundred thousand, I want payment in kind," he murmured near her ear. "I'll be home late, but I expect my wife to be up waiting and ready to perform her wifely duty."

THE NEW COUNTESS of Salt Hendon did not wait up for her husband. She was exhausted, emotionally and physically, from a day that seemed to go on forever. She had entered the bookroom thought by all in the anteroom to be just another petitioner, indeed a newly-employed domestic in the Earl's household, and left its warmth as the sixth Countess of Salt Hendon, feeling no different, yet immediately whisked off to a suite of rooms on the second floor that smelled of fresh paint, glue from newly-hung wallpaper, and that teemed with industry. A dressmaker, a milliner, a *corsetiere*, a shoemaker, a number of seamstresses, and several assistants all toiled away at their various tasks, while workmen busied themselves with arranging beautifully-carved mahogany furniture and hanging damask curtains around a new and enormous four-poster bed.

Jane had never seen a bed quite like it. She was told there was one other, its twin in fact, in the Earl's bedchamber. The intricately-carved mahogany posts stretched up to the ornate plastered ceiling, and there was an elaborate headboard which incorporated the coat of arms of the House of Sinclair. Unlike the dark crimson velvet curtains about the Earl's bed, Jane's curtains were decidedly more feminine, being pale blue and yellow damask. Matching curtains covered the sash windows and complemented the coverings on the chaise longue and the dressing table stool in the spacious closet.

The housekeeper apologized for the lack of a fire in the grates of the closet and the bedchamber. A chimney sweep had been called to investigate what was blocking the flues, possibly old birds' nests from the previous spring. Like most of the rooms and furniture on the second floor, this suite had never been used since the Earl's purchase of the house some four years before. The only occupant on this floor was the Earl himself, but as he spent most of his time when Parliament was sitting at the Arlington Street townhouse he shared with Sir Antony Templestowe, this thoroughly modern and spacious mansion was sadly neglected.

Of course, that would all change for the better now. The house was in desperate need of a mistress, opined the housekeeper with a kind smile at Jane, who blushed and quickly walked on into the next room, a pretty, light-filled sitting room fitted out in the Chinese manner, with peonies and stork wallpaper, matching silk curtains and a carved mahogany chinoiserie overmantel. The housekeeper hoped her ladyship would not object to being fitted for her gowns and necessaries in this room, where there was a good fire in the grate. An ornate screen had been set up in a corner for just this purpose, and beside this screen, looking nervous and self-conscious, stood a young woman not much older, but considerably taller than Jane. The young woman quickly bobbed a curtsy and was introduced by the housekeeper as her ladyship's newly-employed personal maid, Springer.

"Oh, that name will never do, Mrs. Jenkins," said Jane, a smile at the nervous woman who again bobbed a curtsy. "I once owned a beagle who answered to Springer. You must have a Christian name?"

"Anne. It's Anne, my lady," the maid shyly volunteered.

"Relation of Springer, the butler at Arlington Street?"

Anne smiled. "Yes, my lady. That would be my father. He and my mother look after his lordship when he cares to stay at that address." She received such a scowling look from the housekeeper for prattling on that she bobbed another curtsy saying, "Shall I fetch in the dressmaker, my lady? And there's a jeweler come to fix your wedding band, and the shoemaker needs one of your shoes, if your ladyship wouldn't mind... But perhaps your ladyship would care for a dish of tea first, before we begin the fittings?"

"Yes. Tea, and the jeweler. Thank you, Anne," said Jane.

"If you don't need me, my lady, I must get back to the kitchen," apologized the housekeeper. "Cook needs me to finish up the arrangements for tomorrow's dinner after his lordship's tennis tournament, and what with a house full of guests—"

"A houseful? Here? Tomorrow?"

"Yes, my lady. His lordship said not to bother you with the arrangements," explained the housekeeper, "on account of your ladyship having enough to do today. But if you would like to see the menu?"

Jane shook her head. "No. That will be all, Mrs. Jenkins. And thank you for all you've done to make me feel welcome." She gave herself up into the hands of the dozen or so people employed by the Earl to ensure she had a wardrobe befitting a Countess, come the arrival of the first guests for the annual Royal Tennis tournament and dinner.

By the time she was well and truly ready for sleep, she had lost count of the number of gowns she had been pinned in and out of, and the yards and yards of silks, velvets, damasks, Chinese and Indian cottons, and various other fine materials that were too numerous to remember. These wondrous and expensive materials were wrapped around her slim frame and over panniers that encased her slender hips, then expertly tacked and trimmed and taken away to be sewn up by industrious seamstresses.

From behind the ornate dressing screen, the *corsetiere* and her two assistants laced her into various low-cut stays and bodices, until she thought her ribs were cracked. Some were of buckram and whalebone covered in silk and linen, others were embroidered, and many matched the petticoats and were to be worn to be seen. The two French female émigrées then presented for her selection diaphanous chemises, nightgowns with tiny pearl buttons and low-cut necklines trimmed with satin bows and lace, exquisitely-embroidered silk dressing gowns of matching fabrics, and a mountain of silk stockings and garters, all, they assured her with knowing smiles, guaranteed to please husbands and lovers alike.

Jane blushed rosily, pulling the coverlet up to her chin, recalling their sly smiles and confidential giggles, as she had blushed in their company, and drifted off to sleep on the chaise longue in the cold bedchamber. She was not in her enormous new four-poster bed because its new mattress of duck and geese feathers had failed to arrive that day, an oversight for which the housekeeper could not apologize enough, until Jane assured her she would be just as comfortable and warm if a bed were made up for her on the chaise.

The Earl found her here an hour later, in the glow of a guttering candelabrum.

The hum of voices and industry came from behind the sitting room door, where various tradesmen and women were only too happy to work by candlelight in shifts through the night to accommodate his wishes. The covers had slid to the floor, leaving Jane cold and curled up in a ball trying to find warmth in the thin linen nightshift bunched up around her knees, giving him an appreciative view of her slim stockinged ankles and slender feet.

With her hair braided in one long thick rope down her back, and dressed in a nightshift that covered her from throat to wrists, she looked absurdly youthful and untouched. In fact, she did not look a day older than his sister Caroline, who was all of seventeen and a half years of age, a comparison which froze his ardor better than a hipbath of cold water. Not that it had been his intention to disturb her so late. But he was curious to see how she had got on in her new surroundings, and if she had indeed waited up for him as he had ordered.

He really hadn't expected her to obey him and was glad to find her asleep. Though why she was on the chaise longue... No mattress on the bed—and no fire in the grate. He would have words with Jenkins in the morning. No wonder the room was as cold as the deserted square outside.

She would surely freeze if she slept in here all night.

Decided, he picked her up off the chaise longue, careful not to wake her, and was surprised when, in her sleep, she wrapped a slim arm about his neck and pressed herself against him invitingly, finding warmth in his waistcoat. He was all too well aware that under her thin linen nightshift she was naked but for her stockinged legs. Yet, bedding his bride tonight was not his intent. He just wanted to get her warm and go to sleep himself after a tiring day. But as he carried her effortlessly through the opened door that connected her apartment to his, he could not ignore the alluring feel of her garters under his fingers, or the knowledge that from the knees up her lovely thighs were completely bare.

She was so light. He'd forgotten that about her, or perhaps he had made himself forget with the help of a string of casual lovers, all of whom, despite their skill in pleasuring him, were forgotten in the coolness of morning. It was in the coolness of morning that the memory of Miss Jane Katherine Despard was most acute. Kissing her, pleasuring her, the memory of her sweet-smelling skin and the adorable smile and laughing blue eyes that haunted him in his half-waking state. Not tomorrow morning, or any morning after that. He was going to make certain of that.

His bedchamber was warm and inviting, with plenty of light and a roaring fire in the grate. His valet was busying himself in the closet, where two footmen were filling a hipbath with hot water. Andrews was unaware of his master's return until he came through to the bedchamber to turn down the sheets of the enormous four-poster bed, and there discovered, tucked up under the covers, a sleeping beauty. He saw this vision of loveliness before he saw his master, who stood on the other side of the bed slowly unbuttoning his waistcoat, gaze very much fixed on his bride.

Without a word or a look, the valet turned on a heel and went back into the closet, where he threw back in one mouthful the nightly drop of brandy he had set out for the Earl.

"Andrews, is there the remotest possibility I own a nightshirt?"

"A nightshirt, my lord?" repeated the valet, pouring the Earl a fresh glass of brandy, then taking from him his divested waistcoat. He knew full well the Earl had never worn that particular article of clothing a day (or more precisely, a night) in his adult life. Still, he managed to keep the surprise out of his voice. "I do believe I may be able to find a nightshirt, though as to its condition…"

"Just get it," Salt said abruptly as he pulled his shirt up over his square set shoulders and dropped it into his valet's willing hands.

He went over to the hipbath and stared at his reflection in the warm still water, hands on narrow hips, wide flared bare back displayed for his valet's admiration. "I must be mad," he muttered at himself. "What man on his wedding night puts clothes on to go to bed with his bride? Mad!"

The valet thought so too.

SIX

T HE POST BOY RINGING his eleven o'clock bell signaled the last collection of mail for the day, and shattered the still and freezing night air. It was much too cold in this fashionable quarter surrounding Grosvenor Square for itinerate sellers, thieves, pickpockets, and drunken Merry-Andrews who usually roamed the streets at this late hour. Even the chairmen were scarce. But then a carriage pulled up outside a particular townhouse in South Audley Street, and out stepped a lady in a fur-lined hooded cape, wearing pattens to keep the muck off her satin slippers.

She had just come from Drury Lane Theatre, where she had enjoyed the attentions of her son's circle of male friends and the admiration of one or two gentlemen nearer her own age, who left their cards and asked permission to call on her the following day. She had no idea what the play was about or the names of its actors, but she had spent the evening surrounded by titled and wealthy males. She was more than satisfied with her foray to the theater.

Her buoyant mood dissolved, however, as soon as the nose-in-the-air porter of this fashionable establishment admitted her. She was not welcome; she saw it on the faces of the porter, the butler and the lady's maid who were all lemon-and-lime faced. She was made to feel inferior and cheap, and her clothes not quite the thing under their steely, disapproving gaze. But she had waited all day for this interview with the high and mighty Diana, Lady St. John, daughter of a Baron, cousin of an Earl, mother of his heir, and related to at least three ducal houses.

This doyenne of fashion and darling of Polite Society had graciously granted Lady Despard five minutes of her time, but only under cover of darkness. But Lady Despard didn't care that she was unwelcome, nor would she have cared had she been shown in via the tradesmen's entrance. She had a message to convey and important news to share with her ladyship, and she couldn't wait to see her reaction. She hoped for venomous tears, at the very least. She got much more.

She was shown up to her ladyship's boudoir because there was a fire in the grate. Ordinarily, provincial visitors were granted an audience in the drawing room at the front of the house, if they were granted an interview at all. Her pattens she left in the hall, along with her cloak. No refreshment was offered her, and the porter was instructed to tell the driver to wait; Lady St. John's visitor would not be staying above a few minutes.

Lady Despard was standing by the fireplace warming her gloved hands when Diana St. John came quietly into the room. She was in *déshabillé*, a brocade dressing gown thrown negligently over her nightgown, and her light auburn hair, full of curling papers, fell to her shoulders. Yet her face, as always, was perfectly made up, even down to the carefully-applied mouche at the corner of her painted lips.

Diana St. John took one look at the woman by the fireplace in her revealing, low-cut bodice and outrageously upswept powdered hair, and smiled thinly. Her exceptional memory had not failed her. She would not have been able to recall the woman's name, but her butler had supplied that. Yet she knew who she was: The wife of a nobody squire and sister of a Bristol merchant—Allenby was his name—and she was stepmother of *that creature*. How gratifying that Lady Despard's beauty had faded more rapidly than her own in the four years since their one and only meeting during the Salt Hunt.

"Been on the town, Madam?" Diana St. John enquired with a crooked smile as she came further into the room.

She did not sit, nor did she offer her visitor a chair, and was displeased when the woman did not curtsy to show her rank the proper respect.

"Drury Lane Theatre, where I saw a most marvelous play by a well-known playwright, but I can't remember either," Lady Despard replied, the inference to her loose morals lost on her. She openly looked Diana St. John up and down. "I was surprised not to see you, my lady. Everyone who was anyone was there tonight. Still, ladies of our age must have at least one night off a week to recover our looks. The London Season must be so fatiguing for you, whereas in Bristol—"

"I don't give a damn about Bristol, nor do I have time for your inconsequential small talk. What is it you want?"

"Fie, my lady! There's no need to be vulgar, to be sure," Lady Despard commented with a pout and, spying her reflection in the looking glass by the fireplace, couldn't resist an admiring glance. "Particularly when I have made the effort to come here at such a late hour with news of interest to you, and suffered a considerable loss to my social calendar—"

"If you've yet to scratch his itch, your prospective lover will look you up tomorrow if you pay him enough. So why have you come?"

Lady Despard took a moment to adjust a small bow in a powdered curl. "Are you aware that my dear brother Jacob was buried a mere three months ago?"

Diana St. John lifted her brow. "And how would one know that, Madam, when you've already dispensed with your mourning? Or didn't you even bother to put on your black?"

Lady Despard was put out. She puckered her painted lips. "Black does not become me. I wore gray to mourn Sir Felix, and that was quite enough. Poor Jacob," she added with a sigh, as if her sad regret made up for her lack of mourning. "He survived the smallpox only to die from complications of the lung. Such a loss to me and my son…"

Diana St. John shrugged a shoulder in callous indifference. "Three months or three years. Allenby's death is supremely unimportant. You don't require my sympathy. No doubt he left you more than you deserve."

Her visitor looked smug. "Twenty thousand, to do with as I please."

Diana St. John dismissed the inheritance with a contemptuous sniff. "Pin money. So? The reason you are here?"

"Twenty thousand to do with as I please, once I have delivered you a message from Jacob. A lawyer awaits in my carriage to ensure I have done as stipulated in my dear brother's will."

"Oh, *please*. Not a message from beyond the grave! What could that moralizing puff piece possibly have to say to me?"

Lady Despard smiled thinly. "I know what you had done to Jane. Jacob told me."

Silence fell upon the room. The only sound, the ticking of the mantel clock.

Lady Despard waited and watched.

Finally, Diana St. John yawned as if bored, and said levelly, "So your brother felt a twinge of regret and was weak enough to confess his part in that tedious melodrama to you. My conscience is clear. I merely carried out Sir Felix's wishes to have the rotten fruit of his daughter's disgraceful behavior got rid of as expediently as possible."

"It was exceedingly interesting to Jacob that you knew of Jane's pregnancy before she had confessed her condition to Sir Felix."

"What of it? Once she opened her legs to Salt it was no stretch of the imagination to suppose a pregnancy would ensue. After all," she said with a small private smile, "his lordship is exceptionally virile."

"You knew Jane's seducer was Lord Salt, when her father did not. Jane told no one. You have made it your life's work to know all about his virility have you not, my lady?"

"I beg your pardon?"

"Lord Salt's habits, more precisely whom he has bedded and when, if he got them with child and how often, and what you did for them and others who found themselves *inconvenienced*."

Diana St. John crossed to the door and wrenched it open.

"I have not the slightest idea to what you allude. You are talking goose fat, Madam! If that is all you have to say, leave before I have you bodily removed."

Lady Despard stayed where she was.

"Betwixt you and me, my lady, brother Jacob didn't give two testers how many whores Lord Salt had impregnated, or what you did to help rid them of their unwanted pregnancies, his lordship none the wiser. But it bothered him greatly that you overstepped the mark with little Jane, who was a virgin."

"The creature should have thought of the consequences of her behavior before she let Salt between her thighs."

"What was the medicinal preparation you supplied to Sir Felix?" She peered into her reticule and took out a piece of paper; this she unfolded and smiled. "Ah! That's it! Syrup of Artem—Artem*isia*." She held out the paper. "There is an address here of your apothecary on the Strand.

Diana St. John gritted her teeth. "I know his address, you insolent slut. Leave! *Now*."

"But I haven't delivered Jacob's message yet," Lady Despard replied with a pout, putting the folded paper back in her reticule, enjoying the woman's growing anger. When Diana St. John opened the door wider, she added with a shrug, "I don't see why it matters now. Not after today's events, but Jacob wanted you to know that placed with his will is a document that names your clients, females who found themselves with child, and the services you rendered them as a terminating midwife; a hanging offence for client and supplier, so brother Jacob's attorneys tell me."

Diana St. John kept her features perfectly composed. It was as if Lady Despard had not spoken. She certainly wasn't about to acknowledge the accusation or the implied threat. "I have a full round of engagements tomorrow. No doubt the heady social scene of Bristol beckons you. Good night, Madam."

Lady Despard still remained by the fireplace. "It seems to me that you are in ignorance of what occurred today in Grosvenor Square."

"Grosvenor Square?"

"You truly have no idea what happened to Lord Salt today, my lady?"

A little of Diana St. John's cold façade cracked. She came back into the middle of the room. "Happened?"

"The Earl of Salt Hendon was married this afternoon."

Diana St. John laughed as if told a good joke. "Impossible!"

Lady Despard blinked at her, unable to fathom what the woman found to be amused by in such news.

"You witless creature! As if his lordship would marry with his family none the wiser. As if I would not know such a momentous occasion was to take place. There is a proper order to such things in our circle. It may be common in the gutters of Bristol—

"What is there that you don't understand, my lady? Lord Salt was married this afternoon. I was there to witness his—"

"You? Nonsense! Why would you of all people on God's good earth be witness to his marriage? Now I know you are talking flummery. I was at Grosvenor Square only this morning. Tuesday he is at home to petitioners. There's always a mob of beggars at his door. And in the afternoon he's at Parliament. He is a stickler for doing his duty, tiresomely so. He wouldn't have time to get married on a Tuesday. Perhaps on a Thursday or a Saturday. But never on a Tuesday. He doesn't even have the time for me, but I make certain I stay an hour; just so he remembers what's important in life, that he has a duty to Ron and to me. Just so he knows I'm there for him…always."

"You haven't asked about the bride…"

"He wouldn't marry without consulting me," Diana St. John continued stubbornly convincing herself, ignoring the leading remark. "He doesn't visit his mistress without me knowing about it. I can tell you when he visits and how many times he mounts his whore in a night. I make it my business to know. And if he so much as looks sideways at an eligible young female, I'm there to make certain the girl takes her interest elsewhere. Luckily, his rakish reputation usually precedes him, which scares the prudish ones away.

"And one can't be too careful when selecting the right woman to be his mistress," she boasted. "She must interest him enough to distract him, but not too much that he can't be persuaded to move on to the next diversion. She has to be unable to bear children, or at the very least not want any brats and know to come to me to rid herself of unwanted offspring, should that tiresome circumstance eventuate. You see how considerate I am of his welfare?" She pressed her shaking hands together and tried to smile. "What with looking out for his political career, which is going ahead in leaps and bounds, sitting for dreary hour upon dreary hour in the Ladies Gallery of the Lords, playing hostess to party political dinners and the like when he requires that of me, not to mention taking Ron to see him as much as possible, and the onerous task of keeping track of his love life, I rarely have a moment to myself. So it is impossible for him to find the time, least of all want to marry behind my back…"

Lady Despard thought Diana St. John raving like a mad woman, and that perhaps her mind had indeed snapped. She had no idea what to say in reply to a sermon on her good works on the Earl's behalf which clearly, even to her lax moral code, overstepped the boundaries of decency at the nobleman's right to privacy. But in the ensuing long silence she felt she had to say something.

"You are all consideration for his welfare to be sure, my lady, but perhaps you could have saved yourself a great deal of time and bother had you just married him yourself."

"Married him?" Diana St. John repeated, as if the question was offensive in the extreme. "Of course I want to marry him, you bloody stupid cow! I've wanted to marry him since I was twelve years old. But a lady does not ask a gentleman to marry her. A lady waits to be asked…"

Lady Despard was taken aback but unsympathetic. "Then you've missed your chance and must take comfort in the fact that you weren't the only female destined for disappointment."

"I've known him all my life and not once has he ever seriously considered the married state," Diana St. John continued, dumbfounded. "Though four years ago he came within a flea's foot, but fortunately I managed to put a stop to that whim before he did something utterly rash and socially unacceptable. Whoever heard of a Sinclair marrying the daughter of a nobody squire? Of course, I attribute that episode to an infatuation for a pretty face. Is that creature still as beautiful as I remember her? She had the most perfect skin, and such gloriously dark thick hair. Too thin and small-breasted, of course, but some men are attracted to the type. One could forgive Salt his momentary lustful lapse, but as for marriage—"

"He married Jane Despard this afternoon, my lady. And yes, she is just as beautiful as your remembrance of her."

Diana St. John stood as stone and stared disbelieving at Lady Despard for a long time. But as that woman merely stared back at her expressionless, fear seized her. "Salt… *Married*? Married? *Married* Jane Despard?" She shuffled to the fireplace, unsteady on her slippered feet and put out a hand to the headrest of the wingchair, the other to her constricted throat. "Oh, God. Oh, God. *Oh, God.*"

"Strange how matters can take a turn," Lady Despard said wistfully. "I should have realized that even when Sir Felix banished her, even when he forced the baby to be quickened before its time, he still loved his daughter. He always used to say Jane was the image of her mother. His first wife was granddaughter of an Irish duke, don't you know? But she married well beneath her by eloping with Sir Felix. It was her death that started his drinking and gambling. Poor Sir Felix. Tragic. Still," she added in a rallying tone, "he wanted nothing less than an earl for Jane and an earl was what he got with his last breath; *your precious earl,* to be precise."

She frowned. Diana St. John looked on the verge of a nervous collapse. "Shall I call for your maid, my lady?"

"Maid?" Diana St. John repeated, dazed.

"Such news has made you unwell, my lady. Perhaps a brandy…"

Diana St. John's fingers gripping the back of the upholstered wingchair were white at the knuckles. This woman had been sent here to do her harm. She was lying. Yes, that was it! She was lying. This was Jacob Allenby's way of taunting her from the grave. She glared at her visitor with menacing intent. "Did Allenby put you up to this? Did he hope to punish me with this lie?"

"It is no lie. Though, when you think about it, it is a fitting punishment for what you had done to Jane." Lady Despard had a flash of insight. "A natural justice of sorts."

"Justice? Ha!" Diana St. John's mind was spinning with a mixture of denial and possibilities. "Let Salt satisfy his lust with that creature, as many times as he likes, much I care! Then watch me have the little trollop banished back to her sodden corner of Wiltshire quicker than you can spell Ranelagh."

"But surely that defeats your purpose, my lady?" Lady Despard asked, confused. "A virile man of Salt's age and abilities is more than capable of making love to his wife several times over on his wedding night. And we both know they can breed. In all likelihood, as you stand there mourning his marriage, he's already impregnated her." She smiled at her own cleverness. "Isn't that what you wanted to avoid all those years ago? If Jane begets an heir where does that leave your son?" She tittered. "And you call *me* the stupid cow!"

Diana St. John was stunned, as if the reality of the wedding night had never occurred to her. She remained upright and composed until Lady Despard was unceremoniously dismissed from her sight. She then collapsed in the wingchair, put her head in her hands and gave herself up to tears of intense hatred and mounting frustration. Much later, when she was wasted of self-pity and drained of all natural emotion, she began plotting her revenge.

SALT HAD NO IDEA HOW many hours he remained awake in the big four-poster bed, lying on his side, staring at the little leaping flames amongst the glowing coals in the deep grate of the bedchamber fireplace. He just knew it was uncomfortable on his wide shoulders. But if he moved and lay flat on his back, or turned on to his other side, there was a very real possibility he would come in contact with his sleeping bride, and he wanted to avoid that at all costs.

The nightshirt definitely helped as a deterrent. What a ridiculous article of clothing! Wide, collarless and with billowing sleeves, it felt more like a sheet with a hole cut in it for his head. No wonder he'd given up wearing them as soon as he'd left Eton. He felt as if he'd been put into adult swaddling; the linen caught round his legs, and there was no way of untangling himself without lifting his entire body off the bed several times. He really couldn't bear wearing the ridiculous thing a moment longer. Surely the bed was wide enough that he could sleep naked and be comfortable without causing a disturbance to his bride?

Decided, he slid out of bed, wrenched the nightshirt up over his shoulders, and flung it in disgust into a darkened corner. Satisfied to be rid of one torment, he raked his shoulder-length hair out of his eyes and slid back under the covers to lie on his back. It was such a welcome relief to evenly distribute his weight that he only managed to stare at the pleated canopy for a handful of seconds before he finally drifted off into a welcome deep sleep.

Twenty minutes later he was wide-awake.

Blissfully asleep, Jane migrated to the middle of the bed in search of warmth. It was a big bed that allowed its equally large owner to sprawl out in comfort, but without the heavy curtains drawn about the four mahogany posts to keep out the still night air, nor the use of a bed warmer to take the chill off the linen sheets, there was little comfort for Jane's slender frame, inadequately covered as it was by a thin nightshift. Even her white stockings were of little use in keeping her warm, stopping as they did just above the knees. But she found the perfect substitute for a hot brick in the form of her husband's warm, naked body. Tall, wide and with plenty of well-exercised muscle, he radiated heat and comfort, and on such a cold winter's night he was the ideal bed and body warmer. The sleeping Jane happily snuggled into him and instantly returned to a state of deep slumber.

The same could not be said for her husband, who kept as still as he possibly could, eyes on the canopy, and tried his best to ignore her soft, lithe female curves. She had her pink cheek nestled against his beefy shoulder and an arm across his torso, while one shapely stockinged leg straddled a brawny thigh. She clung to him like glued paper to a wall. And as if this wasn't enough of a distraction, her raven hair, which had escaped the confines of its long braid, fell about the pillows in a wild mane and tickled his square, unshaven chin.

Ignoring his edict to remain still beside her, because his arm and fingers were tingling from inertia, he shifted his weight amongst the pillows and covers, disturbing Jane enough for her to move with him, then resettle with her head now resting against his chest and an arm about his neck. There was nothing for it but to drop his arm over her.

He closed his eyes, determined to ignore her soft curves and his stiffening erection, and set his mind to recalling the goings on at Parliament that afternoon, particularly Bute's dreary speech about troop deployments, now the war with France was concluded and the Peace about to be signed in Paris; and there was that ridiculous debate over the Commons' adjournment for the observance of St. George's Day on the 31st because the 30th fell on a Sunday.

Ordinarily these musings were enough to put him to sleep faster than a dose of laudanum, but Jane's light regular breathing and the delicious distraction of her body moving ever so gently against him did nothing to dampen his ardor. And when she turned and tried to straighten her bunched up nightshift to untangle her stockinged legs, but with little success, he did the gentlemanly thing and helped her out of the flimsy linen garment. He tossed it across the room to join his crumpled nightshirt.

Half-awake, she remained sitting up in bed facing him, completely oblivious to her nakedness but for her white stockings held fast above the knee with silk ribbons tied in neat bows, and her tumble of lustrous raven-black hair that fell about her shoulders to the small of her back in alluring disarray. With a heavy-lidded drowsy "thank you" and a sleepy smile, she promptly snuggled down beside him again to enjoy the warmth of his body. He wasn't sure how much more of this glorious torture he could endure.

He was about to draw up the coverlet when he couldn't resist admiring his bride's feminine loveliness under the glow of the fire. From stockinged toes to shapely bare thigh, from the rise of her hips to the dip in her waist and up to her small firm breasts, she was utterly arousing and completely captivating—and his. Bland speeches about peace treaties and frustrating debates about the observance of saints' days burst like bubbles as he gently brushed a long strand of soft curl from across the pale pink of her nipple and off her throat.

The scent of soap, of freshly-scrubbed skin and the natural essence of her, made him hover and drink her in. She smelled as delicious as she looked, lying on her side with her hands tucked under her cheek, long black tresses falling all about her. He could almost convince himself that the intervening years had never happened and this was in truth the wedding night he had planned for them to enjoy at his Wiltshire estate. Perhaps if he kissed her the deception would be complete…

He brushed his mouth along her soft warm cheek, and when she blinked and tilted her chin up to him, he did what he had so very much wanted to do for four years—he kissed her mouth.

"What a lovely dream," she murmured through half-open lids.

"Yes, a dream."

She put her arm up around his neck and drew him back down to kiss her again. "You smell nice. You always smell nice."

He smiled. "Do I?"

She licked her top lip.

"Taste nice, too."

He chuckled. "So do you."

"No more talk. Kiss me."

He obliged her, giving himself up to the luxury of a long, lingering and delightfully exploratory kiss as her mouth parted under the pressure of his. She had such soft plump lips. He wanted to go on kissing and caressing her for as long as he was able to resist entering her gloriously aroused flesh, the anticipation of what was to come almost as exciting as the act itself; for he had not kissed another woman the way he kissed Jane.

When he had forced a kiss on her that day on the Hunt two years ago, when she had trespassed onto his land, it was in the belief it would cure his want of her. That if he kissed her, held her in his arms, he would finally be done with her. But even a kiss forced upon her had only increased his misery, for it merely reaffirmed his inadequacy in wanting her. Just as these kisses now with her permission made the wanting of her excruciatingly urgent. If he did not have her there and then he was certain he would go mad.

"Touch me, Jane. *Hold me.*"

She willingly complied, and his entire body ignited. They tumbled on the bed, and when he had her at the precipice of no return, she pressed against him, stockinged legs wrapped around his strong thighs, whimpering for release. He had all the encouragement he needed. He could wait no longer. If he heard her gasp as he filled her completely, it was in the deep recesses of his mind. Yet he was not so far beyond reach that her unguarded admission in the heat of the moment went unheard. It evoked for him the stark reality of their bittersweet union, and served to remind him why they now shared a bed, not because they were passionately in love but because they were legally bound together as man and wife. There was no romance here. But there was definitely lust...

"How could I marry another when you've utterly ruined me..."

Why had she chosen that moment, while they were in the throws of passionate lovemaking on their wedding night, to remind him of the past? Was she intent on emasculating him for defiling her? So be it. He *would* stop. He would leave her dissatisfied. He should... But he was beyond the point of caring. All that mattered was fulfillment. His fulfillment.

In the heat of the moment, in the heat that turned to anger mingled with a throbbing need for physical gratification, all he cared about was filling her, his wife, with his seed, seed barren and wasted, but his seed as her husband. And when release finally came, when they tumbled off the precipice into blissful oblivion, he had the hollow satisfaction of hearing her splinter the cold night air with his Christian name.

"YOU'RE DAMNED IF YOU DO and damned if you don't," was Jenkins the butler's gloomy prediction. He yawned loudly. "What time is it? Three in the morning and not a minute less."

The Earl's valet eyed him with drowsy resentment and again addressed the messenger. "How urgent is urgent?"

The messenger from South Audley Street shrugged. "Urgent. With respect, sir, at this late hour, none of us are in a position to argue the meaning of the word."

The valet leaned his night-capped head back against the wall of the ill-lit servant passageway outside his master's apartment and stared at the door opposite. Jenkins was right. He was damned either way. If he didn't deliver Lady St. John's message, she would cause an almighty fuss and demand his immediate dismissal. If he did, and walked into his master's bedchamber on this of all nights he was confident the Earl would dismiss him anyway. He was not a betting man but he was of the opinion that he would take his chances and incur Lady St. John's wrath rather than disturb his master on his bridal night. Decided, he stepped away from the wall and snatched the sealed parchment from the messenger's hand.

"Tell your mistress her letter was delivered. I'll see his lordship gets it."

The messenger shook his head. "Sorry, sir. I'm not to leave until I 'ave a reply."

"Then find yourself a nice corner to curl up in, because you'll be spending the night!" the valet hissed. "There's no power on this earth that will see me walk through that door on this of all nights. It's his lordship's wedding night, for God's sake!"

The messenger grinned lewdly at the butler but Jenkins decided the lackey was becoming too familiar and needed putting in his place. "You heard Mr. Andrews. Find yourself a corner. His lordship can't be disturbed."

The messenger looked from one to the other and shrugged, unperturbed. "Thing is, sirs, if I don't get a reply within the hour, her ladyship 'as threatened to come round 'ere 'erself on account of the fact that she don't trust you lot 'ere. She said so 'erself. Tell 'em, she said, if I don't get a reply from 'is lordship I'll come round there and disturb 'im m'self. And you know she will."

Yes, Jenkins and Andrews knew very well of what Lady St. John was capable. As the widowed mother of the Earl's heir, her ladyship frequently abused her position of influence. The valet wiped a hand across his dry mouth, and stared down at the sealed note.

"What is so urgent that Lady St. John requires the Earl's presence in the middle of the night?"

"Something about 'er boy vomitin'," the messenger replied. "'is temperature is 'igh too, and 'e's delirious and wanting 'is Uncle Salt. Nothing or no one will calm the little master save 'is lordship's presence."

The valet swore viciously under his breath. He knew the Earl was devoted to Lady St. John's children. When his first cousin and best friend Lord St. John had tragically died from the smallpox four years ago, the Earl had willingly taken on the role of substitute father to the St. John children. The valet knew his master had on occasion left the warmth of his bed in the middle of the night to pacify Lady St. John's sickly son. But this night was different from all others, and Andrews didn't relish the task—in fact he wished he could avoid it, but knew that for wishful thinking.

"Has a physician been called to the boy?" Andrews asked the messenger, feeling the noose of decision tightening about his neck. When the messenger nodded, he sighed, took from the butler his burning taper and went over to the closet door. "Give me a minute."

"So you're going in there?" Jenkins asked with a trill of anticipation. He frowned and shook his head. "Courageous, Andrews. *Very* courageous."

The valet didn't think so. He considered himself the greatest coward this side of the Thames. Heart beating against his chest, he stood on the threshold of the cavernous bedchamber with burning taper in hand and listened for signs of life within. Thankfully the room was quiet now, and all he could hear was the familiar sound of the crackling fire in the grate. It had been anything but quiet and still two hours ago.

He was not a betting man but he would confidently stake a year's wages on his lordship having vigorously consummated his marriage, and to the mutual satisfaction of both parties. He put the taper on the table by the doorway, took two steps, and trod on cloth. Curious, he scooped up the bundle under his foot, and holding it at arm's length, realized he had in his hand a man's and a woman's nightshifts. His face burned with embarrassment, but he did what any good valet worth his coin would do: He folded the articles of clothing neatly and put them over his arm before approaching the four-poster bed in the light of the fire.

Twelve years of service to the Earl had not prepared the valet for the novel experience of disturbing a newly-married couple on their wedding night. Yet, to his great surprise and relief, the Countess was wide-awake sitting on the edge of the bed, back up against a mahogany post, wrapped in a coverlet, her mass of shiny black curls tumbled about her shoulders. She was admiring the Earl while he slept sprawled out in the big bed, a tangle of sheet scarcely covering his sizeable manhood.

Jane blushed rosily upon seeing the valet hovering in the shadows, but made life easy for him by smiling and saying in a friendly whisper, as if it were the most natural thing in the world for her husband's valet to disturb her on her wedding night, "Oh good, you found my shift. I did wonder where it had disappeared. I'll put it on if you'll just turn your back, and then we'll be comfortable."

Andrews did as requested, even going so far as to tiptoe across to a ribbon-back chair to one side of the fireplace where he had laid out one of the Earl's silk banyans. He offered this to Jane, still with his back to her, hand thrust out behind him. She was so quiet, all he heard was the swishing of silk, and before he knew what was happening, the Countess appeared before him, the silk banyan wrapped tightly over her nightshift. The garment was ludicrously large on her, making her appear smaller and absurdly youthful. Andrews had the urge to offer his assistance in rolling up the sleeves so she could find her fingers. Of course, he curbed the instinct, and when she moved away from the bed to the fireplace so they could talk without disturbing the slumbering nobleman, he made her an officious bow.

"Please excuse this intrusion, my lady," he stated, keeping his eyes lowered. "I would not have disturbed his lordship for the world except there is a matter of some delicacy. I am at a loss to know how to proceed without seeking his lordship's opinion."

"It must be important indeed... I'm sorry, but I don't believe I know your name?"

"Andrews, my lady. It's Aloysius Andrews, valet to his lordship. Your ladyship should address me as Andrews."

"Well, Andrews, as I am wide awake and willing to offer you my assistance, do we need to disturb his lordship?"

The valet glanced over at the bed where the Earl slept soundly, then back at Jane's big blue eyes regarding him with frankness. Although he was unconvinced that this young bride would be a match for the social wiles of Lady St. John, she was, when all was said and done, the Countess of Salt Hendon, and that counted for everything in his books. So he told her his dilemma.

Jane listened attentively and asked all the right questions. At the end of his diatribe, Andrews felt he had such a sympathetic ear that he let down his guard and confessed his real fear: That the Earl would dismiss him, and if his lordship didn't, Lady St. John would certainly have him tossed onto the streets.

"Do you truly believe his lordship a fickle nobleman capable of dismissing his most trusted servant after twelve years' good service, all because you failed to inform him at four o'clock in the morning that his godson was vomiting?" Jane asked with a smile.

"When you put it like that, my lady, no, he isn't. He's always been very fair," Andrews replied and felt curiously relieved. "To point out fact, his lordship is the best and fairest master by whom I've had the privilege to be employed as gentleman's gentleman."

"I thought as much," Jane said with confidence. "So what do you suggest we do with Lady St. John's letter?"

"I'd wait till morning," Andrews replied without hesitation. "There's not much his lordship can do for the boy tonight, save get in the physician's way. And if he is delirious, he wouldn't know if his lordship was in attendance on him or not, is my opinion. Besides," he began and stopped, but when Jane continued to smile at him encouragingly he added cautiously, "Lady St. John can sometimes be a bit of a-a panic merchant where her son is concerned, if your ladyship understands my meaning."

Jane understood only too well. Her stepmother was the same with her stepbrother Tom, overprotective and frantic at the first sign of a sniffle, and not much good in a crisis. She suspected Lady St. John made a habit of calling on Salt for male support in her times of crisis, whatever the hour or the inconvenience.

"Then I suggest we leave the letter on his lordship's dressing table for him to read in the morning," was Jane's advice. "If there is any change in the little boy's condition, his mother will no doubt send another messenger with an even more urgent request, and then perhaps we will need to wake his lordship. But until then, let's wait and see, shall we? Does that seem reasonable?"

"Very reasonable, my lady," agreed the valet, standing taller, the cloud of doom and despair rising up off his shoulders.

"Now if you'd be good enough to show me which door leads back to my apartments, I would be most grateful," Jane said conversationally, keeping matters light for the benefit of the valet, who had come into the bedchamber looking most embarrassed and uncomfortable. "In time I know I'll be able to find my own way... This house is so vast, and I've not yet seen a third of the rooms... The fireplace in my bedchamber must be working by now..." And she prattled on in this conversational way until back in her apartment, where indeed there was now a good fire in the grate of the bedchamber fireplace.

The valet left the Countess with a spring in his step. She had managed to put him so much at ease that when he drew back the heavy velvet curtains in the Earl's bedchamber to let in the muted light of a freezing cold January day, he still felt curiously optimistic. The little drama over the delivery of a letter from Lady St. John seemed quite inconsequential as he went about hurriedly dressing his master for the Royal Tennis tournament. Several of the gentlemen players and their entourage of supporters had already arrived and were down at the covered court hitting up. But the night before came back to haunt Andrews when a footman trod quietly into the closet with the news that a very distressed Lady St. John was downstairs and requested an immediate audience with the Earl.

Andrews' gulp was audible, and the telltale flush to his cheeks alarmingly obvious. He continued on with his duties, despite a sidelong suspicious glance from his master, and shrugged the Earl into a Venetian blue waistcoat without sleeves, worn over an open-necked white linen shirt and a pair of thigh-tight woven breeches which allowed for ease of movement when playing Royal Tennis. It only remained to slip the Earl into his soft kid leather tennis shoes. While on bended knee at this task, he was quietly asked to explain if the unopened letter from the Lady St. John on the dressing table was in any way connected to her ladyship's present distress.

The valet did his best to recount his early morning conversation with the Countess without incriminating either of them in the decision not to wake the Earl. Salt remained silent throughout. But when he got up to leave, taking the now-read letter with him, he swore under his breath and so viciously that Andrews felt as if he'd had his face slapped. He only hoped he had managed to save the Countess from the Earl's wrath.

SEVEN

S ALT WAS IN A FOUL MOOD. He'd woken to find Jane gone. That he had expected her to still be asleep in his arms, her luscious curves cuddled up to him, and she was not, put him out of sorts. It put him out of sorts that he should be out of sorts over such a banal circumstance. Eight out of ten married nobles of his acquaintance didn't wake up with their mistresses, and least of all with their wives. He certainly had never stayed the night with a lover, preferring his own bed to sleep in. One night with his wife, a woman who had rejected him and then married him because she *must*, and already he wanted to wake up with her in the morning.

God, what was wrong with him?

But he knew the answer to that. It was simple. He had enjoyed making love to Jane very much. In fact, so much so that he had woken with a throbbing need to make love to her again. He couldn't wait to have the taste and feel of her under him again. He had expected that making love to her would cure him of wanting her. To his utter surprise and annoyance, he found that he wanted her now more than ever.

Yet in wanting her, he felt wretched.

An unsettled feeling had descended upon him since waking, and he'd had time to reflect on the night before. He had been too rough with her. He should have shown more restraint. Taken things more slowly. Waited for her to be fully awake, not seduced her while she was half-asleep. She was not a virgin but she might as well have been; one night of making love four years ago did not an experienced lover make.

He prided himself on being considerate in the bedchamber, and here he was, on his wedding night no less, reduced to the most basic of primal urges with no thought to the inexperience of his bride. Such behavior was unforgivable. Then, so had hers been, to have the audacity to throw her ruin in his face when he was beyond the point of no return. He remained physically and mentally unsatisfied, and that was no way to start the day.

Such brooding thoughts consumed him as he traversed the length of his vast Grosvenor Square mansion, down to the Royal Tennis Court he'd had built at the back of the house. The enclosed tennis court afforded the Earl and his male companions exercise, relaxation and entertainment during the long winter months that Parliament sat, when it was too cold, too wet or just plain miserable weather for horse riding. By repute, the Salt Hendon Tennis Court was the only place in winter for the pursuit of serious sports by serious sportsmen.

A replica of the Tudor Tennis Court found at Hampton Court Palace, the court had a tiled floor, rich wood paneling, and an enormous void that reached up to an intricate wood-beamed roof. Along the length of one high wall, windows were set at an angle to give adequate light, air and space. Along the opposite wall was the Gallery where spectators gathered in individual boxes, fitted out with velvet cushions and soft furnishings, and assigned an attending footman with an endless supply of refreshment. Here wives, daughters, children and mistresses of sporting noblemen lounged at their ease, drinking champagne and wines. From behind the relative privacy of curtains made of soft netting, to ensure rogue tennis balls did them no damage, these pampered females were free to ogle and discuss the merits of the sporting male physique, shown to full advantage in thigh-tight woven breeches, and shirts so wet with sweat that they clung to broad chest, wide back and beefy arm.

The Earl hailed his friends. Four were out on the court with their hickory rackets, about to commence a practice hit-up, the rest of the group milled about the first boxed gallery opposite the Tambour, in conversation with the gathering spectators, while footmen adjusted the lacings of their soft kid shoes, took away frock coats, and offered refreshments on silver trays. But Salt did not join them. He acknowledged their hearty salutes with a wave and strode on, down the length of the boxed gallery in search of his cousin.

He was halfway along the Gallery when Diana St. John appeared through the doorway which gave access to the court. She saw him almost at once and came bustling along the tiles, careful to stay close to the spectator boxes because the four players had begun a game of doubles, serving across the net, the ball hit up onto the angled side wall so that it skittered along the sloped roof of the gallery making a loud series of thumps before dropping down on the opposite side of the net. She stopped in front of the third box. When Salt joined her there, she threw her arms about his neck and clung to him, bursting into tears.

"How is he?" he said without preamble, and pulled her closer to the spectator box, shoulder brushing against the soft net curtain, back shielding her from any stray tennis balls.

Diana St. John remained mute. She looked as if she hadn't slept all night.

"Diana, for God's sake, tell me!" he demanded, ashen-faced, interpreting her forlorn expression to mean her son's temperature had indeed taken an upward leap into feverishness. "Ron's just got a slightly elevated temperature? He'll be all right in a day or two?"

"Oh, Salt! It's been such an ordeal," Diana St. John announced loudly, as if to be heard over the shouts of the tennis players, and quickly dabbed at her eyes with a lace handkerchief, careful not to smudge her expertly applied cosmetics. "I can't begin to tell you what a wretched night I've had. No sleep and the worry. I couldn't stop thinking what would happen if I lost my boy, too. First dear St. John's death, and he in the prime of his life, and now, to lose my son… Oh, I couldn't bear it, Salt. I just couldn't. It would surely kill me."

"But he's all right, isn't he?" Salt asked her stridently. "Just a slightly elevated temperature, nothing more? Nothing to really worry about? Tell me! Diana!"

She nodded and covered her face with her hands before looking up at him with tears in her eyes. "But he was so hot, and I thought... I thought it might be smallpox. That's how it started with St. John. Do you remember? The high temperature and then the sweats... I was so scared. So scared that my boy might have caught the smallpox, too. You can't begin to imagine how dreadful that feeling is for a mother!"

"No. But St. John was my best friend," he answered quietly. "I never want to relive those weeks. It was a nightmare." When she clung to him again, he put his arms about her and hugged her briefly, saying gently, "But nothing is going to happen to Ron. He and Merry were inoculated remember? So it would need more than a high temperature to take the boy from us, now wouldn't it?"

"Us. Yes. *Us*," she answered, seizing on the word. "He means everything to us, doesn't he, Salt? He's your future, *our* future. If something were to happen to him—"

"But nothing will happen," Salt assured her and put her away from him, just as one of the players bounded over their way, arm at full stretch to hit a ball that was coming straight at them. "I think we'd best get off this court before you are hurt."

"I say, Tony, good shot!" came a shout from the court.

There was loud applause from the spectators, one female calling out encouragement and her companions giggling in response.

"Splendid tambour, sir! Well done," offered another voice, much closer to the Earl and his cousin.

But Diana St. John ignored the tennis game going on so close to her, and the fact there was a real possibility she could be struck with the ball, or a player run into her. Nor did she consider it was unfair of her to be in the way of the players. Her gaze did not shift from the Earl's handsome profile, distracted by the game in progress, and her painted lips puckered in disapproval that she should not have his undivided attention.

"I don't know why you couldn't come last night," she said pettishly, mood suddenly changing, and speaking as loudly as before, needing to be heard over the shouts of the players offering each other encouragement. She remained firmly in front of the third spectator box and was pleased when Salt's attention returned to her. "Ron would've settled much quicker had you been there. And poor little Merry was crying and asking for you too; you know how attached she is to her brother. They only have each other... And us. They look on you as their papa. Well, why wouldn't they, when their own dear papa is in heaven? How do I tell two little children that are dependent on you it was too much to ask for their Uncle Salt to come when they are ill?"

"Diana, I..."

She dropped her powdered head then lifted it, tears on the end of her darkened lashes. "Of course, I have no right to question you, to even wonder what could be so important that you could not even send a response to my note, nor should I assume that you care above the ordinary what happens to my children—"

"Now, Diana, you are being unreasonable," Salt interrupted, annoyed, hands lightly on her bare shoulders. "You know very well I look upon Ron and Merry as my own. No one means more to me than St. John's children, and nothing would've kept me from Ron's sickbed had he been truly taken ill—"

"Nothing and no one?" Diana St. John asked hopefully, smiling up at him. "How Ron and Merry would dearly love to hear their Uncle Salt tell them so! They're here today, y'know. I couldn't keep Ron away from your Royal Tennis tournament. Dr. Barlow said it would be all right for him to attend, but we must keep him well rugged up. Are you certain—nothing and no one?"

"Nothing and no one," he repeated, the tension easing in his neck and limbs knowing Ron was not in any danger, and pleased Diana had brought the children along for the day. "Now, will you allow me to remove you from this Court before one or both of us are maimed or mutilated by your brother's heroic displays with a tennis racket?"

A loud shout of "Hurray!" went up near Salt's ear, and he turned to see Sir Antony and Tom Allenby beaming from ear to ear and clapping each other on the back. After shaking hands with their dejected opponents, the winning twosome came across the court toward Salt and Diana St. John. But Tom bounded ahead of Sir Antony, and such was his excitement that he completely ignored the Earl and his cousin to throw back the netting of the third box and lean over the barrier, saying, excited as any ten-year-old schoolboy,

"Jane! Jane? Did you see my final shot? Didn't Sir Antony play brilliantly? He's a crack at placing the ball. None better. Just knows how to tip it over the net, or to up the ball over the service penthouse so it drops in such a way that the fellows on the other side can't get a racket to it! If it weren't for him we wouldn't have won!"

"Now, Tom Allenby, that's a stretch of the truth, if ever I heard one," Sir Antony responded with a good-natured laugh, a nod at his sister and cousin, and a hand on the barrier because he was still out of breath and feeling as if all his muscles had been pummeled at once. "You played some fine tactical shots yourself that I couldn't have managed, and you served the winning point. I say we make a fine team, wouldn't you, my lady?"

"Oh, none better," Jane responded with a smile at the two victors, coming to stand at the barrier, not a glance at the couple less than a foot away. Yet the flush to her cheeks and the fact she did not acknowledge her husband or his cousin was indication enough to Salt that she had overheard every word. This was confirmed when she said with a cheeky smile at her stepbrother, "Although, I'm afraid my view was partially obstructed for those shots that were on the chase one yard line. That's what it's called, isn't it, Sir Antony, the line closest the wall?"

"How good of you to remember my monologue on the King of games that is Royal Tennis, my lady. Most female eyes glaze over when I offer too much detail," Sir Antony said with a smile of approval, and not able to help himself because he was annoyed with his sister's theatrics in monopolizing the Earl's time, added most undiplomatically, "Though I'm not surprised you were denied part of the action, what with m'sister and Salt's large carcass blocking the view."

"Perhaps I shall do what you suggested in the first place, Sir Antony, and watch the next game from the Dedans penthouse gallery?" Jane responded pleasantly, resisting a glance at her husband. "There is a clear view straight up the court from there."

"That's a splendid idea, Jane," Tom agreed. "You'll see it all from there. The next game should prove a real corker too," he added, speaking without thinking through his thoughts, the only bad habit Jane was certain her stepbrother had inherited from his mother, "because Lord Church is up against his lordship, and Art assured me it's the game to watch because they are evenly matched. Despite what Art overheard Lord Church boasting to the other fellows: That today he has the Earl at a distinct advantage because it wasn't *his* wedding night last night!"

Sir Antony laughed with embarrassment at Pascoe Church's smug belief that the bridal night had sapped his rival's strength. But Diana St. John, who felt she had done all she could for the moment to make the Countess of Salt Hendon uncomfortably aware of her and her children's cemented place in the Earl's affections, kept her mouth firmly shut on the topic of her cousin's marriage. In fact she kept her expression so tightly under control no one would have guessed that inside her head she was screaming her anger.

No sooner had she arrived at the Grosvenor Square mansion than Sir Antony had pounced on his sister, informing her bluntly that Salt had been married the day before and that she wasn't to make a fuss. She had replied with a smile of superiority that this was old news and to leave her to her misery. She had then flounced off to the Royal Tennis Court, only for her brother to follow up his warning by forcing upon her an introduction to the new Countess of Salt Hendon in front of a dozen athletic noblemen, who, to a man, were paying homage to the Countess's beauty, as if Aphrodite incarnate had deigned to descend amongst them.

That the creature was just as beautiful and self-effacing as Diana St. John remembered was no real surprise—the Despard woman had forewarned her of that—but seeing this for herself threatened the return of her sick headache of the night before. Years of experience hiding her true feelings from the world enabled her to suffer the indignity of making her curtsy to her cousin's new wife. Despite spending the previous night weeping buckets of bitter tears over the Earl's marriage, today she was cunning enough to wear a mask of supreme indifference.

Her campaign to have the new Countess of Salt Hendon disgraced and disowned before the Earl had impregnated his bride had begun in earnest, and she would be relentless in its execution.

So, as she had done when first introduced, Diana St. John silently curtsied to rank and retreated to the spectator boxes. Once ensconced with her friends, she continued weaving her web of rumor and counter-rumor. The female crème de la crème of polite society were only too eager to soak up malicious whispers about an unknown girl from the country who'd had the effrontery to usurp them and marry one of their own. The Earl of Salt Hendon was not only the most eligible bachelor in the kingdom, but was a prime piece of unfettered male vigor, the likes of which had not been seen since a French chit had captured the heart of that hardened libertine the Duke of Roxton in the '40s.

Sir Antony smiled sweetly as his meddlesome sister flounced off, and said to the Earl, "Well, you'd best prove Pascoe wrong, Salt, because I have a ten pound wager saying you'll trounce him within half an hour."

"Half an hour? Why should I take that long?" Salt murmured in response, distracted by the sight of his bride dressed in one of the many new gowns he'd had ordered made for her, and that now crammed her closet to bursting.

He was thinking how ravishingly pretty she presented in a very feminine sacque-back gown of pale green and pink silk, the tight sleeves showcasing her long, slim arms. And he approved of her elegant hairstyle. Gone were the coils of unfashionable braids. Her waist-length hair was piled softly atop her head, and secured with pearl-headed pins and threaded with matching ribbons, the remainder allowed to cascade about her shoulders in long soft ringlets. But he was mystified as to why she had ruined the effect of the low square-cut neckline of the embroidered bodice that should have flattered her small round breasts, by the wearing of a gossamer fichu bunched awkwardly over her left breast. Surely she only had to ask and her maid would have arranged such a useless article of feminine clothing to better advantage? And then he noticed the square of white linen tucked into the neckline; it appeared to be some sort of makeshift bandage…

Slow to respond to Sir Antony's assertion, he finally added with a frown, "So Pascoe Church is confident of trouncing me?"

"Not exactly trouncing, my lord," Tom admitted, looking to Sir Antony.

"Beating you, certainly, dear fellow," Sir Antony said cheerfully, one glance at Jane and his best friend confirming that he and Tom should make themselves scarce, to allow the couple a moment of privacy. "But I know you'll prove Pascoe wrong. I don't want to lose ten pounds. So, Tom, let's get ourselves cleaned up and repair to the Gentleman's Box to await our next match. And I could do with some refreshment. I'm parched."

"What have you done to yourself?" Salt demanded of Jane in an undervoice, Sir Antony and Tom barely out of earshot.

He put out a hand to lift the fichu to inspect the bandage but Jane backed away from the barrier and resumed her seat on a maroon velvet cushion. The barrier was no deterrent to Salt, who simply vaulted over the low wall and sat down beside her on the bench. He tried again to lift the fichu but she pushed his hand away.

"I… I like it. It's all the rage."

"Nonsense. It's hideous, and a crime to hide such beautiful breasts. Take it off."

Jane blushed in spite of herself at his unguarded compliment, but she did not remove the fichu. "No, my lord. I will not."

"My lord?" He put up his brows. "Well, my lady, I shall remove it for you."

At that Jane did look up at him. "No. Please. I am more comfortable with it on."

Salt frowned at her distress. "What is it?" he asked gently. "Why do you have a bandage hidden under that fichu?"

"Nothing. It's nothing," she whispered, not meeting his gaze and in a telltale sign of her distress, blotches of color stained her white throat strawberry. "Please. You've a tennis match on now and you're wanted."

"If you've hurt yourself I have a right to know," he said gruffly. "What if someone enquires and I can't answer them? Won't I look the uncaring brute?"

"They already have asked," she admitted, eyes lowered to her lap, on the re-sized sapphire and diamond wedding band that now fit her long finger perfectly. "I was clumsy with a tea dish and scalded myself. That will suffice."

"What truly happened?" he asked, ignoring the loud bantering at his back to get a move on or Pascoe Church would win by default.

"It doesn't matter. It couldn't be helped. Please go."

"They can wait. Now show me."

She shook her head, a hand to the bunched up layers of gossamer silk to stop him removing it.

"It's not a request," he stated brusquely.

Slowly, with a sigh of defeat, she dropped her hand into her lap. This time when he went to touch her she did not flinch, but she wouldn't look at him either. He unwound the layers of light silk and let the fichu slide to the floor, exposing the lovely rise of her white breasts in the low-cut embroidered bodice, and the makeshift bandage that was tucked into the neckline covering her left breast. He gently lifted the bandage and his intake of breath was audible.

What had been the unblemished pale pink wash of her nipple now glowed red like veal. A cursory glance suggested a nasty burn. If he'd had his eyeglasses to make a closer inspection he was sure he'd see that the wash of red across her breast was actually a series of tiny red bumps, resembling a painful grazing. In fact, it *was* a graze; he knew at once its origin and he felt his face grow hot. He silently replaced the bandage, scooped up the fichu and put the gossamer layers of silk back around Jane's bare shoulders. He then went down on bended knee before her to better arrange its fall, so that it draped evenly. Crossing the two lengths of delicate material over her breasts, he tied the ends at the small of her back, tucking the excess into the lacings of her bodice. Satisfied that this arrangement was more the fashion amongst ladies of his acquaintance, he remained on his haunches before her and took hold of her hands.

"Jane, look at me," he coaxed, but when she continued to stare at her hands in his, he lifted her chin with the crook of a finger. Still she kept her eyes downcast. Her cheeks were apple red and she appeared every bit the blushing bride on the morning after the night before. It increased his discomfort and concern enough for him to say abruptly, "I should've had the decency to shave. I'm sorry. It was unthinking of me—Do you have ointment? Good," he said with relief at her quick nod. "Did I—did I hurt you when I—not the rash. When I—God, I'm blathering like an idiot!" he said brusquely and got up off his haunches, a hand to his thick chestnut hair as he turned to look out across the tennis court without seeing any of it. He sat down beside her. "I mean—I mean when I—when we—"

"I know what you mean," she interrupted, quietly. "Yes, but only for the briefest of moments," she confessed at his quick intake of breath, adding with a frankness he found inimitable to her, "It's just that we have only made love the once—in truth it was twice in the summerhouse, but just the one time, if you understand my meaning. And it's been four years, so even though making love is quite wonderful, I'd forgotten that the first few moments are-are awkward, and as you are a large man it is only natural—Oh dear! Now *I'm* the one blathering. Please forgive me…"

Jane was up off the bench, face burning with mortification for having the barefaced cheek to comment aloud on the laudable size of his equipage. What must he think of her? They should not be discussing what happened in the bedchamber between man and wife in the wide-open spaces of a tennis court inhabited by upwards of twenty guests. She felt foolish and gauche for confessing to a moment's anxiety. What she should have said was that making love with him last night had been just as wondrous and fulfilling as in the summerhouse, but she could not. No doubt it was perfectly acceptable for his mistresses to point out his size, and to heap praises on his technique and stamina as a lover, but not something he would want to hear from a wife with all the cumulative experience of two nights!

The silence dragged, and when she had the courage to look at him his intense frown told her that he had a disgust of such frankness. Her humiliation was complete when one of the footmen came up to the barrier to remind his lordship that Pascoe Church was waiting and the Earl abruptly changed the subject.

"Andrews went out of his way not to implicate you in Lady St. John's late night note," he said conversationally. "But I believe I have you to thank for allowing me an undisturbed sleep?"

This did make her smile. "So you aren't angry at us for not waking you?"

"Angry? No, I'm grateful, particularly with this tournament today," he admitted. "Diana is just an overprotective mother.

Which isn't a bad thing, but it can be tiresome at times. As you no doubt saw through the netting, she is apt to over-dramatize the situation where her children are concerned. But she means well."

Means well? Jane had to wonder, recalling the effect Diana St. John's strong perfume in the cold anteroom the day before. Was she being foolish to suppose the woman had stage-managed the scene outside the Gallery box knowing she sat behind the netting? She wished with all her heart that Salt was right and that there was no harm in his cousin, but there was something about Diana St. John that made her wary and fearful, and these feelings could not be shaken off so readily.

"There's a dinner after the tournament," Salt was saying. "It's a bit of an ordeal, if you're not used to sitting through thirty courses and political chit-chat. After that, there's a recital. If you don't feel up to it, if you'd prefer to retire early, I'll make your excuses and Diana can step in and—"

"No," she said firmly and smiled. "I'll be fine. Truly."

He lightly pressed her hand, then turned to the court and put up a hand to Pascoe Church, who was swinging his hickory racket about in thin air, as if ready to conquer the entire fraternity of assembled tennis players. He looked back at Jane. "They're calling me for the match. Will you be all right sitting here alone?"

"Yes. Perfectly. Now go," she assured him and watched as he vaulted back over the barrier and jogged across the court.

From the start it was a fast-paced, go-for-the-throat match, with both men equally talented tennis players. The small solid ball was hit hard and fast and was spun in all directions, with the peculiar hazard of the tambour and the angle of wall and floor offering exciting placement options that kept Jane on the edge of her velvet cushion, in anticipation of where the ball would land next. Salt was superior in anticipating the ball's drop, and being taller and longer-limbed than his opponent was able to stretch his racket and get to the ball more often. But Pascoe Church was lighter and faster on his feet and bounced about the court on his toes, reminding Jane of a rooster chased by a determined fox.

There was plenty of vocal support for both players coming

from the Gallery, and Jane soon found herself clapping and cheering along with the rest of the noble spectators. At interval, it was time for the players to change sides and take a few moments of rest before resuming the game. Footmen brought the players hot towels and refreshments, and lackeys ran about with cloths tied to the ends of long poles to wipe the tiled floor dry of sweat.

Many of the Gallery boxes had pulled aside their netting to allow the spectators to lean across the barriers to exchange conversation with their fellow spectators in other boxes, and to speak with the two players. This was a time of much loud conversation, toasting of glasses, and footmen coming and going with bottles of claret and champagne. Then a huge cheer went up amongst the men. Such was the general uproar of cat-calling, giggling and female shrieking at the far end of the court where Salt and Pascoe Church stood catching their breath and chatting, that even Jane leaned out of her box with the rest of the spectators to see what all the fuss was about.

A number of articles of female clothing had been thrown in direction of the two players and had landed at their feet. At least three fans, a fichu, one mask, two reticules, a number of gloves, and even a couple of stockings and garters littered the tiled court. Another glove sailed through the air and landed by the toe of Salt's left shoe. It was not this that he scooped up, but a female stocking and garter. He draped these feminine articles over the stringed head of his racket then held the tennis racket out at arm's length, not unlike holding a sword at the ready, and took a bow with an exaggerated flourish.

Another cheer went up when he proceeded to return the stocking and garter to its rightful owner, several giggling ladies, undoubtedly drunk, denying loudly that such intimate objects were theirs and lifting up their petticoats above the ankles as if it were necessary for them to provide proof of their boastful denials. Jane could not see the female to whom Salt offered his racket with another bow, but there was no doubt as to the significance of the offering when one of the ladies in the box next to Jane's, who was leaning so far over the barrier, fluttering her fan, that her big breasts were in danger of falling out of her low-cut bodice, made an announcement to her companions that Jane heard above the laughing and the cheering further along the Gallery.

"There you have it, Eliza! What did I tell you? Salt's chosen Jenny Dalrymple, and thus ends Elizabeth Outram's reign as *maîtresse en titre*. They never last more than a year; never have."

"They're lucky to last that long, given his sword is rarely sheathed."

There was a series of unfeminine snorts and a burst of raucous female laughter.

"Oh, Eliza! You have such a quaint vulgar way of expressing yourself!"

"How ever does Diana bear with his infidelities?" enquired a third whining voice through the thin wall that divided Jane's spectator box from the next.

"She bears it as we all do," was the haughty reply. "Selective blindness. It's not our place to question a lover's, and certainly not a husband's, straying. It's not as if these lapses mean anything."

"Mine certainly don't."

"Eliza! *Eliza*! Do stop or I'll burst my stays! You teasing girl."

"But what about his bride?" the whining voice asked. "Will she be as understanding as the rest of us? I mean, what do you know about her?"

"You tell me, Susannah. What do any of us know about the little upstart?"

"None of us know anything. Although, Diana did mention something about Salt marrying the little ninny to settle a gambling debt. God! What a waste of noble flesh. On a Bristol Blue Glass merchant's daughter, no less."

"There isn't enough meat on her bones to satisfy a man of Salt's strong appetites. He's always fancied 'em plump-breasted and big-thighed."

"Is that such a surprise when he's as solid as an ox and hung like one too?"

There were gasps of laughter and girlish giggles until the one with the whining voice said, "For a man of Salt's physical prowess it must've been a most unsatisfactory coupling."

"Most unsatisfactory."

"Particularly when a groom has a right to expect his bride to be untouched on their wedding night."

"Whatever can you mean?"

"Diana says that if ever the truth got out... You must promise not a word—"

"Not a word!" came the quick reply in unison.

"It's not something a man wants his friends, and certainly not his political enemies, to discover about the bride. It's all to do with male pride."

"What? The pitcher was already cracked?"

There was a horrified gasp. "She wasn't a virgin on her wedding night!"

"Oh, Eliza! Just when I begin to think your pretty little head is stuffed full of wool you surprise me. You clever cherub! Yes. Spoiled goods."

"How utterly vulgar!"

"Yes. As vulgar as her lineage. What can one expect? Certainly this blue glass has imperfections."

"Clever!"

"Salt's gambling debt must've amounted to a pretty guinea indeed."

"And she isn't even one of us."

"Definitely not one of us, my dear Eliza."

"Poor Salt."

"And poor Diana. Let's not forget Diana. How she must be suffering. But *such* a brave face!"

"Oh, yes! Susannah, you are *so* right. She's been in love with Salt since *forever*."

"Yes, Eliza, we all know Salt is the great love of Diana's life, but we don't say it out loud."

"What a pity St. John came between them."

"Not in all things, my dear Susannah. There is the rumor, which Diana has never denied, that her two brats—"

"—are *Salt's*?"

There was a collective gasp.

"Good God! How extraordinary!"

"But... Isn't there also the rumor he's barren?"

One of the women made a sound reminiscent of a startled

pheasant. "Salt?*Barren*? Don't be a dolt, Eliza! A divine specimen of maleness who can go on and on and on, barren? Ha!"

"Well, even if he isn't barren, who's to know? Diana's friend Artemisia is always quick to put a stop to any unwanted breeding."

"Indeed, Susannah? Interesting. *Exceedingly* interesting."

"Yes, I thought you would find it so. She helped me in a most difficult predicament."

"Arta *who*?" interrupted the whining voice.

The explanation was given as if speaking to a child, or one who did not know the English tongue. "*Artemisia*. Syrup of Artemisia. Surely you've heard of it? Rids one of unwanted brats before they are formed."

"Oh! *That* Artemisia. I thought you were referring to Diana's friend Artemisia."

"Yes, well we were! She is Diana's particular friend. Comes in a bottle."

There was a collective giggle and then silence fell before one of the female voices returned to the question of the paternity of the St. John children.

"He does dote on Diana's brats."

"Yes, he does, Susannah. And quite rightly, too."

"Just like a papa should."

"But you didn't hear that from me."

"No. Not from you."

"It makes perfect sense."

"Perfect sense," two females voices echoed in awed unison.

"The game's afoot! I've thirty pounds on Pascoe Church to win!"

"Eliza! I was wrong," her friend announced with disgust. "Your head *is* full of wool."

EIGHT

As she sipped tea from a delicate porcelain dish in the Yellow Saloon, Jane was still wishing she had pulled away from the wall of the Gallery box and not listened to the rumors and counter-rumors about the Lady St. John and her husband. Watching through the netting it was clear Diana St. John was infatuated with Salt. But did he know it? And were they lovers? She had no idea.

Jacob Allenby had repeatedly lectured her about the hypocrisy rife within Polite Society—that the ruling class was riddled with vice in all its forms, and the Earl of Salt Hendon was just as guilty of the unspeakable sins of his class as the rest of the inhabitants of Gomorrah, as he continually referred to London, and the environs of Westminster in particular. And his lordship had committed the most heinous crime of all amongst his wickedly depraved brethren: He had seduced a virgin and then abandoned her with child.

He had preached this sermon to her so often that Jane became immune to his hellfire and brimstone prophesies. Living in a house in the wilds of Wiltshire, where no pictures livened the walls, fires in the grate were permitted only every second day, and such vanities as looking glasses and feminine fripperies were strictly forbidden, the Earl of Salt Hendon's nefarious lifestyle was a world away. Yet, now that she was the Countess of Salt Hendon, it mattered to her a very great deal, and that bothered her. It bothered her because she was in love with her husband. And because she was in love with him, the sooner she signed the document banishing her to Salt Hall, the better for her peace of mind.

Loud laughter intruded into these musings and Jane remembered she was in the Yellow Saloon, where the ladies had gathered to await the gentlemen who, having finished playing their games of Royal Tennis, were bathing and dressing in readiness to sit down to a good dinner. With their silk and brocade layered petticoats spread out around them, and painted and ivory fans fluttering on flushed upward thrusting bosoms, the ladies lounged about on the arrangement of sofas and wingchairs by the two fireplaces, chatting amongst themselves.

Diana St. John presided over the tea things with all the aplomb of one used to the task. Of course she had made an elaborate display of refusal when the butler and four liveried footmen had arrived with the trolleys stacked with the Sèvres porcelain tea service, plates of sweetmeats and a variety of cakes and pastries, and the teapot and coffee urn on their silver stands. But Jane, not knowing the first thing about playing hostess to a gaggle of sharp-eyed society matrons, was only too willing to allow Lady St. John the honor, even if it did highlight her lack of social skills. Her calm capitulation to Lady St. John's expertise won her a few nods of approval from the older matrons, but the close friends of Diana St. John were all smug smiles at their friend, as if she had won a small victory against the young Countess.

Jane saw these looks of petty triumph but ignored them. She was unable to join in a conversation about politics and people she knew not the first thing about. She wondered if the discussion was being deliberately steered in this direction by Diana St. John and her cohort, for the specific purpose of excluding her. So she drifted over to the window with its view of the square. Here she sipped her tea and watched the traffic of sedan chairs, carriages, and a bullock team with its drivers and dogs, maneuver comfortably about the wide streets of Grosvenor Square.

She was studying the hive of activity that accompanied the arrival of a coach laden with luggage outside one of the townhouses, liveried footmen sent out into the cold to put down the steps and hand down the occupants as quickly as possible to enable them to dash indoors to the warmth of a good fire, when from the corner of her eye she caught a flash of movement through the wide doors that opened into the dining room. More movement and laughter, and Jane moved to the doorway in time to see two children, the son and daughter of Lady St. John, running up one side of a very long polished mahogany table which had been set with silver and crystal for upwards of thirty guests. They were being chased by a man in somber attire, and behind him, walking at a brisk pace, a woman dressed in gray with a severe hairstyle.

Several liveried servants were going about the business of arranging epergnes filled with fruit and flowers equidistant down the center of the table, under the blaze of three candlelit crystal chandeliers. Others were placing warmers and silver servers on two very long sideboards which were up against one wall on either side of a massive marble fireplace, all under the watchful eye of the eagle-eyed under-butler. None of these servants took the slightest notice of the boy and girl playing around the table, nor did they seem to mind. When the St. John children directly affected their particular task, they merely stepped aside and got on with things. The man, whom Jane now decided must be the boy's tutor, and the girl's governess, were quick to come between the busy servants and the giggling children when necessary.

Yet when the boy pushed aside two ribbon-back chairs and dived under the table, quickly followed by his giggling sister, the tutor and the governess lost all patience. Hollow threats to life and limb were made if they didn't show themselves immediately. These threats were naturally ignored by the adventurous children, who made threats of their own to stay under the table unless given sweetmeats and punch immediately. It was only when the tutor pushed up his sleeves and volunteered to thrash the life out of both of them if they didn't surface forthwith, that Jane bravely stepped forward and made her presence known.

The tutor and governess took one look at Jane, recognized in her delicate beauty and embroidered petticoats that she was not a servant, and dutifully, if reluctantly, stood aside from the table as requested. It took the under-butler whispering at their backs, that they were being addressed by the Countess of Salt Hendon, for the tutor to double over 'til his nose almost hit his knees, and the governess to plunge into such a deep curtsy that she almost toppled over. But Jane saw none of this as she had carefully bobbed down, one hand holding the table edge to remain steady, to peek under the table.

"Hello. Do you remember me from the Tower Zoo?" she asked with a friendly smile, the St. John children huddled between the turned legs of a couple of chairs.

"Hello. You liked the lions best," stated the boy, dark eyes wary, as if waiting for the inevitable lecture on bad behavior.

"And your favorites were the elephants," Jane responded.

"I'd like to ride an elephant one day," the boy announced.

"I hear that in India they use elephants much like we use draught horses here."

The girl's hazel eyes lit up. "Do they? Can I ride one too?" she asked Jane hopefully.

"Don't be ridiculous, Merry!" her brother said with derision. "You're a girl. Girls can't ride elephants."

The girl pouted. "If I go to India—"

"Girls can't ride elephants and girls can't go to India. Girls can't do anything."

Merry poked her tongue out at her brother and said sullenly, "I will! I will if I want to!" And looked to Jane for support and said more even-temperedly, "I can go to India if I want, can't I?"

Jane smiled at the girl, saw the mulish look on her brother's face, as if he expected her to agree with him, and said placidly, "It's not a matter of can't, is it? It all depends on what happens when you are a grown-up young lady. Of course, it goes without saying that you'll be a lady of fashion and marry a very handsome and important man—"

"Just like Uncle Salt?" the girl said hopefully, and when her brother groaned, showed him her tongue again.

"Yes, just like your Uncle Salt," Jane said evenly, trying not to smile. "If you marry a gentleman who decides to travel to India one day, then of course you'll go with him."

"If he was important like Uncle Salt, Merry's husband

wouldn't go to India," the boy stated emphatically. "He'd be a nobleman and needed here to run the kingdom."

The girl opened her mouth to speak but Jane spoke first, saying lightly, "That is very true, but perhaps your sister's future husband might be a diplomat, like your other uncle Sir Antony, and travel to India on important business for his King?"

The girl smiled triumphantly at her brother, who had to concede Jane had a point, though he added haughtily, with nostrils aquiver which was alarmingly reminiscent of his Uncle Salt at his most scornful,

"Mamma says diplomatists are all failed political men. Or sent away because they're an embarrassment to their family."

"But surely your uncle Sir Antony is neither?" Jane asked, startled.

"Mamma says Uncle Salt sent Uncle Tony away because he caught him making up to Cousin Caroline." The boy rolled his eyes and crossed his thin legs adding, because this sort of talk made him uncomfortable and the beautiful lady was looking at him queerly, "Whatever *making up to* means. But that's what I heard Mamma telling old Lady Porter, so it must be true."

Jane hid her shock, but she must have appeared stunned for the girl offered her comfort and an explanation.

"Oh, Uncle Tony doesn't mind living abroad. He told me so. And Mamma says Cousin Caroline is much too young to be married." The girl frowned in thought. "But she's soon to turn eighteen. I should like to be married when I'm eighteen. Eighteen isn't too young to be married, is it?"

Her brother added, because Jane was looking confused, "We've always called Uncle Salt uncle, even though he is our cousin. And we call Cousin Caroline cousin, even though she's Uncle Salt's sister, because she's much too young to be called an aunt. It's simple really."

"But not too young to be married, is she, Ron?"

Her brother shrugged. "I don't know anything about that, Merry. But if you want to get married at eighteen, I'll not object."

Merry beamed to receive such praise, and feeling generous asked Jane, "Would you like to join us?" She lowered her voice to a whisper. "But you must be very quiet because we're hiding from

Uncle Salt. He always finds us but not today, whatever he says to the contrary. He'll never suspect we're under his dining table!"

"You're such a slow top, Merry!" accused her brother, an embarrassing glance at Jane. "You can't invite one of Uncle Salt's guests to come under the table. What would Mamma say?"

"Oh, I'm not one of the guests," Jane assured them with a smile. Dropping to her hands and knees, she crawled under the table.

She found it surprisingly spacious between the turned legs of the chairs, and tucking her stockinged legs up underneath her silk petticoats, she was able to sit comfortably with the two children; being small and slender helped. She smiled at the boy, who was regarding her with wary fascination. No doubt he had never seen an adult under a table before. It was a new experience for Jane, too, but she was enjoying herself and felt far more comfortable in the company of these two children than she had with the tedious and incomprehensible conversations in the Yellow Saloon.

"I should've introduced myself. It may come as a bit of a shock to you both, but I'm your uncle's wife. We were married yesterday."

"You don't look old enough to be anybody's wife, least of all Uncle Salt's wife," Ron blurted out, then immediately recanted. "Sorry. I shouldn't have said that."

"Oh, I assure you I am older than I look," Jane said encouragingly. "It's just because I'm not very tall and have small bones, and all the Sinclairs are tall and rather large by comparison."

Merry nodded. "Except for Cousin Caroline. She's short like you and has pretty red hair. But I think you're very beautiful; like a fairy at the bottom of the garden. I like your shiny black hair particularly."

Jane blushed. "Do you? Thank you. Then I suppose you won't mind having me for an aunt? You may call me Aunt Salt, although that makes me sound very old, so Aunt Jane would be nicer. But only if you wish to. I won't be offended if you don't. After all, you don't know me." She stuck out her hand to the boy. "But I should like you both to get to know me better."

Both children looked at one another before the boy willingly shook hands. "I'll call you Lady Salt, if it's all the same to you."

"I'm going to call her Aunt Jane," the girl said confidently, shaking hands with Jane as she glared at her brother, "because I like her and she's too beautiful to be called Aunt Salt or Lady Salt which sounds stuffy, and because Uncle Salt would want us to. You know he would, Ron!"

"It's perfectly all right for—Ron? For Ron to call me Lady Salt, and for you to call me Aunt Jane."

"If you want the lot, it's the Honorable Aubrey Vernon Sinclair St. John," the boy reluctantly volunteered. "Aubrey after my father and Vernon after Uncle Salt's papa, the fourth Earl. Friends call me Ron. You can call me Ron." He pushed his sister's silken arm in a friendly fashion. "This is Merry. Actually it's the Honorable Magna Diana Sinclair St. John. Named after Uncle Salt. Well, his Christian name is Magnus but I guess you'd know that being married to him. We all call her Merry. We're eight and three-quarters and twins, if you hadn't guessed."

Jane had not guessed. Ron was smaller, much thinner and very pale, with dark circles under his eyes, and he didn't appear very robust. He had a serious demeanor, which could be a consequence of his poor health. Yet his brown eyes, sandy hair and long, thin straight nose gave him a great look of his Uncle Salt, which was even more interesting, given the quivering nostrils and the conversation she had overheard in the Royal Tennis Court Gallery. Merry was very different. Merry glowed with vitality, had pink to her cheeks and a bright smile. In every way she was a contrast to her twin. Both were dressed in the height of adult fashion, Ron in lace cravat, richly embroidered waistcoat and black silk breeches. Merry wore a restrictive bodice of blond silk and layers of petticoats embroidered with tiny rose buds. Her hair, thankfully, was not powdered or pomaded, so her auburn ringlets bounced about her shoulders. Jane couldn't help thinking they would have been more comfortable in simpler, looser-fitting garments that allowed for play and movement, as worn by the parish children near her home village, but supposed that their mother dressed them this way when they went out into company.

"Do you have any brothers and sisters?" Merry asked, gingerly touching Jane's fingers.

Jane readily held her hand.

"I have one brother, called Tom. He's here today. He was at the Tower Zoo with me. I'll introduce you both at dinner if you wish."

"We don't eat dinner with the adults," Merry confessed. "We eat in the nursery. Mamma says it shouldn't be called a nursery because Uncle Salt isn't in expectation of having any children to put there. It upsets her to hear it called a nursery. Doesn't it, Ron?"

"Yes, but Lady Salt isn't interested to know where we'll be eating our dinner, or cares what Mamma thinks about the nursery," Ron chastised his sister. He looked at Jane with a self-conscious frown. "Still, it's too bad we have to eat up there alone when all the fun's down here."

"I agree. But perhaps your Mamma thinks it best because you've been unwell and you need to rest?" Jane suggested.

"*Unwell?* Rest?" Ron pulled a face of disgust. "I'm not ill!" Then revised this declaration by saying meekly, "Sometimes I get stomach cramp—"

"—but Mamma gives him medicine and when he throws up he feels better again."

"*Merry.*"

"It's true," Merry assured Jane, snuggling closer and looking earnestly into Jane's blue eyes. "Mamma says Ron's unwell, even when we think he's well, and makes him swallow a horrid-tasting medicine to make him feel better. But you don't like taking the medicine, do you, Ron? But if he refuses to do Mamma's bidding, she has him strapped to the bed and forces the—"

"*Merry.*"

"—medicine down his throat. That only makes you worse, doesn't it, Ron? Because you vomit and vomit. And then Uncle Salt has to come and give Ron a different medicine which makes him feel so much better, when he wasn't really ill in the first place."

"Merry! Stop it!" Ron demanded with angry embarrassment. "Lady Salt isn't interested in Mamma's medicine cabinet!"

"Oh, dear, what a very unpleasant ordeal for you, Ron," Jane said with an understanding smile, hiding her alarm. "Do you know, my brother Tom used to suffer the same fate at the hands of his mother. Mothers worry at the slightest sniffle or sign that their child might be poorly. But you shouldn't be too hard on your mother, either of you. She must love you very much to be so concerned. I'm sure she'll grow out of it and leave you alone soon enough."

"At least Ron can't be blamed for the physician's visit last night," Merry volunteered.

"Oh?" Jane moved closer and tried to sound disinterested. "Were you the one with the high temperature?"

Merry giggled and shook her auburn ringlets. "Me? No! Uncle Salt says I have the con-*constitution* of an ox," she announced proudly.

"It was Mamma with one of her sick headaches," Ron explained reluctantly.

"She's always suffering from sick headaches," Merry interrupted cheerfully. "Clary and Taylor say we give Mamma headaches all the time. So we have to be quiet about our house and tiptoe in the passageways."

"But last night's headache was a terribly awful one," Ron said in defense of his mother. "Mamma's suffering woke the whole house and there was nothing any of the servants could do to help her, so the physician had to be called out in the middle of the night."

"Clary said she was in a raging temper," Merry confided in an awed whisper. "And when that happens, no one can go near Mamma for days. But in this house we don't have to tiptoe at all," she added with a beaming smile. "Uncle Salt lets us run about as much as we want."

"But not in the public rooms," Ron added seriously, "where just anybody can come and see Uncle Salt. And most particularly not on Tuesdays, when there's all sorts of beggars sitting about wanting Uncle Salt to do things for them. Then we must be on our best behavior, because we are Sinclairs and it wouldn't do for a Sinclair to be seen to be common. But as most of the rooms in this house are empty, there's plenty of places to run about and play hide-and-go-seek. That's the arrangement we shook hands on with Uncle Salt, isn't it, Merry?"

"Yes."

Ron sighed. "But it's the nursery for us tonight, because Mamma couldn't bear the disturbance at dinner after her raging temper last night. As it is, she could hardly stand up to make it into the carriage to come here."

"But there's so many people here today making much more of a disturbance than we ever would, so it's hardly fair," Merry complained.

With thirty guests sitting down to a huge dinner and intent on having a good time, Jane didn't think it fair either. And if their mother could survive the continual thud of the tennis ball hitting the roof of the Gallery without reviving her headache of the night before, then why couldn't she tolerate her two children eating their dinner surrounded by feasting adults? Far be it from her to interfere in a mother's edicts. But Jane knew she wouldn't be able to sit through such a dinner, least of all eat anything, with the thought of these two children eating alone in a cavernous, ill-lit and possibly freezing room, if the nursery was anything like the rest of the rooms in this house. She had eaten so many dinners cold and alone that it didn't bear thinking about.

"My lady, the gentlemen have now joined the ladies in the Yellow Saloon," Willis the under-butler informed Jane, squatting to peer under the table. "Would you care for me to help you out of there?"

"No!" the children said in unison, a pleading look at Jane.

The tutor and the governess dared to peer under the table on either side of the under-butler, glowering at the two children with every expectation that they follow Jane out from under the table. But Jane saw the little faces crumple, and she didn't have the heart to ruin their game of hide-and-go-seek.

"Thank you, but I shall remain here until his lordship discovers us," Jane replied evenly. She looked deliberately at the tutor and the governess to ensure they were included in her edict. "And I would be pleased if you would forget we are here, or you will give the game away, and that would give his lordship an unfair advantage."

The under-butler bowed his head in complete acceptance of this order, but the tutor and governess had jaws swinging that, had they been able, would've dropped to the floor when Jane added to the blanked-faced Willis, "If you can manage it, and it isn't too much bother, would you find space at the table for two more covers, next to me, of course." She smiled at Ron and Merry. "It's only fair all the Sinclairs be present at my first dinner, don't you agree?"

With the children nodding their delight, the under-butler went away to do his bidding with perfect composure and the governess and tutor departed to await the first opportunity to inform Lady St. John of these surprising developments.

It was not many minutes later that, amongst the usual to-ing and fro-ing to the table of soft-footed servant activity, the three under the table heard the measured tread and voices of two gentlemen in conversation. The gentlemen came further into the room. In fact, they strolled right up to where the three under the table were huddled. Merry took the unnecessary step of putting a chubby finger to her smiling lips to ensure her co-conspirators remained silent, and hunched her shoulders in delight. Even Ron's eyes lit up and he hugged his knees and wiggled his toes in his black polished shoes.

The two gentlemen in conversation came to stand close by the table. It was the Earl of Salt Hendon and Sir Antony Templestowe. Ron and Merry were in such an ecstasy of expectation of being discovered by their much-loved uncles that they swiftly and silently pushed themselves further back along the length of the polished floor to hide amongst the tangle of chair legs, leaving Jane behind, with the possibility of being the first to be discovered. Yet, she couldn't help but get caught up in the children's excitement. That is until she heard whom the two men were discussing, and then she was glad the children had scampered out of earshot.

She wished herself a hundred miles away.

"HER BROTHER IS A FINE FELLOW," Sir Antony was saying. "And not a bad tennis player for someone who professes to have played only the odd game at Oxford. Are you certain I've not met his mother?"

"Absolutely," was Salt's clipped response.

"Odd. When she came swanning into the library yesterday, I

was convinced I'd met her before. There's something... Are you sure she's never been to Salt Hall?"

"Tony. If you're going to bore on about the vulgar Lady Despard, I'll sit you beside Jenny Dalrymple, who has the brain the size of a pea and about as much conversation."

"Is that so?" Sir Antony laughed. "But what about that stocking and garter business down on the court?"

Salt put his wine glass on the table, just a foot away from where Jane sat huddled. "No doubt Diana thinks Jenny's ideal mistress material. Just like Elizabeth before her and Susannah before that. No brains and all breasts."

"Diana? Yes, I'd heard she took an interest..."

"A diplomatic understatement, dear fellow. Your sister is under the misguided belief she has control over my life, in and out of the bedroom. What she doesn't realize and never will is that I permit her good-natured interference only in matters I deem of little consequence."

Sir Antony laughed again. Jane heard the nervousness in his voice. "Well you've definitely got her fooled, not to mention half of society. Diana plays the part of Countess of Salt Hendon by proxy to the hilt. May I ask why you let her get away with it?"

"It gives her something to do. She was born to be a political hostess. In fact, had she been born a man she would've made an excellent politician. Much more successful at wielding the political dagger than you ever could be."

"Thank you very much!" Sir Antony said, offended.

"I mean that in the nicest possible way, Tony. You have a conscience and I trust you implicitly. That doesn't bode well if you hope to claw your way to the top of the political manure pile here at home. But I will help you rise to ambassador, precisely because of your shortcomings. We need more men like you in positions of influence, and I will continue to do what I can to see this is realized."

"Your faith in my abilities overwhelms me," Sir Antony commented dryly. "Though I'm not sure your speech was entirely complimentary."

"My dear Tony, my ancient pedigree entitles me a seat atop the political poop, where I am best able to put your abilities to good use," Salt drawled with exaggerated emphasis. "To state the obvious, an earldom and more wealth than I know what to do with gives me unlimited influence. I was being complimentary. You undervalue yourself."

"But what of Diana?"

"If she were a man..." Salt replied, an edge to his voice and with the slightest of pauses before he continued in a more conversational tone. "She's very good at organizing my social calendar, something that, quite frankly, bores me beyond belief. But you know as well as I that social calendars are a necessary evil for a man in my position. I will be forever grateful to her for taking on the task, though I did not ask it of her. But I'm not blind to her motivation. That she has overstepped the mark by taking on the role of procuress, I will stop—Oh? So you knew? God! Is nothing sacred?"

"For Diana? About you? Afraid not," Sir Antony apologized.

Jane heard Salt huff his annoyance and watched him take a step closer to the table, so that the toe of his shoe tickled the hem of her petticoats. She quickly gathered the silk layers closer, and in the process knocked a chair leg. The two children drew in quick breaths and Jane held hers, but when the Earl and Sir Antony continued talking, those under the table silently breathed easier.

"I've tolerated your sister's interference in my life since the death of St. John because it has given her widowhood occupation and meaning," Salt said flatly. "I had hoped that in time she would remarry. The fact that she has, as you so bluntly informed me at White's, held out in the expectation that I would ask her to marry me, has made me realize that allowing her to organize my social engagements and play hostess at my party political dinners was an error of judgment. To be blunt," he added on a sigh of admission, "I permitted your sister such license because it stopped her interfering in matters that are far more important in my life."

"Such as your marriage?" Sir Antony asked too quickly and could've bitten off his own tongue. Why was it that he could be the consummate diplomat with others, but with Salt he just blathered like a schoolboy? He tried to make a recover. "If it's any consolation, Diana's taken the news better than I expected. Of course, she pretended she already knew you were married and practically spat in my face for daring to tell her to be on her best behavior. I dare say having guests here today has helped temper her mood. That was a good tactical move on your part."

Salt let out a long breath. He sounded tired. "Putting off the inevitable is what it was. I don't want your sister to suffer any undue embarrassment or distress from my marriage. That I am married is enough of a shock for her to bear right now. When she learns how far I've sunk into the mire, she'll be mortified."

"Mire?"

"That Jane married me *for Tom's sake*."

Sir Antony blustered. "So her brother could inherit what was rightfully his, and finally put food on the table of his loyal factory workers, who had gone without wages for three months? Do you believe that pap?"

Jane held her breath in the silence until the Earl said simply, "Yes. Yes, I do. It's just too pathetic a circumstance to be invented. I'll have a copy of Jacob Allenby's will tomorrow, so I'll find out exactly what hoops that lunatic merchant made his nephew and my wife jump through."

"Makes her less the mercenary bride, then," Sir Antony commented lightly. "She certainly doesn't come across as the type, far from it."

"Tony, whatever way you flavor it, the dose is still hard to swallow. And now I have a wife, Diana can no longer act as my hostess. I am counting on your support to make your sister see reason. She must be eased out of her social commitments on my behalf, and it must be done as gently and as expeditiously as possible, so that she doesn't make a fool of herself and me in front of our friends and family. As it is, she's in there dishing out the tea as if it's her place to do so, and it's not, it's my wife's."

"So you've no intention of sending Lady Salt into the country?" Sir Antony asked, looking hard at his cousin. "You're going to make your wife your wife?" and could have stood on his own foot for again allowing words to flow out without due thought. "What I mean is—"

"I know what you mean," Salt answered wryly and picked up his wine glass. "Lady Salt will remain here until such time as I can take her to Salt Hall," he stated and added, as if needing to justify himself because Sir Antony was looking at him curiously, "Parliament doesn't rise until Easter, so I have no choice but to stay in London until then. Particularly with rumblings that Bute may resign any day, though I don't see that happening for some time to come. He'll hold out as long as he can. His Majesty will convince him to stay on. And because Lady Salt remains in London, my dear Tony, I will expect her to do her wifely duty."

Wifely duty in the bedchamber was what he was thinking. Up until last night as he lay beside her in that ridiculous nightshirt, he had had every intention of bedding and then banishing Jane to Salt Hall as soon as he could make arrangements to have her and her new wardrobe packed up and bundled into his traveling coach. Then they had made love, and now he didn't know what he wanted to do with her, apart from get her into his bed again at the earliest opportunity.

"Do you think her capable of carrying it off, being Countess of Salt Hendon, playing hostess at your dinners, accompanying you to balls and routs and the like?" Sir Antony asked, peering intently at the Earl, who was sipping from his glass and seemingly miles away with his thoughts. "From what I gleaned from her brother, your wife hasn't stepped outside the confines of her little garden in Wiltshire in nigh on four years." He coughed into his hand, embarrassed. "Jacob Allenby was very possessive. Kept her locked up. Feared attracting stray dogs. Not an unreasonable assumption. You must admit, she does have an unworldly quality about her, and that coupled with her undeniable beauty and gentleness, well that's—"

"—an irresistible combination for stray dogs! I appreciate the warning."

"Listen, Salt. I didn't mean anything by it. To tell you a truth, I find her and her brother delightfully frank and unpretentious, which is a refreshing change when you and I breathe air thick with cynicism and flattery. Just think you should keep a wary eye on her, that's all. Though how you are to do so when you have all those Parliamentary obligations…"

"Or appoint a guard dog to do it for me. Perhaps I'll appoint you. In fact, consider it done."

"Salt, be reasonable! You can't make me."

"Yes, I can. As you say, I have far too much to do, and you've nothing better to do while you're in London. Bedford won't send for you until I say so." He put a hand on Sir Antony's shoulder. "Besides, you're the only man I can entrust to help Jane through the emotional wasteland that is Polite Society. Ah! Here's Willis now. Have you seen Lady Salt? Lady St. John mentioned that my wife had wandered in here some time ago?"

"Lady Salt was here, my lord," the under-butler said truthfully. "And it was some time ago..."

"And Master Ron and Miss Magna? Have you seen them?"

Merry's burst of the giggles and Ron's furious whispered hush saved the under-butler from any further distress. Salt dismissed him with a jerk of his head and turned to Sir Antony with a finger to his lips before saying casually,

"Not only has Lady Salt vanished, but so too have those wretched brats, Ron and Merry. I ask you, Tony, were there two more annoying children in all of London?"

"Oh, surely not only London?" suggested Sir Antony, playing right along and nodding when the Earl signaled at the table. "I'd go so far as to say that they would put the French to shame. I've seen French children. Mere harmless gnats by comparison to our Ron and Merry."

There was another stifled giggle and another hush and scrape of a chair as Merry pushed her brother sideways for pulling a face at her. Jane tried to calm them both and they settled again. But Salt had heard them and seen the chair move near where Jane sat hunched, so thought he knew the children's exact location.

"Gnats, you say, Tony?" Salt answered, shifting to the left and ready to pounce. "If French children are gnats," he announced loudly as he ducked, lowered a shoulder and thrust a hand under the table and made a grab for a child, "then Ron and Merry St. John must be rats for taking up residence under my table. And lousy rats at that for being so easily caught! Come on out and receive justifiable punishment, rats!"

This pronouncement was accompanied by loud squeals of delight and much thrashing about and movement of furniture. Ron and Merry watched with delight as Jane was caught about the ankle. They were well out of Salt's reach, but still they scampered away to the other side of the table with shouts that no rats by the names of Merry and Ron were to be had in this particular dining room.

Sir Antony joined in the fray, running around to the other side of the table to head off an escape, much to the fascination of the liveried servants and those curious guests who had spilled in from the Yellow Saloon at the sounds of chairs being knocked over, and much squealing and shouting.

"Two rats here, my lord!" Sir Antony shouted out, thrusting aside two chairs and going down on his haunches to peer under the table. "Egad! Two very big rats in residence indeed, and only a cat the size of a Tower Zoo lion would be able to catch 'em. Come out, rats! Come out before the lion of Grosvenor Square makes a meal of you both!"

There were more squeals of delight when Sir Antony made a lunge for Merry, who shrieked so loud Ron clapped his hands over his ears. Shielding his ears made him slow to escape and he managed to get himself caught by his Uncle Tony, who grabbed him by the sleeve of his velvet frock coat, only to have Merry pulling Ron by his right upturned cuff to try and break their uncle's grip. But Sir Antony tugged harder and suddenly there was the ominous sound of ripping cloth as he tore a rent in the stitching at the shoulder of Ron's frock coat. With nothing to hold on to, Sir Antony shot backwards and skidded on his backside across the polished wood floor. Ron was free, and he and Merry laughed to see their uncle in such an undignified pose; stockinged legs in the air and sprawled out in the middle of the floor at the feet of the startled under-butler.

"Aha! Caught!" Salt announced with satisfaction, and firmed his grip on his rat's ankle, while looking over the top of the table between two elaborately decorated epergnes to see what all the fuss was about. More than a dozen guests and as many servants were gawking at the high-jinks in his lordship's dining room. "Tony? Tony, do you have the other rat?" he called out with a laugh as his rat kept wriggling and wasn't about to give up the fight. "I hope so! Or my rat gets tickled to death until his fellow capitulates! Tony? Where are you? It may be a very long torture indeed," he said with mock menace to his rat as he tightened his hold on a slim ankle, "if you, my dear rat, don't let go of that chair leg and come quietly!"

He pulled his prisoner by the stockinged ankle swiftly toward him, caught up a bunch of her petticoats and hauled her out from under the table and up over his shoulder in a smooth and easy operation. Shoeless and kicking, her stockinged feet and slim ankles on display to the world, he demanded she stop struggling, and to keep her legs from kicking and her silk petticoats from billowing out, he placed an arm under her bottom and held her to his shoulder. This also stopped her from slipping completely over his shoulder and onto her head.

There wasn't much fight in his rat now because she was laughing and protesting at one and the same time. She beat at his back with her fists and told him, while upside down and voice muffled into his velvet frock coat, that he was a brute and a fiend and she wouldn't give in, whatever tortures he inflicted. Rats stuck together! All this did was make him laugh harder, and he so far forgot himself that he smacked his rat's bottom in mock anger and said he would go on meting out due punishment until she gave up the whereabouts of her fellow rats.

"Salt, put me down!" Jane pleaded, though she was enjoying herself hugely. "My head is spinning and I feel faint!"

There was more squealing and laughter from the other side of the table when two heads appeared and they saw the Earl with his Countess up over his shoulder, giving her a mock thrashing. They jumped up and ran round the table, ignoring their governess, their tutor and even their mother, who broke from the crowd of stunned onlookers to go after her children, demanding that they stop all this nonsense at once and act the well-bred gentleman and young lady they had been brought up to be. But Merry and Ron were too caught up in the moment and were intent on freeing their fellow rat from the Earl's imprisonment. Sir Antony, too, who was now on his feet and recovered his dignity, brushed down his silk breeches and adjusted his lace cravat, then came across to join his niece and nephew, his sister ignored.

By the time they reached the Earl, Salt had slid Jane to her stockinged feet and let her go, once he was certain she had regained her balance. As for her dignity, seeing the mute faces of their audience, she wasn't at all certain that would make a recover any time soon, and she turned away to pin up her mussed hair. Her fichu needed adjusting again, her petticoats were crumpled, she had no idea where her satin slippers were, and she couldn't hold her head up because her face was flushed with embarrassment.

What Jane was doing under the table, Salt could hazard a guess, looking at his mischievous niece and nephew. He knew the moment he had a good grip on her ankle and pulled her towards him out from under the table that it was his wife in his arms, but he was too caught up in the moment to give two testers who saw them.

"You didn't catch us at all, Uncle Salt!" Merry announced proudly, coming to stand before the Earl and staring up into his flushed face. "Ron and I were too quick for you and Uncle Tony, weren't we?"

Salt smiled down into her upturned smiling face and pinched her small pointed chin. "Much too quick, Merry."

"And it was a good hiding place wasn't it?" Ron asked anxiously, a look over his shoulder at his mother and the two servants bearing down on them. "You'd no idea we were there under your feet all the time, did you, Uncle Salt?"

"No idea at all. One of the best hiding places you've found, without doubt," Salt assured him. "And you were so very quiet." He glanced at Jane. "All *three* of you."

"We were as quiet as rats!" Merry announced, and looked about for approval at her cleverness.

"Aubrey and Magna Sinclair St. John!" Diana St. John announced, sweeping up to her children. "I am very disappointed in you both," she said sullenly. "Where have your manners flown? Did I not tell you about Mamma's sick headache? And here you are running about your uncle's dining room like a couple of street urchins. You will go with Clary and Taylor to that room upstairs where you usually eat, and you will conduct yourself in a manner befitting a Sinclair. That is all. No. I don't want to hear your excuses. Go."

"Yes, Mamma. Of course, Mamma," both children mumbled in unison, a fearful glance up at their mother. But just as the tutor and governess stepped forward, Merry broke from her brother's side and ran to the Earl and caught his hand and pointed at Jane.

"She said we could have dinner here with you."

"Merry," her brother whispered, "it's not *she*, it's Lady Salt."

"But I want to call her Aunt Jane," Merry counted. "She said I could!"

"Magna! Aubrey! How dare you carry on like rabble! Give your uncle the proper respect and do as you are bid and say good-night!" Diana St. John ordered, and signaled again to the governess and the tutor to take her children in hand. "You know very well you don't eat in the dining room when we have guests, and that's the end of it!"

Obediently, Merry curtsied and Ron bowed to the Earl, their gaze cast to the floorboards. But Merry did not let go of the Earl's hand and was somewhat comforted by the fact that he did not let go of her hand either. It was then that Jane stepped forward and calmly addressed their mother.

"I told Merry and Ron they could eat their dinner here with us." She looked at the Earl and then at Diana St. John's marble countenance. "It's just that it must be very lonely eating alone in the nursery. And cold, too, if I know anything of this house."

"What could you possibly know about this house? You've only been in it five minutes!" Diana St. John whispered viciously in Jane's face, self-control lost for the briefest of moments, then masked instantly by cool-indifference. She added haughtily, and loud enough for the assembled guests to hear, "I do not appreciate interference in my children's welfare, my lady. I am their mother. I know what is best for them."

Yet the brief loss of control, and the fact her children feared her, provided Jane with a glimpse behind the woman's mask. It made her inwardly shudder. If Diana St. John put her mind to it, she was capable of wielding more than a political dagger to get what she wanted. Jane decided it was time to be brave for the two little eager faces that looked at her expectantly.

"I'm so pleased you no longer have the headache that called out a physician in the middle of last night," Jane said pleasantly, looking Diana St. John in the eye. "Then again, watching the tennis match could not have helped...?"

Lady St. John's hazel eyes opened wide, then narrowed to slits and her painted mouth twisted up in a smile. "You may think yourself very clever—"

"Let it be, Di," Sir Antony hissed under his breath. "Don't make a fool of yourself."

Diana St. John smiled sweetly at her brother and tapped his sleeve with the sticks of her ivory fan. "Foolish boy! Trust you to trip over your flat feet for a pretty face."

Salt smiled encouragingly at his godchildren, who were staring up at him in anxious expectation, then turned wearily to their mother. "Diana, take Tony's advice. I see no harm in the children being present. And as Lady Salt has kindly given Ron and Merry permission to sit at the table with the adults, they may do so. But they must be on their best behavior," he added, a mock frown down at the two now suddenly happy children, who nodded up at him enthusiastically, "and do as Lady Salt bids them, or they will find themselves consigned to the nursery."

"I won't allow it!" Diana St. John blurted out before she could stop herself. "Clary! Taylor! Take—"

"But as this is my house and my table," Salt said very quietly, "it is not your place to say otherwise."

"But they are *my* children," Diana St. John stated, and in a show of defiance, pulled her son and daughter from their uncle's side and gathered them to her petticoats. "I will do with them as I see fit."

Salt inclined his head to her with excessive politeness but there was ice in his voice. "I suggest we not mince words, my dear. St. John left his children in my sole custody."

Lady St. John blanched and instantly let go of Merry and Ron, who, after a small hesitation, ran to the Earl and hugged him. She was on the verge of tears of rage as she watched her children go hand-in-hand with Salt to the foot of the table, but force of personality kept her temper in check. Before retreating to take her place at the table, just as the butler announced dinner was served, she said very quietly to Jane,

"You are nothing but a hiccup in his life. Annoyingly present, but eventually hiccups disappear, by whatever means necessary, and then one can't remember ever having had them."

NINE

"Don't worry about Diana" Sir Antony assured Jane over the pea soup. "Salt's marriage has given her a severe shock, I won't deny that. But she'll adjust. She has to. She has no alternative."

But Diana St. John believed she did have alternatives. As she sat through the long dinner seated just a few places away from the Earl at the head of the table, surrounded by the titled and politically powerful, she had the satisfaction of seeing the new Countess of Salt Hendon consigned to the furthest end of the table, where obedient wives sat and played hostess to the nobodies: The old, the young and the politically insignificant. Why her brother chose to play the chivalrous idiot by sitting himself on the Countess's left amongst the worms, Diana knew not, but thought perhaps he hoped to gain the Earl's favor by keeping the little wife company. But as Salt did not once look his wife's way, and spent the evening talking politics with Diana and their mutual group of friends, she decided that her brother's little ploy had gone awry.

And while she was chatting and laughing and fluttering her fan very prettily, and holding court amongst the politically influential, she learnt an interesting piece of information from Lady Porter, whose favorite pastime was being up on all the gossip involving Westminster's upper-servants. Diana had recently lost a very good upstairs maid by the name of Anne Springer to Jenny

Dalrymple, and it just so happened that the elder sister of this Anne Springer was Lady Porter's dresser. But it was Lady Porter's adamant belief that Diana's very good upstairs maid had not gone to Jenny Dalrymple at all, but was here in this very house, newly employed as the Countess of Salt Hendon's personal maid, to be closer to her betrothed, one Rufus Willis, under-butler to Lord Salt. Lady Porter was insistent. After all, her source, Anne Springer's sister Janet, was impeccable.

Come time for the ladies to retire to the Long Gallery to sip tea, leaving the gentlemen to their port, Diana St. John disappeared for half an hour. She found her way through the public rooms to the labyrinth of dimly-lit passageways that led to the very private rooms occupied by the Earl and Countess one floor above. Here, in the freshly painted and prettily furnished rooms that were the Countess of Salt Hendon's apartments, she discovered her very good upstairs maid Anne.

The young woman was in amongst a plethora of exquisitely embroidered petticoats in a variety of rich fabrics and colors. A dozen pairs of shoes in matching fabrics were lined up along the polished wood floor, and on the sofa were neatly stacked piles of stockings and all manner of female fripperies. She was humming to herself and busily hanging, folding and putting away her ladyship's extensive new wardrobe. With her were two dressmakers and a milliner. They sat huddled together with needle and thread, under the light of a branch of candles by the warmth of the fireplace, putting the finishing touches to a couple of bonnets and bodices.

Diana St. John screwed up her mouth at such overindulgent spending on a creature who in her eyes wasn't worth her housekeeper's cast-offs, and summarily dismissed the dressmakers and milliner to a back closet with threats of their bills remaining unpaid if ever they opened their mouths to her presence. When her very good upstairs maid Anne dropped into a respectful curtsy, she was delighted to see real fear in the woman's eyes.

"I don't have time to waste on why you told my housekeeper a falsehood about your present employment," Diana St. John stated coldly, circling the woman with a menacing swish of her wide hooped petticoats. "Suffice that if you render me a small service I will forget that you are a liar, and thus I won't need to inform the Earl, and you won't be thrown out on the streets, where deceitful servants belong."

"My lady, I—"

"Did I ask you to speak? I don't have time, idiot! Listen. You can form your letters? Good. You will make a note of the Countess's every move. And I mean *every* move. I want to know everything there is to know about her, from her favorite color to her preferred breakfast beverage; what time of the day she rests, goes riding; who gets her custom; in particular who visits her and why; but most importantly, when and how often his lordship avails himself of his marital rights."

Anne blinked and wondered if she had heard correctly. "My lady?"

"You will also keep a detailed record of when Lady Salt has her monthly courses—"

Anne shook her head vigorously, but kept her eyes lowered. "Oh, no, my lady, I couldn't! I—"

"—and, most importantly, when she stops menstruating. I need to know the exact day of the month."

"My lady! Oh please don't make me! *Please,*" Anne protested, blushing to the roots of her brown hair. "I can't tell you—I can't report on them doing-doing *that,* or on her ladyship's courses. I can't—"

Diana St. John grabbed the woman's upper arm hard and stuck her face in hers. "Yes, you can and you will, or I will inform the Earl that the Countess's new personal maid lifts her skirts for the under-butler."

Anne was horrified. She burst into tears. "Never! Never! Mr. Willis is an honorable man, my lady. We have never—not before marriage. We are betrothed."

"Stop blubbering, girl! You won't be betrothed for much longer if you're both dismissed from service."

"Oh, please, my lady, no. Mr. Willis has worked so hard to get to where he is as under-butler. One day he hopes to—"

"Stop whining!" Diana St. John demanded and let her go with a shove. "If you want this Willis to rise to the dizzying heights of butler, you had best do as I say, or both of you will be out on the street without a reference and nowhere to go. No one will employ either of you, not if I have any say in the matter. The only vocation open to you both will be as whore and pimp." She rested her chin on the closed sticks of her ivory fan and pondered a moment before glancing slyly at the quivering maid. "He availed himself of her last night, didn't he? Do you know how many times he mounted—"

"No! No! Of course not, my lady!" Anne interrupted, shaking hands to her tear-stained face. "I do not listen at doors!"

"You will, if you want to keep your position," Diana St. John stated unsympathetically. "Willis can then continue to dream of becoming a butler in some third-rate household, and both of you will be fed and warm the rest of the winter."

Tears were streaming down Anne's face and she sniffed loudly. She knew she had to submit to Lady St. John's outrageous demands. She had worked long enough in the St. John household to know her ladyship meant what she threatened.

With an uncompromising mistress who expected her servants to obey her without question, the St. John children fared no better than the servants, the little boy most of all. Most shocking was the fact her ladyship fed her son a "strengthening" medicinal that more often than not necessitated a visit from the physician to cure the boy of an ill he suffered needlessly at the hands of his overprotective parent.

As for Lady St. John's temper tantrums, few of her servants had actually witnessed one at first hand, but those that had never forgot. Most sought other employment immediately. Anne had witnessed one such fit of temper and had pleaded with her father to find her another position. She could not stay in a house where the mistress tore up the bedclothes and pillows, scattering featherdown everywhere, and slapped her personal maid's face, all because she could not go to sleep without a sapphire and diamond locket that she kept under her pillow at night.

Three upstairs maids and Lady St. John's personal maid, with a red welt across her cheek, had been ordered to tear up the bedchamber until they found the precious piece of jewelry. Anne had been lucky enough to find the locket. It had slipped down the back of the carved headboard, and was lodged between the mattress and the carved backing board. It was an intricate piece of jewelry, beautifully wrought, with a large gleaming sapphire set into a gold back and surrounded by diamonds. Anne had it snatched out of her hand without so much as a "thank you". Her maids were then dismissed with the screaming threat that if ever the locket went missing again from under her pillow, Lady St. John would dismiss her entire household staff.

Anne had been miserable in that house, and when her father found her the position of lady's maid to the Earl's new wife, who turned out to be a soft-spoken young woman with a sweet nature, Anne considered herself the luckiest girl alive. But there was no escaping the ruthless Lady St. John. Nor did she feel she could approach the Countess, who was young and inexperienced and unlikely to believe a new servant over the Earl's particular cousin. And she certainly didn't want trouble for her betrothed, Rufus Willis.

Yet, the thought of watching the Countess's every move, of recording her intimate relations with the Earl, turned her stomach and made her say bravely,

"Please, my lady, don't make me do this… Lady Salt has been so good and kind to me."

Diana St. John swept to the door. "So good and kind in fact that she'll never suspect her maid." With a flick of her wrist she opened out her ivory fan. "Did you know these are the worst January frosts on record? People are literally *freezing* in the streets…"

SALT HAD THROWN ON A red silk banyan and sat at his dressing table filing his manicured nails, glad the day was over. He had enjoyed the tennis immensely, particularly winning against that prosy dandy Pascoe Church. But the dinner was tedious. The talk of the political maneuverings of Rockingham and Newcastle, and speculation over whether the King's favorite, Lord Bute, would or would not resign held no particular interest for him that night, despite Diana's attempts to keep him in the political argument. He was too distracted to be bothered offering more than the barest of comments—distracted with wanting to know what was going on at the far end of the long table, where his wife held court with Ron and Merry, Sir Antony, his secretary and Tom Allenby.

He had been unable to see past the tall silver epergnes, although he heard the occasional outburst of loud laughter from that end of the table. And twice the children came to visit him, which he thought charming; Merry sitting on his lap and Ron leaning against his shoulder, intent on telling him what a wonderful time they were having being with all the grown-ups. They assured him they were on their best behavior. He could ask Aunt Jane if he didn't want to take their word for it. They told him simply that they liked Lady Salt very much, and that her brother Tom was a capital fellow who knew a lot about ships and blue glass.

Later, when the gentlemen joined the ladies in the Long Gallery for the recital, he was the last to arrive and found Pascoe Church deep in conversation with his wife. Sir Antony, Arthur Ellis and Tom Allenby were all strategically nearby, not unlike mastiffs guarding the master's bone. He had to smile to himself at the looks on their faces. None of them were pleased that the silver-tongued Pascoe was intent on monopolizing Jane's time. Most of the ladies had gravitated to the opposite side of the room where Diana held court. Merry and Ron were perched stiffly on the sofa beside their mother, and by their gloomy expressions, not happy to be there.

Salt felt obliged to rescue them from their enforced good behavior. He spent the hour before the recital playing at snakes and ladders with them, at the far end of the Long Gallery, sitting on the rug in front of the second fireplace, where he and the two children could make as much noise as they wanted without disturbing the adults.

By the time the last of the guests had left for the evening, Jane had retired, and he sat over a brandy with Sir Antony in his book-room. Finally, Sir Antony bid him a good night and went up to his rooms off the first landing. With Tom Allenby and his mother staying at the Earl's Arlington Street townhouse, Sir Antony's usual abode when in London, Salt had given him quarters at his

Grosvenor Square mansion, a circumstance the congenial Sir Antony took in his stride.

It was Sir Antony's throw-away comment about Jane as he bid him good night that decided Salt to seek out his wife before he went to sleep. No wonder the Countess was a slight little thing, what with her sparrow's appetite. She ate nothing more than a bowl of pea soup at dinner, saying the food was far too rich for her, as she was used to very plain meals, and only one course at each sitting.

"I ask you, Salt," Sir Antony continued on a huff of disbelief as he set aside his empty brandy glass, the quantity of wine drunk before, during and after dinner loosening his tongue. "What rich merchant worth his moneybags eats plain meals? And one course only? Tom confided that his uncle permitted Jane a fire only every second day. Can you imagine such a frail butterfly eking out such a frugal existence? Not to mention Allenby leaving a will so bizarre it defies comprehension," he added as he staggered to the door. "And it gets better, y'know. Wait till you read it! I mean, I would need to see it in ink before I believed your merchant neighbor left Caroline ten thousand pounds. Yes, I knew that would make you sit up and take notice! Yes, your sister Caroline, Salt. Young Tom confided in me that Caroline was bequeathed such a sum by his uncle, and for the life of us we don't know why. If you ask me, two and two just don't add up to four where Jacob Allenby was concerned. Good night."

Salt was of the same opinion. He was completely astounded by Sir Antony's confession and was inclined to think too much brandy had fuddled his brain. Still, Jacob Allenby's resentment went deep where the Earls of Salt Hendon were concerned and mentioning Caroline in his will was just the sort of squalid revenge the merchant was likely to exact from the grave. As for keeping Jane cold and fed plain meals...

He tossed aside the nail file on the cluttered dressing table, dismissed Andrews for the evening, and padded through to his wife's rooms, telling himself he hadn't wished her a good night. Besides, he wanted to make sure she was putting liniment on his nasty handiwork of the night before. God, he had been an unthinking ass... If the food was too rich for her, then why hadn't she said so? He had a kitchen staff of twenty, not including the pastry chef, baker and scullery servants. Cook would've obliged her with a bowl of potatoes with lashings of butter, if that was to her fancy, silly girl!

Not finding her in the bedchamber, he went through to the dressing room and discovered her just out of her hipbath and drying herself behind the ornate dressing screen. Puddles of water had followed her the short distance from bath to screen, and there was the distinct smell of scented soap in the air.

Salt propped himself by the fireplace to wait and was pleasantly surprised to discover that the long looking glass behind the screen was at such an angle that from where he stood it was possible to view the candlelight goings-on in the shielded dressing area. He would definitely have the looking glass repositioned tomorrow, but not tonight.

He watched his wife drying herself by the light of a candelabrum, tackling an overlarge bath sheet that was clearly made for someone of his size and width. When she accidentally stepped on a trailing corner and it flew out of her hands to the floor and she scolded the towel as if it were animate, he smiled indulgently. He wondered why she had taken the prudish step of going behind a screen when it would have been much more comfortable and warm to dry herself before the fire. But such thoughts evaporated when she bent at the waist to quickly pick up the bath sheet.

His intention of scolding her for not eating her dinner, and wishing her a good night before returning to his cold four poster bed, vanished as he felt himself stir. Mesmerized, he watched her toss aside the bath sheet then turn to the looking glass. Catching a glimpse of something about herself in the reflection, she moved closer and put up her hands to carefully remove the array of pins that held up her waist-length hair. Salt's discomfort increased, as she stood on glorious display, naked and unselfconscious before her reflection. And when she let down her hair, leaning forward before tossing her head back so the raven-black mane tumbled, untangled, to the small of her back, he was determined to share her bed.

He wasn't sure how long he stood by the fireplace admiring her, dazed by the fact that this most beautiful and utterly captivating woman was finally his wife, but it was long enough for her personal maid to squeak a cough and run behind the screen with head bowed. He quickly turned to the fireplace, face aglow with embarrassment to be caught out furtively admiring his wife, the maid's intrusion just as effective as an icy dip in the Thames.

"His lordship? Here? Oh! Why didn't you say you were here, my lord?" Jane called out, hurriedly wriggling into a thin cotton nightshift and throwing on a silk dressing gown without bothering to button it up.

She dismissed Anne with a smile, saying she should get some well-earned sleep, as she looked quite tired. She hoped she hadn't given her too many tasks in the one day? She then thanked Anne for staying up so late and said she would decide in the morning what she wanted to wear tomorrow.

"You don't have to thank your maid for carrying out her duties," Salt told her with a laugh, as Anne hurriedly left the room with head bent and quietly closed over the door, leaving it ajar. "She stays awake until her tasks are complete. If that means her ladyship arriving home from a ball at three in the morning and must needs be undressed, then so be it."

"I truly do feel for Andrews' position," Jane quipped, standing beside him and warming her hands at the fireplace. "No wonder he's so efficient. It's fear, not devotion, that drives him."

Salt frowned, realized she was in jest and playfully tugged a long silky lock of her hair, saying with a smile, "And will fear make her ladyship eat her dinner? I'm told you ate only a bowl of soup. That's not enough to sustain you."

"I assure you, the portions your servants dish up could feed me for a week. Well, not a week, precisely, but a bowl of soup and a handful of bread was my usual dinner. So you needn't glare at me in that way."

"What sort of deprived household were you living in that a bowl of soup constitutes dinner?" he demanded incredulously. "Didn't that man look after you properly? It's just as well he was a chair-ridden cripple. His sort of ruthless economizing could not have sustained a wife, the expense of a mistress and the demands of any brats from both!"

Jane's throat constricted and she looked away. "I'm sure Mr.

Allenby could have learned a thing or two from you. Susannah, Elizabeth and Jenny don't have any complaints, do they?"

He grabbed her arm and spun her to face him. "We weren't talking about me, but that man—"

"I would prefer not to talk about him," she answered quietly, meeting his brown eyes. "Ever."

His brows snapped over the bridge of his long bony nose. "Did he mistreat you? Tell me."

She swallowed and shook her head. No, she wouldn't tell him. Not yet. She couldn't. She didn't want his pity. She didn't want him to be kind to her out of a sense of sympathy for the life she had led under Jacob Allenby's protection. How he had treated her as a whore in need of solid correction; how she had had to listen to his endless sermons on the Earl of Salt Hendon's immoral ways: That she was much better off as she was than as the wife of an unfaithful husband. So she held back her tears and kept the tremble out of her voice to say cheekily,

"I'll tell you if you tell me about Susannah and Elizabeth and Jen—"

"Don't be absurd!" he said with a huff of embarrassment and let her go. "That's another matter entirely."

"Oh?" she said curiously. "I'm supposed to ignore the existence of these women whom you consort with, and yet it bothers you that Jacob Allenby gave me a roof over my head when my father would not?"

"Of course it bothers me!"

"Why?" she asked simply. "I may have been tossed onto the streets by my father for one night of illicit passion, but in the intervening years you've cavorted with—how many women?—ten, twenty, thirty, possibly more. Not all at the same time—though— given half the chance…"

"You've no idea what you're talking about!"

Jane sighed. "No, I really don't know anything about orgies." She looked at him openly, as if considering the matter. "And I don't ever want to know. So, please, if you must participate in such activities, I would prefer you do so here, in London, and not in Wiltshire." When Salt goggled at her in disbelief, unable to respond, she giggled behind her hand saying, "I may be a complete novice in the marital bed but I am not *ignorant*."

"Marriage is no laughing matter!" he snapped. "It is to be taken *very*seriously."

Jane immediately lost her smile. He was mutinous, as if she were the guilty party. She wondered what he meant. His idea of marriage was surely quite different to hers. She may have had stars in her eyes as an eighteen-year-old, but when he had broken off their engagement those stars were quickly extinguished. And just so she never forgot what it was like to fall in love with a nobleman, Jacob Allenby had painted for her a very clear and gloomy picture of what life would be like to be the wife of a wealthy and vigorous nobleman who could have any woman he wanted. She thought she had prepared herself for this marriage, but she was wrong. She really could not bear the thought of sharing him.

She guessed he was naked under his red silk banyan. It gaped wide at the throat to reveal an expanse of bare chest, and where the banyan ended at the knees, his strong legs were bare. With his light-chestnut hair tumbled about his shoulders and that intense, long-sighted gaze that made him dip his high forehead to look at her, he was devastatingly handsome. Such good looks coupled with his skill and stamina as a lover, of which she was now acutely reminded after their lovemaking of the night before, made it easy to understand why the Susannahs, Elizabeths, Jennys and most certainly the Dianas of Polite Society, were all ears-over-toes in lust with him.

She did not think fidelity and constancy were part of his marriage vocabulary, as she brought her gaze back up to his brown eyes. She might take their wedding vows seriously, even consider them romantic and heartfelt, but men of the Earl of Salt Hendon's stamp would see the exchange of wedding vows much as they did any contract, legally binding and entirely to their advantage.

"I do not disagree with you, my lord," she replied quietly. "Indeed, I would go further and say that wives take their marriage vows far more seriously than do their noble husbands."

"Now you are showing your ignorance of the nobility," he said and looked away into the fire, as if the topic were distasteful to talk about openly. "Noble wives are deceitful; husbands are uncomplicated about their sexual needs. Trust me. I know."

She did not doubt his first-hand experience. His mistresses must have a husband somewhere and at sometime. She mentally sighed and wished he would just pick her up and carry her to bed and make love to her. All she wanted at that moment was love, laughter and sharing the physical expression of that love with him. She did not want to think about his love life with other women. For this night at least he was exclusively hers.

She could not predict the future, whether he would remain hers for one week or two, perhaps a month, so she was prepared to jump right in and enjoy him and their time together without fear or favor. But she was no fool. She was not prepared to wait until he had had enough of her, then play the cast-off passive wife when he returned to his usual way of life. Tom had told her at dinner that he and his mother had taken a house just around the corner in Upper Brook Street. Lady Despard intended to remain in London a further six weeks before Tom returned to take her back to Bristol. Jane had every intention of leaving London with them. She just hoped Salt didn't tire of her before then. She didn't want to be around when he cast her aside for his newest favorite, nor suffer Diana St. John's gloating triumph when he did.

Love and laughter and making love—that's what she needed tonight.

"Of course, I'm sure you have no regrets making love to all those women," she said in a light conversational tone, knowing she was goading him terribly. "Not to mention the orgies, where you probably don't remember how many women you cavorted with. But did it never occur to you that there was the possibility of you contracting some terrible social disease from such cavortings?"

"Of course it occurred to me!" he bristled, angry embarrassment overriding whatever shock he felt at her raising such a topic. "What do you think me? Mad?"

Jane looked to the ornate plaster ceiling and tried hard not to smile. He was even more handsome when out of sorts and embarrassed. "Jacob Allenby told me once about a type of pox that often infects lotharios, and if left unchecked will send you mad. He says that's what killed King Henry—"

"We are not having this conversation!" he snapped.

"But if I can't have this conversation with my husband, then who can I have it with?" Jane asked earnestly, looking up at him expectantly.

He cleared his throat, ill at ease yet knowing she had every right to a response.

"You have no need to be concerned," he said haltingly, dragging a hand through his hair. "I've never... That is, I have never consorted with a common prostitute. As for the others... I was—*I am*—extremely careful, and since October when I—we—I haven't —as I said," he added abruptly, seemingly unable to complete a sentence under her steady gaze, "you have no need for concern."

"How *very* comforting," she said, seemingly unimpressed. She picked up on the month of October, the month they had officially become engaged, but for the moment was content to push that to the back of her mind in her pursuit of teasing him mercilessly. "But what about the women you have consorted with? Did you ever stop to ask them if they were just as considerate?"

"I beg your pardon?" he said, horrified at the thought, his awkwardness increasing with every sentence she uttered. He had never been spoken to with such frankness, a habit that was all her own, and he certainly had never openly discussed his love life with anyone. And here was his bride questioning him about his sexual history, no less! He was too dumbstruck to be furious.

"Did it never occur to you that your mistresses and any of your casual lovers might have caught something from their other lovers?" she continued with all the casualness of one discussing the day's menu with the housekeeper. "It's all very well for you to tell me you're disease free, but what about Elizabeth and Susannah and—"

"Enough! This conversation has gone far enough!" he growled. His brow furrowed. "How do you know their names?"

"Or were they expected to give you a full medical history before you bedded them?" she added, backing away from him to the bedchamber door. "Names?" She shrugged. "I was under the dining room table while you were talking to Sir Antony, remember? And the spectator boxes of your Royal Tennis court have very thin walls. You'd be surprised what I learnt from your gaggle of female admirers."

He was appalled. "They are not my admirers and—"

"No? Well you certainly can't blame them for ogling you in your tennis breeches, which, by the way, leave nothing to the imagination—"

"—I wouldn't take it as read the tittle-tattle of a bunch of frustrated hens. Nothing?" he added, face deepening to a nice shade of puce. "*Nothing* at all?"

"Nothing at all," she stated, and was surprised he was self-effacing at being so openly admired. A dimple showed itself in her left cheek. "So I shouldn't believe that little theatrical display, either? I've never seen so much female underclothing in full public view before. And on a tennis court no less!" She smiled sweetly, a hand to the doorjamb. "It was very chivalrous of you to return Jenny Dalrymple's stocking and garter. No doubt she'll be only too pleased to offer up a full medical history now that you've offered her the post of mistress." She put up her little nose, not expecting an answer, and, turning on the balls of her bare feet, disappeared into the bedchamber, saying over her shoulder with a toss of her long hair, "Not very romantic, but quite sensible under the circumstances."

He stared after her, speechless. He didn't have an answer. What had been a piece of tomfoolery and gamesmanship on the sporting field of battle had been reduced by his wife to a boy's tawdry prank. Pascoe Church had not only had his eye on Salt's previous mistress, he had also been pursuing Jenny Dalrymple. He knew returning Jenny's stocking and garter with a flourish would put Church off his game. That was the sum total of his intent.

He had not told a living soul, he barely admitted to himself, but taking that kiss from Jane without her permission during the Hunt had had serious repercussions for his virility. To his troubled amazement, and growing fear that there was something wrong with him, he lost his hearty appetite in the bedchamber. That's not to say he was a monk. But since the previous October, when the date had been set for the exchange of marital vows in the first week of January, he had eschewed his mistress. He blamed Jane, just as he blamed her now for the healthy resurgence in his sexual appetite.

He was still frowning at the bedchamber door, when Jane peered back into the dressing room with a mischievous twinkle.

"I don't know why you're standing there waiting. I'm not about to ask you for a physician's report, if that's what's stopping you from joining me in the marital bed."

"You little witch!" he exclaimed, tension easing in his limbs. He came to life as she disappeared again and strode through to her bedchamber. "I should thrash you, madam wife!"

"As you did in the dining room?" She chuckled and skipped to the four-poster bed. "You see me all aquiver with terror, my lord!"

"Not only a witch, but a strumpet and a shameless baggage to boot!"

She darted out of his way and scrambled up onto the mattress, using the damask curtains to pull herself up. He grabbed for her, caught at her dressing gown, which easily slipped off her shoulders, and was left with a handful of silken material, while she stumbled about on the mattress in her thin linen nightshift laughing at his inability to catch her. At that, he clambered up beside her, picked her up and dumped her amongst the pillows. She threw a feather-filled pillow at him and he caught it before it connected with his chin. Now they were both laughing and before she could scuttle away, he pinioned her wriggling body to the bed, straddled her thighs and held her wrists above her head.

She smiled up at him with an impish grin. "Shall I oblige your lordship by rolling over so you can smack my behind?"

"No, my lady," he murmured, dipping to kiss her full lips, the intensity in his brown eyes both exciting and frightening her. He let go of her wrists and slid down the length of her body to kiss the instep of her dainty foot, his kisses progressing along her shapely leg as his hands slid her thin nightshift up over her knees, then gently parted her thighs. "I have a much slower and exquisite torment in mind."

TEN

WHEN THEY FINALLY DRIFTED off into a deep sleep, wrapped in each other's arms among a tangle of bed sheets and pillows, it was the early morning, in those few hours of utter quiet when it was still dark and there were no carriage wheels, not even the clip-clop of horses' hooves, to be heard on the cobblestones in Grosvenor Square. Jane slept soundlessly, snuggled up in her husband's warmth, but the Earl, who had fallen into a deep sleep only to stir a handful of hours later, lay wide-awake in the final glow of the dying fire in the grate, staring unseeing at the pleated canopy above his head. He was befuddled, bewitched and bewildered by his bride, and it scared him half to death.

His heart thudded against his chest, just as it had when he spied the seventeen-year-old Jane amongst the gentry assembled to see the hunt on its way; she had literally taken his breath away. He was overjoyed to discover that her astonishing beauty was matched by her decency of character and a forthright yet gentle nature. Here was a girl who was as honest as she was beautiful, untouched by cynicism and flattery. He had pursued her, courted her, and ruined her on her birthday. To all outward appearances he had played the lothario landlord to the hilt. But this time it was different. She was different. He was different. He had fallen immeasurably in love, and wanted to marry her and make her his countess.

He asked her to marry him and then lost his head in the summer-house, forgetting his upbringing as a gentleman, and made love to her.

Why had she not trusted him to return from London? Did she think so little of his character that she believed him capable of taking her virginity with false promises of love and then abandoning her? What manner of man was he to her? How was it she had accused him of breach of promise when he had not broken off their engagement? Why had she not waited for his return? She confessed her ruin to her father and been cast out of his house, and he had the locket returned as proof of her fickleness. He had been disbelieving and devastated when he learned she had accepted the protection of Jacob Allenby, a man he despised above all others. It did not make sense. It still did not make sense to him four years on.

He felt betrayed.

Reason yesterday he was intent on having her sign a document that laid down rules by which she would live as his wife and countess, rules to demoralize and humiliate and make her a virtual prisoner on his estate. He wanted to punish her for breaking off their engagement, for betraying his love, and yet, today he could not get enough of her.

But he would not allow her to get under his skin, to have his hopes and dreams shattered a second time. He would content himself with bedding her. In bed he knew exactly how she felt, what were her needs and desires, and could have his own strong carnal appetite satisfied into the bargain. And if the previous two nights were anything to go by, where lust was concerned, neither of them need look elsewhere ever again. Lust, pure and simple, he understood. Lust was uncomplicated. Lust could be satisfied. Lust would do them both just fine.

He slept past noon and woke completely rested. Sprawled out in Jane's bed in the semi-gloom, a new fire in the grate but the curtains yet to be pulled back to reveal the wintry sky, he was content to think of nothing more arduous than what he would eat for breakfast. He was well aware that his long-suffering secretary would be awaiting him in the library, appointment book open, and with a stack of correspondence requiring an answer, his signature or to frank, but for once in his life he was going to ignore pressing matters of state and eat a leisurely breakfast with his wife… Who was not beside him.

Where was she?

Frowning, he threw off the covers, found his banyan, covered his nakedness and scraped his hair out of his eyes. He poured cold water from a patterned jug into the porcelain bowl on the bedside table and splashed cold water over his face. Feeling reasonably awake, he went in search of her. He forgot that at this hour, not only was his secretary going about his duties his whole household had been up for half the day and were all busily engaged at their tasks.

Several of his household servants were assembled in the Countess's pretty sitting room under direction of Willis, the under-butler, who had been assigned to offer her ladyship a gentle guiding hand with her new responsibilities and duties as Countess of Salt Hendon. Expert guidance in all matters servant-related would ensure his lordship's house was disrupted as little as possible. The butler couldn't agree more, and was only too pleased that the Earl had given Willis the job of taking the young Countess in hand, leaving him to the more important task of seeing to the Earl's needs. Naturally, Willis did not mention that attending on the Countess would give him the opportunity of coming into contact with his betrothed, Anne.

Two footmen, the housekeeper, her ladyship's personal maid, and Rufus Willis were all standing on the edge of the Aubusson carpet by an arrangement of chaise longue, sofa, and wingchair near the fireplace. Willis and the housekeeper were sorting out the week's menus with Arthur Ellis, who was seated on the edge of a pink-striped chaise longue, the Earl's red leather-bound appointment book opened out across his knees. But his attention, like everyone else's in the room, was focused on the Countess, who was curled up in front of the fireplace.

Dressed in a froth of embroidered shell-pink silk petticoats, she had kicked off her silk mules and had her stockinged toes to the warmth of the fire. Her hair was in "undress", one thick rope-like braid down her back with the ends bound up and secured with a pink silk ribbon. She was dangling this silk ribbon just out of the reach of a fluffy white kitten with black-tipped ears. Every so often she would drop the ribbon within reach of the ball of fluff so he could paw at it, sink his little white teeth into it, and pretend to capture it. Jane would then disentangle the ribbon and pull it up out of the way again, laughing at the kitten's antics as it jumped up on its hind legs only to flip over and land on all fours. She would then scoop it up, pet it, nuzzle it, then set it down again to begin the game again.

Despite her preoccupation with her new and fascinating playmate, she was listening attentively to the views of Willis and the housekeeper on whether to serve the Lords of the Admiralty, the Chancellor of the Exchequer and the Privy Council their dinner before or after the Council meeting. It was the Earl's turn to host the nuncheon, but given the Chancellor's weak stomach, not to mention the propensity of several of the Lords to drink too much before the meeting had even commenced, there was debate as to whether it was a sensible idea to eat first. But eating first meant that there was the likelihood of several of the Privy Councilors suffering severe postprandial torpor. The meeting would then drag on far longer than desired by the Earl, who had an engagement to attend the theater that same evening.

"Why not serve nuncheon during the Councilors' meeting?" Jane suggested, taking her attention from the kitten but still dangling the ribbon to keep it distracted. She glanced at the secretary, who had his elbows on the appointment book in his lap and his gaze on the feisty ball of fluff. "Of course it will be more difficult for you to keep minutes of the meeting, Mr. Ellis, what with footmen going to and fro with dishes and their lordships distracted by the food, but I see it as the only way of keeping the majority of the Councilors content. Naturally, I know nothing of such matters, and you will have to seek Lord Salt's approval for the scheme, but it may just allow his lordship to wind up the meeting in time for him to change for the theater."

The housekeeper and under-butler looked at one another as if the idea had not occurred to them but was just the answer they were looking for. What was Mr. Ellis's opinion?

But Arthur Ellis hadn't heard a word. He was too enthralled watching the Countess playing with the black-and-white kitten, a gift from a new-found admirer; one of many gifts to have arrived that morning, but by far the best received. There were posies, cards of invitation, scented handkerchiefs, a fur muff, a gouache fan, and several parcels yet to be unwrapped. The kitten had been delivered in its own velvet-lined basket, with a porcelain dish and a pint of fresh cream. There was a note tied to the basket:

> *Pascoe, Lord Church,*
> *sends his compliments to Jane,*
> *Countess of Salt Hendon.*
> *May she prove a good mother to*
> *Viscount Fourpaws.*

The secretary wasn't sure what was meant by the note, but he had a very good sense that contained within it was a message for the Earl, and that his employer would not be pleased, however much the Countess might delight in Lord Church's gift. He had the uncomfortable satisfaction of being proved right when the Earl shocked the assembled company by appearing in the doorway unshaven, undressed and unimpressed.

"Mr. Ellis? What is your opinion of my scheme?" Jane repeated, and smiled when the secretary gave a start, nodded and dropped his gaze to the appointment book.

When Willis repeated the Countess's idea for the Privy Council nuncheon Arthur Ellis quickly concurred, saying he was only too pleased to take the minutes of the meeting during nuncheon, the food being a welcome diversion for those Councilors who had a tendency to digress from the topic—a circumstance that particularly annoyed Lord Salt.

Dipping his quill in the ink pot of the Standish placed on the chaise longue beside him, he made a note in the margin of the appointment book. He was about to move on to the next matter on his agenda when every servant in the room suddenly registered mute astonishment, became as stone, then dropped to a curtsy or doubled over in a bow, gaze on their shoes. When the Countess scrambled to her feet with a radiant smile, the secretary knew immediately who was at his back. He shot up off the chaise, open appointment book hugged to his chest, and with the sudden depressing realization that he had pressed wet ink to the front of his best brown wool waistcoat.

"Bloody Hell!" Salt exclaimed, bringing himself up short and retreating to stand in the doorway at the unexpected sight of half a dozen of his upper-servants occupying his wife's sitting room. Despite his embarrassment at being in a state of undress, the kitten intrigued him. "Where did you find such a ferocious animal, my lady?"

"His name is Viscount Fourpaws," Jane told him, brushing out the creases in her petticoats. She scooped up the mewing kitten and presented him to her husband. "I'm sure he thinks he is very ferocious, which is all that matters."

Salt held the tiny bundle of white fluff in the palm of one large hand and unconsciously tickled its throat with a long finger. "I see her ladyship has received more than a kitten by this morning's post," he commented, not surprised by the array of gifts and flowers piled on the sofa and scattered over the carpet. He had a fair idea who they were from. At the tennis tournament every male present had complimented him on his wife's beauty and grace. He smiled down at Jane. "And who sent you this brute?"

"Lord Church," Jane told him simply, and retrieved the note that had been tied to the kitten's basket. "See… Oh! How silly of me, you don't have your eyeglasses," she apologized.

Salt slipped the card into a pocket without reading it, looking even more uncomfortable, if that was possible given he was unshaven, his hair fell unbrushed about his shoulders, and he was naked under a flimsy silk banyan.

She took back the kitten when he held it out.

"Return it," he ordered and addressed his secretary. "Ellis, I'll see you in the bookroom in an hour." Then turned on a bare heel and strode off through Jane's apartments to his own.

Jane followed, kitten clasped to her silk bodice.

"You can't be so mean-spirited! Just because I made a slip of the tongue about your weak eyes—"

"I'm not that puerile, you silly girl!" he answered gruffly, marching onwards.

"If you want the truth, you are just being stubbornly unreasonable about wearing your eyeglasses in public. Poor eyesight is nothing of which to be ashamed. Not when you are perfect in every other way. Everyone has some physical flaw they do not like and cannot alter."

"Ha! Thus spake perfection herself!"

Jane frowned. "Now who's being childish? Just because I have a pleasing countenance does not mean I don't have flaws. I wish I were taller and plumper, like most females. And my mouth—I don't like it. I have a perpetual pout. It makes me look the spoiled child. Don't laugh. It's true."

Salt stopped at the door to his rooms and faced her with a smile. "I like you just the way you are, Jane, *particularly* your lovely mouth. But the kitten must be sent back."

She blushed at his simple compliment. "And you're just as handsome wearing eyeglasses," she said shyly, looking up at him. "The kitten stays."

"How can you say that when you've only ever seen me wearing the damn bloody nuisances once, and that was years ago! The kitten goes."

"I must be one of the few people to have ever seen you in your eyeglasses. So it's not something to forget, is it? You're just being stubborn. I won't send the kitten back."

He leaned his wide shoulders against the doorframe with a huff, and pulled out Lord Church's note and held it up to her. "What does it say?"

She read the note aloud.

"Dear Pascoe," drawled the Earl with a twisted smile. "He is all consideration for your welfare, my lady. He makes my wife a mother when I cannot. The kitten most certainly will be returned."

He wrenched open the door and kept walking until he reached his closet. To his surprise, Jane followed him through to this most private of male bastions. When Andrews saw the Countess he immediately downed shaving blade and leather sharpening strap and covered a bowl of soapy water with a hand towel. With a bow, he retreated to the dressing room to occupy himself until such time as the Earl was ready to be shaved.

"You believe by sending me the kitten he is having a cruel joke at your expense?" Jane asked calmly, stroking Viscount Fourpaws because he was mewing and probably in need of another bowl of cream after all his exertions with the ribbon. "But if you make me return him, won't Lord Church know he has gained his object?"

"It doesn't mean I have to accept his substitute for a child!"

Jane tilted her head in thought. "How does Lord Church know about the physician's diagnosis?"

"Who doesn't know?" he retorted flippantly, flinging out an arm. When she continued to look up at him expectantly he added, "Amongst the nobility, news that an earl is incapable of producing an heir is *gazetted*." He rubbed his cheek, grimaced at the feel of stubble under his fingers, then ran a hand through his uncombed hair, and was similarly disgusted at this want of grooming. "Now if you would allow me, I'd like to make myself presentable," he added, much subdued. "I have a full afternoon of appointments, and then a prior engagement at the theater."

"Have you ever wondered if the physicians may have got it wrong?" she asked quietly, ignoring his request for her to leave him to dress. "Perhaps you may have fathered a child or-or children, but because a physician says otherwise, you haven't bothered to even think that these children could be yours?"

Salt smiled uncomfortably and casually flicked her flushed cheek. "God help me, Jane, but your disturbingly frank questions would unnerve a lesser man. First you lecture me on catching a social disease, and now you raise the possibility that I may have unintentionally fathered a bastard or two. Is no topic sacred?"

"Not between husband and wife," Jane answered with a bashful smile, but her smile faded thinking how best to explain the rest of her thoughts.

She was utterly convinced he had never received the locket with her note telling him of her pregnancy. But how to broach this topic without blurting out the truth and revealing the whole heartbreaking story and the very real possibility of not being believed? He might even think her demented! Perhaps it was best if she just plunged in at another point that might help convince him that he was every bit as fertile as the next man. It was only halfway through her disjointed speech that she realized she had taken the wrong approach altogether, but by then the damage was done.

"From the little I overheard yesterday at the tennis tournament, there is a great deal about the activities of the nobility I do
not understand," she said conversationally, taking a turn about her
husband's expansive closet, the kitten now asleep in the crook of
her folded arms. "It seems that as long as a married woman is
discreet, she can have an affair with, say for argument's sake, her
husband's best friend if she so wishes and no one bats an eyelid.
Surely, if this is the case, and the woman becomes pregnant, how
does she know who is the father of her baby—her husband or her
lover?"

Salt loosely folded his arms across his chest, brown eyes fixed
to Jane's slightly flushed face. There was an edge to his voice. "I
would know."

"But that's just it. If the physicians have got it wrong and you
are fertile, then you wouldn't know. You could very well be Ron
and Merry's father, and how would you know? Only if their
mother confessed the truth to you, and she's unlikely to do that
because her husband was your best friend." She was rattling on
now because Salt was staring at her, face devoid of natural color.
"Ron does have a great look of you, and that could easily be
explained because his father and you were first cousins. Of course I
never met St. John so I don't know if you and he were much alike
and he may very well be their father, but I'm not the only one it
seems who has asked the question. So you see, you could be able
to father a child, but because you believe the physicians you
haven't suspected that you are just as virile as the next man."

"When you accused me of breach of promise I thought I could
stoop no lower in your eyes. I see that I was wrong," he enunciated
very quietly, and in a voice that froze Jane's marrow as he came
towards her, "Now you accuse me of cuckolding my best friend
and closest cousin. Not only that, but impregnating his wife with
my offspring. If it was not so despicable it would be laughable."

"But if you and Lady St. John were lovers and you can father a
child—"

"It is immaterial to this argument whether I can father a child
or not!" he spat out, grabbing her shoulders hard and jolting the
sleeping kitten awake. "I may be blind, but it's you who needs
spectacles of comprehension! What you fail to see, what has failed

to penetrate beyond your beautiful façade to your brain, is that St. John was my best friend."

"That does not stop Diana St. John being ears-over-toes in love with you!"

"Regardless of his wife's infatuation for me, I would never cuckold St. John, even in death," Salt stated flatly, backing her towards the door. "St. John knew this. To his bitter disappointment, he also knew he could trust me better than he could his own wife! So, Madam, your argument about my fertility falls flat."

Jane stared up into his brown eyes. "Ron and Merry are two lovely children, and if not St. John's, then I wish they were yours."

"They are not," he stated emphatically. "That statement of fact should snuff any flame of hope you may have held that I could give you a child." He let her go, a sudden dryness in his throat, and jerked opened the door that led back to her apartments. "You'll have to content yourself with mothering that little brute in your arms. He's mewing for milk. You'd best do your duty by him. Now, please, be good enough to leave me in peace with my deficiencies."

Jane did not move. She did not take her gaze from her husband. Absently, she stroked the kitten, hoping to distract it from its hunger pains a little longer.

"Do you not sometimes harbor doubts about the physician's opinion?" she persisted, adding in a halting voice, "That perhaps— if two people love one another deeply enough—their prayer for a child will be answered?"

At that, Salt dropped his gaze from staring over her head to look directly into her eyes, big, blue eyes swimming with tears. She was utterly wretched and hopeful at one and the same time. He didn't doubt her misery was genuine. It caused him to experience a stab of inadequacy so acute that it hurt his chest. How ironic that he'd had the same wishful thought she'd just voiced after making love to her in the summerhouse. He had asked her to marry him, aware that he could not give her children, and yet recklessly believing that perhaps, if they loved one another enough, their union would be blessed.

What romantic claptrap!

He was well aware of the ten-year joke whispered amongst

society that the lusty Earl of Salt Hendon couldn't even get a whore with child. The odds entered in White's betting book was a hundred-to-one against that he would father a son; fifty-to-one he could get a mistress with child; twenty-to-one he would remain childless.

Yet he couldn't help a twinge of wanting the impossible. What he wouldn't give to make Jane pregnant, to see her grow plump and round with their child. But that possibility didn't bear thinking about because that meant growing plump and round with another man's child. And that, for him, would be hell on earth.

He felt as wretched as she looked. With inadequacy came bitterness and anger.

"But you do not love me, Madam. You married me for Tom's sake and I obliged your father's dying wish and made you a countess. There is the sum total of our union. That we enjoy physical pleasure as husband and wife is mere serendipity. Content yourself with that. It's a rare commodity amongst our kind and more than most husbands and wives of noble marriages have in common."

Jane bowed her head to quickly wipe away tears, then resolutely lifted her chin.

"You know that's not enough—for either of us."

"Don't. Don't goad me," he said through his teeth. "I *cannot* father a child. I will *never* have a son. You will stay *barren*. Our marriage is destined to remain *childless*. How many ways do you want me to say it?" he added, gripping her upper arm, unintentionally twisting the silk of the tight sleeve under his long fingers and making her wince with pain. He jerked her closer. "Don't ever play me for a fool. Understand? You belong to me, and only me. The males in my family have ever been uxorious, but I don't believe in miracles. Find yourself pregnant and I won't hesitate to kill the father of such ill-begotten offspring. Hold to that thought. It will keep you a faithful wife better than any chastity belt." And with that he put her out into the connecting room and slammed the door.

~

Jane didn't see her husband for the rest of the day. She hadn't really expected to receive a visit from him that night, he had been so angry with her. But he came to her bedchamber in the early hours of the morning and slipped under the covers. When she drowsily asked after his day he apologized for waking her, said he had read Jacob Allenby's will and that Tom was very fortunate to have her as a sister, then told her to go back to sleep. Of course, neither of them could, and they lay awake in the dark, each acutely aware of the other, yet unsure if physical contact was wanted after their acrimonious parting earlier that day. Still, Jane was reassured by the fact he had chosen to seek her out and not gone to his own bed, or worse, to another's.

She wasn't sure who made the first move. All she remembered was that as she drifted off to sleep she was wrapped in the warmth of Salt's body. And later, in the dawn light, she was woken by his caresses and soon they were making love. Both craved touch, as if pleasuring one another was the only way of communicating forgiveness for the harsh words spoken earlier. Yet nothing was said, and when they finally drifted back off to sleep in each other's arms, satisfied and satiated, it was with a bittersweet contentment; despite forgiveness, matters remained unresolved between them.

And so they settled into a pattern of sorts in their first three months as husband and wife.

The Earl spent his days caught up in the political machinations of Whig and Tory factions and the negotiated Peace Settlement with France, carrying out parliamentary obligations to committees and to those who owed their sinecures to his patronage, and the endless round of social engagements that did not require the presence of his wife.

He confined himself to attending the male-only card parties and dinners of his friends, most of whom were unmarried, or if married, had been leg-shackled into arranged marriages where it was customary for husband and wife to lead separate lives, only coming together for a ball or a rout where social etiquette required that both parties of the union attend. Even Salt's good friend the Earl Waldegrave, who was madly in love with his wife Maria, spent his social hours with his male friends at the Club, or at Strawberry Hill, the home of Waldegrave's uncle-in-law Horace Walpole. He encouraged Salt to do likewise.

That the newly-married Earl of Salt Hendon was seen about town without his wife was not thought the least bit odd. Except, that is, by those romantically-minded ladies who considered it a crying shame that such a handsome, virile nobleman had not made a love match, and by a select few male friends who dined occasionally at the Earl's Grosvenor Square mansion. They had met the new Countess of Salt Hendon and were of the opinion the Earl was keeping his beautiful bride from the country locked up in his London residence to have her all to himself.

It did not go unnoticed by close friends and political rivals alike that when the Countess of Salt Hendon did venture from her gilded cage, she was mobbed by the admiring masses, eager to catch a glimpse of London's latest beauty. And it was not the Earl by her side fending off the hordes, but the Earl's best friend. Be it a ride in the Green Park, attendance at a performance at Drury Lane Theatre, a shopping excursion up Oxford Street to purchase a half a dozen pairs of gloves and three new fans for her ladyship's slender wrist, or even a visit to the tombs in Westminster Abbey, Sir Antony Templestowe was Lady Salt's constant companion and champion.

Eyebrows were raised, tongues began to wag, and the venom to drip about the young Countess and her husband's cousin the diplomat. Sir Antony did not return to Paris to rejoin Bedford's entourage, but remained in London paying court to his best friend's wife. That the Earl was not in the least concerned with this state of affairs and was rarely seen in public with his wife set Polite Society wondering if there was substance to the rumor that the Countess's outstanding beauty was overshadowed by her dim-wittedness, and thus Salt kept her locked away for fear of what she might say or do in public that could embarrass him.

Diana St. John fanned the flame of this rumor, commenting to all who enquired after the Countess that as there was nothing between her ears but wool, was it any wonder a nobleman of Salt's intellect and political acumen considered his new wife dull in the extreme? That Jane was self-effacing, kind, and always polite, but not quite certain what to say when confronted with the verbose compliments of strangers, particularly the fawning attentions of gentlemen, only seemed to confirm Diana St. John's spiteful précis.

It did not help the Countess's cause that when she was not out and about taking sight-seeing forays with Sir Antony, now the January frosts and a bracing February had given way to a warmer if blustery March, she liked nothing better than to spend time in her apartments. With Viscount Fourpaws asleep on her lap she embroidered, sketched or read. Sometimes she was content to curl up in the window seat and watch the traffic and pedestrians in the busy square below her sitting room window. The activities of this vast, noisy city were a never-ending source of fascination for a girl brought up entirely in a quiet corner of Wiltshire.

Yet time alone was precious. Willis spent part of every day tutoring the new Countess in the ways of running a great household. He answered the all-important questions: Which upper servant held the keys to the wine cellar? What was the precedence required at the dinner table? Did a Scottish Dowager Duchess outrank an English Baroness? These questions were easily answered by those brought up from the cradle knowing their place in society, but a complete mystery to the daughter of a country squire. Willis also proved a veritable font of information on important people and places he considered it necessary her ladyship should make it her business to know.

While Sir Antony considered it his duty to keep his best friend's wife entertained, Jane's stepbrother, Tom, who had returned to London from Bristol at the end of February, came to afternoon tea every second day. He told her all about his latest adventures out and about in the metropolis, but in truth kept a brotherly eye on her.

Tom often brought Billy Church with him to afternoon tea, and sometimes Arthur Ellis would join them. And when Hilary Wraxton and Pascoe Church made weekly visits on the pretext of enquiring how Viscount Fourpaws was getting along, Jane found herself in her sitting room surrounded by half a dozen young men. This was how Sir Antony discovered her when he poked his powdered head in to share a cup of tea, and quickly joined the group, a wary eye on Pascoe Church. But he was soon caught up in Tom and Billy's retelling of their experiences in the riots at Covent Garden Theatre, and when Hilary Wraxton was invited to share one of his poems with the group, Sir Antony was laughing along with the rest of the assembled company.

Salt never visited his wife's public rooms during the day, but most evenings he dined at home. Yet he and Jane never dined alone. Sir Antony, despite residing at the Arlington Street Town-house, had most of his dinners at Salt's Grosvenor Square mansion. Some nights Arthur Ellis joined them, usually to go over Salt's appointments of the next day, and once a week Diana St. John deigned to come to dinner with her two children. On other days, she made a point of arriving in company when Salt had open house dinners and at least ten of his colleagues and friends sat down at his table.

On these occasions, Lady St. John sat herself on Salt's left hand and was content to leave Ron and Merry to the Countess. She would then spend the entire meal monopolizing the conversation with witty anecdotes about politics and people unknown to Jane. She was determined to outshine the new Countess, but Jane never rose to her bait, showed not the slightest annoyance that her husband's cousin dominated the assembled company, or that the Earl, Sir Antony and Lady St. John frequently indulged in a politically-charged argument for the sake of it.

Instead, Jane quietly listened to the conversations around the table, gave her opinion if asked, and spent most of the meal listening to Ron and Merry prattle on about their days. She took a keen interest in their activities and had become such a favorite of theirs since the hide-and-go-seek incident under the dining room table that when they visited their uncle on Tuesdays, they would ask to be excused from the bookroom so that they might visit the Countess's sitting room, where, as they told the Earl, they were permitted to play with Viscount Fourpaws and listen to sickly poetry delivered by a fop in an iron wig.

Diana St. John was all for her children annoying the Countess.

It meant she could monopolize the Earl's time. It was on one such open Tuesday, with the cold anteroom full of hopeful men patiently waiting the Earl's pleasure and Ron and Merry gone upstairs, that Diana half-reclined amongst the cushions on the chaise longue by the warmth from the fireplace closest to the Earl, who sat writing at his mahogany desk, his secretary standing silent at his left shoulder.

Her velvet petticoats, richly-embroidered with silver thread, fell in a sweep to the floor and she had kicked off her matching mules, her stockinged toes pointed to the flames. Her careful coiffure rested against a closed fist, a fat auburn ringlet falling across her low-cut décolletage, while she languidly fluttered a filigreed ivory fan and prattled on about the latest on-dits swirling about drawing rooms concerning the Princess Augusta's affair with Lord Bute.

This was how Sir Antony discovered the occupants of the bookroom when he put a diamond shoe buckle across the warm threshold. That his sister was holding court did not surprise him; that his cousin continued to indulge her did. He raised an eyebrow at the low cut to her bodice that revealed the dark pink tinge of her nipples, and the manner in which she reclined on the chaise was a clear invitation to seduce. That his friend continued to write without once looking up, and was providing monosyllabic replies to her questions, was evidence enough of his level of interest. It never ceased to amaze Sir Antony that for an intelligent woman, his sister was a complete dunce when it came to the feelings of their cousin the Earl.

"Good God! It's a Tuesday and you're wearing your eyeglasses," Sir Antony exclaimed in awe, making his presence known with an outburst that was far from the measured question he had had in mind to ask.

"Oh! So you are," Diana commented with surprise, a glance at her brother who had sat uninvited opposite her.

Salt peered over his gold rims, then returned to reading the final paragraph before putting his signature to the document. He stood to allow his secretary to take his place to set the ink with a sprinkle of pounce powder, and came around to sit on a corner of his desk, eyeglasses still perched on the end of his long bony nose.

"It appears that I was being stubbornly unreasonable about wearing my eyeglasses in public—"

"You were," agreed Sir Antony.

"Thank you, Tony—and that, so I am informed, poor eyesight is nothing of which to be ashamed—"

"It isn't. Sensible advice."

The Earl's lips twitched. "—when I am perfect in every other way."

Sir Antony grinned. "Ah! Well, I'll leave that subjective estimation to your fair and frank admirer."

Salt gave a huff of embarrassed laughter. "Yes, she is *bruisingly* frank."

Diana St. John glanced from one male face to the other with no idea they were referring to the Countess. She sat up with a frisson of expectation, completely misreading the mood. "How unfair of you not to tell me Salt's latest interest!" she pouted at her brother then looked at the Earl. "So who is it? Jenny? Frances? Margaret?"

Salt removed his eyeglasses and pocketed them, a glance over his shoulder at Ellis. "Leave the rest. I believe you are wanted elsewhere. We can deal with the Rockingham papers later this afternoon."

Sir Antony took the opportunity to glare at his sister and shake his powdered head, but Diana St. John was oblivious to the warning and leapt right in. "Oh, Salt, please don't tell me you've made that Morton creature your latest interest! I couldn't bear it. She'll positively gloat when I next see her in the Mall."

"I wasn't about to tell you anything of the sort, my dear," the Earl said flatly, all humor gone. He addressed Sir Antony. "I presume you are also wanted elsewhere?"

"Oh! So you hadn't forgotten your engagement this afternoon?"

"Not at all. Were you sent to fetch me?"

"No."

"You perhaps presumed I had forgotten? For shame, Tony!"

Sir Antony smiled. Inwardly he was jumping for joy. It was something the Countess had let slip on one of their many excursions beyond the Grosvenor Square mansion that alerted him to the favorable turn of events within the Earl's household. He had become very fond of Jane and he genuinely enjoyed her company for its own sake. That she loved the Earl, he was in no doubts. Being a romantically-minded young man he hoped that one day her feelings for his cousin would be reciprocated.

A sennight ago she had inadvertently revealed that she and the Earl had begun spending their evenings after dinner in the book-room, where her husband was teaching her to play at chess. A small domestic detail in itself, but knowing the Earl as he did, Sir Antony saw this gesture as a huge hurdle for the matrimonial harmony within the Salt Hendon household. Which would mean he was a step closer to fulfilling his own matrimonial plans, his motives being not entirely altruistic. And just then he heard the name of the very object of his desire and dreams. Shaking his mind free of romantic ruminations, he heard his sister say in all seriousness, as she slipped on her mules,

"But surely you cannot have any objections to George Ruther-ford as a suitable match for your sister? He is worth fifteen thou-sand a year, not a penny less, and has an estate in Ireland that's the size of Surrey! Caroline could do worse."

"Much worse. But she can do better."

"Got anyone in mind?" Sir Antony asked, and inwardly cursed himself for he heard the edge to his own voice.

Salt regarded him steadily. "No. But when I do, you will be the first to know, Tony."

Diana shut her fan with a snap. "At almost eighteen, Caroline is practically on the shelf—"

"—where she will remain until her twenty-first birthday and not a day before."

Sir Antony made his cousin a small bow of understanding. "Three years is not such a stretch when she has the rest of her life to be married." And abruptly changed the subject. "We had best not keep her ladyship waiting. I believe the entertainments are due to begin on the hour in the nursery."

Diana St. John could barely say the word, but curiosity got the better of her. "N-Nursery? What entertainments?"

"Surely Ron and Merry told you all about it, Di?"

She shrugged a bare shoulder at her brother. "Possibly. They are always prattling on about inconsequentialities—it gives one the headache. None of it bears remembering."

Salt paused, a liveried footman holding wide the door, and regarded her steadily. "It is the anniversary of their father's birth. Had he lived, St. John would have turned four-and-thirty today."

ELEVEN

SUCH WAS THE CACOPHONY coming from behind the double doors that led into the rooms designated as the nursery, that it brought Salt up short, Sir Antony and Diana St. John at his back. But it was not the noise, it was this section of the house that made him hesitate. He had not set foot on the third floor since inspecting the house just before purchase some four years ago. He could not even remember the configuration of the rooms, how many there were or how they had been furnished, if indeed they contained any furniture at all. He seemed to recall the selling agent telling him that with a coat of fresh paint, pretty wallpaper with matching curtains, and a good fire in the grates, the rooms would do very well indeed for a brood of growing noble children.

He had not given the rooms another thought, until now. He had even dismissed as farcical Diana's refusal to mention the rooms by their designation as a theatrical means of protecting any feelings of inadequacy he had at being unable to father a child. Yet, now faced with crossing the threshold, he had a twinge that Diana's affected display of refusal was not so melodramatic after all, for it seemed laughable to be holding a birthday memoriam for a dead father in a nursery that would remain for him as silent as the grave.

Still, he could not disappoint Ron and Merry.

He had two fingers to the door handle when Diana pushed past him in a crush of petticoats to fling wide the doors. She misinterpreted his hesitation for embarrassment at being forced to enter a wasted nursery. Her own smoldering anger that the Countess had somehow deliberately set out to taunt her by using the very rooms she so despised was enough to make her drop her guard and speak without thought to her words or her audience.

The door banging hard against the wallpapered wall did not stop the chatter and movement. Those who heard Lady St. John's outburst above the din dropped their jaws, and a few little faces crumpled with fright at the sight of the angry lady. In one sweep, Diana took in the assembled company, adults taking tea and seedy cake, while children played skittles or statues under the guidance of their nannies and tutors at one end of the long room. All were happy and content and enjoying themselves. The warmth and color, the freshly-painted walls and upholstered furniture, the Turkey rugs covering the floorboards where small children took their first steps and chubby babies crawled, all made her seethe with resentment. Then she recognized the young woman standing beside Jane and her hazel eyes widened with new knowledge, then narrowed to slits of mischief.

She saw the Countess before Jane saw her.

"Well! How like you to unsettle his lordship's household with a pathetic display of domestic felicity!" and with a hand to her throat and a look of shocked disbelief that would have done any actress proud, she turned to the Earl with a swish of her petticoats to say in a loud whisper, "There's Lady Elisabeth Bute *that was*. The silly creature has invited the *Bute* sisters!"

Sir Antony had seen the married daughters of the Earl's polit-ical rival almost upon entering the room, and though it raised his eyebrows in surprise he was not so dismissive or so accusatory. How was Jane to know the connection? Both young ladies were married women, and thus used their husband's surname. Their presence in the house of their father's political nemesis was indica-tion enough that they looked upon Jane with great favor, and were prepared to weather the displeasure of their statesmen father by visiting her home, than it did about the Countess of Salt Hendon's lack of political acumen. Sir Antony was surprised his sister could be so blind to the gesture. Yet, he thought with a depressed sigh of resignation, where Salt was concerned it was his sister who was the simpleton.

Jane did not catch the content of Diana St. John's outburst, only her derisory tone. She had been in conversation with Lady Elisabeth Bute Sedley, whose much-admired newborn son was cradled in her arms, and because Lady Elisabeth's two-year-old daughter was intent on seeking her mother's undivided attention with as much chattering as possible. A grubby fist was clutched to Jane's petticoats, while a nurse tried to untangle the chubby fingers free from the delicate silk. Thus when Jane swiveled on a silk-slippered foot, baby cradled in her arms, it was not in answer to Diana St. John's spiteful remark but in expectation of seeing her husband.

Her blue eyes lit up and her smile widened, but fell away when Salt merely blinked at her as if she was a stranger. When she saw him sway, face blanched as white as the elaborately tied cravat about his throat, she carefully placed the sleeping infant into the waiting arms of its wet-nurse, scooped up the two-year-old who was taken away by her nurse, and scurried across the crowded room to his side.

Sir Antony had Salt by the elbow. "It's all right, dear fellow. I have you."

"It's… I'll be fine directly," the Earl muttered, mortified to be so weak-minded as to be affected by such a trifle as the sight of Jane with a baby in her arms and another tugging at her skirts.

He swallowed and took a deep breath, and for want of something to mask his momentary feebleness, he glanced about the room, seeing people without seeing faces. But his heart would not quiet and continued to pound hard against his chest, and no wonder. He had suffered a shock. The recurring dream he had been experiencing every night for a fortnight had come to life before his very eyes. Not entirely accurate, for in his dream (or was it a nightmare?) Jane was heavily pregnant. But the infant in her arms and the child clinging to her skirts were just as he had conjured them up in his disturbed sleep. So vivid and repetitive was this dream that one night he had woken in a lather of perspiration and immediately escaped to his own rooms to douse his body with cold water.

The very next night he had stayed away from Jane's rooms, and the night after that a late parliamentary sitting had given him a reason to dine with Sir Antony and spend the night at his Arlington Street townhouse. Alone in a cold bed, staring up through the darkness at the plastered ceiling, he had ruminated over the reasons for the recurring dream, and come to the realization that it was guilt that haunted him, guilt at marrying Jane when he knew very well he could not give her children. He had denied her motherhood to serve his own selfish need. Guilt was eating away at him. He who had spent his life commanding and receiving at will felt utterly helpless for the first time in his life. He had no idea what he could do about it, and that made him utterly miserable.

"You are just in time for the puppet show, my lord," Jane said brightly, as if nothing was amiss, but exchanged a worried glance with Sir Antony, who had relinquished the Earl's elbow to allow Jane to take his arm. "Mr. Wraxton was all for commencing the afternoon's entertainments but Ron and Merry would not listen to his entreaties. They said we must wait for you, and so we have."

The crowd parted to allow the Earl and Countess to pass to the far end of the room, and then closed ranks, swallowing them up in a sea of silk before Diana St. John could follow. That she was shown the backs of these perfumed and patched parents of precious brats did not greatly bother her, only that they had dared to side with the Countess against her. As it so happened, being left stranded at the back of the room gave her the perfect opportunity to slip away unseen to seek out the Countess's maid.

Jane guided Salt to a corner of the room where the adults had seated themselves on an arrangement of ladder back chairs, in front of which were half a dozen children cross-legged on plump cushions—all before a raised platform that had upon it a marionette theater. Nurses, nannies, and tutors stood off to one side with their smaller charges and babes in arms, while servants in livery scurried about with food and drink on silver trays for members of the audience.

"Uncle Salt! Sit here next to Tom. Sit here! It's about to start!" Merry demanded eagerly, grabbing for the Earl's hand.

"Not the puppet show," corrected Ron with a roll of his eyes. "We have to sit through a yawning poem first."

"But you are just as eager as the rest of us to see Mr. Wraxton's iron wig," Merry countered. "Isn't he, Aunt Jane?"

Salt cleared his throat as he took a swift look about the long room, with its fresh coat of powder blue paint, sprigleaf patterned wallpaper and soft matching curtains. He smiled down at his wife. "All your endeavor, my lady?"

"I cannot claim all the glory. Tony, Merry, Ron and Tom proffered their expert opinion on decoration. Although I suspect Ron and Tom will deny any involvement in such a womanly venture. Tony is made of sterner stuff."

This made Salt laugh, a glance over her dark hair at her stepbrother who gave a shrug of defeat. "I do not doubt it. Not a very manly pursuit to own to poring over swatches of fabric."

"Speak for yourself, Salt," Sir Antony quipped, quizzing glass plastered to an eye and a wink at Tom. "You'd be surprised how many pretty girls occupy the counters of drapery shops."

"Uncle Salt! Sit!" demanded Merry, pointing to an empty chair central to the row as she scrambled on to one of two tasseled cushions at the claw-and-ball foot of his chair. "Aunt Jane? Aunt Jane! Here! Here!"

Jane let go of the Earl's arm and would have stepped away to take her place on the cushion placed between Merry and Ron, but he grabbed her hand.

"Are you abandoning me, my lady?"

Jane looked down at his possessive hold on her wrist. "I—The children have reserved a cushion and I promised…"

He let her go and sat where requested with an outward flick of his frock coat skirts. "Naturally they have placed you at my feet, which is only right and proper."

Jane glanced up, saw the wink and turned away to sink down on a cushion beside Merry. Salt leaned in to whisper at her ear before settling back to enjoy the performance.

"I would gladly trade places if it were in my power to do so."

His words were still reverberating in her ear as Hilary Wraxton minced across to stand center stage dressed in a canary yellow frock coat with matching breeches, diamond paste buckles in the large leather tongues of his red-heeled shoes, and carrying a lace handkerchief. He unfurled a parchment and held it out at arm's length, then cleared his throat as if about to make an announcement as town crier. But it was at his head that all eyes were glued. He was wearing a full-bottom wig, all tight brown curls and festooned above each ear with yellow ribbons.

A strident elderly female voice cut into the stunned silence.

"What's that you say, dear boy? Iron? The fellow's wearing an *iron* wig?"

"Can't tell 'em from the real thing."

"What? You must be mad! It's bloody obvious the thing ain't real!"

"Steady! Ladies and brats present."

"Sorry."

"Ha! Ha! Can't tell horsehair from the real thing so why should iron be any different. Aye? Still. Ridiculous creation."

"Hope the poetry is better than the finery."

"It's an *Ode*."

"*Ode*-or. Ha! Ha!"

"Oh do be quiet and let the fellow get on with it!"

"Yes, do!"

"What's it called, this Ode?"

"*Ode to a Bloody Obvious Iron Wig*. Ha! Ha!"

"Not amusing at all, George."

"What's that you say about a carriage, dear boy?" came the same strident elderly female voice. "I thought we were talking about wigs?"

"Do listen, Aunt! Hilary's *poem*. It's called an *ode*, and it's about a carriage."

"Good—Lord!"

"*Shhhhhhh!*"

The children were being better behaved than the assembled adults, who giggled behind fluttering fans and guffawed into lace handkerchiefs. Jane glanced over her shoulder at the Earl.

"You see the level to which poor Mr. Wraxton has had to descend to garner your patronage, my lord."

Salt playfully tugged one of her curls.

"Wearing an iron wig at a children's tea party is certainly descending, my lady. But why does Hilary require my patronage?"

"Oh? You *have* neglected him! Poor Mr. Wraxton will be devastated if he discovers his poetry accumulating in your book-room remains untouched and unread."

Salt continued to play with her hair.

"I've been rather preoccupied of late… If *poor* Mr. Wraxton wishes to place blame, he had best place it at your elegant feet. No! You cannot argue with that. Now do stop distracting me," he added loftily, eyes on the stage. "I must give my full attention to Hilary's ode." In the manner of a sultan, he waved a languid lace covered hand for Mr. Wraxton to begin his recitation: *Ode to a Well-Sprung Carriage.*

> *Oh, thy torment of a rut in the road*
> *To the muck and manure, the slush and the slurry…*

IT WAS USUALLY AFTER DINNER, when tea and coffee were taken in the Long Gallery and her children drew Salt and Sir Antony—and that creature with her big blue eyes and radiant complexion—and any of the guests who had a mind for childish pursuits, to play at charades, that Diana St. John quietly disappeared upstairs to the Countess's private chamber.

She was never away for more than half an hour at a time. And when she returned without ever having been missed, it was in a brooding temper. Because as hard as she fought to remain a force in the Earl's life since his marriage, with her disruptive Tuesday visits with her children in tow, being within his orbit at all the same parties, party-political dinners, routs and theater evenings, there was one area of the Earl's life that remained off-limits and beyond her control to influence. She might continue to insinuate herself into his waking hours, but his nights belonged very much to his wife, and much to her angry disgust, only his wife.

That he had not strayed one night from the marital bed since his marriage gnawed away at her day and night. She tried to convince herself that to a man of Salt's experience and strong appetites, physical gratification was as necessary and as mundane as satisfying hunger and thirst, no more and no less. But when the Countess's personal maid reluctantly told her that the Earl had not only spent every night since his marriage with his wife, but always stayed the entire night in her bed, Diana St. John began to realize with bitter disappointment that such long-held, cold-blooded beliefs could be applied to Salt's lovers, but not, it seemed, to his wife.

Hiding her anger, frustration, and intense jealousy behind a mask of indifference, she bided her time. She waited for the maid to tell her the inevitable news she dreaded to hear, and yet desperately wanted to know, so she could finally do something to put an end to her misery. The anticipation was almost worse than the news. After three months of being told there was no news to tell, Diana St. John was beginning to suspect the maid was holding out on her.

"Are you absolutely certain?" she demanded fiercely, backing the maid into the Countess's closet and shutting over the door. "You're not mistaken? She's not keeping the news from you?"

Anne sniffed loudly, feeling wretched at abusing the young Countess's trust for the umpteenth time, yet so afraid of this woman, who stood so menacingly close her legs wobbled with fear, that she did her bidding without question.

"Her ladyship hasn't said a word to me."

"That doesn't mean she isn't breeding, nitwit! You're supposed to look for signs, *anything* that might give me a clue."

"Yes, my lady," Anne replied meekly and cast her gaze to the floorboards.

Diana St. John frowned and tapped the closed sticks of her fan in the palm of her hand as she took a thoughtful turn about Jane's dimly lit closet. She came back to the maid, who was too scared to look her in the eye.

"But from what you've been telling me he's been mounting her every night," she added silkily. "Sometimes twice in a night. So it stands to reason that such a healthy, vigorous male as his lordship would've planted enough seed to start a garden of brats by now… God, one wonders where he gets the stamina, what with parliamentary sittings and debates and those long late hours spent alone in his bookroom poring over sinecure paperwork…"

"Not alone, my lady," Anne interrupted, latching on to mention of the bookroom and prepared to confide an interesting turn of events, if it meant diverting this woman from what was more momentous news. When Diana glared at her and waved her fan to and fro, for her to continue, she said with a swallow, "Her ladyship has taken to spending an hour before bed in the bookroom—"

"*What?*"

"—the bookroom with his lordship."

"*No.*"

Anne recoiled at the ferocity of the denial and backed away as Diana St. John began to pace again.

"That's my room, *our* room!" she growled, and such was her caged fury that she snapped the delicate latticed carved sticks of her fan with thumb and forefinger. "That's where we spend *our* time. What's she doing in there?"

"Mr. Willis tells me his lordship is teaching her ladyship to play at chess."

Diana St. John blinked. "Chess? Why would he spend his time playing at chess with that simpleton?"

Anne bit back a retort about kindness not being an indication of idiocy.

"What else can you tell me?"

"Her ladyship sometimes takes her embroidery with her to the bookroom to—"

"Not that, you ridiculous creature! What else can you tell me about her besides the fact she opens her legs and is playing chess?"

Anne winced at such crudity and racked her mind for some other piece of news.

"They-they talk in bed…"

"Talk? *Talk?* In *bed?*"

"Yes, my lady. When his lordship first comes to the bedchamber they talk; sometimes they talk for well over an hour."

Diana St. John was bewildered and she voiced her bemusement aloud. "But what could they possibly have to talk *about?* Why would he want to talk to *her?*"

"I am sorry, my lady, but I cannot hear what they talk about, I just hear them talking."

Diana St. John's brow was still furrowed, as if this piece of information was so incredible as to be disbelieved. So much so that Anne rattled on for fear the woman would turn on her with violence.

"One night last week his lordship didn't come to her ladyship's bed, my lady," she said in a rush, hating herself for being such a telltale.

This pronouncement ended Diana St. John's preoccupation, and she stopped her pacing and looked the maid up and down with interest. "Did he not? Now that *is* a *very* interesting piece of news indeed," she purred with satisfaction. "Do you remember the precise night?"

"It was two nights, my lady. Wednesday night and Thursday night."

Diana St. John's brow cleared and her eyes shone. She looked past the maid's shoulder at some distant point. "Wednesday *and* Thursday night! Well! Well! Better still! Two nights left *all alone*. Two nights he was with someone else…"

"Oh, I don't think so, my la—"

"What would you know to the contrary?"

Anne felt the sting before she realized she'd been struck. She crumpled against a dresser drawer, a hand to her smarting cheek. "Andrews—Andrews is his lordship's valet and he said on one of those nights his lordship came home in the early hours of the morning and not wanting to disturb her ladyship, stayed in his own bed and—"

"And? And? That's only one of the two nights accounted for! And? Speak up! Speak up! I haven't got all night."

"The-the second night, my father Mr. Springer, he's the butler at the Arlington townhouse, said his lordship dined with Sir Antony Templestowe and then stayed the night in his old suite of rooms on account of the very late hour."

Diana St. John clucked and cooed and smiled. "Well, little Anne. You have managed to engage two households in spying upon their lord and master; every servant with their beady little eyes to the keyholes! Well done!" Almost instantly her face darkened. "The servants know this, but I presume her ladyship has been too timid to enquire of her husband's servants as to their master's whereabouts on those nights?" When the maid nodded, she sighed her satisfaction. "Good. Her reticence will serve me well." She stuck the end of her broken fan under Anne's chin. "You still have not told me what I want to know."

"My lady?"

"Tell me what I want to know or I will return downstairs this instant and inform his lordship in front of his guests that I found the Countess's personal maid on her knees for the under-butler!"

Anne curbed the desire to burst into tears to reply haltingly, "Her ladyship—her ladyship hasn't had her womanly courses since-since marrying his lordship." She prattled on because Diana St. John's face had taken on a deathly hue, "And she is off her food, my lady. And this past week she's been feeling queasy and faint, more so in the mornings. She's more herself after she's nibbled on a dry biscuit and taken a cup of weak black tea, though she hardly sips more than a mouthful at best..."

"His lordship doesn't suspect does he?" she asked anxiously, giving the maid's arm a shake. "She hasn't told him?"

"No, my lady."

Diana St. John breathed an audible sigh, "*That's* something to be thankful for in the creature's reticence! No doubt waiting for just the right moment to give him the good news," she said sarcastically and laughed. "Fool!" She stared at Anne, saying matter-of-factly, "Tomorrow morning I will send a lackey with a small package. Inside the package you will find a blue bottle of medicinal syrup. You are to put a teaspoon of this medicine in the dish of black tea you prepare for the Countess. Make certain you stir it thoroughly. You may have to give her another dose the following morning. All being well, the medicine will do its job to everyone's satisfaction." She looked the maid up and down with a haughty frown. "You don't have any questions, do you?"

Anne shook her head and dropped her chin. "No, my lady," she answered obediently and curtsied. "I understand you perfectly."

Diana St. John gave the girl's reddened cheek a perfunctory pat and swept out of the Countess's apartments and down the wide staircase to rejoin the dinner guests in the Long Gallery, wretched her worst fears had been confirmed, that the Countess of Salt Hendon was with child, yet relieved the wait was over and she was now able to do something about it.

No sooner had Anne closed over the door to the closet than she rushed across to the darkest corner of the room, where out into the candlelight stepped Mr. Rufus Willis, grim-faced and determined. He had wedged himself in the space between two mahogany tall boys, out of sight, yet well able to hear the conversation between his betrothed and the Lady St. John. It was the first time he had ever eavesdropped on his betters, but he had put aside his principles, deciding that the seriousness of the allegations Anne had brought against the Earl's cousin called for drastic measures.

He gathered the weeping Anne to him, and after a few moments of holding her, stepped back and handed her his handkerchief.

"Wipe your tears, my dear," he said calmly. "We don't want her ladyship to suspect."

"I can't take much more of that horrid woman, Rufus." Anne sniffed. "I know you have cautioned me not to talk about his lordship's cousin in such a fashion but do you not now see what a horrid, nasty creature she truly is? I wish I could tell her to her face. I wish I weren't such a coward. She knows now about the babe and that's what we wanted to avoid all along!" She gripped the under-butler's sleeve convulsively. "Now do you believe me, Rufus? Now do you see that she means her ladyship harm."

"Yes, my dear. I believe you," confessed a grim-faced Willis. "And you are not a coward. It took great courage to tell me about Lady St. John. Now I must return to my duties before I am missed. On no account are you to administer the medicinal syrup to her ladyship. As soon as the opportunity arises bring the package to me."

Anne followed her betrothed to the servant door. "You mean to give it to his lordship?"

"Yes, my dear. Have no fear, when the time is right, his lordship will be provided with all the evidence required to know his cousin is an extremely wicked and treacherous woman." He lightly kissed Anne's reddened cheek. "Be brave, dearest Anne. The Countess needs our support now more than ever."

Anne smiled shyly but said fearfully, "Be careful, Rufus. Lady St. John is so blinded with love for his lordship that she is capable of harming whoever stands in her way."

"Yes," Willis agreed. "But Lady St. John is not in love with his lordship, my dear. She is obsessed with him. That makes the situation far more perilous for those he cares about, and even more dangerous for Lady Salt now she is with child."

JANE WOULD HAVE BEEN GREATLY surprised but oddly comforted to know Willis's opinion of the Lady St. John, because it so matched her own feelings of apprehension—for herself, her husband and most importantly for the new life she was now carrying. She dared not confide to a soul she was with child. Not until she had told the Earl. She was so happy to think they were to have a child, but the fear of losing this baby as she had lost the first, and of her husband's incredulous reaction to the news, made her wary and hesitant. First she had to break him of the stubborn belief he was infertile.

She had considered confiding in Sir Antony to whom she had become close since he had been appointed to watch over her. She had teased him several times about his new role and he had insisted he much preferred to be in her company than return to Paris. If the truth be told, shopping in Oxford Street, and attending readings of absurdly odd poetry by Hilary Wraxton in his iron wig, were vastly more entertaining than listening to the monologues of the parsimonious Duke of Bedford. Besides, the longer he remained in London the more likely the chance he would be invited to Salt Hall for the Easter break, and there see the Lady Caroline Sinclair. Of course, this hope he kept secret until he found himself confiding to Jane his muddled feelings for Salt's sister.

"Salt doesn't want Caroline to have her come-out until next Season," explained Sir Antony, stretched out on the chaise longue in Jane's pretty sitting room. He was watching her seated in the window seat, head bent over her needlepoint. "That's understandable given she don't turn eighteen until the summer. He thinks her too young."

"What do you think?"

Sir Antony gave an involuntary laugh. He still found Jane's blunt questions disconcerting, though refreshing. "It doesn't matter what I think."

Jane glanced up at that, needle and thread suspended. "But if you love Lady Caroline it matters a great deal, doesn't it?"

"It's not that simple, my dear," said Sir Antony and sat up, dropping his stockinged legs to the floor and in the process disrupting Viscount Fourpaws, who had been curled up asleep on a cushion at his feet. When Jane smiled, he confessed hesitantly, "I am in love with Caroline. But I don't know if she is *in love* with me. She thinks she is, but she is young and lived a sheltered life at Salt Hall. I cannot be certain her feelings are fixed. Salt's very protective; treats her like a daughter. Well, that's to be expected given old Salt up and died when Caroline was still in swaddling. She was barely six years old when her mother passed away. So Salt's the only parent she's ever had."

Sir Antony was suddenly bashful and scooped up Viscount Fourpaws, who had been brushing up against his stockinged leg, and absently scratched its ears. "Salt's in the right, regardless of Caroline's protests to the contrary. She should have her Season in London, go out in Society, meet gentlemen, dance at assemblies and balls, and have young bucks falling at her feet. She needs to discover where her true heart lies."

"And while she is having her Season, you will wait in the wings hoping she will grow up a little, and in the end, choose you?"

"Yes. Sounds simple, doesn't it? I think I will go away. Take a posting to the Hague or St. Petersburg."

"Will I like Caroline?"

Sir Antony smiled. "I hope so. In many ways she's much like her peers. Loves a party, adores clothes, knows how to use her feminine charm to wrap a gentleman round her little finger, Salt in particular. In other respects she's different from other females, but that may be a consequence of her sheltered upbringing. She loves nothing better than to have her dogs to heel and go mucking about on the estate or galloping off around the countryside with her brother. Between you and me, I believe Salt encourages her boyish pursuits. Wants to keep her reined in for as long as possible before he unleashes her on the unsuspecting male populace."

He smiled at a memory, adding, "No two siblings could be so different and yet have greater affection for each other. Whereas Salt is serious and hard-working, one would think on first meeting Caroline she is feather-headed and indolent. But they do share a quick brain, and she's just as conscientious as Salt about the welfare of tenants and those who rely on the Sinclair largesse. And they both have kind hearts."

He put Viscount Fourpaws back on the chaise longue and leaned forward, still rapt in his topic.

"She informed me only last summer she wants to travel and that my chosen career as a diplomat will suit us both perfectly—the managing baggage!" he added lovingly, and sat back with a huff of laughter. "Hasn't stepped outside Wiltshire but already has our passage booked for the Bosphorus! Have you ever heard the like?"

Jane had not, and if Sir Antony's extolling of the Lady Caroline's virtues were to the life, Jane couldn't wait to meet this fascinating girl. She finished a stitch and wove her needle lightly into the fabric to hold it in place for another day.

"So Salt is prepared to allow Caroline to choose her husband?" she asked with practiced indifference. "I thought perhaps, she being a great heiress, he might consider an arranged marriage. One of those political matches between two wealthy noble houses."

"Ha! Now that's the sort of cold-blooded union Diana encourages Salt to make for his sister. But not Salt. Deep beneath our Earl's noble chest beats the heart of a hopeless romantic. Not that he lets on. Besides," added Sir Antony, oblivious to the ready blush to Jane's cheeks, "Caroline wouldn't be party to such a union, even if Salt threatened to beat her into submission. Not that he ever would, but you get my meaning."

"Does—does Salt know about Caroline's plans to marry her diplomat?"

"Know? He has a fair notion of my feelings," Sir Antony

confessed. "But as to knowing Caroline's wishes... I dread Caroline falling in love with someone else, but in many respects I also dread the day I ask Salt for Caroline's hand in marriage. He and Caroline are as close as father and daughter, and like the stern, protective father, he'll be reluctant to give her hand to me, despite me being one of his closest friends."

"Every father is apprehensive about giving his daughter into the care of another man. That's to be expected. But he'll recover."

"I'm eight years her senior, my dear."

Jane laid aside her needlepoint.

"Twelve years separate Salt and me, and never once did I contemplate age as a barrier to falling in love with him. Neither should it bother you, if you truly love Caroline, and she you."

Sir Antony threw up a lace-ruffled wrist with a huff of disbelief. "That's all very easy for you to say, but I vividly recall Salt citing the age difference between the two of you, and the fact you lived a sheltered existence at Despard Park and never had a London Season, as prime examples of why you baulked at marrying him all those years ago. That's why he is determined Caroline must have a London Season. He will not permit her to marry until she is one-and-twenty, and thus is old enough to know her mind *well and truly*. I'm prepared to wait out those three years, if it means she has well and truly settled her affections on me."

"For a gentleman who professes to being a diplomat, you are woefully tactless. By the by, even at eighteen years of age I *well and truly* knew Salt was the only man for me. So the argument about age does not wash."

Sir Antony's jaw swung wide and in two strides he was beside Jane on the window seat and holding her hands.

"God, I'm an unthinking ass. Forgive me. I should be stripped of my sinecures and made to walk the diplomatic plank for—"

"—speaking candidly? Not by me. But I suppose frank speech is not seen as part of the diplomatic armory, is it?"

"No, for upsetting you, my dear. The last thing I wish to do on this earth is distress you." He kissed her hands, pressed them gently and would not let them go. "I should not have been so flippant with your feelings. We have been enough in each other's company now that I feel we have become good friends." He smiled into her blue eyes. "And I know that you truly do love my cousin. I see that love reflected in your face every time he walks into a room. If one day I receive but a thimbleful of such emotion from my wife, I will be a contented man. No. Don't hang your head. I want to offer you my help. Perhaps if you would allow me to understand what went wrong between you and Salt all those years ago, we could put our heads together and clear the mire…"

Jane took a few moments to find her composure, Sir Antony's kind words drying her throat, but she wasn't given the opportunity to respond because the sitting room door opened and in walked her husband, dressed magnificently in a dark blue velvet frock coat with silver lacings. His hair was powdered and tied with a black ribbon and across his chest was the blue riband of the Most Noble Order of the Garter; a number of lesser orders and decorations pinned to the breast of his silver-embroidered waistcoat. He looked up from the flat rectangular box in his hand and frowned as Sir Antony and Jane sprang apart and were uncomfortable; Sir Antony on his feet and Jane to pick up her discarded needlepoint.

"You're not wearing powder," he stated, an eye on his wife's simply dressed hair, swept up off her lovely neck and affixed with many pins and a couple of strategically placed diamond-encrusted clasps, a weight of dark curls falling about her shoulders.

"No, it does not agree with me or my complexion," she replied simply. She poked her small, silk-clad foot out from under yards of soft blue watered-silk. "But I am wearing shoes with a two-inch heel so I can at least stand beside you and look the part, although I doubt I shall be noticed beside such a wall of decoration."

"Blinding, ain't they?" commented Sir Antony, with seeming irreverence for his best friend's noble orders. He brushed down the sleeves of his frock coat and stretched his white-stockinged legs. He too was dressed in his best silks and wore hair powder to attend the Richmond ball, the quantity of lace at his wrists and throat compensation for his lack of noble orders. "Poor Andrews must've bloodied his thumbs pinning all that lot on. Or does he wear gloves to catch the drips before they splatter the noble chest?"

"That Florentine green frock coat becomes you better than you know, Tony," Salt said with a crooked smile, and handed Jane the velvet-covered box. "Those petticoats are very fetching," he commented, an understatement given Jane could only be described as breathtakingly beautiful in a low, square-cut bodice with tight sleeves that accentuated her slim arms and back, and matching blue silk petticoats. He smiled down at her; a smile Sir Antony had come to notice the Earl kept exclusively for his wife. "Your choice will complement the locket very well."

"Locket?" Jane heard herself say, heart thudding against her chest as she stared at the flat box now in her hand. "What locket is that, my lord?"

"The Sinclair locket."

Returning this family heirloom surely signified he had traveled a long way down the path to putting their past behind them, and was now prepared to go forward with her into the future. It brought tears of happiness and memories of the last time he had given it to her, in the summerhouse, when he had proposed to her.

"Where... Where did it come from?" she asked, slightly dazed, and hesitated to pry open the lid.

"From the family vault. Where else?"

"No. Before it was put back in the vault. After—"

"Sir Felix returned it," he interrupted quietly.

Jane was nonplussed. "My father? I do not understand."

"Sir Felix returned it at my request."

"At your request? You requested it be returned? Why?"

The Earl was uncomfortable. He glanced fleetingly at Sir Antony, who was pretending an inordinate interest in the manicured nails of his right hand, before meeting Jane's open look. "I thought it right and proper, after I received word from Jacob Allenby that you had ended our engagement and were living under his protection."

Jane's gaze never wavered from his handsome face. "I did not end our engagement, my lord, nor could Mr. Allenby tell you any such thing."

Salt put up his brows, half-incredulous. "Why do you say so, my lady?"

"Because I told no one we were engaged. You asked that I keep our engagement to myself until your return. And so I told no one."

"Then I wonder how Mr. Allenby came by such vital news?"

"I wonder at that too, my lord. He wrote to you?"

"No."

"Then may I know by what method he communicated my supposed wishes?"

He inclined his powdered head, unperturbed by her bluntness. "Through a family intermediary."

Jane swallowed. "Family intermediary?" she repeated softly, up on her heels, a shaking hand to her bare throat. But she knew whose name he would utter even before she asked. "May I know the name of this family intermediary?"

"Diana received the locket from your father—What is it? Are you unwell?" Salt asked, taking a step forward.

Jane blinked up at him, the enormity of what he had just told her making her skin crawl cold and hot at one and the same time. She glanced over at Sir Antony and saw that he was staring fixedly at her; her husband was doing likewise. What could she say? How was she to be believed over Diana St. John, who was Sir Antony's sister and who had known Salt all her life? Still, she could not let the matter rest when she knew the truth of the lie.

"My father knew nothing about the locket. He was kept in ignorance of our engagement. I-I waited as long as I could and then when you did not return I sent the locket with a note as you had instructed me to do as soon as I realized I was… When I knew about the… When I—" She faltered, too overcome to continue, pushed the box back at Salt and scurried into her dressing room with a shaking hand covering her mouth to stop a sob.

Anne dropped the pile of linen she had scooped up into her arms and quickly helped Jane to her dressing stool. Without a word, she poured her out a glass of lemon water and held it to her mouth, because the Countess's hands were shaking. After a few sips and a couple of deep breaths Jane was more herself. Holding her hands tightly in her lap and with her back straight, she tried to compose herself and collect her thoughts.

She now knew Salt had not received the locket, sent to him when she was two months with child. She reasoned that Diana St. John must have taken delivery of the locket upon its arrival at the Arlington Street townhouse. And she was certain that Diana St.

John would have known about the secret compartment, just as she had made it her business to know everything there was to know about the Earl of Salt Hendon.

And the more she thought on it, the more convinced she was that it was Diana St. John who, knowing about the secret compartment, had read her note, and conveyed its message, not to its rightful recipient, but to Sir Felix. She had always wondered how her father had discovered her pregnancy, now she was almost certain who had told him. How Lady St. John had managed to convey the news without divulging that Salt was the father of her child was something Jane was sure took all the woman's cunning. For had Sir Felix ever suspected it was the Earl of Salt Hendon who had seduced and impregnated her, he would have gone hot-foot to London and demanded the nobleman marry her.

It was years later, when she was living under the protection of Jacob Allenby and her father was dying, that Sir Felix learned the appalling nature of what he had done. In what Jane thought a most cruel act, Jacob Allenby told her father that the unborn child he had ordered destroyed was not of indeterminate lineage but in fact belonged to Lord Salt. He had murdered the Earl of Salt Hendon's heir, and Jacob Allenby hoped Sir Felix burned in hell for his crime.

Jane did not doubt that Diana St. John would have removed and destroyed the little scrap of paper informing Salt of her pregnancy before returning the locket to its rightful owner. The evidence she needed to convince her husband he was capable of fathering a child, that she had been pregnant before, was lost forever.

TWELVE

"JANE? JANE, ARE YOU perfectly well?" the Earl asked, coming through to the dressing room. He saw the maid hovering over his wife and laid the box aside on the cluttered dressing table. "If I'd known the family bauble would affect you so, I'd not have brought it out." He took hold of her hand and found it cold, yet when he gently touched her forehead she was burning up, despite her face being deathly pale. He went down on his haunches before her. "Perhaps it would be for the best if you stayed home, what with the unseasonably cold weather—"

"No! I want to accompany you to the ball," she answered and took a deep breath. She forced herself to look at him with a bright smile. "I'll be fine. Truly. I'll wear that lovely fur cloak you gave me just last week. That should keep me warm. It's just…" She couldn't finish the sentence and was glad when her maid jumped in with an excuse, which instantly alerted Jane that Anne knew about her pregnancy.

"Her corset, my lord!" Anne blurted out in explanation as she dropped into a curtsy and kept her eyes to the floorboards. "I've been lacing her ladyship's corsets too tightly of late. That would account for her dizzy spells and-and paleness. It will only take a moment to set it to rights."

"Yes, that must be it," Jane agreed when Salt stood up but was unconvinced. She placed a hand on the lid of the box. "I'll leave this until you can put it on for me."

When she was left alone with her maid, Jane quickly pried open the lid of the box, and there, nestled on a bed of velvet was the Sinclair locket, a single large sapphire surrounded by diamonds and set into an oval of gold. The setting was suspended on a gold chain set with smaller diamonds and sapphires. It was a magnificent piece of craftsmanship and drew an awed gasp from Anne.

With shaking fingers, Jane turned over the sapphire, trying not to disturb the sit of the chain too much in the box, and searched for the tiny point of gold which was the catch that, when pressed, opened the secret compartment behind the sapphire. But as hard as she looked, as much as her fingers ran deftly around the gold lip of the claws that held the precious stones in place, she could not find the catch. It had to be there, it couldn't just disappear. She knew how the catch worked, remembered exactly where it was, so how was it that it wasn't there now? It didn't make sense until Anne said conversationally,

"It's so beautiful, my lady," she cooed, "I never thought I'd see the like of such a locket again after leaving Lady St. John's house —" She shut her mouth when Jane's head snapped up. She bobbed a respectful curtsy. "I spoke out of turn. Please forgive me, my lady. Should you like another sip of lemon water?"

Jane shook her head. "Go on, Anne. Tell me about this other locket."

"Yes, my lady," Anne replied and obediently told Jane about Diana St. John's dramatic reaction to misplacing her locket adding, "Her ladyship was in a state of the greatest agitation, as if her whole health and happiness was bound up in that locket. Her ladyship keeps it under her pillow and sleeps with it wrapped around her wrist every night, without fail. She never wears it out, but she's never without it. She even takes it with her when she goes to stay in the country."

Jane turned the locket back to its face and studied it in silence. Sir Antony had told her once that the treasure trove of jewelry dripping from ears and around the throats and wrists of the wives of nobles were mostly exacting copies of the originals, which were locked away for safe keeping; the copies made from paste so as to foil attempted theft by pickpockets, disgruntled servants, and above all, hold-ups by highwaymen. So this, too, must also be a very good paste copy, substituted by Diana St. John for the real locket. But why make the switch? And why hadn't Salt noticed? Jane wondered if he had examined the locket closely since its return—if indeed he had even bothered to put on his eyeglasses to do so.

ABSENTLY, SHE FINGERED THE false sapphire and diamond locket as she stared out of the carriage window at the passing traffic of carriages, sedan chairs and men on horseback. Rugged up in her new fur cloak, she wondering how she was going to recover the real locket from Lady St. John. She would have to visit the woman's Audley Street House, but when, and what reason could she possibly give for visiting a woman who clearly disliked her? She would need to take Anne with her—Anne knew the house and the servants. Perhaps she could go on the excuse of taking Ron and Merry on some particular excursion about the city? She would ask Sir Antony to accompany them, but not tell him about recovering the locket, that would add validity to her visit...

"Share your thoughts, my lady?" Salt asked quietly.

He was sitting diagonally opposite Jane, Sir Antony beside him. He wasn't surprised when she slowly turned her head to look at him blankly, her thoughts seemingly miles away.

He hadn't taken his gaze off her since they had set off from Grosvenor Square for Richmond House by the Thames. He knew her mind to be anywhere but on the present. He wondered if he had left her alone too often during the day over the past three months. He had been a great deal caught up with parliamentary business and a host of committee meetings, but he had purposely kept his distance, so he told himself, to allow her to find her feet as the new Countess of Salt Hendon.

The real reason, however, was far more selfish and self-destructive.

By leaving her very much to herself during the daylight hours it was as if he were waiting for disaster to strike. What that disaster could be, he had no idea. It somehow seemed he was not entitled to the happiness he felt when he was with her. He might not be at home much but he knew his wife had been crowned queen of the fairies by a group of young, artistically-minded, wealthy young gentlemen who had pretensions to artistic greatness, and with nothing better to do with their time but write poetry, act out plays and fawn over the Countess of Salt Hendon's beauty. He was kept informed of their comings and goings and had even now read a number of Hilary Wraxton's poems, all of which he knew were a source of great mirth at the Countess's afternoon teas. Salt considered them harmless confections of fun, but he wasn't particularly pleased that the iron-wig-wearing Wraxton's most recent string of poems all centered on his Countess, whom the aspiring poet had the absurdity to call his "fair faerie queen".

Yet, from the reports regularly given him by Arthur Ellis, Willis the under-butler, and by Sir Antony, Jane never put herself forward, never flirted with these young men, and never had her head turned by their constant compliments of her beauty. In fact, she treated such worship with the grain of sand it deserved, maintaining a cool, if kind-hearted, distance from her admirers. His own observations of his wife at dinner parties and the like confirmed this, and yet he still felt ill at ease, that if he allowed his defenses to drop completely, his hopes and dreams would again be shattered.

He had no real basis for his apprehension, only the past experience of their broken engagement, which she emphatically denied she had instigated. It's not that he disbelieved her, but it did not make sense: One and one did not make two. Yet the more time he spent in Jane's company, the less he cared about the details of the broken engagement and what had occurred in the past or who was in the wrong. He just knew his future happiness and contentment rested with his wife.

He repeated his question just as the horses slowed and the carriage turned into the forecourt of Richmond House.

"I was thinking about Ron," Jane replied and turned from the window to look at him, "and how well he has been looking these past few weeks."

Salt was surprised. "Ron?"

"Yes. He had color in his cheeks at the nursery party, and he played *three* games of skittles with the Spencer boys. *And* he ate two slices of pie."

"*And* he was rolling around on the floor laughing along with the rest of us at Wraxton's absurd poetry," Sir Antony stuck in. "*Ode to a Well-Sprung Carriage*, indeed! God help us all when we have to listen to his next piece of piffle!" When the noble couple looked at him as if seeing him for the first time, he grinned sheepishly. "You did offer me a seat in your carriage. Can I help it if I have eyes and ears?"

"He had no color whatsoever at three in the morning!" Salt said with asperity.

Sir Antony glanced at Jane before looking at the Earl. "Called out to his bedside *again*?"

"Yes."

"How many times has he been ill these past few months?"

Salt shrugged at the question and was ashen-faced. "Too many times. Last night he had one of his worst attacks yet."

"I'm sorry to hear it," Sir Antony said grimly. "Poor little chap. Poor you, to be inconvenienced at such an hour," he added with a huff of laughter, thinking the Earl had to be the unluckiest bridegroom in London, to be dragged from the arms of his beautiful bride at such an inauspicious hour, to attend on a sick little boy who had no consideration for his uncle's newly-married state. Yet he was all admiration for Salt's devotion to the boy, and for the Countess's tolerance.

"Er—apologies," he muttered in response to the Earl's embarrassed glare of disapproval.

Sir Antony turned his profile to the undraped window and the view of the congested line of horses and carriages queuing up one behind the other at the wide steps of Richmond House, and where Jane was staring, a blush to her cheeks. Still, he could not help voicing a thought that had been niggling at him for some time now. He was surprised when Jane stared at him with wide blue eyes of shock, as if she, too, had had the same thought, yet had dared not voice it aloud for fear of it being true.

"Merry said an odd thing to me at the tea party... Made me think. Made me think damn hard," he mused, turning over his closed snuffbox in his left hand. "Observation of a child, but acute nonetheless. Not that she would have had the foggiest notion of its importance…"

Salt sat forward on the upholstered bench and adjusted his cravat in anticipation of the carriage door opening and the steps being put in place for them to alight. "Out with it, Tony! This isn't the time or place for a fireside chat."

"Merry predicted Ron would be ill that very night."

"Not surprised with three games of skittles and two slices of pie!"

The Earl's flippant remark was ignored.

"What did she say to you, Tony?" Jane asked quietly.

Sir Antony glanced down at his snuffbox then across at Jane. "To be precise, she said a couple of things. Told me matter-of-factly that Ron would be ill later that night, all because Uncle Salt was so happy—that it was always like that. Whenever you are happy," he said, addressing the Earl, "Ron is ill. Can you believe it? Words out of the mouth of a babe!"

"What did you say by way of reply?" asked Jane.

Sir Antony threw up a lace-covered wrist. "Don't recall. Some tripe to dismiss such a notion as absurd."

"It is absurd!" Salt stated angrily. "Merry and Ron are children with childish thoughts. The idea that Ron becomes ill all because I am happy is in itself laughable, in the worst possible sense of the word!"

"Is it?" Sir Antony enquired levelly. "Is it truly that absurd? Think about it. I have—long and hard. I've put some twos together. You said yourself that Ron has been ill too many times."

"Tony, what else did Merry tell you?"

Salt looked at Jane in some surprise. "You believe there is some truth to Merry's prattle, my lady?"

Jane and Sir Antony exchanged a look before she said calmly, "Yes. Now that Tony has voiced his concerns, I will add mine to his. And I cannot dismiss out of hand a child's remarks, not when that child is Merry, who is wise beyond her years and suffers to see her brother ill."

It was the Earl's turn to throw up a lace-covered wrist. He sat back against the upholstered headboard and ignored the rapping on the carriage door. "Well, Tony? What else did Merry say?"

Sir Antony took snuff and sniffed. Finally composed, he met his best friend's expectant if slightly skeptical look, and did not baulk. "That her mother did not like to see you happy; it made her angry and gave her the megrim." He glanced at Jane, but addressed the Earl. "And that since marrying Jane you are always happy, which means her mother is always angry, and that because she is angry she makes Ron sick."

The rapping on the carriage door became insistent but Salt ignored it, hard gaze fixed on Sir Antony. "You realize you are talking about your sister."

"I am unlikely to forget the connection. And as her brother I do believe I am able to see her more clearly than—and you will pardon my bluntness—you do, who will always see her as St. John's widow and mother of his children. I believe there is substance to Merry's chatter." He glanced at Jane, "And so does your Countess."

"I do not want to discuss this any further here or now. It is my wife's first public engagement and I want it to be a pleasant one."

Sir Antony inclined his powdered head. "As you wish, but this state of affairs must be discussed at some time, and soon. As you rightly pointed out, we are talking about my sister and, let us not forget, the welfare of my niece and nephew."

"Ron and Merry's health and happiness are my prime concern."

"Then on that we agree. Now do open that door before the poor fellow loses what's left of the skin on his knuckles."

The carriage door swung wide and the steps set in place by a liveried footman. Another footman handed the Countess out of the carriage, and Salt wrapped her arm around his and led her across the forecourt to join the queue of guests filing into Richmond House. Sir Antony took his leave of the noble couple, and spying two cronies from the Northern Department, sauntered away to talk politics.

Jane barely noticed his departure, such was her distraction with the noise and bustle of carriages arriving and departing, of linkboys with tapers lighting the way for the many guests resplendent in silks, powdered wigs and elaborate hairstyles, all making their way inside the Duke of Richmond's waterside mansion.

She was determined to enjoy this, her first ball in London, but knew also she must be on her best behavior, that it would not do to wear her excitement on her sleeve. As this was her first official engagement as the Countess of Salt Hendon, she was acutely aware that all eyes would be upon her. Not all eyes would be friendly, particularly the friends of Diana St. John, who would be waiting for the young Lady Salt to commit some social faux pas so they could commiserate with Lady St. John on the Earl's misfortune in marrying such a rustic miss.

Jane glanced up at her husband, and seeing his frown realized he must still be ruminating over Merry's confidences to her Uncle Tony. She was determined to divert him. After all, if she were to enjoy herself tonight at this fireworks ball in honor of the Peace of Paris, he must enjoy himself, too.

"Do you know, my lord, I have just come to the sudden realization that I have no political conversation and know even fewer people than Viscount Fourpaws! Who, I might add, is the only Viscount of my acquaintance who literally purrs when I prattle. Will your friends think me dull company?"

"I am not entirely happy to discover my wife is being purred over," he said with a laugh, brow clearing, and held her close as a couple of liveried footmen dashed across their path and disappeared between two carriages to assist new arrivals. "I do not think you dull company, and that's all that matters."

She gave a practiced sigh. "But unlike Viscount Fourpaws, you never seek my company during the daylight hours, so you cannot know if I am a dull conversationalist or not."

"That's unfair, you little wretch!" Salt replied, ignoring the smiling nods of several powdered noble heads in the queue up ahead who were trying to catch his eye. He spoke close to her ear, so she could hear him over the din. "We talk every night in bed."

"That is of no account," Jane threw at him, pretending an interest in the long line of stony-faced liveried footmen, standing shoulder-to-shoulder like marble statues along the gravel path and up the wide steps, though she was very pleased he was put out by her accusation. She hoped he could not detect the blush to her cheeks in the dusky light. "Conversation is not the reason for your visits. Though I have no complaints about the order in which you conduct business."

"Business? Good God, you think I view my nightly visits to your bed as-as *business*? Another item on the agenda to be marked off when completed?"

Wide-eyed, Jane blinked up at him, gouache fan brought out from under her cloak to flutter prettily and stir the wispy tendrils of silken black hair about her beautiful face. She pretended ignorance. "Don't you, my lord?"

"Of course not!" he blustered.

"Oh? But I am reliably informed that making love to one's wife is a husband's *tedious obligation*."

"You certainly know how to pick your moment for one of your frank conversations, my lady," he stated in a clipped voice, finding it difficult to express himself in the middle of a public space, surrounded by a hundred faces known to him. "It's never been an obligation to make love to you, and it is anything but tedious," he replied earnestly. "It is a pleasure and a privilege." When she dropped her chin into her shoulder, he added gently, "Jane, I come to your bed because I want to—*very much*."

Jane did not trust herself to speak and clung to his silken arm more tightly. She stared blindly out across the activity of footmen running here and there, of ladies adjusting the useless novelty of flimsy aprons tied loosely over petticoats, and of gentlemen giving a tug to the points of their elaborate waistcoats, and saw it all through a mist of happiness. Despite the excitement of her first public social engagement in her husband's company, she wished they were at home before the fire in his bookroom, alone. There she could freely throw her arms about his neck and tell him how much she loved him—had always and only loved him.

Salt, misinterpreting her silence because he had said more than he had intended, but nothing he did not hold as truth, self-consciously stretched his neck, wrapped in its tightly-bound cravat of intricate Brussels lace, and swallowed.

"If I'm becoming a nuisance, you need only say so."

"Oh, I will," she answered, with her ready sense of the ridiculous, composure returned. This brought his head down with a snap to stare at her hard. She tried not to giggle at his look of self-conscious contrition. Impulsively, she went up on tiptoe and swiftly kissed his cheek, saying with a gurgle of laughter, "Absurd man! The day I consider you a nuisance, consign me to Bedlam."

He grinned and pinched her chin.

But the smile died on Jane's face the instant her heels were back on firm ground. By kissing her husband in public she had committed, what Mr. Willis had warned her, two of the cardinal sins of Polite Society—of allowing emotion to rule good breeding, and of showing genuine affection for one's spouse in public. She went to apologize, flustered and embarrassed, thinking Salt would not appreciate her spontaneous and very public display, acutely aware that more than a dozen powdered heads had caught the kiss, and with raised eyebrows were staring at her with curious disapproval from behind fluttering fans and beribboned quizzing glasses.

Her one small impulsive kiss had the opposite effect on the Earl. Caught up in the moment, he saw only his wife and was completely oblivious to everyone and everything else. He bent to nuzzle and whisper near her ear. "If this wasn't Lady Salt's first ball," he murmured, removing her cloak to hand to an attentive footman, for they had arrived indoors, "I'd take her to the carriage and have my way with her, here and now."

Momentarily forgetting her embarrassment, Jane faced him, all wide-eyed fascination. "In the carriage? Here and-and now?"

He pretended a sudden interest in the sit of one of a dozen small silk bows sewn down the front of her low-cut water-silk bodice. Deftly, he straightened the largest bow at the neckline, and allowed his pinkie to lightly caress the swell of her bare breasts. His words were all for her.

"Unfortunately, my lady will have to wait that delight until the end of the ball. I have poor Andrews' bloodied fingers to think about. I'd never get these orders pinned back in place."

As he surreptitiously caressed her breasts, Jane was gripped with a sudden frisson of desire and she quickly moved back into line, picking up a handful of her silk petticoats to ascend the wide stairs into the ballroom of Richmond House, without ever remembering her feet touching the floor. To her shame and surprise she couldn't wait for the ball to be over before it started. Nor could she resist an impudent remark to her husband while they waited in line to be announced by the sonorous, nose-in-the-air butler.

"Do you think we would be missed if we gave our excuses and departed early?"

Salt was unable to hide his grin as they stepped forward at the butler's announcement to the assembled company of the arrival of the Earl and Countess of Salt Hendon. He kept his square chin perfectly level and stared out into the void of dazzling light from hundreds of candles and colorful movement that was the noble crowd, yet he managed to wink at Jane. "Behave yourself tonight, Madam wife, and I'll make certain the ride home is worth every dip in the road."

Jane would have been hard pressed to give an accurate account of her first ball of her first London Season, because from the moment she moved into the blaze of candlelight of the ballroom, with its blur of color and light, noise and music, and endless chatter, she was swept up into an evening of introduction, conversation, and dance. Not since the Salt Hunt Ball on her eighteenth birthday had she enjoyed herself so much. The four years of somber solitude and austerity as the charitable ward of the crippled merchant manufacturer Jacob Allenby were finally laid to rest, with her husband by her side and the crème de la crème of Polite Society welcoming the new Countess of Salt Hendon with open arms.

Everyone agreed the handsome colossus that was the Earl of Salt Hendon and his exceptionally beautiful and very graceful bride made the perfect couple. Everyone, that is, except the Lady St. John.

DIANA ST. JOHN kept her distance from her noble cousin for most of the Richmond Ball while he remained by his wife's side. She flitted from group to group, seemingly oblivious to the Earl's existence, which, friend and foe alike agreed, was most uncharacteristic. It was universally expected that at Society functions Lady St. John remained only one person removed from the Earl of Salt Hendon at all times. No one knew if he noticed her always in his orbit, or not. For the most part he seemed to treat her as if she were part of his shadow, and got on with his life. Everyone wondered if she would remain part of his shadow now that he had a bride, more beautiful and much younger than the handsome statuesque Lady St. John.

Resplendent in a Venetian red and gold sack-back gown with three tiers of lace cascading from elbows to plump wrists, Diana St. John spent the entire time the Earl and Countess of Salt Hendon danced the minuet with her back to the dancers. She engaged the Florentine ambassador in conversation, who kept his gaze leveled at her breasts, magnificently displayed in a low square-cut bodice, a string of rubies and diamonds nestled in her cleavage. A confection of powdered curls, a gouache painted fan, and her distinct perfume were the finishing touches to her resplendent ensemble. She laughed, she chatted, and she was witty and full of life, so much so that more than a few guests commented on her high spirits. The only person to see through the façade was her brother.

Sir Antony was confronted by his sister in an anteroom off the main vestibule as soon as his well-shod foot touched the marble parquetry inside Richmond House. She demanded to know why she had not been invited to share the carriage ride with him and Lord Salt. Sir Antony suffered in silence her barrage of verbal abuse. She was furious to be informed that the Earl had brought his wife to the Richmond Ball. To argue that their noble cousin had every right to bring his wife was pointless, so Sir Antony kept his opinions and his arguments to himself.

He never won with Diana, and he had long since given up trying. He wasn't by nature a coward, nor was he lazy, but he had learned from an early age that his elder sister had the ability to take a point of view and twist it to suit her own ends. It didn't matter if her opponent had right on his side—by the time Diana had finished arguing, her opponent came round to her way of thinking, even if it was through sheer exhaustion and a need to escape her constant onslaught. Ethical considerations of right and wrong never entered her mind. It only mattered that she got her way. The only time Sir Antony ever saw her back down from a stubborn belief, indeed concede defeat in an argument, was with the Earl; and that was only because she had been besotted with their cousin since the schoolroom and would do anything to win his approval.

Many of their friends and family wondered why such a strong-willed, handsome creature had settled on marriage with the mild-mannered Aubrey St. John. Sir Antony knew. St. John was Salt's closest paternal cousin and best friend, and the pair were as insepa-rable as close-knit brothers. When it became clear to Diana that Salt would never offer for her, she chose the next best thing, or so she thought, in marrying Aubrey St. John. Lord St. John was not Salt, but he had been very much in love with Diana. The marriage was a disaster from the beginning, not least because, for all her outwardly overt sexual playfulness Sir Antony suspected his sister was frigid.

The marriage quickly soured, even before the birth of the twins. Sir Antony was in no doubts that it was Diana who had pushed a wedge of mistrust between her husband and the Earl, and so firmly that it was not until St. John was dying that the two men were reconciled. St. John had not said much about the rift at the time but once, when in his cups, he had confided to Sir Antony that Salt had counseled him against marrying Diana, but he would not listen. Salt had been right all along.

Sir Antony hoped that the Earl's marriage would, at long last, throw the cold water of truth in his sister's face, and awaken her to the indisputable fact that the Earl of Salt Hendon was forever beyond her reach. However, Diana's response to the marriage not only surprised but also shocked Sir Antony to such a degree that he feared for her sanity. She conducted herself as if the Salt Hendon marriage was a small, not insurmountable, problem that could be overcome if she just put her mind to finding a solution. At her very worst, particularly in the company of their mutual friends, she put on a very public façade of careless indifference, acting as if Salt's marriage had never taken place. She was acting that way tonight at the ball and he had to stop her before she made a fool of herself before three hundred people.

Just before the commencement of the country-dances, standing in the refreshment room by a Corinthian pillar and pretending an interest in the crowd through his quizzing glass, Sir

Antony tried to reason with his sister. She was talking with Pascoe Church, amongst others, and Sir Antony deliberately bumped her elbow so that she swirled about to see whom it was. He nodded at Pascoe Church, smiled at his sister, and took her firmly by the elbow, and led her to a quiet corner by a French window. Here he let her go and again took up his quizzing glass.

"How very sporting of you to allow Salt breathing room tonight," he said chirpily.

Diana bristled. "Heard the expression "give enough rope", brother dear?"

"Salt's never danced at the end of any ropes."

"Fool! Her. The moment he steps away, she's bound to hang herself."

Sir Antony turned his quizzing glass from the glittering crowd to his sister. "It doesn't look as if he wants to leave her side, does it?"

"He can't afford to, more's the pity. An organ grinder has more confidence in his monkey!"

Sir Antony couldn't help a laugh of disbelief and he shook his powdered head. "You go on convincing yourself of that, Di. I suppose he isn't by her side because that's where he wants to be?"

"Don't be a dullard, Tony. Wants to be? You never were quick on the uptake, were you? If Salt hadn't got you that sinecure in the Foreign Department I despair of where you would've ended up."

With a sigh, Sir Antony let the quizzing glass drop on its riband and picked up two glasses of champagne from a passing footman's silver tray. He gave one to his sister, and raised his to her. "Comfortably ensconced at White's behind the pages of a newssheet minding my own business, I suspect."

Diana St. John's painted mouth twisted with disdain. "You were such a disappointment to Papa."

"We all can't be Queen of the Amazons, my dear," he replied mildly. "Oh, you could. No doubt about that, Di. But there's one thing you'll never be, and that's Countess of Salt Hendon. The post's been filled—*for life*."

"I so *hate* you, I'd like to throw this champagne in your inept face."

"Go ahead," he stated and indicated the crowd breaking up

into groups for the country-dances beyond the pillars in the ballroom. "At least then this lot would see your soft center and know
that underneath your sparkling display of indifference you have a
heart. Di, please, before you douse me in French vinegar, listen,"
he added, all pretense dropped. "You must leave Salt alone, for
your own sake as much as his. You need to make something of
your life. You could marry any grand nobleman in this room in
need of a wife and be a great political hostess; what a formidable
pair you'd make! But there's one nobleman you will never have,
under any circumstances."

Diana St. John stared at her younger brother a full five seconds
before she replied. Sir Antony thought he detected a whisper of
emotion in her face, until she opened her mouth, and then his
shoulders slumped at the futility of trying to make her see reason.

"I settled for second best once before. Never again."

"St. John loved you to distraction, Di, and you know it! Poor
chap. He knew your heart belonged to Salt, that you foolishly
married him hoping to make Salt jealous. Didn't work, did it?"

"He deserves better than that skinny county chit who's now on
his arm," Diana St. John ruminated, ignoring her brother's
pointed comments. "He was almost trapped by her four years ago,
until I intervened to save his career and his name. And I won't sit
by and allow her to ruin his political ambitions now, not after all
my hard work to see him rise to greatness."

"*Your* hard work?" Sir Antony was laughingly incredulous. He
threw back the last drops of champagne and deftly off-loaded his
glass on a passing footman. "I suppose Salt had nothing to do with
his own success?"

"He needs a female who can help him achieve even greater
political success. Someone just as adept at playing the political
game. A hostess who isn't afraid to be ruthless and cunning if
required to further his career."

"Has it never occurred to you, Di, that what a nobleman of
Salt's position and abilities needs in a wife is someone who cares
about him, not his political posts, or whether he'll rise to be First
Lord of the Treasury, or form government with a pack of petty
corridor-whispering, backstabbing noble rabble. A wife who
doesn't meddle in politics, who, at the end of the day, makes him

feel content and untroubled." Sir Antony peered at his sister. "No? Not ringing any bells of St. Clemens in that pretty head of yours, sister of mine?"

"Salt may have married a wide-eyed stick insect, but he need not be distracted by her," Diana stated as if her brother hadn't spoken, depositing her glass of champagne on a silver tray that was being offered to her. "If he wants distraction, I can provide him with any number of females chafing at the bit to fill the position of mistress."

"Your services in that area have never been sought or required," Sir Antony remarked dryly. "And as he hasn't strayed from the marital bed since the day he was married, his carnal wants are being admirably fulfilled by his wife."

"That just proves she's ill-bred. Noble wives are not there to play harlot for their husbands. Husbands take their carnal appetites elsewhere. That's what whores are for."

Sir Antony rolled his eyes to the ornate ceiling on a sigh.

"Father lamented Mother had all the carnal cravings of a Scottish salmon."

"He'll soon tire of her," Diana went on, ignoring her brother's remark, "whether she plays the whore for him or not—he always tires of his whores."

Finally Sir Antony's frayed temper snapped. He gritted his teeth and turned glittering blue eyes on his sister. "For God's sake, Diana! Stop calling her that. She's his *wife*."

Diana teasingly tickled her brother under the chin with the pleats of her fan. "Ooh! Such *emotion*, Tony! Got you under her whore's spell, too? That would explain the latest gossip circulating drawing rooms—while Lord Salt is hard at work making speeches in the House, you are hard at work between Lady Salt's thighs."

Sir Antony snatched his sister's fan and flung it to the floor in abhorrence.

"Never. *Never* repeat that piece of filth again," he growled. "Lady Salt is deeply in love with her husband. I believe her to be honest and true. And even if in your blind jealousy you have convinced yourself that she could be disloyal to Salt, you should never have believed it of me, your own brother! I could never cuckold my best friend."

"Sir Lancelot to Salt's King Arthur to be sure, Tony!" Diana announced dismissively with a trill of laughter that had the few remaining guests lingering by the refreshment tables turning to stare with interest at brother and sister. "But it's not what *I* believe that matters. It's what Salt believes about his little whore-bride, isn't it?"

"For the last time, Diana," Sir Antony stated, beyond patience. "Leave them alone—for your own sake. Salt has tolerated your interference in the past because it has been harmless, if annoyingly persistent. This is an entirely different game you're playing at, and one you are destined to lose. I give you fair warning: Overstep the mark with his wife and he'll never forgive you—ever."

Diana shrugged a bare shoulder and changed tack. "You think I give a groat about that insipid milkmaid being Countess of Salt Hendon? My dear Tony, what I do I do, and have always done, for Ron."

Sir Antony was skeptical. "It's what you do to Ron that bothers me."

"I beg your pardon?" Diana St. John was uncharacteristically startled.

For the first time in their conversation, Sir Antony sensed that his sister was paying attention. "Here's another warning you should heed, Di. If your son continues to be ill, if you continue to have Salt called out at all hours of the night, you may find your children removed from your care."

"Are you *drunk*? I am their *mother*. Salt would never take them from me.*Never.*"

Sir Antony held her gaze. His mouth grim. "Fair warning, Di."

She turned her chin, and out of the corner of her eye spied the Earl at the edge of the dance floor in relaxed conversation with that old roué Lord March, the perverse wit George Selwyn, and his mentor and good friend Lord Waldegrave. The Countess was nowhere to be seen. He was happier and more content than she had seen him in many years. In fact, since that fateful Hunt Ball at Salt Hall when he had proposed to Jane Despard. It made Diana St. John sick to her stomach.

It was time she made her move on the Countess and stopped squandering it in vapid conversation with her brother. Still, she couldn't resist a parting remark, to exert her superiority over him, as always, and calculated to send his mind into a spin of conjecture. She snatched her fan from an obliging footman, who had scooped it up off the polished floorboards, flicked it open, and with a bunch of her silk petticoats in one hand, said to Sir Antony with a smug smile, before she swept off to the ballroom, "Salt's whore-bride has a dirty little secret. She's with child. But whose brat is it?"

SIR ANTONY'S JAW SWUNG wide at this startling pronouncement and he watched his sister traverse the ballroom, stopping to say hello to an old Dowager Duchess with gout here, kissing the powdered and patched cheek of a dear friend in a towering toupée there, playfully rapping her fan across the knuckles of an old roué who bowed over her outstretched hand, then exchanging smiles and pleasantries with a Lord of the Admiralty before disappearing from view onto the terrace. She was the most amiable and animated beauty in the vast sea of noble silks and powder, and an altogether different being from the one Sir Antony knew as his sister, and it bothered him greatly.

Her throw-away news that the Countess of Salt Hendon was with child made him oblivious to the footman who stood waiting at his elbow. The servant had been standing there for some time. Indeed, he had been the one to retrieve Lady St. John's fan from the floor. The only sign that he had heard the whole of the heated discussion between brother and sister was the redness to his ears. In every other respect he remained blank-faced. Inside he was bursting with news and couldn't wait for the ball to end, to exchange these juicy tidbits with the staff below stairs. He now stepped forward and presented the still gaping Sir Antony with a sealed letter.

Sir Antony had the letter in his hand a full minute before he realized it was there, and when he turned to enquire of the servant who had sent it, found himself alone by the French window. He broke the seal, mind still abuzz, but when he opened out the single sheet of paper and saw the familiar handwriting, his mind cleared of all else. Reading the two sentences caused his heart to flutter, and he beamed from ear to ear. Quickly, he put the letter in an inner pocket of his frock coat.

Five minutes later he was making his apologies to his hosts, the Duke and Duchess of Richmond, and before a powdered head could turn to wonder why the diplomat was making a hasty retreat from the social event of the winter thaw, Sir Antony was out the front door and in a hackney headed for Grosvenor Square.

THIRTEEN

J ANE LEFT THE GLITTERING ballroom for the fresh air of the expansive terrace with its breathtaking views of the Thames, mind bubbling over with so many new faces and names that she was sure she would forget them all by morning. She was in search of her stepbrother, whom she spied earlier in the ballroom in company with Billy Church. He had waved to her, but she had been caught up in a round of endless introductions and small talk, everyone it seemed who was anyone eager to meet the Earl of Salt Hendon's bride. She had lost sight of Tom in the press of the crowd and it was only later, after Pascoe, Lord Church, had taken her out for a country-dance, and Salt was busily engaged in conversation with Lord Waldegrave, did she feel able to slip away.

Tom was said to be on the terrace, but so it seemed was half the guest list. Couples had spilled out of the house to walk the gravel paths or just stand by the iron railings to admire the view, considered one of the finest in all London. Liveried footmen scurried about with trays of refreshment. Others stood to attention either side of the wide steps that took guests from one flat expanse of terrace to the next until they finally arrived at the jetty, where bobbed colorful barges and boats that had brought guests from lower down the Thames.

The enormous shoals of floating ice that had blocked the river in January were now melted, so all manner of water craft plied the congested breadth of the Thames, from small two-man row boats, to ships under sail and covered barges festooned with colorful bunting. At the foreshore of the river to the horizon everywhere was brick and stone, the red roofs of buildings, and church spires piercing the milky blue sky. Rising majestically above this conglomeration that was the city of London stood St. Paul's, the cathedral's glorious dome dwarfing everything that surrounded it, the magnificence of which never failed to draw a breath of amazement from this superlative vantage point, from residents and visitors alike.

Jane drew breath now as she took in the sprawling vista of river, city and darkening sky. She carefully descended the steps that led down to the next section of terrace closer to the water's edge, a clutch of petticoats in her hand, and glad she had come outside before nightfall shrouded the view in a dark blanket, and the cold air finally penetrated her bones. Strategically placed tapers lined the terrace walks, ready to be lit the moment the signal was given, to ward off darkness and cold. And out in the water bobbed a flotilla of barges, packed with fire rockets and Catherine wheels, all intended to light up the night sky, however briefly, and shower the guests in flecks of tiny lights: The much anticipated finale to the Richmond Ball.

Music drifted out from the ballroom. Laughter and conversation in the open air competed with the noise of water traffic and sounds of a city that never slept. Jane had at first thought she would never be able to sleep at night with the constant and varied noises around her, everything from carriage wheels rumbling along the cobbles, cattle being herded to market, sellers advertising their wares in their sing-song voices, to the pitter-pat of pattens that kept a lady's silk shoes from town filth. But since her marriage, she had slept very well indeed, in no small part due to her husband's warm embrace.

Instinctively, she lightly fingered the sapphire locket about her throat and wistfully thought about the baby she was carrying.

"You think that trinket holds any meaning for him?" a voice purred in her ear.

Jane spun about, saw a flash of red and gold silk and was

suddenly nauseous. Dizzy and disorientated, she stuck out a hand to hard grip the iron railing that was the only barrier between her and the plunge to the embankment below. It was the overpowering scent of the woman's perfume, not the words hissed in her ear that had her flustered.

Diana St. John had cornered her where two iron railings met at right angles. She stood behind Jane, her wide petticoats penning her in and blocking her escape. To the casual observer it appeared as if the two women were admiring the view from opposite compass points while in conversation.

"That trinket has no more meaning for Salt than that garish wedding band he was forced to slip on your finger," Diana St. John continued flatly, hazel-eyed gaze riveted to Jane's face. "His mother wore the Sinclair locket on State occasions and to significant balls such as this because it was expected of her; another social trapping of her position in society. But she considered it an ugly heirloom. It suits you perfectly."

"Is there anything I may do for you, my lady?" Jane asked quietly, blue eyes holding the woman's gaze, while she stirred fresh air onto her face with her fan in an attempt to ward off the waves of nausea that came and went with Diana St. John's strong scent carried on the river breeze. Perhaps if she let the woman say her piece she would then leave her alone?

Diana St. John's painted mouth thinned and she cast a significant look over Jane's shoulder at the flowing river. "Aside from drowning yourself? No."

Jane swallowed. "If I have offended you in any way…"

"Offended me? Your existence offends me!"

"Why?"

"Why?" Diana St. John repeated, disconcerted. How dare this wisp of a woman, who had the bad manners to put up her chin, ask such a blunt question? Who did she think she was? "Surely you know the answer. Or are you as wafer-brained as you are scrawny? He deserves better than you. He deserves someone befitting his noble blood and rank, someone of whom he can be proud, who holds to the same convictions and ambitions. He deserves—"

"—you?" Jane interrupted simply. "I am sorry he did not

marry you years ago, my lady. Then perhaps you would not hate him."

"*Hate* him?" Diana St. John jabbed Jane's beribboned stomacher with the closed sticks of her fan. "What do you mean, hate him? I *love* him. I've always loved him!"

"For a woman who professes love, you spend a great deal of your time needlessly interfering in his life—"

"How dare—"

"—and finding ways to punish him for not loving you in return."

Diana St. John was rendered speechless. She itched to slap the Countess of Salt Hendon's beautiful face. A terrace crowded with the crème de la crème of Polite Society forestalled her.

"Clever," she finally managed to say in a low voice and held firm her fan to Jane's belly. "Got a dirty little secret to tell me, my lady?" she taunted, again jabbing the fan into her. Jane opened wide her eyes and instinctively tried to move away but was trapped by the iron railing in the small of her back. Diana St. John's smug smile reappeared. "I'll lay good odds he's blissfully ignorant of the brat you're carrying, just as he was four years ago."

"Yes, I am pregnant with Lord Salt's child, my lady," Jane replied with a calmness that belied her anxiety. "You can be the first to congratulate us."

"Congratulate you? Dear God, I'll see you and the bastard burn in hell first!"

"How is that you know I conceived Salt's child four years ago?" Jane asked in her blunt way, though it took all her self-control to remain calm, stunned as she was by the ferocity of the woman's vitriol. "I told no one Magnus was the father of my child."

"That was a dim-wit's mistake, but one I applaud wholeheartedly. Had you sense, you would've confessed all to Sir Felix, and your father would have run hot-foot to London, and forced Salt to marry you. By protecting *Magnus* you caused the death of his child. Good Lord! You didn't even possess the guile to keep your legs closed to him until he had you up before parson. More fool you."

"Perhaps I was a fool. Perhaps I am in some way to blame for my baby's death, but… I was naïve and so desperately in love, and believed myself loved in return…" When Diana St. John gave a snort of disbelief, Jane added quietly, hoping to see a spark of humanity in the beautiful painted face, "What about the birth of your twins, when you first held Ron and Merry in your arms? Did you not love your babies so much it hurt?"

"What sentimental tripe!" Diana St. John said dismissively, then smiled knowingly, prodding Jane again with her fan. "My children are worth a great deal to me, a very great deal because Salt loves them as if they were his own. My son is Salt's heir. He would do anything for my son; leave his bride in the middle of the night to comfort me by Ron's sickbed. Don't think he won't continue to do so for as along as I want him there, out of your bed and beside me. In that there is no contest. You will never win."

Jane regarded Diana St. John with horrified fascination to think she saw her children as merely a means to an end, that end being Lord Salt's time and attentions, that it was a contest worth winning just to have the Earl attending on her sick son in the middle of the night.

Jane voiced a disturbing notion that had been forming in the back of her mind since that day in the freezing anteroom when she was overcome with nausea at the scent of Lady St. John's perfume. "You were there the night I miscarried. Your voice—your perfume, I remember both distinctly."

"Drink it in, my lady," Diana St. John purred, enjoying intimidating the Countess, whose face had lost its healthy glow. Perhaps if she tormented her a little while longer the woman might collapse from nervous exhaustion which would bring on a miscarriage. "It's a very distinctive scent, is it not? Most men adore it. It's blended for me by a little apothecary on the Strand; very talented German; perfumer, apothecary and supplier of all manner of substances to rid oneself of unwanted ills. Does it make you feel very, *very* green? For shame! Let me give you something to expel your nausea. I assure you it works every time. Sir Felix was very grateful for my guidance, and of course he couldn't have been more pleased with the medicinal I provided."

Jane was dismayed. "You supplied the medicinal that quickened my baby?"

"You should be obliged to me that the matter was taken care of so expeditiously."

"*Matter? Expeditiously?*" Jane fought back tears hearing her dead unborn baby referred to in such a cold-hearted way. "Have you no conscience? I lost my baby that night."

"Aren't you listening, you stupid creature?" Diana St. John sneered. "You didn't lose it. The bastard was quite rightly disposed of on the orders of Sir Felix."

"Did it mean nothing to you that Magnus was the father?"

"It meant *everything* to me. Are you bird-witted? It was precisely because it was his child that it had to be removed."

"And you profess to *love* him?"

"Yes, *him*, not his ill-gotten offspring. The loss of one barely-formed child is nothing in the grand scheme of things. Women miscarry every day. Babies die. It's a fact."

Jane shivered with a mixture of fear and revulsion. The sooner she escaped this woman's evil aura, the better. Years of being eaten up with jealousy and bitterness had turned Diana St. John's heart to stone. It was clear the woman had lost all sense of right from wrong, and any means—interfering in the Earl's life, in Jane's life, taking the life of the innocent, their baby's life—was acceptable, if it achieved her ends.

"Remove your fan, my lady," Jane ordered.

Instead of doing as requested Diana St. John jabbed a little harder at Jane's stomach. "There's no guarantee this one will be delivered full-term. No guarantee at all. Just because it was conceived in wedlock does not give it protection. Many hazards can befall mother and child before birth—"

"How dare you threaten me!"

Diana St. John prodded again, but this time had the fan knocked out of her grasp as Jane pushed past her. Instantly, Diana St. John thrust out a velvet arm to the iron railing and blocked Jane's exit.

"I haven't finished with you yet!" she hissed.

"But I have finished with you, Madam," Jane replied firmly. She looked significantly at Diana St. John's obstructing arm and then up at the woman's painted face. "Have you forgotten where we are?"

Surprisingly, Diana St. John had done just that, but she was so intent on putting this little upstart in her place, to show her that she was worth less than nothing and that the Earl of Salt Hendon did not care a tester for his country bride, that she was beyond caring who was peering down at them from the terraces.

"You smug little slut! You think you are the object of a singular devotion? Ha! He has finally tired of you. It is a fact of life, and one you had best get used to. Noblemen of Salt's ilk possess strong carnal appetites and thus are incapable of remaining faithful. And why should they when they can have the pick of any litter? Cast your mind back a sennight—Wednesday and Thursday nights to be exact." When Jane gave a start and half-turned, she smiled thinly. "Ah, so you are not so stupid as I first supposed. Then you will appreciate that I have made it my business to know where Salt spends each and every night of the year, and with whom. So when I tell you what I know, I am merely stating facts."

When Jane stared at her mutely, she smiled her satisfaction.

"Good. We understand one another. Then know this: On Wednesday and Thursday night last week, when he did not return to Grosvenor Square and to your bed, and you spent the entire night alone, possibly and stupidly waiting up for him, he was with his latest mistress. She has been very patient and he has shown great forbearance over the past three months. You should count yourself fortunate to have received that much of his undivided attention. But now the honeymoon period is over and he has done his duty by you as a bride. Now he will return to his usual way of life, the way of life Society expects of a nobleman in his position."

"Jane? Jane! There you are!"

"Tom?"

Jane saw her stepbrother coming lightly down the wide terrace steps through a blindness of tears. She was so eager to get to him and away from this evil woman that she pushed with two hands on Diana St. John's arm, as if it were a gate that could be swung wide on its hinges. But before she could go to him, before she had taken more than two steps in his direction, Diana St. John had caught the lace flounce at her elbow.

"You're being sent to rot in the country. It's just as well, isn't it? Because he'll never believe the brat you're carrying is his," she announced gleefully in Jane's ear. "Not in a thousand nights, not after all the barren lovers he's had over the years. It's so much easier to farm out a bastard in the wilds of Wiltshire. You'll never see it again and he'll never want you back in London after—"

"What are you doing down here in the shadows?" Tom scolded his stepsister good-naturedly, reaching her just as Lady St. John let go of Jane's arm. She brushed past him in a billow of red and gold silk, a lovely smile directed his way. He nodded to her ladyship and took Jane's hand, and turned to lead her back up the terrace steps. "You're half-frozen! Salt's been looking for you everywhere. The fireworks are about to commence and the best views are to be had from up there on the top terrace. And we'd best fetch your cloak. We'll miss the rockets if you don't hurry—Jane?"

He turned when Jane stopped at the foot of the steps. He peered at her more closely. It was only then that he saw that she was deathly white and that her cheeks were stained with tears.

"Jane? What's wrong? What did that woman say to upset you?" he asked, a swift look up at Lady St. John who was sweeping up the stairs just as the Earl of Salt Hendon was descending them.

She waylaid him, a hand possessively on his upturned velvet cuff, her petticoats pressed against his silken leg. She was talking to him in a rush, and he looked over her carefully constructed coiffure to see Tom and Jane huddled together on the lower terrace. Tom frowned. Tomorrow could not come soon enough. He turned back to his stepsister, to confide in her he had just told the Earl a few home truths, but not to worry, his lordship seemed to take it in his stride.

Although, being rather foxed, Tom was not absolutely sure the Earl's silence was thunderous fury or dignified acceptance. Whatever, tomorrow he would set matters straight. He had documents to wave under his lordship's fine nose. His uncle's lawyers had presented them to him with the understanding that Jacob Allenby intended them for the Earl, but only if Tom thought it in the best interests of his stepsister to do so. Tom had every intention of presenting them to the Earl in his bookroom tomorrow, and that would settle the matter and it need never be discussed again. His lips, and everyone else's would be sealed. Jane's happiness depended upon it.

Jane did not understand a word of Tom's garbled speech, not least because her encounter with Diana St. John had left her nauseous and emotionally drained. What she did understand was that her stepbrother had accosted Salt on a public terrace and had left that impromptu interview with no idea if the Earl was angry or not, which told Jane her husband was very angry indeed with Tom. She wished she felt better able to quiz Tom but the relief of being out from under Diana St. John's sinister orbit was enough to make her light-headed. Tom's voice became very far away as she tried to stay upright. She was certain if he fetched a glass of lemon water she would feel much better. But before she could ask him her eyelids fluttered, her knees buckled and she crumpled into Tom's arms in a dead faint.

AN ACRID SMELL OPENED Jane's eyes. She screwed up her mouth and pushed away the hand that held the burnt feather under her nose and tried to focus and get her bearings. The last thing she remembered was Tom telling her he had approached Salt on the terrace to tell him a thing or two, and then everything went black. Now there were voices and light, and what seemed to be a hundred faces peering down at her from way up in the stars of a night sky. She was lying on the small patch of lawn to the side of the terrace steps, cradled in Tom's lap. Several liveried servants were peering down at her, under the light cast by a flambeau held by a footman, as was every man and woman leaning over the iron railings of the terrace to better view the theatrics of the Countess of Salt Hendon's faint at her first public engagement.

"Help me up, Tom," Jane murmured, cheeks now aglow with embarrassment at being the main attraction at the Richmond Ball.

"You fainted," said Tom, stating the obvious as he eased her into a sitting position. He handed her a tumbler of punch. "Drink. You'll feel better."

Jane took the tumbler, suddenly very thirsty. She thrust the empty tumbler back at a footman. "Please, Tom. Help me up before Salt finds out I've made a spectacle of myself."

Tom smiled apologetically. "Too late."

The nobleman in question, a head taller than the crowd of onlookers surrounding them, pushed through the contingent of liveried footmen, Jane's fur-lined cloak draped over an arm, and went down on bended knee to throw the cloak over her bare shoulders.

"Jane? Are you all right?" Salt asked anxiously, concern overriding formality. He deftly buttoned the cloak before lifting her chin to look in her eyes. "What happened?"

"I fainted. Silly me. I'm feeling much better now."

"Fainted? How? I mean, what happened to make you faint?"

"One minute Jane was talking with Lady St. John by the railings, and the next she fainted dead away," Tom said with a shrug, trying to make light of it for Jane's sake. "She don't eat much, y'know, and what with all the excitement tonight, she had a dizzy spell."

"Diana mentioned you and she had an unpleasant conversation. What did you say to upset her?"

"Upset *her*?" Jane could hardly believe her ears.

"Not everyone appreciates your frank approach," he scolded gently as he helped her to stand. "Best to stay out of her way."

Jane pulled the fur-lined cloak tightly about her. "I am only too happy to do so. If she would only stay out of mine!"

Salt scowled, Jane's retort confirming what he had first thought when from the top terrace he had spied his wife and his cousin having a very public *tête-à-tête* on the lower terrace: Diana had sought her out. He was momentarily embarrassed. "My marriage was a huge shock… She hasn't yet come to terms with my changed circumstances… Given time, she will accept you as my wife. She has no choice."

"Lady St. John's feelings toward me are unimportant," Jane confessed. "My only concern is how you feel…" She couldn't bring herself to continue when Salt swallowed, dropped his gaze and turned his head ever so slightly away from her. Her frankness would not be rewarded this time. She would have to content herself with the return of the Sinclair locket for now. She glanced at Tom, who still hovered in the background, and said with deep mortification, "I'm sorry. I had no right to embarrass you and in such a public place. I really must learn to curb my tongue. Perhaps I should've stayed home as you suggested."

"Yes, perhaps you should have," Salt responded gruffly, taking hold of her hands, which were as cold as blocks of ice. "I warned you about the unseasonable weather and still you came out of doors without the proper covering. You're half frozen. Idiotic not to have had your cloak fetched."

"Yes. Idiotic," Jane repeated forlornly.

"And Tom's right. You don't eat enough. No wonder you fainted. Half-starved and under-dressed. It was as well Tom was keeping an eye on you," Salt continued, and pulled her closer to put an arm about her slumped shoulders. "I turn my back for five minutes' conversation with Waldegrave and Selwyn, and you wander off to disappear out of doors without a thought for the night air, and without telling me where you were going."

"How unthinking of me," Jane responded bleakly.

Salt saw Tom about to rush to his stepsister's defense, but with a wink and a smile over his wife's bowed head the young man shut his mouth. He walked her to the steps that led up to the main terrace where the guests had assembled awaiting the start of the fireworks, and said with a feigned mocking sigh, "Not only do you wander off, but you have the temerity to faint in full view of the world. How I am going to keep my noble head up for the rest of the evening, I know not, madam wife. And you ask me whether you should've stayed home tonight? You tell me!"

By now Tom was smiling along with the Earl, but when he caught the look of shame on his stepsister's face he knew with a shake of his head that Jane had not fallen in with her husband's gruff cajolery and thought him in earnest. This soon became evident to Salt when Jane turned in the circle of his arm and buried her face in his silver-threaded waistcoat, ignoring the numerous orders and decorations pinned to his chest that chaffed her delicate skin.

"Oh, Jane! *No*. I didn't mean it," Salt quickly reassured her. "I was funning with you, you silly girl! I wouldn't have let you miss this ball for anything," he added soothingly, cradling her in his arms.

He looked about and saw a vacant bench in a shadowy spot

beside the base of the broad stairs. "You go on up," he said to Tom. "We'll watch the fireworks from down here. And Tom, I look forward to a continuance of your views tomorrow evening. Good night."

Noise and light made Jane jump and turn her head in her husband's embrace to the wondrous view of skyrockets and Catherine wheels lit from barges anchored on the river. They lit up the black sky like a thousand of the brightest chandeliers. She watched the display snuggled in her warm cloak beside her husband. His strong arms about her were the greatest source of comfort and warmth, and her embarrassment at having fainted in full view of Polite Society completely forgotten as she ooed and aahed with the rest of the crowd at such a wondrous display of brilliant lights. It was so entertaining that for a few moments at least she was able to put to the back of her mind her confrontation with Diana St. John.

Yet her mind would not be quiet. She could not put off for much longer telling Salt about the baby. With her light frame, she would soon begin to show. What she did not know, could not predict, and what made her ill with anxiousness, was what would be his response. As to her husband's whereabouts the two nights he had spent apart from her, her heart told her not to believe a woman who was intent on destroying any vestige of happiness in the Earl's life. Her head reasoned that as the Earl had made her no promises of eternal devotion, and his past was littered with mistresses, what made her believe that she was the object of a singular devotion as Diana St. John rightly pointed out? He may have professed to loving her four years ago, but not once had he uttered those magic words since their marriage.

"Do you know, I have never sat still and silent at a ball before," Salt announced with something akin to awe. "It is rather enlivening." He beamed down at his wife, as if given a new toy. "I will lay the responsibility for this novel diversion at your feet, my lady."

His handsome smile stopped Jane's breath; it was so genuine and heartfelt that she impulsively touched his cheek.

"Magnus, kiss me."

He brought his mouth down to hers, saying on a murmur, "It would be my very great pleasure, Lady Salt."

. . .

BEFORE THE SPARKS FROM the last skyrocket had showered the night sky and fallen extinguished into the icy Thames, the Earl and Countess of Salt Hendon had slipped away to their waiting carriage, where Jane surprised her husband by putting her arms about his neck and saying,

"Tell John to take the long way back."

"Are you sure?"

Jane gently kissed his mouth. "Quite sure."

"But—your fainting spell… It might be wiser if we just returned home as quickly as possible."

Home. Jane mentally smiled at the word but pretended to be disconsolate. She removed her arms from around his neck and sat back on the velvet-upholstered bench with her hands in her lap to gaze at her fingers.

"I understand," she said with a practiced sigh. "You're tired. It's been a long evening. For a man of your age, I suppose tiredness is to be expected."

"I—beg—your—pardon? Man of *my* age? I'm only four-and-thirty!"

Jane kept her chin down because she was on the verge of a fit of the giggles. He was aghast, as she knew he would be. She never failed to unbalance him. Served him to rights for playing the same trick on her on the terrace and pretending to be angry.

"You needn't concern yourself I'm-I'm disappointed," she continued, barely able to contain her mirth. "We-we can always take the long way home some-some other time, when you're feeling more up to it."

"*Disappointed?*" Salt growled. "*Up to it?* You little wretch!" he added in an altogether different voice and grabbed her to him. "Don't ever think I'll be taken in by your tricks again! Two can play at your game! On the terrace, I did a splendid job of bamboozling you, if I do say so myself. Admit it, you thought I was truly angry with you."

Jane snuggled into his embrace. "I admit to nothing, my lord."

"What? Must needs I spank an admittance out of you?"

Jane kissed his cheek. "If that is your whim, my lord."

Salt shook his head with mock displeasure, then took her breath away by crushing her mouth under his.

With the steps gone and the carriage door finally closed, it only remained for the Earl to give his driver the appropriate signal. Still kissing his wife, he lifted his arm to rap twice on the wall behind his head which separated the occupants from the driver up on his box, then made two more raps in rapid succession.

The horses were given their heads and the carriage lurched forward.

Jane came up for air and asked curiously, "What signal was that?"

"Too tired indeed," Salt murmured and kissed her again, fingers tugging at the lacings of her silk corset, his other hand outstretched to draw the heavy curtain on the window and the world.

FOURTEEN

WHEN THE EARL'S CARRIAGE finally pulled up outside his Grosvenor Square mansion, it was mud-spattered, the horses were spent and his driver John was in need of a well-earned jug of ale beside the kitchen fire. The under-butler, the porter and two drowsy footmen came out of the house to welcome the Earl and Countess home. Willis waited under the portico with the porter, who held up a flambeau, while the footmen stepped forward, one to set the steps in place while the other went to open the carriage door.

A short, sharp sentence and a solemn shake of the head from the driver and the two footmen stepped away to stand beside the porter and await the Earl's pleasure. Willis took one look at the driver, who dared to wink and grin lewdly at him, and he frown-ingly turned on a heel and disappeared back indoors out of the cold to have words with the butler.

In Willis's opinion, it was beyond everything decent that the Earl should bring a whore he had pleasured in his carriage to the front door of the house he now shared with his young Countess. It stretched Willis's patience and moral fiber to breaking. If it weren't for his deep regard and respect for Lady Salt, so he told Mr. Jenk-ins, who stood sleepy-eyed but listening in the marble-floored entrance vestibule, he would give notice forthwith.

And what, pray tell, was Mr. Jenkins' opinion, given his lordship's younger sister, the Lady Caroline Sinclair, had arrived from Wiltshire not five hours ago and was now resident in this house? And if the unexpected arrival of the Earl's sister wasn't enough to try the patience of a martyr, how did Mr. Jenkins intend to handle the delicate matter of Lady St. John's urgent missive that her son was on his death bed, and that the Earl present himself in South Audley Street at once.

The butler shrugged his narrow shoulders and kept his thoughts to himself.

When the porter opened wide the front door and in stepped the Earl, Rufus Willis had to swallow his words.

OUTSIDE IN THE CARRIAGE, the carnage of various articles of clothing strewn about the padded velvet interior, from discarded panniers to a gentleman's silver waistcoat pinned with decorations of the highest order flung in a corner, suggested a frenzied urgency to the occupants' lovemaking. Nothing was further from the truth. Everything had occurred with a deliberate slowness, as if the cogs of a clock moved at half-speed. From undressing each other in the darkness, to making love, each action and reaction was savored. Every exquisite sensation—sight, touch, smell and taste—was enjoyed for its own sake, while the carriage bumped and rattled across the uneven cobblestones of the deserted city, then out along the muddied roads of the newer squares and streets of the wealthier occupants of the parish of Westminster.

Stripped of his finery, gloriously naked and deep inside her, there was so much tenderness in his hands and in his mouth as he caressed and pleasured her, and in his words when he confessed his overwhelming need of her, that Jane was able to delude herself that he would be forever hers and hers alone. And when she finally tumbled off into oblivion with him, somewhere in the fog of satiated desire she heard her name, and the one tiny, but oh so precious, sentence he had not uttered to her since he had asked her to marry him all those years ago.

His declaration, which should have made her supremely happy, only served to stir her doubts because he had declared himself not in the coolness of daylight but in the darkness of a moving carriage in the heat of passionate climax, his mind and body in turmoil. Although she had no experience of other men, she instinctively knew that what was said in the intense heat of lust could not be believed until repeated in the stillness of a clear head and restful body.

Staring unseeing at the ceiling as the carriage turned into Grosvenor Square, Jane was oblivious to the fact that while she mentally ruminated in the darkness, Salt was propped on an elbow watching her intently. He wondered for the umpteenth time why he could make this utterly beautiful and thoroughly beguiling creature respond to his every intimate caress, yet she continued to keep him locked out of her thoughts. It was no surprise then that when the carriage finally came to a halt under the portico and he lightly touched the locket about her throat, she gave a start and brought her blue-eyed gaze down from the carriage's padded ceiling to his face, her smile enigmatic.

"Home," he said with a smile, pulling on his drawers.

He buttoned up his breeches, and helped Jane to sit up before struggling into his crumpled shirt. But he did not bother with his stockings or his shoes, and ignored his waistcoat and frock coat. He found Jane's chemise flung over a cushion and helped her wriggle into it, but when she put out a hand for her bodice he tossed it aside and instead placed the fur-lined cloak about her shoulders.

She gave a start, appalled.

"You are in jest! I cannot leave here in nothing more than my chemise and stockings!"

"That's why I gave you the cloak," he responded cheerfully and opened the carriage door, letting in a great rush of chilled early morning air. "Besides, what's important is around your neck. The rest can be replaced."

Jane remained seated, hugging the cloak tightly about her slender frame, despite Salt having descended the steps to stand barefoot on the cobbles. She put up her brows.

"And what of your Most Noble Order of the Garter, my lord? Shouldn't his lordship throw that around his neck? After all, it's just as important and can't be replaced."

"No," he stated simply and grabbed her wrist. "I have what's important here."

He yanked her through the doorway. The cloak slipped off one shoulder and Jane squealed and grabbed at the fur as if her life depended upon it. But Salt would not be deterred, and in one swift and easy movement her threw her, startled and protesting, over his shoulder, an arm across the back of her bare thighs to keep her squirming legs still, a hand pressed to the cloak to ensure it slipped no further.

"If you keep wiggling about," he said with a laugh as he turned and strode past the two gaping footmen and a red-faced porter who silently opened the door, "I give no guarantees that we will make it upstairs with our dignity intact."

"Dignity?" Jane tried to rise up to stop the blood rushing into her ears, only to flop forward in defeat. "Magnus! Stop this at once!" she demanded in a strident whisper, thumping his lower back with her balled fists. "Be reasonable! Think of the example to the servants! What will they think of us? *Magnus?*"

"I do so like to hear you call me by my Christian name," he said conversationally, ignoring Jane's ineffectual thumps.

HE STOOD IN THE WIDE expanse of the marbled entrance hall as if it were the most natural thing in the world for the fifth Earl of Salt Hendon to arrive home at three o'clock in the morning in nothing more than a crumpled white shirt hanging out of his breeches, bare-legged and barefoot, with his protesting Countess slung over one shoulder, her shapely stockinged ankles and feet on display.

The dumbstruck butler, under-butler, and porter all exchanged a swift, eyebrow-raising glance that confirmed what they all privately thought: Not only was the Earl in his cups, but his Countess was tantalizingly naked under her cloak. It made them stay back, the butler holding Lady St. John's unsealed note at his side and waiting the appropriate moment to interrupt the couple.

"No one calls me Magnus," the Earl was saying, finally sliding Jane off his shoulder and down the length of his hard frame to allow her to stand on her own two feet.

Her arms remained up around his neck and her barely-covered breasts were deliciously pressed to his chest. He continued to hold her tightly against him, a hand in the small of her back so the cloak, which had now slid to her waist, exposing her narrow back through the thin linen chemise, did not reveal more tantalizingly bare flesh.

"Not even my mother called me Magnus, not when I was in short skirts and leading strings, not ever. I was Lacey while my father was alive, Viscount Lacey. Always Lord Lacey."

"How very sad. A child deserves to be called by his Christian name, especially by his parents," Jane responded, looking up into his brown eyes. "That's what makes him *him*. Not some cold and distant title that has belonged to his forebears for generations."

He bent to kiss her gently. "Somehow I knew you'd say that," and in a more rallying tone, "Not a very manly name is Lacey. Magnus has more presence and is much more manly, don't you think?"

"Oh, much more manly!" she mocked. "Just as manly as Salt. Though I prefer Magnus."

"Do you know," he added with a huff of laughter, surprising himself, "I do believe my family have quite forgotten I have a Christian name."

"You are being absurd again!" Jane announced with a giggle. "Of course they know your Christian name, it's just that they choose not to use it because they prefer you to remain atop your noble pedestal; it adds to their self-consequence."

"Pedestal?"

"The pedestal you inhabit as the most noble Earl of Salt Hendon; where you and your noble nostrils live most of the day."

"Noble nostrils? Good God, do I have noble nostrils?"

"Only when you're being pompous and when you're angry. Then they quiver."

He laughed out loud at that, as if told a good joke, displaying a perfect white smile. "Thank you. I must remember that when next I show my displeasure." He dipped his head and brushed the tip of his nose against hers and said seriously, "And when I'm not living atop my pedestal, where am I?"

Jane blushed and lowered her lashes. "In bed with me." And

just as quickly added with a smile, because she felt she had gone too far with her candid observations, "Besides, your family must approve of the name Magnus because you have a beautiful little goddaughter by the name of Magna."

"Poor Merry! To be saddled with such a name." He effortlessly lifted her into his arms. "I hope you will go on calling me Magnus —in and out of the bedchamber," he murmured.

She leaned her cheek against his shoulder and snuggled up to his neck, where traces of his spicy masculine fragrance remained, her disheveled hair a mass of tumbled curls and loose pins, and closed her eyes. "Only if it's mine to own," she responded, feeling very sleepy cradled in his arms. "No one else... to have it."

"No one else," he muttered and kissed her tangle of hair.

He had a large bare foot on the first step of the curved stair, when from the first landing there came a squeal of undisguised delight that had Jane instantly wide-awake and struggling out of Salt's arms to stand half-concealed behind him. The owner of the squeal came sailing down the stairs, one hand to the polished balustrade, an elaborately embroidered pink silk dressing gown over her night shift, and over her bright copper curls a lace night cap was tied lopsidedly under her pointed chin.

Jane blinked and wondered if she were witness to an apparition. The girl was not much younger than she, and although she possessed the Sinclair coloring, her pretty features had more in common with an Allenby than a Sinclair.

"What the devil are you doing in London?" Salt growled and suffered the girl to throw her arms around his neck. "I hope you dragged the long-suffering Dawson with you and half my laborers as outriders?"

"Of course!" she announced cheerfully and released him. "Dawson refused at first to accompany me, but I told her I'd come up to town without her anyway and now she's quaking in my rooms convinced you mean to dismiss her. Of course I told her that's rot." She stepped back and ran her wide-eyed gaze over the Earl, from bare feet to dressed hair, and cocked her head in mock disapproval. "You went to the Richmond Ball with your hair powdered but without your stockings and shoes?"

"Don't be vile, Caroline!" Salt snapped in embarrassment.

Jane muffled a giggle into the Earl's shoulder, instantly warming her to the girl, and clutched the fur-lined cloak more tightly about her naked body.

"He calls me *Caro-line* in that pompous way when he's uncomfortable," Lady Caroline confided with a smile, then had the temerity to wrinkle up her little nose with its dusting of freckles to brazenly appraise the half-concealed Jane from tumble of dark hair to small bare feet. "You're much shorter than I remember, possibly because I've grown, but you're still utterly lovely," she remarked, as if they were known to one another. "You're quite the loveliest garden sprite to have lived at the bottom of our garden, isn't she, Salt? When I say *our* garden, of course I mean Salt's vast seat in Wiltshire; but you know that. Did you ever see us, on the hill overlooking your quaint little cottage? We were on horseback under the stand of old oaks. We'd rest our mounts there. But that was just an excuse so Salt could catch a glimpse of his garden fairy—that's you, by the way—tending your garden—"

"Caroline! For pity's sake!"

Lady Caroline rolled her eyes, not at all abashed at making the Earl's ears go very red. She made her curtsy to Jane and said matter-of-factly, "I'm Caroline Sinclair. Salt's *long-suffering* sister. You can call me Caro. Even Salt calls me that when he's being pleasant. Which isn't often enough, let me tell you!"

"Call you impossible, insufferable, and intolerable!" he retorted, face ablaze with color at the public revelation of details he'd rather leave unsaid. He quickly introduced Jane, adding wearily, "Caro, you really have chosen the most awkward time to land on my doorstep, not to mention the fact you disobeyed me in coming to London."

"I'm truly sorry, Salt, but my news couldn't wait," she said, not at all apologetic. "Besides, now you're married it makes all the more sense. By the by," she said, changing tack, "how did you manage to pry the Sinclair locket from Cousin Diana's talons?"

Jane put a hand to her throat. "This is paste."

Salt's head snapped round at Jane, and then almost at once looked back at his sister when she said coolly,

"I didn't think she'd give it up without a fight."

"I beg your pardon? Will someone tell me what you are talking about?"

Both women exchanged a look. It was enough to make them firm friends.

"I believe your sister knows more about the Sinclair locket than we do, my lord."

Salt frowned and waited for Caroline to explain.

"Diana keeps the Sinclair locket under her pillow. She has done so for years. I know, because once I stole it from its hiding place, if you can call taking back what is rightfully yours stealing, and got whipped for my troubles."

"She *hit* you?"

Caroline shook her head at her brother. "No. She had her lady's maid do that for her."

Salt was aghast. He looked at Jane and seemed to read her mind. He lifted the sapphire with one finger. "No secret compartment in this one…"

Jane swallowed and shook her head.

"But in the other one, the real one, you placed a note in the secret compartment for me."

She did not trust herself to speak. Her blue eyes filled with tears and he had his answer.

Gently, he brushed a strand of hair from her flushed cheek. "I want to ask you… But perhaps in the morning, when we've both had a good night's sleep, we will be better able to discuss the past…"

Jane nodded.

Intuitively, Lady Caroline knew this quiet exchange between her brother and his wife was a momentous one. Yet she was still young and selfish enough to believe her news was so important that it could not wait. After all, she had come all the way from Wiltshire to tell her brother, and she wasn't about to go off to bed again, having been woken at three in the morning, so she just blurted out what he needed to know sooner rather than later.

"Salt! Do you want to know why I came up to London?"

"Do I?" the Earl responded with a tired sigh, turning to look down at her. "Could it not wait until morning?"

Lady Caroline beamed mischievously. "I came to tell you that

Captain Beresford has asked for my hand in marriage and I have accepted him."

Salt stared at her in utter disbelief. And if Jane hadn't been stunned by Lady Caroline's smile of absolute confidence, that the Earl must accept this news as a *fait accompli*, she would have enjoyed her husband's hot-headed response.

"Captain Barefaced-Cheek can ask for the whole of your damned spoiled carcass, for all I bloody well care, but he won't get a hair on your head!" Salt exploded angrily. "And for this you disobeyed me and came up to London? *I* have a mind to whip some sense into you!"

"It won't do you any good. I'm no longer a child!" Lady Caroline pouted with her chin high in the air, adding for dramatic effect, "I am a woman."

"Ha! You're a child until I say otherwise."

Lady Caroline rolled her eyes and crossed her arms, not at all intimidated, nor did she seem to think he meant what he said. Jane had to admire her pluck.

"You're as beastly and as prejudiced as Tony," Lady Caroline said without heat, which surprised and alerted Jane, who expected a tearful tantrum at the very least. "Just because Beresford is a penniless war hero, you dismiss him out of hand. And it's not as if you know him. He only moved into the neighborhood two years ago."

"Whether I know the Captain or not is inconsequential; more important is that I know *you*," Salt countered and would have said more except for Jane's fingers on his crumpled shirt sleeve.

"Perhaps it would be best to continue this engaging discussion over breakfast?" she suggested quietly at his shoulder and couldn't suppress a shy smile. "You will never win an argument, however sound your case, in your present state of undress."

Her calm reasoning instantly soothed Salt and he smiled down at her before turning back to Lady Caroline with a weary sigh. "Her ladyship is quite right, Caro. This discussion can wait. I'm very pleased to see you here safe. But go to bed and, for God's sake, wake up in the morning with some common sense."

Lady Caroline took the Earl's stern directive in her stride and gave his stubbled cheek a perfunctory kiss. "I've missed you too, glum chops."

"Glum chops? How dare you knock me off my pedestal in front of my wife with that old nursery nick-name," he responded with a huff of embarrassed laughter. "You haven't called me that in years."

"Pedestal?" Lady Caroline frowned in puzzlement at Jane, who couldn't meet her gaze, then said to the Earl with guilty pleasure and a wide, impish grin, "Well, not to your face."

"You little viper!" Salt retorted and pinched her cheek a little too hard, goading her with, "Glum always wins, remember?" before bounding bare-foot up the stairs ahead of her.

Lady Caroline took the bait, and with a squeal of delight turned tail and fled up the staircase after him, pink dressing gown trailing behind like a cloak, nightcap outrageously askew. Salt stopped on the first landing and lay in wait. Jane watched him grab his sister about the waist and effortlessly lift her up and spin her about, she squealing and he laughing, before putting her down, whereupon there was a friendly exchange of words before he kissed her goodnight. Caroline gave Jane a friendly wave over the balustrade before disappearing from view.

Jane came up the wide stairs at a more leisurely pace, clutching the fur-lined cloak tightly about her slim form, mind whirling with possibilities as to how it came to be that the Lady Caroline Sinclair resembled the females of the Allenby family. It certainly made her wonder anew, as she drifted off into a deep sleep snuggled in her husband's arms, at the feud between neighbors merchant and noble, and at the bequest left to Caroline in Jacob Allenby's will.

WHEN SHE WOKE NEXT morning there was only one question about the Lady Caroline Sinclair she wanted answered, but she woke very late and to the novel experience of being alone in her bed. Usually she was up and dressed and ready for the day well before her husband stirred, a consequence of Jacob Allenby's edicts on how she must live while under his protection: Early to bed and early to rise, plain food, few creature comforts and plenty of industry to keep mind and body occupied. A thriving herb and vegetable garden, a storeroom full of jars of pickling and preserves, and enough hard-wearing stockings sewn to warm the legs of an army of poorhouse women were testament to her benefactor.

As she sipped her dish of black tea and nibbled on the dry biscuit Anne customarily left on a silver tray on the bedside table, she had a vague memory of her husband's warmth curled around her in the big four-poster bed, only for him to be up and gone in the next instance, or so it seemed to Jane in her half-waking state: Loud whispered conversation and being told to go back to sleep, and something about a note from Diana St. John and Salt off to South Audley Street to Ron's bedside yet again.

Finishing her tea, and with her nausea more settled, Jane felt better able to face the day, and after washing her face and hands with the tepid water in the porcelain bowl beside her bed, she went through to the dressing room in search of her maid to help her bathe and dress for the day. What she found was the startling sight of Sir Antony sprawled out on the chaise longue by the French windows, a silken arm across his face to shield his eyes from the light, and with Viscount Fourpaws curled up asleep on his stomach. He was dressed in the rich clothes and powdered wig he had worn the night before to the Richmond Ball. Given the crumpled state of his cravat, the deep creases to his black silk breeches, and the fact he was unshaven, Jane knew he had not been to bed since leaving the ball.

Taking his presence in the second most intimate of her rooms in her stride, she threw an embroidered silk dressing gown over her thin nightshift and sat before her dressing table looking glass to brush her waist-length hair free of tangles. She wondered if Sir Antony was asleep and guessed he was not. That he was spread-eagled across the chaise longue and avoiding daylight simply meant that he had drunk too much the night before, and this, coupled with lack of sleep, had given him an excruciating headache. She knew this to be so when the silver-backed hairbrush caught on a knot in her hair and fell with a clatter amongst the clutter on the dressing table. Sir Antony's body convulsed, sending the kitten fleeing to the safety of Jane's lap.

He groaned loudly and shifted amongst the cushions to sit up, wig outrageously askew. It was an effort and when he was upright he leaned his elbows on his knees and put his unshaven face in his hands, feeling bilious. Finally, he managed to lift his head and smile weakly.

"You see me at my most damnable, my lady. I can sink no lower," he announced. "Forgive me, but I had nowhere to go. Well, nowhere else I preferred to lay my weary and battle-scarred carcass."

"You could do with a dish of black tea," Jane said cheerfully and rang the little handbell on her dressing table that summoned her maid. "It helps me better able to face the day when I am feeling green."

"I doubt it will help me. I am not green. I am purple, yellow and puce, a sort of slime. But I am willing to try anything, particularly if it has the power to restore my dignity."

Anne came and went, and if Jane had not been attending to Sir Antony she would have detained Anne because the woman was miserable. Her face was blotchy and she kept her eyes lowered. That her maid's misery was compounded by the fact her mistress was entertaining a man other than her husband in her rooms never occurred to Jane.

"The tea has helped, thank you," Sir Antony said gratefully, balancing the delicate porcelain dish and saucer on his silken knee.

Feeling more himself, he noticed Jane for the first time. His unshaven cheeks burned hot and his mouth went dry finding her sitting before the looking glass in a flimsy silk dressing gown with her thick, raven-black hair tumbled to her waist; a delectably arousing sight normally reserved for a husband's eyes only. He put his thudding head in his hand and felt an even greater fool. He would never be offered another diplomatic posting, least of all rise to ambassadorial rank, if he didn't pull himself together, mentally as well as physically.

But he wouldn't even get a Channel crossing if he didn't make it through the day without Salt discovering him in the Countess's dressing room. He shouldn't have invited himself in, but he felt he had to see her. Hers was the voice of calm reason, and he needed calmness and reason in his life at that very moment. He certainly couldn't speak to Salt about his sister Caroline's shock announce-

ment she was engaged to be married. He knew Jane would under-
stand. Yet, when Jane made a light remark about the Lady
Caroline, he forgot he was on the brink of being called out by the
Earl for matrimonial trespass and ground his teeth.

"I was introduced to Lady Caroline earlier this morning," Jane
announced casually, brushing her hair forward over one shoulder
in preparation for braiding. "You were quite right. I liked her on
sight. She's full of life and, it would seem, surprises."

"Surprises be damned!" Sir Antony growled. "She has the
nerve to send round a note to the Richmond turnout telling me
she's in London and to come at once, which I did. Throws herself
in my arms telling me how much she's missed me, then announces
in the next breath that Captain Bossy Boots Beresford has asked
her to marry him!"

"And you took the news badly?"

"Of course I took the news badly!"

"And you permitted Caroline to see that you took the news
badly?"

"I told her precisely what I thought of such an intemperate
match—"

"She would have enjoyed that," Jane murmured.

"—and what I thought of her so-called suitor."

"Even better."

"I ask you: The man has a limp, a war injury from the
Hanover campaign, and struts about the county—if one can limp
and strut at the same time—six years after he was pensioned off,
still playing the war hero!" Sir Antony retorted, frustrated rage
making him oblivious to Jane's pointed remarks. "He has less than
two thousand a year to live on, with only limited prospects of
inheriting a very healthy aunt's modest estate in Somerset, if and
when she drops off the mortal coil, which won't be any decade
soon. Caroline is worth in excess of fifty thousand pounds, and
lives in a Jacobean palace a Continental prince wouldn't turn his
nose up at. Whatever she asks for, Salt provides. Her idea of
economy is to buy only two-dozen pairs of new silk stockings on
any given day instead of three! Does that sound like a match made
in heaven?"

Jane hid her smile and said calmly in mid-brushstroke, "But, as you said yourself, she does love dogs and horses and mucking about the farm. That would seem to suit Captain Beresford?"

"Of course it suits Beresford, but what he fails to understand is that once Caroline turns eighteen and is launched into her first Season, dogs, and horses and farm muck don't stand a chance!"

"But if they are in love..."

Sir Antony was instantly on his feet. The empty dish and its saucer balanced precariously on his silken knee crashed to the floor and smashed unnoticed. Viscount Fourpaws sprang from the comfort and warmth of Jane's lap and beat a retreat into the next room to take refuge amongst the bank of feather pillows on the big four-poster bed, his usual resting place.

"In love? She isn't in love with him!"

"No, she isn't in love with him," Jane agreed.

Sir Antony's anger burst like a soap bubble. Totally deflated, he sat down, blinking. "She isn't?"

Jane wondered at the workings of the male mind. She did not have to wonder about Caroline's thought processes. She reasoned the girl was young after all, and if anything like Jane's stepmother, the only other female Allenby of Jane's acquaintance, then she would have woken up this morning very proud of herself for the damage she had wrought the night before. She had gained her objectives. She had discovered the true nature of Sir Antony's feelings for her, and the Earl had flatly refused her engagement to Captain Beresford. Jane did not doubt the existence of the good Captain, or the fact he might have designs on marrying an heiress, he may even have feelings for Caroline, but she doubted very much if he had asked her to marry him. And if he had, then he truly was a fortune hunter and Salt would deal with him very swiftly.

"How do you know she isn't in love with Beresford?" Sir Antony asked in wonderment. "You only met for the first time last night." When Jane smiled and continued brushing her hair, he perched forward on the chaise longue and said hopefully, "She confided in you. She's had second thoughts about the Captain."

"No. As you said, I only met her for the first time last evening. Naturally, Salt was furious and told her in no uncertain terms that he would not countenance a union with the Captain. Caroline took this in her stride and wasn't to be dissuaded."

"As only she would! But if she isn't in love with Beresford, why is she putting me through this-this *torture?*"

So much for Sir Antony calmly telling her he would wait until Caroline had had her Season before declaring himself. Jane smiled to herself. Poor Tony, he had best take himself off to St. Petersburg, or ask Caroline to marry him immediately, or develop an armor-plated sensibility to see him through Caroline's flirtatious Season amongst the young bloods and fortune hunters who would court her. She would surely flaunt each and every one of her suitors in his face, all to get his reaction. And if he did react, then woe betide him ever gaining the upper hand in that union.

"She is trying to force your hand, Tony," Jane said simply. "And by informing Salt of the Captain's intentions, she is ensuring that when you do get up the courage to ask Salt, he will be heartily relieved that his sister is to have a husband that is acceptable to him, and not a social pariah. Of course, if Caroline were truly in love with the Captain I don't think Salt would be too concerned about the man's measly two thousand a year. Being generous and devoted to Caroline, he would provide them with a house and sundry other comforts that Caroline cannot live without, if she were to marry a war hero of modest income."

Sir Antony wasn't so certain but he lost his mulish look. "You think?"

"I think," Jane said brightly. She turned away from the looking glass to face him. "Unfortunately, your angry reaction to her news means you've played into her hands."

"Scheming baggage!" Sir Antony grumbled good-naturedly. "I should've had my eyes open! But I was so happy to see her after all these months that it never occurred to me she would ill-use me in that way." He grinned and shook his head. "Thinking about it, she's had months to plan her campaign, hasn't she? I suppose I ought to be flattered."

Jane laughed behind her hand. "Very flattered. And the situation is not unsalvageable. To my mind, you can do one of two things: If you are set on marrying Caroline, immediately declare yourself and hope that Salt will acquiesce, given Caroline hasn't had her Season; or, if you are still uncertain about making a commitment until she's had her Season, to satisfy yourself that she knows in her own mind that it is with you she wishes to spend the rest of her life, then you must coolly accept her plans to marry the Captain."

Sir Antony pouted. "Must I?"

"Why, of course! On no account must you allow her to see that the Captain bothers you. My guess is, she will keep up the pretense of being in love with the Captain for as long as it takes for you to declare yourself, and if you do not break to her will, she'll give some excuse why the Captain proved unsuitable and move on to another wholly unacceptable marriage proposal. All to wear you thin."

Sir Antony rubbed his unshaven chin and smiled ruefully. "I'm feeling rather thin now…"

"You may have to accept a posting to Stockholm to distance yourself from her teasing," Jane ended with an encouraging smile, Sir Antony looking as ill as she felt when she'd woken up. "Of course, if you do decide to run off to the Continent, you will have Salt on your conscience. The poor man will be left alone to deal with Caroline's hordes of admirers."

"Oh, I shan't feel guilty. Why should I when he has you? You'll provide him with all the support he needs to get him through the whole unpleasant business of launching Caroline on an unsuspecting society."

Jane turned away, a blush to her cheeks, and searched for a silk ribbon amongst the clutter on her dressing table. Unable to find one, she fiddled unnecessarily with several jars, saying hesitantly, "He… He may have to cope without me… I-I may be indisposed…"

"Egad! I'm an unthinking ass," Sir Antony responded and dropped to his silken knees beside the dressing table at her feet. "Of course! The baby! Your confinement will be around the time the Season begins, won't it? Diana told me," he confessed when Jane's blue eyes widened in surprise. "I have no idea how she found out, but she knows, and now so do I." He smiled ruefully. "It's not my place to ask, and you don't have to answer me, but why, my dear, haven't you shared this momentous news with

Salt? He'll be beside himself with joy to know he is to be a father."

Jane gazed at her hands clasped in her lap. "He doesn't believe in miracles."

"Miracles?"

"You may recall that ten years ago Salt had a rather nasty riding accident that left him bedridden and in a great deal of pain. The bruises and severe swelling to his—to a particular part of his—"

"I remember," Sir Antony cut in to save her any further embarrassment. "In fact, my eyes are watering in sympathy. Any man's would."

Jane nodded, grateful for his interruption and continued.

"You may also recall that the physicians who attended him at that time advised that as a consequence of the-the injuries sustained, it was unlikely he would father a child."

"Did they? Bunch of charlatans! What would they know?" Sir Antony replied with an encouraging smile. "Well, obviously not much because they've been proved wrong. If I was Salt I'd have the wholly jolly lot of 'em struck off the medical register for being quacks and frauds. He could do it too, y'know."

This did force a laugh from her. "You make it sound so simple."

Impulsively, Sir Antony caught at one of her hands. "It is simple," he said gently. "When two people are deeply in love, miracles can and do happen. And if he doesn't believe that," he added in a rallying tone, and at Jane's watery smile kissed her hand, "then he doesn't deserve you! He must have gruel for brains!"

"Or no brain at all," drawled the Earl.

Jane snatched back her hand and shot up off the dressing stool, mortified. It was the way her husband was regarding her with a steady, unblinking gaze, a gaze that shifted momentarily to Sir Antony, who had overbalanced with shock and fallen back against the chaise longue, an arm stuck out to grope the silk cushions to keep himself upright.

Jane wondered how long Salt had been leaning in the doorway and guessed, by his readily given quip, he had just walked in on

Sir Antony's final undiplomatic pronouncement. He had come from his apartments, having bathed, shaved and changed into a chinoiserie frock coat that matched the magnificence of his Richmond Ball dress. For all his outward appearance of the noble courtier, there was a dullness to his brown eyes as they continued to regard Jane steadily, and his gaunt, tired expression suggested that what he needed was not another day of political machinations but a good night's unbroken sleep.

Jane finally stepped forward, worry about Ron outweighing any feelings of embarrassment she had at being caught in *déshabillé* in her dressing room with her husband's best friend. "How is Ron? Were you able to settle him?"

"Salt!" Sir Antony suddenly blurted out in the silence.

"Do get up, Tony," the Earl responded flatly, coming further into the room as Sir Antony scrambled to his feet and set his wig to rights, then stood to attention like a naughty schoolboy. He addressed his wife. "Ron was sleeping peacefully when I left him tucked up in bed just a little after sunrise. I promised that if he is very much better this afternoon, he and Merry can stay the night in the nursery. They are both looking forward to seeing Caro."

"What? Ron was ill *again*?" Sir Antony blurted out. "Egad! That's two nights in a row! No wonder you look fagged to death." He glanced from Salt to Jane and back again, all embarrassment at being caught trespassing in the most private of the Countess's rooms extinguished with his concern for his nephew. "Salt, you really must put a stop to Diana's nonsense, or I will. If you don't believe what I told you in the carriage about your happiness and—"

"I believe you."

"—Diana's petty jealous anger and Ron's illness—Oh! You do?"

"Yes. I merely had to have the blindfold removed to see what's been going on, for which I thank you—and my wife."

Jane touched the Earl's embroidered upturned cuff. "You have taken the matter in hand?"

"Yes," he responded, but said no more because he was not to be diverted from his displeasure at Sir Antony's trespass. His gaze flickered from his wife's state of undress to the broken dish and saucer by the chaise longue, and then fixed on his best friend. That he chose to deliver Sir Antony a short, sharp dressing down in the French tongue signaled to Jane that he was not only furious, but had no wish to sully her ears with his derogatory vitriol. The contrition on Sir Antony's face confirmed her suspicions.

"You have the damned *idiocy*, no, ill-mannered *selfishness*, to invade these private rooms unshaven and still in your ball costume, and I am no longer left wondering why the latest *filth* circulating drawing rooms has it that you are *tupping* my wife?"

"Salt, I—"

The Earl raised an imperious hand. "*Je ne veux pas t'écouter.*"

"But—*Parbleu!* You must listen to what I have to say! It isn't what you think! I was only—"

"You are not privy to my thoughts. *Va-t-en!*"

Sir Antony bravely drew himself up and looked the Earl between the eyes. It was an unnerving and unpleasant experience for a young man who worshipped his mentor. He openly eyeballed him nonetheless. "The reason I came uninvited and unwanted here is because I needed—"

"Your needs are supremely unimportant to me at this moment," Salt interrupted, and continued in English, a glance at Jane to see if she was attending. "If you think I don't know you got yourself pickled last night, all because of Caro's absurd announcement and, feeling sorry for yourself, came here seeking my wife's sympathy for your pathetic behavior, then it is you who have gruel for brains. You will go to Arlington Street, get yourself together, change into something befitting a man who has aspirations to strut the diplomatic stage in St. Petersburg, and be back here in my bookroom within the hour to meet with Count Vorontsov. His Excellency has condescendingly permitted you an hour of his precious time. Now get out and allow me a moment's peace with her ladyship."

"He really was in a dreadful state of anxiety," Jane said in defense of Sir Antony when left alone with the Earl.

"That's no excuse for his ungentlemanly conduct," he said, a pointed stare at her free-flowing hair, brown-eyed gaze dipping to her breasts and fixing on her bare toes. His eyes came back up to her flushed face. "When I am not here, her ladyship's maid should be with her at all times. I had presumed Willis had given the Countess the lecture on what rooms of her apartments are public and those that are strictly private, off-limits to everyone except her husband. I won't have my wife the subject of servant gossip."

"And what about me, my lord?" Jane asked, chin up.

Salt frowned. "I am talking about you."

"No. You are talking *at* me, as if I am someone quite removed from this poor creature that is gossiped about by servants. Although… I don't know what the servants could possibly find to gossip about the Countess of Salt Hendon that would outshine the Earl's performance last night. He makes love to his wife in his carriage, carries her indoors, both of them practically naked, and in full view of his lordship's butler, under-butler and a handful of footmen. Not to mention being caught out in this morally depraved state of undress by a young lady yet to make her come-out. No, I fail to see what the servants could possibly find to gossip about her, when his lordship has provided a surfeit of servant gossip about them both."

This forced a tired laugh from him, and he drew her into his embrace and kissed her forehead.

"Touché, my lady. I can always rely on you to bring the planets back into alignment. But I'm still annoyed at Tony," he added seriously. "I may consider him family, but only I am permitted the arousing sight of you in undress with your hair down your back."

Jane blushed and dropped her chin. "Is that what you said to him in French?" she asked shyly. "Poor Tony was in such a state over Caroline's teasing pronouncement that she is engaged to Captain Beresford."

He sighed his annoyance and took Sir Antony's place on the chaise longue, avoiding the broken tea dish and saucer, and drew Jane to sit beside him. "I really do wonder at Tony's ability to withstand the rigors of diplomatic life abroad if he can't put two coherent sentences together in my company when I'm displeased with him. I'm told he's a very competent and astute politician, and I do trust his judgment, but…"

"It's that pedestal," she replied, snuggling up to him. "You need to let him see that you can climb down off it from time to time. When you're displeased you could intimidate the Sun King. And your nostrils quivered."

"Did they?" Salt laughed with genuine good humor. "Poor Tony. But if he thinks, after all these years, I don't know he is wig-over-toes in love with Caro, then he truly does have gruel between his ears!"

"What are you going to do about it?"

Salt smiled slyly and stifled a yawn. "What any good parent worth his coin would do. Let him sweat it out for as long as it takes him to get up the courage to approach me. Besides, I want Caro to have a Season and receive at least a dozen inappropriate marriage proposals before she settles on Tony."

"How cruel, but how utterly fatherly of you!"

He looked down at her hand in his and played with her fingers, saying quietly, "You have a hundred questions for me about Caro, don't you?"

A hundred questions Jane certainly had. But there was only one question concerning the Lady Caroline Sinclair that was uppermost in her mind. As always she took the direct approach.

"Whose child is she, Magnus?"

FIFTEEN

J ANE'S QUESTION ELICITED an embarrassed laugh, but the
Earl was not smiling.

"As always, Lady Salt, you are woefully frank."

"There is no other way of asking, is there?"

"God help me when Caro has her come-out," he responded,
continuing to avoid the question. "I'm dreading that day's arrival.
She'll have ten suitors on her hook by the end of the first week."

"Your apprehension is only natural. Any parent of a girl of
marriageable age must feel the same way," she answered matter-of-
factly, ignoring his equivocation for the time being. "Parents want
their daughters to travel down the right path to matrimony, to
find an eligible gentleman of the same social standing. But such
eligibility does not necessarily mean a happy marriage, does it?
Those parents who truly care for their daughter's happiness give
equal weight to the suitability of the husband, as well as to his
eligibility, don't they?"

"Yes. I want Caro to make a suitable match, but equally I want
her to be happy," he answered quietly, still playing with her
fingers. He looked into her eyes. "Not an aspiration your father
had for you, was it?"

Jane smiled ruefully, face hot with embarrassment for a father
for whom she had been a sad disappointment.

"True. My personal happiness was never a consideration for Sir Felix. But in those few moments I spent in your sister's company, it is evident your relationship with Caroline is very different from the one I had with my father," she continued, determined not to be diverted from her original question. "I would never have dared call my father *glum chops* in that playful way, in any way. Nor would he have responded by chasing me up the stairs in an equally playful manner." Her brow furrowed. "I don't understand why I see the resemblance between Caroline and the Allenbys when others do not, but perhaps it is because I have lived amongst them for most of my life. Caroline and my stepmother could be mistaken for mother and daughter."

Salt let go of her hand. "Caro is nothing like Rachel!"

Jane smiled.

"Now who needs spectacles of comprehension, my lord? I was not referring to my stepmother's lax morals or her need to have her beauty constantly praised. You may think me quite depraved for thinking so, but it is my belief that had my father not been a-a drunk and been more attentive to his wife's needs... For all her vanity and silliness, my stepmother did love my father..." She paused and swallowed and bravely went on under his unblinking gaze. "If he'd paid more attention to her in the bedchamber, I doubt she'd have gone elsewhere."

"My dear Lady Salt," the Earl said with mock indignation. "You shock me. When did you reach this most startling conclusion?"

Jane lowered her gaze. "Since our wedding night," she confessed. "I enjoy making love with you because you have made it enjoyable for me." She smiled up at him from under her long lashes, saying demurely, "You know full well you have thoroughly ruined me, my lord."

Salt's eyebrows drew sharply over the bridge of his long thin nose, Jane's compliment evoking an echo of her words that first night together as man and wife, words he now realized he in his guilt had totally misconstrued. His face grew hot. "Ruined? *Spoiled. Indulged.* That's what you mean," he said gruffly, shame making him sound harsh.

"Yes. Yes, of course," she replied with a start, wondering why he was suddenly ill at ease by her honest confession about his prowess as a lover. She impulsively kissed his cheek. "It was a compliment, silly. Now tell me about Caroline—"

"Jane, I—"

"—and her connection to the Allenbys."

"No one sees what you see because it is too fantastical to be believed. The Allenbys and the Sinclairs have not spoken or socialized these past eighteen years, despite living on neighboring estates. Yet, Caro's resemblance to the Allenbys is strong enough that Tony, who met your stepmother on only one occasion, asked me if he had met her before. Who could have foreseen at her birth that she would take after the Allenbys in form and the Sinclairs in coloring?"

"That doesn't answer the question."

"No. It doesn't. Do you want to hazard a guess?"

Jane shook her mane of hair. "No, because the answer I give might be the right one, and I don't want it to be true. And because it is a sordid tale, and not one either family is proud to own, is it? Caroline's true birth has been concealed to protect her, perhaps her parents, too, and thus she has been presented to the world as your sister."

The Earl smiled crookedly and pulled a lock of his wife's hair. "Not too wide of the mark, my clever girl."

"Jacob Allenby had two female relatives," she said, mind ticking over with possibilities and arithmetical equations. "There was Rachel, my stepmother, Jacob Allenby's sister, but given Caroline is almost eighteen and eighteen years ago Rachel was already married to my father. There would be no need for her to give up a child had she been unfaithful, because she could easily have passed it off as belonging to her husband. And then there was Jacob Allenby's only daughter Abby—Abigail—but she died of consumption when just fifteen years old..." Jane frowned and softly bit her lower lip in thought. "Unless your father was a complete reprobate, I cannot imagine he seduced Abigail..."

"My father was a proud, cold man but a reprobate he was not. He married late in life to a young wife, which was not exceptional amongst his peers, but he was devoted to my mother, which was unusual. Ah, here is your morning chocolate, my lady."

Jane's maid came through from the dressing room carrying a tray which had upon it a brandy for his lordship and a mug of hot chocolate and a couple of dry biscuits on a plate for her ladyship. She silently placed the tray on the table by the sofa, bobbed a curtsy, quickly scooped up the smashed pieces of tea dish and saucer and scurried away.

Salt gratefully savored his brandy, a questioning eyebrow lifted at Jane as she nibbled on a dry biscuit.

"If this is how you sustain yourself, you will fade away. If you're hungry, what you need is a good wedge of venison pie or big bowl of pea soup. Not a few crumbs on a plate."

"Oh, please, no! Just the thought of pea soup makes *me* green," Jane pleaded. She warmed her hands about the mug of hot chocolate, unsure if the beverage would make her ill or not. She didn't much feel like drinking milk. Another dish of black tea with a slice of lemon was what she craved. But the biscuits were welcome. Suddenly she was struck with the most awful thought. Looking at the Earl, she could barely speak. "Not-not Jacob Allenby and-and your *mother*…"

Again he laughed out loud. "You have the most refreshingly wicked thoughts, my darling!" He shook his head. "Most definitely *not* my mother." He put aside the brandy, took the mug of chocolate from her hands and set it aside too, then possessed himself of both her hands. His gaze never left her blue eyes.

"Abigail Allenby was Caro's mother. Abby, St. John and I were all just fifteen when Caro was conceived. Just children ourselves… Before the rift, before Caro's conception, when St. John and I came home from Eton for the holidays, we would roam the countryside: St. John and myself, Abby and a couple of the younger village girls and boys, much like Robin Hood's merry band. Tony was too young and Diana too Lady High-and-Mighty, even at that young age, to lower herself to muck about in haylofts and up trees. She teased St. John and me mercilessly about our preference for the company of tenant farmers' brats and children from the local village. She was forever finding excuses to rat on us to my father.

The Sinclairs and the Allenbys would not have mixed in the same social circles in London or Bath, or Bristol for that matter, but in the country, as you know, it is quite usual for county families high and low to socialize at local events, the hunt, fairs and the like."

"Is-is that where Caroline was conceived—in a hayloft?"

His smile was grim. "And here was I wondering how best to tell you! I guess that's where it happened. I don't rightly know. The last time St. John and I saw Abby was just before we returned to Eton at Michaelmas. She must have been at least three, perhaps four months pregnant then, but she didn't say a word to us. At Christmastime, Father came up to London without my mother, with the startling news I had a baby sister. St. John and I didn't think anything of it, boys don't, but then… My father thrashed me within an inch of my life for bringing the family name into disrepute. He never laid a hand on St. John. He never did.

"St. John was not the most robust of fellows. So I took the whipping for both of us. I didn't mind. It was possibly worse for St. John because my father made him watch while I was flayed. I suppose Father expected a confession. Neither of us said a word because we didn't know what we had done to enrage him. Well, I certainly had no idea then. Father left St. John to deal with my bruised and bloodied carcass, and with the crude pronouncement that I could sow as many wild oats as I pleased with any whore that took my fancy, but be damned if he was going to shelter any more ill-begotten bastards."

"And Abby? What of her? Did she die of consumption?"

Salt smiled crookedly and looked down at Jane's soft hands in his.

"Abby turned to your stepmother, her aunt, for help when she realized she was pregnant. Jacob Allenby ordered Abby to say nothing about the child until a date had been set for the wedding." Salt gave a huff of angry embarrassment. "Rachel and Jacob Allenby used Abby's pregnancy and the threat of exposure to force my father to agree to a hasty marriage between us. They had no idea whom they were dealing with. Father didn't take kindly to threats. He threw Allenby out of his house and off his lands."

"And Abby? What happened to Abby?"

"What do you think a toad like Jacob Allenby did with an unmarried daughter who was with child? Conscienceless prig disowned her! What use was she to him when the Earl of Salt Hendon refused to make an honorable woman of her by marrying her into his family? He cast her out of the family home to fend for herself. She, a gently-bred young girl of fifteen with nowhere to turn! She went to her aunt, hoping she would take her in. Not your stepmother! Lady Despard also turned her back on the poor girl. Abby ended up on our doorstep. Against my father's orders, my mother took her in and cared for her. Abby died three days after Caro's birth. Needless to say it was my mother's idea to make Caro my sister. I don't know how she won over my father to her scheme, but she did."

Jane dropped her gaze to their hands, to his long, tapered fingers with their perfectly manicured nails, and she knew she was crying. She could not stop. She was crying for Abby, and for Caroline because she had never known her real mother, and for herself, because she wished she had had someone as kind and as understanding as Salt's mother to take her in and protect her and her unborn child when she had found herself pregnant four years ago. Never in her wildest imaginings did she think her father would have her unborn child destroyed.

Before she realized what was happening, she was in Salt's arms and he was tenderly wiping her face dry of tears with his white handkerchief. But she didn't want him to hold her at that moment. She wasn't sure how she felt about his affair with Abby Allenby and the part he had played in keeping from Caroline her true parentage. So she pulled out of his embrace and took the handkerchief to wipe her flushed face dry before staring at him resolutely.

"Did you never think that the child growing up as your sister might not be your sister at all? Didn't you think to do the sums? Did you never wonder why Caroline had the coloring of a Sinclair but the looks of an Allenby?"

"No," he answered simply. "Why would it occur to me?"

"I should hazard a guess that the possibility of impregnating your lovers has never occurred to you!"

"Jane, I do not understand why you are upsetting yourself over this. I grant the tale is a sordid one and Abby's death a tragedy, but Caro has never suffered for being my sister, ever. My mother loved her as her own. I love her as any brother would love his sister. She wants for nothing. God, even Jacob Allenby showed he had a conscience in the end when he had the audacity to leave his only grandchild ten thousand pounds in his will; the dowry he had stripped from Abby when he disowned her.

"Believe me or not, but I was five-and-twenty before I figured out for myself that Caro was not my sister. I'd come down to Salt Hall for Caro's ninth birthday. She was running up the drive to greet me, as she always did, with her arms outstretched, playing at being a swallow or robin red breast or some such bird that had taken her fancy at the time. Her copper curls were bouncing about her thin shoulders and she was so happy to see me. And then it hit me, literally in the chest. The breath was knocked out of me. She was the likeness of Abigail Allenby. And then I knew: My parents were not Caroline's parents. Abby was Caro's mother." He gently touched Jane's hair. "I just want you to understand—"

She shifted out of his reach, along the chaise longue, not wanting the touch of him, white handkerchief twisted up in her hands. "What? That you learned your lesson with Abby Allenby's ruin? That you took the advice your father beat into you and henceforth confined your whoring to women of your own class and paid courtesans who knew how to keep themselves from falling with your bastards?" She gave a little sob that broke in the middle. "How ironic that the one and only other time you allowed lust to rule good sense you again impregnated a gently-bred girl from the counties! Though you quickly came to your noble senses. You weren't fifteen anymore and you were the Earl, and once returned to London and your life here, Wiltshire could well have been the Americas for all you cared, so it would have been easy to forget me—"

He came to life at that. He had been staring hard at her, trying to make sense of her emotionally charged denunciation, knowing she was overreacting but not knowing why. She was so pale and shivered in the thin chemise and dressing gown that he wondered if she had caught a chill the night before from the breeze blowing off the icy waters of the Thames. He heard her accuse him of not only impregnating Abigail Allenby, but also impregnating her, and it was such an astonishing accusation that he was incapable of absorbing it there and then. So he seized on the one fact he could deal with and his anger extinguished all thoughts and consideration for her welfare.

"For God's sake, Jane!" he growled in frustration. "Abby wasn't the Allenby I was rutting in that hayloft. It was your bloody stepmother Rachel!" He gave a huff of embarrassment as he took a turn about the room, stopped at the fireplace and set another log atop the burning embers for want of something to cover his mortification at blurting out such a confession. "Truth told, Abby wasn't the only one to lose her innocence in that hayloft…"

There was a long awkward silence between them; the only sound, the spit and hiss of coals as the fire leapt into new life. Jane stood beside him and lifted her palms to the radiant warmth. She stated what he had not.

"St. John is Caroline's father."

"Yes." He looked down at her then. His smile was sad. "As a boy, St. John had a mop of red curls. Caroline has such a mop… She has his eyes."

"Did he know he had a daughter?"

"Like I did, he figured it out for himself much later. We made a promise never to tell anyone, never to tell Caroline. Now I have told you."

Jane nodded, as if it did not need to be said that she too would never divulge Caroline's paternity.

"So my stepmother knew you were not Caroline's father, and yet she colluded with Jacob Allenby to try and force your father to have you marry Abby?"

"Yes."

"And when that scheme did not work out, she and Allenby disowned Abby?"

"Yes."

"I do not wonder why you detest her. Poor Abby."

She saw Salt give a start and turn his shoulder, and realized they were not alone, that her maid stood in the doorway, eyes downcast.

"What is it, Anne?"

"Lady Sedley's carriage will be here on the hour, my lady."

"Oh!" Jane turned to the Earl. "I must bathe and dress or I will be late for our excursion to the Strand. Lady Elisabeth is taking me to view the Society's picture exhibition. She tells me I must see *The Death of General Wolfe*, a piece by a new painter George—George Rom-Rom*ney*, as she thinks him such a prodigiously fine master of the brush and that I should sit for him." When her husband frowned she added with a frown of her own, "Surely you cannot object to your wife being seen in the company of a married daughter of your political rival? After all, wives and daughters are above petty politics, surely?"

Salt inclined his head. "As to that, my wife is certainly above anything petty."

Jane blushed at the compliment, adding with a smile as she sat before her looking glass and began to brush her hair, "I am told in confidence that Lord Bute is tired unto death of the slights against him, when all he wants is what is best for the King—" She paused at Salt's huff of disbelief "—and what is best for the country. Elisabeth believes it to be so, and who am I to disabuse her? She is loyal to her father, which is as it should be. Caroline would defend you to her dying breath, would she not?"

"Just so, my lady."

"Elisabeth also confided that her father is done with politics. Lord Bute means to resign all his commissions come April."

Salt lifted his brows in surprise. "Is that so, my lady? Then you have managed to discover what I and others on both sides of the political fence have been trying to do for months."

Jane stopped in mid-brushstroke and smiled sweetly at his reflection. "Perhaps his lordship should spend more time in the nursery."

He pulled aside the weight of hair from her neck and stooped to kiss her nape, murmuring, "Believe me, Jane, I would like nothing better in this world than to spend my time with you in the nursery."

Jane decided the moment had come to tell him about their

baby, and was about to do so when she caught sight of her maid's reflection in the looking glass. Anne was still standing behind them, nervously wringing her hands and looking miserable. She was staring at the Earl, and although her mouth was moving as if in speech, no words were audible. Jane realized she was rehearsing a monologue, so turned on her dressing stool, a warning glance up at her husband.

Salt beckoned the woman forward, wondering what his wife's maid could possibly have to say to him that could not be discussed with his butler or his housekeeper, or with her mistress the Countess.

"My lord, I must speak with you," Anne announced nervously and bobbed a curtsy before launching headlong into her speech for fear that if she drew breath, or looked up into the Earl's face again, she would lose her way and not be able to deliver her very important message. The fear that Lady St. John was, at any moment, on her way to Grosvenor Square to find out if she had carried out her orders made her resolute. She could not take another interrogation by that evil woman, and as she had not administered the contents of the small bottle to the Countess's dish of tea as ordered, but given it unopened to Mr. Willis, Anne knew the time to act was now.

"My lord, Mr. Willis craved an audience with you today and was told by Mr. Ellis that there was no possibility of Mr. Willis being admitted to your lordship's bookroom, because your lordship had a prior engagement with the Russian ambassador, and then her ladyship's brother, Mr. Allenby, is to come to play at tennis and to stay to dinner. And what with the Lady Caroline come to stay so unexpectedly, and putting the servants in a minor commotion on account of finding places for the Wiltshire servants, Mr. Ellis advised Mr. Willis to take the matter to Mr. Jenkins, who as butler is the right and proper person to be admitted to your lordship's bookroom to discuss servant matters. But as Mr. Willis explained to Mr. Ellis, the matter was not only urgent but was most certainly not for the ears of Mr. Jenkins or, for that matter, any servants' ears, but only for your lordship's ears.

"Whereupon Mr. Ellis ordered Mr. Willis to tell him his business. Mr. Willis resolutely refused to do such a thing because, with all due respect to Mr. Ellis's position as your lordship's secretary, to divulge the matter to Mr. Ellis or any other person save your lordship, would not be right and proper on account of the matter being of such a *particularly* delicate nature. So you see, my lord, it is very, *very* important that Mr. Willis speaks with you *today*."

Anne loudly drew breath and bobbed another curtsy, and dared to bravely look up into the handsome impassive face above her before dropping her gaze again, wringing her hands and with her heart beating so hard against her ribs that the blood drummed in her ears. She wondered if it was a flicker of a smile the Earl displayed, or the beginnings of a frown; either way, she had managed to get his attention, which was all that mattered.

"Well—Anne," Salt replied, a quick glance over at Jane to see if he had correctly remembered the woman's name, "if Willis is of the opinion that the matter is of such a *particularly* delicate nature that it cannot be dealt with by Jenkins or Mr. Ellis but is for my ears only, and that the matter is of some urgency, then see Willis I must. Be good enough to tell Willis to present himself at my bookroom at once, before the Russian ambassador arrives, and he will find me alone and at leisure to speak with him."

Anne bobbed another curtsy, but she was far from happy with this outcome. She glanced anxiously at the Countess, then raised her eyes to the Earl. Her throat was dry from extreme nervousness, making her voice rasping and halting. "With the utmost respect, my lord, what you suggest is not possible. For you see, my lord, Mr. Willis *always* accompanies her ladyship everywhere whenever her ladyship ventures from the house unattended. That is to say that whenever your lordship is not with her ladyship, or Sir Antony is not with her ladyship, then Mr. Willis is-is *duty bound* to attend on her ladyship."

"Willis's loyalty is to be commended. However, I am confident upon this occasion that her ladyship will spare Willis—"

"No! Please, my lord, *no*. You cannot make Mr. Willis *choose*. He must do his duty by her ladyship and especially at this *most* particular time…" She dared not look at the Countess and kept her gaze on the Earl. "By doing his duty to her ladyship, he does his duty to you, my lord."

Salt was stunned by such abruptness in a servant that he

almost reeled back in shock. However, he managed to reply very quietly, "Have Willis present himself at my bookroom before dinner. He will find me there alone. Now off you go," he added uncomfortably and when the maid had scurried away into the closet to gather together her mistress's clothes for the outing, turned on Jane. "Good Lord! I've never heard such a tumble of words, and said with such sternness, from a maidservant. I don't see why you should have a giggle at my expense at the recalcitrance of your maid!"

"Climbing down off your pedestal wasn't that difficult, was it?"

"Difficult?" he replied, nostrils aquiver, trying his best to look offended. Yet, he couldn't stop a lopsided grin. "Not if you are there to catch me should I have the misfortune to take a tumble from such a lofty height."

She smiled at his reflection. "Always."

"Then you had best come to the tennis court when you return from viewing pictures. Tom is sure to beat me at my own game, given I have had less than three hours sleep in the past twenty-four."

But it wasn't Tom who next knocked the Earl from the dizzying heights of his noble plinth; it was his discarded mistress, Elizabeth, Lady Outram, come to call on the young Countess of Salt Hendon to open her eyes to the veracity of life as the wife of a lothario nobleman.

"Mr Wraxton? Mr. Wraxton? Are you awake, sir?"

It was Arthur Ellis and he was gently nudging Hilary Wraxton's Malacca cane with the toe of his shoe, hoping to wake the poet. Hilary's Wraxton's snoring was so loud that his sonorous nasal blasts reverberated in the cavernous vestibule off the downstairs withdrawing room and out into the expanse of the main entrance hall. Lined with marble statues of Greek gods and Roman emperors, and portraits of long dead noble Sinclairs, the vestibule was not a room in the cozy sense of the word that one would want to curl up in and fall asleep, but more a museum where one sauntered about to view the impressive life-size busts of the Emperor Augustus, Marcus Aurelius and Caesar, or gazed at the Elizabethan and Stuart full-length pictures of previous Earls of Salt Hendon.

The secretary had just come from his employer's bookroom where the Russian ambassador and two of his equerries, Lord Salt, and Sir Antony had been ensconced, speaking in the French tongue for three hours. Mr. Ellis prided himself on his fluency in the French language, after all he had a first in languages from Oxford, but the flow of conversation had tested his linguistic powers and given him the headache. His Excellency the Count had stayed to nuncheon and enjoyed himself so much that he invited his noble host and Sir Antony to dine with him the following week. And to bring the oh-so-vivacious Lady Caroline Sinclair with them, and of course Lady Salt, whose company he had not had the pleasure, although he had the pleasure of an introduction at the Richmond House ball—such astonishing beauty was forever remembered.

Salt had graciously accepted His Excellency's invitation, though privately he was not so certain Caroline would be alive to see the light of another day, he so wanted to strangle the life out of her for coming into the bookroom uninvited. His annoyance was tempered by Sir Antony's acute observation that Caroline's behavior was no less reprehensible than that of his own dear sister Diana, who made it her business to interrupt the Earl's at-home days every Tuesday; and Diana didn't have the excuse of the over-confidence of youth and naivety. And as Count Vorontsov seemed very taken with Caroline's enthusiasm for all things Russian, and the fact she was attentive and laughed very prettily at all His Excellency's long-winded stories, Sir Antony told Salt he really had nothing to complain about. To which the Earl wanted to retort that love was blind and the sooner Sir Antony ordered Caroline to stop encouraging the attentions of Captain Big-Boots Beresford, married her, and swept her off to St. Petersburg, the better for his peace of mind.

Peace of mind.

That's what he craved most these days. The thought of the Easter break and taking Jane and the children to Wiltshire to muck about on the estate occupied his thoughts. As the butler and two footmen helped the Count with his sword and sash and into his mink-lined greatcoat, Sir Antony was having a last word with one of the Russian equerries. Salt nodded distractedly when Sir Antony mentioned he was taking Caroline for a turn about the park for some fresh air before dinner. He came out of his abstraction when he saw his secretary disappear into the vestibule, from where emanated the discordant sounds of what could only be described as a muffled bugle, but was in fact heavy snoring.

"Salt! Good! Wanted a word," Hilary Wraxton announced, wide-awake and staring beyond the secretary at the Earl who strode into the vestibule with a quick look around. "Here! You! Be useful. Hold this," he ordered the secretary and pushed his Malacca cane onto Arthur Ellis. From an inner pocket of his blue watered-silk waistcoat he produced a thick sheaf of small parchment squares tied up with a pink ribbon. "Poems for her ladyship. One a week for a year," he announced proudly and held them out to the Earl. "Would have penned more; no time. Pascoe says I can write more from Paris and Venice and Constantinople, if we get that far."

"Thank you, Hilary," the Earl said placidly, accepting the wad of poetical writings and instantly handing them off to his secretary. "Why must her ladyship have one a week?"

"She looks forward to my recitals. Told me so. I admit reading 'em herself ain't the same as me reading 'em to her, but she'll just have to bear up under the disappointment."

Salt suppressed a grin. "Yes. She will be disappointed. Paris. Venice. Constantinople?"

"Pascoe is taking me, well *us*. Actually, come to think on it," he mused with a frown, as if the idea had just popped into his head, "I invited myself. Lizzie don't mind. Says I'll be company for Pascoe when she's sleeping. Sleeps a lot, Lizzie. Dare say that's the price of fading beauty: Beauty sleep at two in the afternoon. You know the type, Salt. Pascoe's turn to put up with her." He gave a sudden snort of laughter that startled the secretary into dropping the Malacca cane, and it clattered loudly on the marble floor. "Sporting of you to let Pascoe have her all to himself. Between us, he's always been ears over toes for Lizzie; wouldn't let on to you. Not while you and she were—*you know*…"

The Earl wondered if Hilary Wraxton was being more obtuse than usual or whether it was just overtiredness on his part that made the poet's conversation even more unfathomable. But mention of Lizzie and Pascoe in the same breath and Salt realized the poet was talking about Elizabeth, Lady Outram, whom he had not thought about since he left her drawing room in Half Moon Street the day before his marriage to Jane three months ago; it could well have been another lifetime.

"When do you leave for the Continent, Hilary?"

The poet jerked his powdered head at the closed double doors leading into the blue withdrawing room, where stood two liveried footmen. "Any moment I shouldn't wonder. Coach loaded up with portmanteaux; horses hitched for Dover. No sooner had I made my bow to Lady Salt than Pascoe shoves me out here to kick me heels with the cold marble so she can have a private word with her ladyship. What about is anybody's guess. Females!"

"My lord," Arthur Ellis interrupted, "there is the tennis match… Mr. Allenby arrived some thirty minutes ago. Jenkins sent him directly to the tennis court…"

"Thank you, Arthur. Who is having a private word with Lady Salt?"

The poet seemed not to hear the question because he had suddenly noticed that Arthur Ellis was holding tight to his Malacca cane and grabbed it from him with a scowl, as if the secretary had meant to keep it. "Gift from Pascoe. Can't have it. He'll have my guts for garters."

"Wraxton! Who is with Lady Salt?" the Earl demanded, though he had a fair idea who it was, he just didn't want to believe the woman had the audacity to come to the house he shared with his wife, and that Pascoe had allowed it. Worse, that she had come with the specific intention of speaking to his bride.

The poet stared at the Earl as if he was the village idiot.

"Lizzie. Lizzie Outram. You *knew* her before Pascoe. Remember? Salt?"

But the Earl was not attending him. In five strides he was at the double doors. In three more he was inside the room unannounced. Standing by the fireplace was Pascoe, Lord Church, and a few feet away, by the arrangement of chairs, the under-butler

Willis, grim-faced and with his hands behind his back. And there, standing by the striped sofa was his forsaken mistress Elizabeth, Lady Outram, in *tête-à-tête* with his wife. Both women looked about at the sudden intrusion; Elizabeth Outram to drop into a respectful curtsy, Jane to regard her husband with a tremulous smile and a deep blush to her throat and cheeks that sent his heart racing and his mind reeling.

SIXTEEN

AN HOUR EARLIER, while the Earl was ensconced in his bookroom discussing the terms of the Peace and Continental politics, the Countess had returned from the Strand to the news that Pascoe, Lord Church, and his shadow Hilary Wraxton had come to call on her and were waiting patiently in the downstairs blue withdrawing room. It had been suggested by Jenkins that the guests return on a more suitable day, but as the butler pointed out to Willis, who had come in off the square behind the Countess and her maid, the gentlemen were adamant that no other day would do; they were departing for foreign climes almost at once.

Willis would have excused himself to prepare for his meeting with his lordship, but when Jenkins added that there was a third occupant in the withdrawing room, and she a female unknown to any of the servants of his lordship's household, but on sight looked an interesting individual, Willis was alerted. *Interesting* in the butler's vocabulary meant highly unsuitable company for the young Countess, and so exchanging a worried glance with Anne, Willis decided that it was in the best interests of the House of Sinclair to follow the Countess into the room. He made a lame excuse about having left the Countess's appointment diary, of which he was keeper, in that very room, and perhaps when the visitors had departed her ladyship would do him the kindness of going over one or two matters that required her urgent attention. Before the Countess could object, her maid piped up with the suggestion that she would bring her ladyship a dish of Bohea tea with a slice of lemon.

Jane had had such an enjoyable afternoon strolling the picture exhibition with Elisabeth Sedley that she was determined the rest of the day would continue the same way. Even the inquisitive Society patrons, who jostled with one another to catch a glimpse of the beautiful Countess of Salt Hendon in the flesh, and whose closeness of perfume and pomade caused her morning sickness to be more acute, could not dampen her spirits. She had been grateful for the presence of Willis and Anne, for though they were distracted with one another (being on an outing together was truly a novelty), Willis always had one eye on the Countess and her comfort. So it was not in Jane's nature to deflate the man's concern by fobbing him off. She graciously accepted him at his word, though she found his excuse flimsy in the extreme, because she had a deep suspicion Anne had confided her pregnancy to Rufus Willis and that her condition had brought out the man's protective instincts; he had become her self-appointed guardian angel.

It was in this capacity the under-butler entered the room, took a swift look about, and seeing a couple by the French window with its view of the expansive square, took up a position by the clavichord which was left of center to the room. As the Countess came across the parquetry the couple moved towards her, and they all met on the deep Aubusson rug under the chandelier. Pascoe, Lord Church, in jockey boots and a traveling frock coat of brown velvet, bowed over Jane's outstretched hand and then introduced Lady Outram, who curtsied to rank.

Jane smiled at them both, only briefly allowing her gaze to linger on Pascoe Church's companion and her striped petticoats and bodice of Florentine apple-green and cherry-red silk that showed her ample breasts to best advantage. Carefully-applied cosmetics made it difficult to determine her age, though she was not in the first flush of youth. That said, she was still a very beautiful woman who knew her own worth and expected others to know it too.

"May I offer you tea?" Jane asked, indicating the arrangement of sofas by the fireplace. She sat and the couple did likewise, side-by-side on the sofa opposite her. "I have been standing all morning looking at the most wonderful pictures and now my feet demand I rest. If you do not want tea, I can send for coffee?"

"Thank you, my lady," replied Elizabeth Outram. "A dish of Bohea would be most welcome before our journey."

"We are on our way to Dover," Pascoe Church offered, "and then on to Paris. Hilary and I could not quit London without taking our leave of you, and I insisted Lizzie make your acquaintance. As to when we will return to England..." He shrugged and looked at his female companion. "We may settle in Florence for a time."

"Church has a cousin at the Embassy there," Lady Outram offered. "But we mean to marry in Paris."

"Oh! How delightful!" Jane said with genuine pleasure. "I do wish you both health and happiness. But I fear I do not have your talent for gift-giving, Lord Church, so you will have to settle for a Sèvres tea service or a piece of silverware."

Pascoe Church was suitably contrite. "As to that, my lady, I fear my jest was in very poor taste, and had I known you better *then*, I would never have sent—"

"I will not allow you to take back your gift. Viscount Fourpaws is very much part of the family. Ron and Merry St. John look forward to their visits with his fluffy lordship, and spoil him with all manner of morsels from the kitchen. Why, even Salt has grown accustomed to Fourpaws, for he tolerates him to curl up at the foot of our bed in the morning—"

"Tea, my lady!"

It was Willis and he had rudely cut off the Countess mid-sentence, judging the run of conversation too personal for present company, but in so doing, drawing attention to the comfortable intimacy between the Countess and her noble husband. If she realized her social faux pas, Jane kept it to herself, and while doing the honors with the silver teapot and chinoiserie porcelain tea dishes, made polite conversation about the couple's travel plans. She was, however, acutely aware of the intense scrutiny of her female guest.

The woman said very little, allowing Pascoe Church to talk freely while she sipped at her tea and appraised the young

Countess over the rim of her delicate dish. Always abreast of the latest fashions, be it in fabric, style or cut of the cloth, Elizabeth Outram judged Jane's pretty silk petticoats with delicate fruits of the vine embroidery to be not overtly ostentatious of wealth, position or power, yet the richness of the embroidery and the way the day-gown was molded to the Countess's lithe frame spoke volumes about the expertise of her dressmakers. She wore no jewelry about her throat or from her small ears, yet none was necessary for such unblemished skin. Her only adornments were a bejeweled wedding band and a pale yellow silk riband threaded through her upswept glossy black hair.

For the wife of one of the richest noblemen in the country and thus with access to all manner of extravagant fabrics, gowns and jewelry, the Countess was self-restraint personified. But it was not only her choice of attire that intrigued Elizabeth Outram but the young woman herself.

She observed that Jane sat with back straight and hands lightly in her lap; that her head tilted ever so slightly to the left when listening; that her blue eyes were kind and her smile genuine; that despite her youth, she was self-possessed; that she exhibited genuine interest and truly enjoyed their company. Indeed, there was no artifice in her manner whatsoever. Yet, what surprised Elizabeth most was that the young Countess was precisely as Pascoe had described—beautiful inside and out.

If she were to find fault, it was with Lady Salt's mouth. Despite being full and ruby red, her top lip was too short and her bottom lip too full so that when she wasn't smiling she appeared to be always pouting. But to men, one man in particular, such a mouth would be intoxicatingly inviting. Elizabeth Outram well understood why the Earl demanded nothing less than this mouth to kiss.

Tea savored and drained, Pascoe Church's female companion placed the delicate dish on its little saucer and put both on the low walnut side table to unfurl her fan and flutter air across her breasts. She had come to a decision, and turned to Pascoe to make a request when a barely visible servant door cut into the wallpaper beside the fireplace squeaked opened and a powdered head appeared, diverting the tea drinkers in the direction of the fireplace.

"*Pssst.* Pascoe! I found one!"

It was Hilary Wraxton and he climbed out of the servant corridor, leaving wide the door so that the dark narrow passage and the stairs beyond were on public view. He tottered across to the sofas in his heels, brushing down the sleeves of his silk frock coat, with his powdered head bent forward to check that the four horn buttons to the fall of his breeches were done up. Willis immediately crossed behind the poet to close the servant door and received a scold for his tractable efficiency.

"Oi! Not so fast! Not so fast! Lord Church may want use of the pot! It's a long way to Dover, my man. A long way indeed."

Pascoe Church rolled his eyes and by a lift of his brows let it to be known to Willis that he was to close the servant door.

"I don't know why you would not wait, Hilary," Pascoe complained. "It's not as if we won't stop at an inn along the way."

"An inn?" Hilary Wraxton was horrified. "I can't pee at an inn." He jerked a thumb over his shoulder. "Perfectly good *pot de chambre* in there. Clean. Just how I like 'em."

"Wraxton! Must you?" It was Lady Outram whose face had fired red under her rouge.

"Well, yes, Lizzie, I *must.* Perfectly reasonable. Perfectly natural, a call of nature." Hilary Wraxton made a low bow to Jane, the lace at his wrists sweeping the rug. "Don't you agree, my lady?"

But Jane was giggling behind her fingertips and could not speak, not because of the poet's blunt pronouncements but at the look of horrified embarrassment on the faces of her under-butler and Lord Church.

"How will you travel across the Continent if you cannot make a call of nature when we stop at an inn?" Lady Outram enquired.

The poet, who had perched uninvited on the padded arm of a wingchair, jabbed at his temple. "Up here for thinking, Lizzie. I am not just a man of letters, but of ideas." He beamed at the Countess and said confidentially, "Had my man pack the family *pot de chambre.* Heirloom. Passed down from father to son since Scottish James sat upon the English throne. Painted with the family crest. *On the inside.*"

"How-how *sensible* of you, Mr. Wraxton," Jane managed to reply, finding her breath and dabbing at her damp eyes. "A definite must for a trip to the Continent. Who knows what amenities are to be found, or not, at a foreign inn."

"Attend, Lizzie! Pascoe! Her ladyship understands. Knew you would, my lady."

"Please, my lady, I beg you not to encourage him," Pascoe Church complained good-naturedly.

"Oh dear. Mr. Willis's frown tells me that I am in his bad book for finding humor in Mr. Wraxton's candid conversation," Jane confided. "Forgive me, Lady Outram. I am still quite new to my role and Mr. Willis is helping me to behave as I ought. But to own to a truth, if I am not myself, I find I make an even bigger muddle of my elevation."

"What did I tell you, Lizzie; breath of fresh air," the poet stated, as if Elizabeth Outram had ever doubted his word. "And what did Pascoe tell you? What!" He put his closed fist to his left breast and with his eyes to the ornate plastered ceiling sighed dramatically. "Her ladyship's sweet nature makes her beautiful *inside* and out."

Again Jane giggled, but this time she managed to say with a grave face, "How will I survive my days without your devotion and your poetry, Mr. Wraxton?"

The poet's gaze came down from the ceiling and he plunged a hand into the pocket of his frock coat and struggled to remove a wad of parchment tied up with ribbon. "See, Pascoe! I told you she would not be able to—"

"Enough, Hilary," Lord Church said stridently and pushed the wad of parchments back into his friend's pocket, Willis a step behind him should he require assistance. He took his friend by the elbow. "Time to make your farewell bow to Lady Salt."

Elaborate leave-taking exchanged, the two gentlemen visitors disappeared out into the marble gallery, the poet heard loudly to complain that he had left the best bit 'til last and it was all Pascoe's fault he was not able to execute his grand finale. Lady Outram remained, suggesting to the young Countess that they take a turn about the long rectangular room so that she could stretch her legs before the long carriage journey to Dover. They set off arm-in-arm, leaving Willis to stoke the fire to new life, a troubled eye on her ladyship.

"I am so pleased to have made your acquaintance, my lady," Elizabeth Outram confessed. "When Church first proposed that he bring me to call on you, I was most reluctant for reasons that will become apparent when you know who I am, or more precisely *who I was*. Church is the dearest of gentlemen, and I am very fortunate he wishes to marry me despite my *interesting* past. He has always maintained he loved me, but I dismissed such talk as a lover's throw-away compliment. But since Lord Salt gave me my liberty, I've had these past three months to devote myself singularly to Church, and we both came to the realization that we suit each other very well, very well indeed. Oh dear, I have shocked you."

"No. Well, *yes*," Jane admitted with a shy smile as they paused by a floor-to-ceiling mirrored wall opposite the French windows. "But, please, do not think I have taken offence. It's just that I lived a sheltered life in the countryside before coming to London to marry his lordship; though not so sheltered that I am unaware there are ladies who take lovers; just as gentlemen take mistresses." She was puzzled. "But I own to being a little simple because I do not understand when you say Lord Salt gave you your-your *liberty*?"

"I was your husband's mistress."

It was a straightforward response but totally unexpected, and it stopped Jane's breathing. In fact, for the briefest of moments, she forgot where she was. She just knew she had to remain calm; she must not react. She gazed over Lady Outram's left shoulder, across the room to the undraped French windows, having no wish to look at the woman beside her. She did not realize that only a few feet away Willis was hovering by the clavichord. He had followed them up the room and had pretended an interest in tidying the sheets of music on the padded clavichord stool.

Willis saw the Countess take a deep breath, and place a hand lightly to the base of her throat. That small movement brought him closer, close enough to notice signs of her acute embarrassment; across her décolletage and halfway up her throat the porcelain skin was stained with smudges of strawberry. Two sentences into Lady Outram's continued conversation and he knew the reason behind the Countess's silent distress.

"I was wretched when Salt ended our agreeable connection. What mistress wouldn't be when her most talented lover announces he is to marry? Not that he showed me a singular devotion. Jenny, Susannah *and* Eliza were just as devastated to learn of his plans. But we never thought he would marry." Lady Outram mistook Jane's silence as a sign for her to continue. She took Jane's arm and resumed their leisurely stroll of the perimeter of the decorative room. "I had every expectation of keeping his interest for at least another Season, so naturally I was the one to be most offended when he came to take his leave. Of course, I had not seen you *then*, or knew the first thing about you to make me believe Salt's marriage was anything but a contractual arrangement to beget an heir. It seemed perfectly sensible that we should be able to continue our-our *understanding*. Many a nobleman has married with no thought of giving up his mistress. Why should they? Wives are for breeding. A mistress knows how to pleasure a lover."

Elizabeth Outram glanced at her silent walking companion who stared straight ahead, saw the stain of deep color across her décolletage and reasoned it was only natural for a young bride to be uncomfortable by such candid conversation. Yet, it did not stop her forging ahead, her voice a little softer than before, but still loud enough to be heard by Willis, who was just one stride behind, ears burning brightly.

"But Church cured me of my petulance and misguided belief. Darling man. He said it was perfectly reasonable for a woman to be both wife and mistress if her husband loved her. That's when I decided to marry him. It was only when Church told me your Christian name that I was able to make sense of Salt's *particular* behavior. And that's when I knew I had to see you before our travels."

Jane finally found her voice.

"My—*name?*"

"Most certainly. Knowing your name answered everything."

"Did-did it?"

Lady Outram patted Jane's silken arm. "I fear I am about to truly test your fortitude, my lady, but you must believe me when I tell you that my confidences are for the greater good. They will help ease your mind so that you need never have a single doubt about your noble husband." She glanced slyly at Jane. "You may have come from the depths of Wiltshire, but even there I am confident Lord Salt's reputation with the fairer sex was well-known…" This was met with silence but when the red stain rushed up into the Countess's cheeks, Elizabeth Outram smiled to herself and continued. "Of course, you must not breathe a word of what I am about to confide in you to anyone, particularly not his lordship. Church remains ignorant, which is how it should be, so it is very important that it stays between us."

Jane slowly nodded her assent with a mixture of stomach-churning aversion and ghoulish anticipation as to what this woman could possibly add to her revelations that would be more outrageous than what she had already confided.

"When I reflect upon it," Elizabeth Outram ruminated matter-of-factly, fluttering fan coming to rest momentarily across her ample bosom, "it is quite humiliating to my self-worth to realize that while I was *entertaining* Salt his mind was elsewhere. To be precise, his *mind* was on someone else. As a young bride, I have no doubts that Salt has been a most attentive husband in the bedchamber so that you are now aware of his considerable abilities between the sheets. His stamina and *consideration* for a lady's pleasure—"

"My lady, *please*." Jane's voice was barely above a whisper.

How this woman, this former mistress of the Earl, thought her revelations were for the greater good, Jane could not fathom. It was one thing to know Salt kept a mistress, indeed had women flocking to take on such a role, and to tease him about the conse-quences of such philandering, and quite something altogether abhorrent to come face-to-face in her own home with a past mistress intent on sharing confidences about the Earl's prowess as a lover.

Her immediate thought was that Diana St. John had somehow convinced this woman to seek her out in the malicious hope of making mischief. Yet as soon as Jane had this thought she dismissed it because she genuinely liked Lord Church, and she could not imagine he would be involved in any scheme to upset her. And as he was to marry her husband's former mistress, Jane decided that whatever confidences Elizabeth Outram wished to share with her were meant, despite their shocking nature, with the best of intentions. So despite her desire to run from the room with her fingers in her ears, Jane remained outwardly perfectly composed and inwardly trembling with trepidation.

"His stamina and *consideration* for a lady's pleasure has rightly bestowed upon him the reputation of a consummate lover," Lady Outram continued smoothly as if Jane had not uttered a syllable. "And as a married woman you cannot be ignorant of a particular moment while making love when a man is at his most *vulnerable*. If he utters anything intelligible it affords a rare glimpse of his innermost feelings. And at the *crucial moment*, Salt was never with me, he was with *Jane*. He was with *you*. It's *always* been you…"

Jane did not trust herself to speak. She was in equal measure utterly appalled and strangely reassured. Such was her distress that in her distraction she was unaware they had traversed the entire room and returned to the fireplace, where Pascoe Church had been warming his hands for ten minutes and pretending an interest in the little leaping flames.

Lady Outram signaled playfully with her fan to her betrothed, who raised his quizzing glass in acknowledgement, and disentangled her arm from Jane's so she could stand before her.

"You do love him, don't you?" she asked rhetorically.

Jane finally looked the woman full in the face. "With all my heart."

Elizabeth Outram smiled. "Church said you did. He said he knew it the first time he saw you in Salt's company." She rested her fan lightly against her pointed chin and regarded Jane pensively. "The first and only time *I* saw you in each other's company was at the Richmond Ball. It was obvious to all—indeed it was *the* topic of conversation for the evening that the Salt marriage was not a marriage of convenience as was first supposed. And then we saw you from the terrace while we were watching the skyrockets. You could've been anywhere—sitting on the moon, much you both cared for anything or anyone but each other! He was kissing you on the mouth and in full view of the world. That's when we all knew."

"Knew?"

"That he loves you so very much."

"My Lady?"

It was the Earl, and he stood just inside the blue withdrawing room, the liveried footmen holding wide the double doors to reveal Hilary Wraxton conversing with Mr. Ellis in the marble gallery beyond.

"My lord! You are just in time," Jane responded, coming to life on a quick breath. With a welcoming smile she swept up to her husband. "I'm so glad you've come."

Salt's concern deepened into a frown seeing the deep blush to his wife's cheeks and throat. "Is—Are you—Is everything—"

"I have been wishing Lord and Lady Church a safe journey," Jane interrupted conversationally, eager to relieve him of any anxiety he felt on her part. "Well, they soon will be lord *and* lady," she confided in an under-voice in response to his startled glance, and continued in a neutral tone loud enough for all to hear, "They are off to the Continent with Mr. Wraxton. Paris is their first destination, to be married by a priest, and then on to Florence for their honeymoon where Lord Church has a cousin at the consulate."

The tension in the Earl's wide shoulders eased. He bowed civilly to Lady Outram as one does to an acquaintance, but was able to smile at Lord Church with a raise of one mobile eyebrow. "A papist ceremony, Pascoe?"

Lord Church shrugged and was sheepish. "Churches have remained loyal to Rome since Bonnie Prince Charlie crossed o'the water. Don't tell me you didn't know?"

"I did. And it doesn't alter our unique friendship," said Salt, another glance at Lady Outram. "Nothing will. I wish you both very happy."

Lord Church bowed with a flourish of his lace-covered wrist as the Countess and Lady Outram swept out of the room before them. He came to stand beside the Earl, who was looking at the Countess as she conversed with Hilary Wraxton, who was bowing over her outstretched hand. He plastered his quizzing glass to one eye, as if to better view his friend's wife, and could not resist a parting shot at her noble husband.

"You don't deserve her, Salt, but she is very deserving of you. *Au revoir, mon ami.*"

TOM AND THE EARL WERE seated in their shirtsleeves and tennis breeches, damp backs against the wall, recovering breath and strength, and drinking a well-earned ale after an enjoyable and hard-fought contest on the Royal Tennis Court. Tom decided there was no better time to broach the subject of his stepsister's present and future happiness. The large nobleman was tired but relaxed and not at all annoyed with him for his drunken outburst at the Richmond Ball. Still, he decided to ease into voicing his concerns by first announcing that he had finally decided on the perfect wedding gift for the couple.

"It came to me the other week," Tom told Salt. "I'd been wracking my brains to think of a suitable gift for someone who has everything he'll ever want or need, and that would also appeal to Jane. And then I had it—"

"There really is no need…"

"—the cottage. The cottage Jane lived in while under my uncle's protection. Jane had a miserable time there and you must loathe the very sight of the place too. So I'm having it torn down and moved brick by brick further up the valley, closer to Allanvale. Once it's remodeled and added upon, it will make a dower house for my mother. If ever she gets to live in it." Tom rolled his eyes and gave an embarrassed half-smile. "I have a suspicion she won't long be Lady Despard. She'll be remarried by Christmastime, and to some aging fop who has gout but is generous with leaving the purse strings untied. I've no objection. I just want her to be happy. As I want Jane to be happy. I told the workmen to have it leveled before you take Jane to Salt Hall at Easter time."

"Thank you. That truly is the best wedding present you could give us. You're the best of brothers, Tom Allenby," the Earl said simply and stuck out his hand, adding with a smile as they warmly shook hands, "You must have been a comfort to your sister while she lived under your uncle's protection."

"Me? Egad! I wish! If that's what you think, then my suspicions are well and truly confirmed. Jane hasn't told you about her life, if you can call it that, in that house, has she?" Tom asked rhetorically. "Just like Jane to keep it to herself, for fear of distressing you..."

"Go on. Don't spare my feelings."

"The first year Jane spent under Uncle Jacob's roof, he wouldn't allow me—*anyone*—to visit the cottage. And then when he did grant me permission, my visits were supervised and only allowed four times a year. Seeing her in those plain gowns, with her head covered, eating sop and with no pictures on the wall, and my uncle preaching his sermons about sins of the flesh and vanity and greed and eternal damnation and the like, it burned me up, never mind going to hell. To my mind that was hell on earth for a young beautiful girl who had the world at her feet one minute and no expectation of a happy life the next. Don't think me anything but God-fearing, but my uncle was a zealot of the fire-and-brimstone school of paying one's dues to the Almighty, and he was hell-bent on making Jane pay for her sins."

He stopped to down the last of the ale in his tumbler, an eye on the Earl, who had pulled his damp shoulder-length hair out of his eyes and was frowning quizzically at him as if he had not the slightest idea what Tom was talking about. It made Tom blurt out belligerently,

"I may have needed a goodly quantity of claret to confront you last night, my lord, but I don't this afternoon. So I'll just say my piece, before Jane gets here, because I don't want her distressed or to feel the slightest embarrassment. What I have to say ain't pleasant. But I'm thinkin' you've been enough in her company, have formed a high regard for the sweet-natured loving creature she is, that what I tell you won't matter a jot now. Do I make myself plain, my lord?"

"I understand you don't want to upset her so I suggest you just come out and say it."

"All right. I will!" Tom announced and swallowed because the

Earl's quiet voice was much more menacing than if he had shouted at him. He took a deep breath and launched into his speech.

"It may come as a complete surprise to you, living as you do surrounded by sycophants and toadies and painted females, who have the *appearance* of beauty but scratch the surface and they're rotten, rotten to the core. Jane is as good-hearted as she is beautiful, and nothing my uncle or her father or you say can make me see her differently!"

"I agree, and if you would allow me to tell you how much she—"

"And if she's forgiven you for breaking off the engagement—"

"Stop there, Tom Allenby!" the Earl growled and sat up. "I am utterly sick of being accused of breach of promise. I will say to you what I have said to your sister many times over: I did not break off our engagement, nor did I write a letter to that effect. A letter that now mysteriously no longer exists because it did not exist in the first place!"

Tom stuck out his chin. "Yes it does, my lord!"

"It's Salt, Tom. Call me Salt. You are Jane's brother and thus my brother-in-law."

This somewhat deflated Tom's belligerency yet he managed to put enough firmness in his voice to say flatly, "It does exist because I have it."

"I beg your pardon?"

"With your seal upon it too!"

Salt was incredulous. "In my handwriting?"

"I don't know what your writing looks like, but Uncle Jacob assured me the letter was genuine. He gave it into my safekeeping on his deathbed."

Salt was skeptical. "And you have this infamous letter here?"

"Not on me," Tom said defensively. "But I can have it fetched from Upper Brooke Street."

"If you would."

"Consider it fetched! In fact, I've been wondering what to do with it ever since Uncle Jacob left it to me. You're welcome to it!" Tom threw at him, unsure what made his blood boil more, the Earl's raised eyebrows of incredulity, or the fact the nobleman's noble nostrils quivered with distaste that Tom had had the bad manners to contradict him. It gave him the impetus he needed to vent his feelings on the subject of his stepsister's happiness.

"I'd prefer the wretched piece of paper be turned to ash, for all the grief it's caused Jane. I'm certain she would like nothing better than to forget the existence of that letter and its consequences. In fact, I'll lay you odds she forgave you years ago, because that's the sort of girl she is. But it stands to reason you should be just as fair and not hold one tiny mistake against her. Mistakes happen and no one can foresee at the time that an error of judgment will have such far-reaching consequences. She certainly didn't. How could she?

"It was her eighteenth birthday and she was an innocent. God knows why it's up to the weaker sex to protect their virtue and fend off the unwanted attentions of a pack of lecherous dogs. Jane never asked or sought out such attention! She wasn't old enough or wise enough to know any better. Her father sent her off to your Hunt Ball without a chaperone and without any cautionary warnings about the roués on the prowl for a bit of vulgar velvet at such functions. And I wasn't there to protect her. I should have been there to protect her!"

"It's all right, Tom," Salt said, a gentle squeeze of the young man's shoulder when he bowed his head and turned away to dash a sleeve across his flushed face. "No one can blame you for what occurred. You're absolutely right. Errors of judgment do happen. I asked your sister to marry me at that Hunt Ball and she accepted, and that should've been enough. But I lost my head in the moment and..." He frowned self-consciously, murmuring, "Well, it seems the rest you know..."

Tom gave a huff of impatience.

"Jane doesn't know that I know and she'd be mortified if she ever found out I did. She likes to think of me as her little brother, and that's fine with me if it gives her peace of mind. My mother told me what happened to Jane. I guess she felt I was owed the true explanation for why Jane ended up under my uncle's protection after Sir Felix disowned her. But she only discovered the extent of Jane's fall from grace after Uncle Jacob's death. Under the terms of his will he charged my mother with a commission to Lady St. John—"

Salt was incredulous. "Diana St. John? What possible commission could your mother have for Lady St. John *from* Jacob Allenby?"

"I don't rightly know. All I do know is that it has everything to do with Jane…"

The Earl's look of utter confusion and frowning silence convinced Tom that his noble brother-in-law was not being duplicitous and so he continued.

"After my mother discharged her commission to Lady St. John, she gave into my safe keeping a document that Jacob Allenby instructed I pass on to you, if and when the need arose."

"And has that need arisen, Tom?"

Tom eyed the Earl with mild hostility. "Yes, my lo—er—Salt, I believe it has. I mean to have that document fetched along with the breach of promise letter. You can do with them as you see fit. My only concern is for Jane. If it's all the same to you, I'd like your word the conversation we are about to have remains between us. Will you give me your hand on it, Salt?"

"Willingly."

The two men shook hands.

Tom's face reddened and he said in a rush to hide his unease, "There was never any likelihood of Jane's fall from grace being linked back to your Hunt Ball. Sir Felix was just as determined as you to keep a lid on any potential scandal. So it was—it was —*cowardly* of you to send Lady St. John along to be satisfied on your behalf that the Sinclair name remained unsullied. That woman should never have been involved in Jane's misery and shame!"

The nobleman balked at the accusation of cowardice, and was instantly furious that this young man had the impudence to level such a serious charge at him. No one had ever spoken to him with such disrespect. But just as quickly, he quelled his temper, remembering the pedestal Jane told him he inhabited. With great self-control he climbed down from his nobility and ignored the sneering insolence in Tom's voice to say evenly,

"I wholeheartedly agree with you. I am at a loss to understand Lady St. John's involvement in my engagement to your sister. As to being a coward… I would never send another on my behalf; and certainly never entrust Lady St. John with any task that involved your sister's welfare. No. Just hear me out and then you can go for my throat if need be.

"The morning after I proposed to your sister I was urgently called away to London. Lord St. John had contracted the smallpox and, after a short illness, died. I had a widow and two small fatherless children thrust upon me, not to mention his affairs to get in order. I'm sure you'd appreciate that what was happening back in Wiltshire was a thousand miles from my thoughts at the time. That's not to say I'd forgotten my obligation to your sister. I had to temper my happiness and delay my future plans until I'd sorted through the grief caused by St. John's death.

"I wrote to Jane explaining my situation but never received a reply to my correspondence. The next I knew, your sister was living under Allenby's roof because her father had disowned her. It still puzzles me to this day why your sister chose Allenby's protection to mine."

"Does it?" Tom gave a dismissive snort. "Does it truly puzzle you? Do you honestly believe Jane had a choice? Your letter breaking off the engagement left her with *none*."

"Don't you see that whoever wrote that despicable breach of promise letter did so to make certain Jane did not seek me out?" Salt replied with great patience. "Believe me, Tom, had I been made aware of her predicament I would have done everything in my power to save her from such ignominy."

Tom eyed him with resentment. His voice was very flat. "You should have thought about the potential for a-a *predicament* before you-you *deflowered* her, my lord." When the nobleman blushed scarlet, Tom had his answer. "No one told me. I worked it out for myself. It wasn't difficult, because I know Jane. And Jane being Jane, she would never have surrendered her virtue to just any man, only to the man she loved above all others."

"Listen, Tom... What happened in the summerhouse—It may present to you, to-to others, to *most* people, as a lascivious nobleman's calculated seduction of an innocent girl; a quick tawdry rut by the lake. But it wasn't like that... *Nothing* could be further from the truth. When—when two people are in love—when they are caught up in the moment, it's as if... They forget everything

else; they forget there may be consequences to their actions...
They... They—God, this is difficult to explain!"

He scowled self-consciously and covered his face with his
hands before drawing his fingers up through his damp tussled hair.
Despite the searing burn of shame to his ears, the dry throat and
the abject chagrin of trying to explain himself to a skeptical audience of one, he met Tom's steady gaze openly and continued,

"You sitting there looking like a stunned trout, worse, like a
son being delivered a lecture on the birds and the bees, when you
know full well how honey is made, doesn't help one's heartfelt
confession. I have nothing to say in my defense that won't make
you think me the veriest cad. But I ask you, no, I *implore* you to
believe me when I say that I have castigated myself a thousand
times over for not having the willpower to wait until we had been
up before a parson. All I can offer in my defense is that I was so in
love with your sister that I did not think; I allowed my heart to
rule my head. I do not ask your forgiveness, just your understanding... Tom? Tom, what is it?"

Tom did not doubt the Earl's sincerity, that he was speaking
from the heart. What astounded him and drained the color from
his face was the fact that the nobleman had no idea, indeed
remained blissfully ignorant of Jane's appalling predicament and
the paramount reason why her father had disowned her. He was so
surprised he just blurted it out with no thought to the effect such
brutal honesty would have on his noble brother-in-law.

"You didn't know Jane was pregnant with your child?"

SEVENTEEN

"*Pregnant? Jane?*"

Tom nodded dumbly in response to the Earl's disbelieving and explosive exclamation.

"My Jane, pregnant? Jane. *Pregnant.*"

Bewildered and disorientated and still muttering to himself, Salt glanced around: From high-racked ceiling to polished tiled floor, to the netting shielding the gallery boxes and out across the expanse of court to the sloping tabor wall. It was as if he had no idea where he was. He stood up; Tom did likewise. He blinked, motionless, as Jane's accusatory words earlier that day screamed in his head… *you allowed lust to rule good sense… you impregnated a gently-bred girl from the counties…* He now understood what she meant and the reason for her tearful distress. Such was the enormity of this new and powerful knowledge that he was seized with an overwhelming panic. He forgot how to breathe.

Tom was transfixed by the intensity in the nobleman's handsome face. It was evident he was experiencing a range of emotions while trying to make sense of such a profound revelation. Yet, Tom was determined, he owed it to his stepsister. No matter how disordered the Earl's state of mind, he would hear the whole sordid story of Jane's fall from grace.

"You ruined her virtue, but to Sir Felix's way of thinking the far greater crime was that his daughter had been impregnated by

an unnamed seducer. Jane would not name you. She kept quiet
—*has* kept quiet all these years. Because of her refusal, Sir Felix
said he had no use for her. He treated Jane as if she was a used,
worthless thing: A-a *whore*. But he treated her unborn babe far, far
worse."

Tom's voice broke on the last word and he took a deep breath
before continuing, following close on the Earl's heels. The
nobleman lurched forward, as if drunk, and staggered up the
court, breathing short and quick, shoulder pressed to the wall to
prop himself up. It was as if he was trying to escape from Tom's
revelations, but Tom would not let him go. He was far from
finished with his lordship.

"Sir Felix said no daughter of his was going to give birth to a
bastard. I asked my mother how Sir Felix discovered Jane was
pregnant." Tom gave a bark of incredulous laughter. "An unsigned
letter! Can you believe it? I hardly credit it possible that some
fiend could betray Jane in that cowardly way. It's wicked! Sir Felix
waved the letter under Jane's nose. She did not lie to her father.
Poor Jane had struggled to keep her condition a secret for as long
as possible. She was waiting for you, *you* to come and fetch her
away and you never did. Your letter breaking off the engagement
had sealed her fate and the fate of her unborn child."

"T-Tom, for *pity's sake*."

But Tom was so overwrought he did not hear the Earl's plea,
nor did it register that the words were rasped out between shallow
breaths. He was blind to the sheen of cold sweat on the nobleman's forehead. He watched without seeing as the nobleman slid
down the wall, legs buckling under him, as if they were no longer
able to support him. All Tom cared about was making the Earl
aware of what Jane had suffered, and that he blamed him just as
much as he blamed Sir Felix and Jacob Allenby for the loss of her
baby.

"She was given a herbal concocted by a squalid apothecary,
tricked into believing it was a medicinal that would help her
morning sickness," he continued, squatting beside the Earl, who
was slumped against the wall. "Poor Jane! She was so trusting of
her nurse that she drank it without complaint, unaware that the
foul tasting brew would quicken her babe before its time. She was

four months pregnant with *your* child, and the next day that child was *dead*. She could've died too. God knows what agony and anguish she endured and all because *you* abandoned her! You promised her *everything* and gave her *nothing*. You... you..."

Tom surrendered to his emotions. Anger spent, and with nothing left to say, he dropped to the tiles beside the traumatized nobleman and hung his head in his hands, oblivious to the Earl's distressed and deteriorated state.

Salt had a fist clenched to his chest where sharp pain would not abate. His breathing was shallow and ragged as if air had been punched from his lungs, leaving him gasping, making it impossible for him to take in air without great effort. Hot and dizzy of mind, heart pounding in his ears, and with his body shivering uncontrollably, day suddenly became night and he lost consciousness.

"My lord? Mr. Allenby?"

The shout came from the other end of the tennis court.

It was Arthur Ellis. He and a liveried footman had entered the Royal Tennis Court at the far end, where abandoned on a bench were a couple of empty ale glasses, two tennis rackets, numerous leather balls and the gentlemen's discarded frock coats. The secretary and servant strode towards the curious sight of Tom Allenby and the Earl slumped against the wall under the high set windows that allowed sunlight to stream across the court. Their stride broke into a trot when it became apparent their master was having difficulty breathing, and then into a run when he passed out.

"Tom? My God, what's happened to his lordship? *Tom?*"

The secretary fell to his stockinged knees beside the Earl and frantically tugged at his master's cravat, unraveling the intricate folds of linen, before moving on to undoing the horn buttons of the damp linen shirtfront.

"Tom, what did you do to him?"

Tom lifted his head, red-faced and glassy-eyed. With a blink he slowly regarded his friend as he ministered to his noble brother-in-law who was out cold next to him. He made no comment and dropped his head.

"Fetch a bottle of brandy and send for a physician!" Arthur Ellis barked out over his shoulder at the hovering footman, who was off running down the court before the secretary had turned to continue his assessment of the Earl's condition.

He reasoned that his master had suffered some sort of paralysis of the heart, and if something wasn't done immediately to wake him up there was every chance he would not make a recover. Arthur knew his employer had had very little sleep the two preceding nights, called out to the bedside of his godson, had spent hours in conference in the French tongue with the Russian ambassador, before a grueling session of Royal Tennis with a young man thirteen years his junior—in Arthur's opinion, a recipe for a heart attack if ever there was one.

The secretary glanced at Tom as he took the nobleman's pulse. "His heart is still working, thank God," he said with an audible sigh. "He may well have just passed out from exhaustion. Tom, what happened, damn it!"

"He suffered a shock," Tom muttered, "and fainted."

"I can bloody well see that! But how—"

"Magnus? *Magnus?*"

The two men turned.

It was the Countess.

She rushed across the tennis court as fast as she could manage in a confection of embroidered petticoats and satin slippers, dropping to the tiles in a billow of layered silk beside her unconscious husband. Ignoring her brother and the secretary, who began to offer garbled explanations, she gathered the Earl up in her embrace, his head in her lap, a hand to his hot damp forehead, then to his flushed cheek, and finally to his cold wrist to feel his pulse, all the time speaking soothing words she hoped would see him open his eyes and look at her.

"Breathe, Magnus. Please breathe," she whispered, smoothing the damp hair off his face and dropping a kiss on his mouth. "Slow, deep breaths. One breath at a time." When his eyelids flickered, she glanced up and stuck out a hand for the tumbler of brandy the footman was nervously pouring out under the secretary's direction. "I have some brandy for you. Just open your eyes and look at me. Good. Keep breathing, slowly. No. Don't try and move; a sip of brandy first. That's good. Slowly. Sip it."

She smiled down at him and kissed him again when he smiled

up at her. She was not smiling when she looked up at her brother and Arthur Ellis and thrust the tumbler back at them.

"Tom? Mr. Ellis? What did you do to him? Couldn't you see he is exhausted? He's been up all night. Mr. Ellis! You should have sent the ambassador away early," she threw at Arthur, and then glared at Tom and back at the secretary before addressing them both. "He needs rest. He needs sleep. You should *not* have played him at tennis, Tom! You're not blind! You could see how he was. You should have declined the invitation. Why are you both standing there gaping at me? Mr. Ellis! Where is his lordship's physician? Tom! Be useful and find Willis and Mr. Jenkins. You," she said, addressing the footman, "find Andrews and have him prepare his lordship's bath. We must get Salt to his rooms where he can be comfortable."

The footman turned and fled. Arthur Ellis stared at Tom. Both men flushed up with guilt, opened their mouths to protest, threw each other a meaningful glance, before staring dumbly down at the engaging sight of the small ferocious kitten-like Countess with the bear-sized Earl in her silken lap. They could find nothing to say in their defense, nor was Tom prepared to elaborate on his discussion with the nobleman. He was about to follow the footman's example, turn tail and flee to do his stepsister's bidding when the Earl spoke.

"Jane?" he said wonderingly, as if seeing her for the first time. "Jane." He lifted a hand to her cheek. "My Jane... Tom isn't to blame. The fault lies with—"

"Oh, hush!" Jane pouted. Seeing a natural even color return to his clean-shaven cheeks she vented her relief as she and Tom helped him to sit up, propping him against the wall. "No, it is *not* Tom's fault, and it is *not* the fault of Mr. Ellis. It is *your* fault, bloody obstinate man! You knew you were worn out when you came home this morning after being with Ron all night, but you foolishly insisted on seeing the Russian ambassador. Tony and His Excellency would have understood and come another day if they knew of your exhaustion. Better they have the hope of seeing you again than for you to-to drop—to drop dead on me! You should have gone back to bed. Instead, your stubborn idiotic pride to do your duty—No!" she said with a sniff and quickly forced the tears to the back of her eyes. "I am *not* crying! I am angry. So—so very, *very* angry with you, Magnus, I could—"

"I love you, Jane."

It was a simple sentence, said simply. She wasn't at all sure he was in his right mind, or that he was restful of body, but it was all she had ever wanted to hear him say in the cold light of day since her eighteenth birthday. She smiled into his tired brown eyes and unconsciously sighed her contentment. Tears ran down her flushed face and she kissed his hand and pressed it to her cheek.

"I love you so very much I *hate you* for frightening me in this way!"

Salt pulled her onto his lap and kissed her, then could not resist rubbing the tip of his long nose against hers. It was a natural, intimate gesture he used when they were alone together, and it never failed to make her heart swell with joy. Yet Jane saw that he was still not entirely himself, and his grave expression gave her pause for thought. Her smile faded.

"Are you perfectly well? Would you care for another drop of brandy?"

He shook his head, distracted, a frown between his brows as he traced her full lower lip with his thumb. "What manner of man must you think me? I've been so manifestly self-absorbed, and you… When I think what you…"

He swallowed hard, closed his eyes and looked away, unable to complete the sentence.

Jane realized that whatever he might say to the contrary, what he needed was rest. She glanced up at her stepbrother, whose gaze had shot to the ceiling rafters the moment the noble couple embraced, while the secretary had turned to the sound of hurried footfall coming across the tennis court. It seemed as if a regiment had been summonsed, but in fact it was his lordship's valet Andrews, followed by the butler, followed by the under-butler, and behind Willis, the Earl's physician, and breathing down Dr. Barlow's back, three burly footmen. All were brought up short by the sight of the Earl seated on the floor with the Countess on his lap. When the physician began rummaging in his doctor's bag, Salt put up a hand to forestall him, and the portly gentleman stepped back in line to wait.

"Ron and Merry will be here on the hour," Salt was saying to Jane, tucking a loose strand of black hair behind her ear. "I want you to keep them with you while I speak to—to their mother. On no account are Ron and Merry to leave this house."

"You are taking the children from her?"

"Yes. It is necessary."

Despite the decision being the right one, Jane was distressed at the thought of Ron and Merry being separated from their mother. "Will they—will they be permitted to see her again?"

"If and when I deem the time is right. And then only under close supervision." When Jane frowned, he added reassuringly, "It is for the best. Ron won't pull through another episode like last night if he remains in her care."

"Her obsession with you has unhinged her, I think."

Salt swallowed, Tom's revelations still painfully raw. "Yes," he said quietly. "More than I could ever possibly have imagined." He kissed her hand and rallied himself sufficiently to force a smile. "I have so much to say to you, but I must put my affairs in order first. They will be resolved today, that I promise you." He flicked her cheek. "Now you must leave me and see to the children."

She nodded, though she was reluctant to leave him. He appeared recovered from his faint, but there was a hardness to his face which still lacked color, and a look in his eye, something akin to sadness, that she could not fathom. He was certainly preoccupied with something or someone. Perhaps it was with Lady St. John and the task of separating her from Ron and Merry. She so wanted to tell him about their baby, but again sensed this was not the moment. She would wait until the evening. Such momentous news deserved to be announced when all other considerations had been dealt with, and it would surely give the children and the family a happier focus.

"What is it, Jane?"

"Nothing that won't keep until this evening."

He helped her to stand.

"Keep? A secret, Jane?"

She shook out her petticoats and smoothed down the sit of her bodice. "Not a secret, a surprise."

He frowned. "I do not like surprises."

She went up on tiptoe and kissed his cheek. "Then you had best be sitting down with a good cup of tea when I tell you."

"Tea, Jane? If I need to be seated, perhaps cognac would better suit the occasion?"

"Yes. Cognac or Champagne. Either would be perfect. Now I will go and make ready for Ron and Merry." She glanced over at the huddle of men who were pretending an interest in their shoe buckles, then looked back at her husband. "You must allow Dr. Barlow to examine you. Play nice. Promise."

At that he laughed and pinched her chin. "Promise."

At the Gallery door she blew him a kiss.

The Countess was barely gone from the tennis court when the Earl turned on Tom.

"I need those documents at once. Don't send a servant. Fetch them yourself. Show no one. Tell no one. Arthur! After you have dealt with the correspondence left on my desk, make yourself useful to her ladyship. On no account is Lady St. John to be admitted to the Countess's sitting room." He waved a finger at the three burly footmen. "Take those three with you. Andrews! Why are you here and not readying my bath? No! Don't speak. Go. Jenkins! Show Dr. Barlow the street.

"My lord! I protest! I must examine you!"

"Don't be absurd. Jenkins?"

The butler had the physician by the elbow.

"But her ladyship entreated that you play ni—"

The Earl took his shoulders off the wall to stand tall. His nostrils quivered. "This is playing nice, Barlow. Good day. Why are you smiling?" he demanded of the under-butler whose gaze immediately dropped to his shoe leather. Salt glanced over the servant's bowed head. Satisfied the dismissed servants were out of hearing range, he returned his attention to Willis. "I have a commission for you. It must be carried out at once and in the utmost secrecy."

"Yes, my lord."

The Earl held the younger man's gaze. Although Willis showed a perfectly neutral expression, his clasped hands would not be still. Salt's lips twitched. "I have not forgotten you are itching to speak with me in confidence. It will have to wait until I have had my bath and you have returned from your errand. Don't go to the book-room. Come up to my private apartments. Andrews will admit you." He had a sudden thought and climbed down off his pedestal. "It can wait, what it is you want to discuss with me, can it, Rufus?"

Willis was so astounded that the Earl knew his Christian name that he nodded dumbly, never mind that what he needed to tell the Earl was a matter of life and death. He reasoned that he had the blue bottle securely locked away in a cabinet and three burly footmen had been sent to guard the Countess's sitting room, and as she would be surrounded by family, her ladyship and her unborn child were safe from any immediate malevolence from the Lady St. John.

"Yes, my lord. Yes, it can wait."

Salt squeezed the under-butler's shoulder. "Good. This is what I want you to do…"

TOM HAD NOT NEEDED a second prompting to do the Earl's bidding. He was off across the tennis court at a run and disappeared through the door at the far end of the Royal Tennis Court into the corridor that connected the Gallery boxes. Here he collided with Diana St. John.

She gave a little start and pulled her petticoats to her to allow Tom to pass. But she did not move aside and blocked his exit. Flustered, she dropped her fan, which Tom retrieved, then made a show of brushing down her petticoats before asking if Tom knew the whereabouts of Lord Salt. She had a most urgent need to see him. It was about her son Ron, and so it was very important his lordship be told at once. Did Mr. Allenby know his direction? None of the servants seemed to have any idea, and as the butler and the under-butler were both missing from their posts, there was not one servant who could oblige her; such a disorderly house-hold. No doubt the young Countess would, in time, fathom the simple intricacies of household management, but it must be such a disruption for Lord Salt, not to mention a nuisance, when his lordship had so many more important matters to occupy his time, running the country for one.

Tom was about to protest and defend his stepsister but decided he did not have the time to waste on this woman, and so his response was blunt and he did not linger.

On his return to Grosvenor Square with the documents safely sequestered in a deep pocket of his frock coat, Tom came to the uneasy realization that Diana St. John had been heading away from the Gallery, not going to the Royal Tennis Court as she had intimated. She must have been secreted in one of the Gallery boxes eavesdropping on the Earl's conversation. Waylaying Tom was a ploy to fluster him from knowing the truth and to gain her time. Once he put the documents safely in the Earl's hands, he resolved to go immediately to Jane's apartments.

Diana St. John got to the Countess first.

WHEN WILLIS WAS SILENTLY USHERED into the warmth and opulent splendor of his master's private apartments, the Earl had discarded his tennis shirt and breeches for clothes more befitting his rank and surroundings. If this noble colossus, dressed in velvet and silver lacings magnificence didn't put the tremble into Willis's knees, then the rigidity in the Earl's handsome features certainly had the ability to turn the under-butler's limbs to frumenty. He also had the distinct impression that whatever the physical malaise his master had suffered on the tennis court, it was now well and truly vanquished. The Earl was again totally in command of his physical and mental faculties. This only increased the under-butler's discomfort. Face-to-face alone with his lordship was a world away from waiting on the young Countess, who not only made him feel at his ease and was open to taking his advice, but also valued his opinion. He felt anything but easy and inclined to confidences with an implacable human edifice that had five hundred years of blue blood pumping through his veins.

His master was preoccupied with reading a document by the light streaming in through an undraped window. So he patiently waited at the edge of the deep carpet and took an interest beyond the cavernous sitting room to the dressing room where the valet was fossicking about an enormous hipbath. Andrews stopped and stared the under-butler up and down with a you're-not-wanted-here, nose-in-the-air raise of his eyebrows that only increased Willis's discomfort. Downstairs, Aloysius Andrews was a force to be reckoned with, and the only servant permitted to do and come and go as he pleased. Still, he had no place overhearing what Willis had to say, and his frowning disapproval was noted by the Earl, who let it be known by a look over his gold-rimmed spectacles that Andrews was to take himself off.

Finally beckoned forward, Willis wondered if his legs would carry him across the room, particularly when at that moment the nobleman tossed the folded document onto a walnut side table with a sharp expletive that made the under-butler wince. His hands were shaking when he placed a leather pouch and a small, fine-necked blue glass bottle on the walnut side table. And when the Earl slipped the pouch into his frock coat pocket without checking its contents, then stared at the blue glass bottle with a significant questioning raise of his eyebrows, Willis audibly gulped.

An hour later, the under-butler emerged from his lordship's private apartments on the brink of nervous collapse. Jenkins, with Andrews at his back, set upon him in the servant passageway, demanding to know by what right Willis had gone behind his back in seeking an audience with their noble employer without his permission. Willis stared at the butler expressionless, white-faced, and thin-lipped. He wiped the beading of sweat from his upper lip but said nothing. When he proceeded to walk off, Jenkins demanded he remain where he was or face instant dismissal for insubordination. Rufus Willis turned, and with a slight bow quietly informed the astonished Mr. Jenkins and the jaw-slackened Andrews that it was quite unnecessary for him to go to so much trouble. He, Willis, no longer held the position of under-butler in this Grosvenor Square mansion; he would be gone by the end of the week. He then turned on a low heel and walked away with as much dignity as he could muster.

~

ARTHUR ELLIS FOUND THE Countess of Salt Hendon in her pretty sitting room curled up with her needlework amongst the cushions in the window seat. The St. John children were playing with Viscount Fourpaws in front of the marble fireplace where radiated the warmth of a roaring fire. The children were laughing and happy, teasing the kitten with a length of ribbon, and the Countess was utterly captivating in a froth of sky-blue satin petticoats that flowed onto the floor, her shiny black hair piled atop her head and threaded with matching sky-blue satin ribbons that were the same color as her lovely eyes.

It was a thoroughly delightful and calm domestic scene, and a welcome change for the secretary after the earlier drama down on the tennis court with his noble master suffering a seizure of some kind followed by his friend Tom Allenby charging into the book-room unannounced, brandishing parchment. When told the Earl was in his private apartments taking a bath and could not be disturbed, Tom winked at him and said his noble brother-in-law would certainly see him, in his bath or no, and dashed off, the secretary's protests falling on deaf ears. And on the way to the Countess's rooms via the servant passage, because it was quicker than taking the main stair and meant there was no likelihood of coming face-to-face with a lingering petitioner or unwanted after-noon guest, he had come upon Rufus Willis being harassed by Mr. Jenkins and Aloysius Andrews. He looked as if he had just been delivered news of his own execution.

What Arthur wanted more than anything was a cup of Bohea tea, a slice of seedy cake, and the Countess to smile upon him reassuringly. She seemed to read his mind because she was regarding him with an understanding smile as he straightened from a weary bow. She offered him a seat on the striped sofa.

"Mr. Ellis! You've come to join us for tea," Jane said with a bright smile, setting aside her needlework but remaining in the window seat. "But I'm afraid you are a little early, or are we late?"

"Ellis is early," Ron announced, flinging the ribbon at his sister because he didn't want to be seen playing with a kitten by one of his uncle's male functionaries—after all he was almost nine years of age—and because it was Merry's turn to amuse Viscount Four-paws. "Besides, we're waiting for Tom Allenby."

"He's promised to tell us all about the manufacture of blue glass," Merry volunteered, scooping the kitten into her arms, "so we'll know all about it when he takes us on a visit of his factories. Have you been to Tom Allenby's factories, Aunt Jane?"

"No, but I should like to. Perhaps we can all go together?" Jane suggested. "Shall you come with us, Mr. Ellis? Or has Tom already taken you to his Bristol manufactories?"

Arthur was slow to respond. In fact, he had not heard a word Jane said. He was staring openly at her. There was something about her today, something he could not quite put his finger on. She was radiant. Yes, that was it. Radiant. She'd had that same radiance four autumns ago when he had visited Tom at Despard Park, around the time of the Salt Hunt Ball.

"It's bad mannered to stare, Ellis," Ron stated flatly, leaning against the window seat close to Jane.

"Everyone stares at Aunt Jane, Ron," Merry responded matter-of-factly. "She doesn't mind. Do you, Aunt Jane?"

"A-apologies, my lady," Arthur stammered. "Tea-tea and c-cake would be most welcome, thank you."

"It's perfectly all right for the unwashed to stare, because they know no better," Ron lectured his sister. "And they aren't ever likely to come across a fairy because they don't own gardens. But it's wrong for servants to stare. Uncle Salt would not like that at all."

"Mr. Ellis is not a servant. He's a *secretary*," Merry corrected her brother.

"Fairy?" Arthur Ellis enquired diffidently, an eye on the Countess. "Whoever said such a thing, Master Ron?"

Ron shrugged a thin shoulder. "Caroline said—"

"—Uncle Salt found Aunt Jane at the bottom of his garden," Merry interrupted, "amongst the flowers. Cousin Caroline said that's where fairies take their tea, made from crushed dandelions, and that Uncle Salt picked Aunt Jane because she was by far the prettiest and nicest fairy he—"

"Don't be a widgeon, Merry! Fairies don't drink tea. They drink…"

Arthur Ellis took the opportunity in the ensuing argument between the twins about tea and fairies, real or imagined, to seek the Countess's attention. "My lady, a word in private, if I may," he asked, a pointed glance at Ron and Merry.

The twins were not so wrapped up in their argument as Arthur Ellis had hoped. The loud chorus of disapproval that greeted his suggestion had Jane up off the window seat and brushing down her petticoats.

"Dear me! What a great noise about very little. No. Stay where you are. The tea things will be here shortly, and so will your Cousin Caroline. Mr. Ellis and I will go through to the dressing room. Besides," she added, picking up a handful of her petticoats and bustling through to her dressing room, "I must find out if Anne has returned. She went on an errand and was away so long I did my own hair. Perhaps she—"

Jane was brought up short in the doorway by the startling sight of her personal maid being stood over by Lady St. John, who had the girl by the upper arm and was giving her a good shake.

"My lady? Why are you in my private rooms?" Jane demanded. "And by what right are you abusing my maid?"

"Your maid, madam, is a thief and a liar," Diana St. John announced. "She stole something from me of great sentimental value, and I want it returned or she'll hang!"

"My lady, I did not steal—"

"*Liar!*"

"Unhand her, my lady," Jane ordered. "It is not your business to seek out my servants and mistreat them, whatever you think they may have done. You come to me with your concerns first."

"Good Lord! Two minutes a countess and you are an authority on how to treat miscreant servants? You really should leave such matters to those who have the experience to deal with the likes of this insolent creature."

"Thank you, but I don't need your advice." Jane led her maid a little way off. "Do you have Lady St. John's property?" she asked gently. "Please, don't cry. I will believe what you tell me, Anne."

That brought Anne's head up and she sniffed. "I did not steal what does not belong to Lady St. John, my lady," she whispered and stared at the Countess meaningfully, a quick glance at Diana

St. John. "Mr. Willis returned the article to his lordship as he was requested to do."

Jane held the maid's gaze. "Returned?" When the maid nodded and lightly placed a hand at the base of her throat, Jane understood. "Thank you, Anne."

"And the blue bottle?" Diana St. John enquired boldly of the maid. "What did you do with the blue bottle?"

Standing behind the Countess, Anne felt brave enough to look Lady St. John in the face. "Mr. Willis has that too, my lady."

Diana St. John took a step forward, teeth and hands clenched. "That was a singularly stupid thing to do, you little fool!"

"Regardless of your opinion of my maid's actions, you see that she does not have what it is you want," Jane answered calmly. "I believe you are required in his lordship's bookroom…"

"I was sent to fetch you, my lady," Arthur Ellis said and nervously stepped forward, saying to the Countess with a significant look, "His lordship was particularly desirous of Lady St. John's company and has been patiently waiting for her in his bookroom."

Diana St. John's smile was superior. "To think he spent the entire night at my house and now demands to see me again not so many hours after he left," she cooed with delight. "You poor wretch, just three months a bride and already he has lost interest. I predicted as much. Those two nights this past sennight that he strayed from your bed—"

"He was with me at Arlington Street," Sir Antony explained, strolling further into the now crowded dressing room, twirling his quizzing glass on its riband. "Two late sittings of Parliament and dinner both nights with yours truly. He was worn thin, so thin that I was able to persuade him to spend the night in his old rooms. Apologies for keeping him from you, my lady," he said to Jane with a bow and sidled up to his sister, saying under his breath, "Your mischief-making is as stale as yesterday's loaf, Di. Give it up before you embarrass yourself further."

"Milk sop," Diana St. John hissed and with a swish of her petticoats turned and swept out of the room, saying cryptically on a sigh, "If you want something done, best to do it yourself."

Unperturbed, Sir Antony shrugged and looked at the secretary.

"Three brutes are guarding her ladyship's sitting room door. Can you enlighten us, Ellis?"

"Please do not be alarmed, my lady," said the secretary. "The men have been posted on his lordship's request should Lady St. John attempt to re-enter these rooms at the conclusion of her interview with his lordship. They have been instructed to keep all comers from your door."

"Fat lot of good they proved to be!" Sir Antony rightly pointed out. "Dratted fellows tried to keep me from joining the tea party, and me dressed in fresh powder and frock coat. The tea party, I might add, is in full swing out there. Looks like you could use a strong dish of Bohea, Ellis," he added good-naturedly with a slap to the secretary's thin back, a wink at Jane as he led Arthur back into the sitting room.

So much for the effectiveness of three burly footmen keeping all and sundry away! Arthur knew when to bow to force majeure. He also knew what was expected of him and quietly perched on a corner of a sofa, gratefully accepting a dish of tea, a beady eye on the Lady St. John, who, far from dashing off to the Earl's book-room as requested, had taken it upon herself to sit by the teapot. With the help of her daughter, she distributed the dishes of tea and the assortment of almond and ratafia biscuits, seedy and lemon cakes amongst the assembled company.

Jane made no attempt to dislodge Diana St. John to take her rightful place in front of her own tea things, despite her great annoyance that the woman had the barefaced audacity to remain in her sitting room and assume control of proceedings. Instead, she quietly returned to the window seat and picked up her needlework, deeming it best for all concerned, particularly the twins, to humor Diana St. John, letting her believe she was in control if it kept her calm until the Earl had the children away from her. The woman's openly hostile behavior towards Anne was indication enough that she was more unstable than Jane had at first thought.

She was so lost in her thoughts that she failed to notice the Lady Caroline had taken up residence on the chaise longue, where she sat with Ron, giving Viscount Fourpaws a good scratch behind both ears, until she began verbally sparring with Diana St. John, not the most conducive activity to maintaining a calm environment.

"Does anyone know why Salt's been in his apartments since forever?" Lady Caroline asked, gathering up her froth of silk petticoats in expectation of Sir Antony sitting beside her. When he chose to warm his hands in front of the fireplace she pouted but pretended not to notice, adding, "Perhaps he's taking a well-earned nap?" a sickly-sweet smile directed at Diana St. John. "Who can blame him when he was awake most of the night playing at nursemaid."

Lady St. John selected a sugared plum from a bowl amongst the clutter on the tea trolley. "Caroline, you have no right questioning Salt's devotion to my son."

"Oh, it's not his devotion to Ron that concerns me, Cousin," Lady Caroline responded, a genuine smile at Ron.

She gave him the kitten and eyed Diana St. John resentfully. She had never cared for Diana, who had made a habit of monopolizing her brother's time and attention since she could remember, and she remembered a great deal. It was only four years since the death of her favorite uncle St. John. He had always taken the time to talk with her as if her thoughts and opinions were important to him, which is how Salt had always treated her, as a person, not as an object to be owned or ignored as if she were part of the furniture, which is how Diana saw her and thus dismissed her existence as unimportant. Thus, it did not matter to Diana that Caroline saw and heard how she mistreated St. John, their heated arguments, the overt flirting with every male visitor to Salt Hall, but most particularly of all how she monopolized Salt's time and attention, which made Caroline loathe her all the more.

She glanced at the Countess, who was curled up in the window seat with her needlepoint, and saw an opportunity to aggravate Diana where it hurt most.

"I love what you have done with the nursery, my lady. And I can't tell you how happy I am that my brother has finally married because I was despairing of ever becoming an aunt." She glanced at Sir Antony with a sweet smile that did not deceive him. "Salt will make a wonderfully devoted father to his own brood, don't you agree, Tony?"

"I am sure he will oblige you, Caro, by filling the nursery to overflowing," agreed Sir Antony, ignoring the Countess, who blushed up with embarrassment, but not his sister who gave a huff of dismissal. "My dear Diana, swallow a stone?"

"Good! I do so want lots of nephews and nieces," Lady Caroline responded then changed the subject before Diana, who was glaring at her with slit-eyed hostility, had time to go in for the attack. "Tony, what was it you were saying about Willis? Surely Jenkins has it wrong?"

"Had it from the horse's mouth, so to speak."

"Rufus Willis has been with us since forever," Lady Caroline argued, puzzled. "He was born at Salt Hall. His father and his grandfather were our stewards. He gave me my first pony ride. And Mamma sent him off to Rugby because he was so bookish. He was meant to go on to Cambridge, but then Mamma died and his papa got ill. I said he should talk to Salt. His brain is wasted as an under-butler—"

"Oh, don't be utterly beetle-brained, Caroline!" Diana St. John said dismissively. "Waste money on a servant's education? The man should be glad he has a roof over his head." She gave Merry a plate of almond biscuits to offer Jane. "Care for a little biscuit, my lady?" When Jane instinctively pulled back from the strong smell of almond paste but still managed to smile and say thank you to the little girl for the offer, Diana smiled crookedly. "Perhaps a lemon tart would better suit your palate? Merry! Take this lemon tart to her ladyship."

"Rufus Willis is one of the most well-read men of my acquaintance," Jane stated, taking a nibble of the lemon tart then putting it aside because she had lost her appetite for sweet pastries. She picked up her needlepoint again. "I hope Salt will do something for him, Caroline."

"Lord, yes, of *your* acquaintance, to be sure. You're as buffle-headed as Caroline!" Diana replied, annoyed Jane had discarded the tart. "Next you'll be telling us Salt married you for your *sweet nature* and not because he had a momentary lapse of reason." She sipped at her tea thoughtfully. "In my experience, unquenchable lust for a beautiful object has often been the downfall of many a great and powerful man. I never thought to see Salt sink so low…"

Lady Caroline was up on her heels. "How dare you speak about my brother and his wife in such a-a *crude* and-and *undignified* manner! Salt married Jane because he loves her; much you would know about *that*."

"Caroline, you are an overindulged, spoiled child who—"

"Enough," stated Sir Antony very quietly, glancing up from the carpet where he was helping Ron detach a thread from the ribbon that had caught in the kitten's claw. "Caro is in the right, Di. You owe Lady Salt an apology."

"Please, we all must remember where we are," Jane said quietly, a significant glance at Ron and Merry, who had been riveted to the conversation. "Tony, what was it Jenkins told you about Willis? He has not taken ill, I trust?"

"Worse. Dismissed from his post. Willis is no longer under-butler in this household."

Just as Sir Antony said this, Anne, who had come through from the dressing room with a fresh reel of cotton for her mistress, burst into tears and fled the room on a strangled sob.

"Thank God such a maudlin creature no longer lingers in my household," Lady St. John announced with satisfaction as she busied herself pouring out milk into various tea dishes. "The woman's a dripping spout of woes."

Lady Caroline stared in disbelief from the Countess to Diana St. John and then went up to Jane, mindful of the twins' presence. "You can't let her get away with making such horrid remarks about you and my brother," she whispered. "She owes you an apology, and if you don't stand up to her, she will think you weak and be forever managing you."

Jane put aside her needlepoint and drew Caroline to sit beside her in the window seat. "If I thought it would be of any use I would do as you suggest, but…" She glanced over at Diana St. John, who was absorbed with corking a small blue bottle that she then slipped into her reticule. "She is not well. Anything I say will only inflame her. I do not expect you to fully understand, but please, we must wait for your brother, who is the only person capable of controlling her." She looked over at Sir Antony and asked about the under-butler.

"Kitchen gossip," Sir Antony apologized. "Willis left the house without telling Jenkins his direction, and when he returned, he was summonsed to Salt's private apartments where he spent over an hour locked up in close conversation. When he emerged, his face was so white it looked as if it had been dipped in flour and he was shaking like a Jelly Surprise, *and* he couldn't put two words together. Whereupon he again left the house and has not been seen since. I might add, that whatever Willis said in that interview left Salt in a blind rage. Andrews confided to Jenkins he had never heard such a vulgar tongue expressed with such eloquence."

Lady Caroline smiled at Jane and glanced slyly at Sir Antony, saying with feigned thoughtfulness, "Perhaps I will ask dear Captain Beresford to employ Willis…?"

Sir Antony did not rise to the bait. He put his dish back on its saucer, saying charmingly, "You do that, sweetheart. Perhaps, given the circumstances of this love affair, your Captain might even take on her ladyship's personal maid so Willis and she can be together again. Now wouldn't that make for a romantic foursome?"

"Yes, how romantic indeed!" Lady Caroline threw at Sir Antony as if he had made the best suggestion in the world. "I must write to the dear Captain at once about poor Willis. He is so understanding about such matters. No doubt when I inform him of the circumstances behind Willis's dismissal he will jump at the chance to be of service to me."

"I believe a note to the dear Captain is just what you should do, Caroline." Jane dimpled, entering into the girl's teasing of Sir Antony. "And be certain to inform him that the romantic notion of keeping Anne and Rufus together was the idea of Sir Antony Templestowe."

Sir Antony bowed. "I aim to please you both, dear ladies."

"When did the feelings of servants ever amount to anything?" Diana St. John said dismissively and smiled at Jane. "You have not touched your tart, my lady. Perhaps the dish of tea my daughter graciously gave you will help you feel more the thing. Merry! Don't hover! Offer the cakes to your uncle then you may stand here beside my chair. No, Ron! Merry!" she snapped when her daughter offered cake to her brother. "No cake. Your brother is still too weak to digest any food. Remember what the physician advised."

Jane picked up the dish of tea Merry had placed on the window seat beside her, ignoring Diana St. John's intense gaze.

"You truly do not look at all well, my lady," Diana St. John said silkily when Jane hesitated to drink the contents of her tea dish. "Tea is most beneficial when one is out of sorts. Don't you agree, Antony?"

"Merry, if you would be so kind as to return this dish to your mamma." Jane smiled at the little girl. "I do not take milk."

"My dear Lady Salt, I assure you that *with milk*, the tea will do you a great deal of good," Diana St. John insisted. "Merry! Lady Salt *will* drink the tea with milk."

"No. I will not," Jane stated firmly, holding Diana St. John's gaze, and the tea dish on its saucer at arm's length for Merry to return to the tea trolley. "Thank you, Merry."

"Merry! Do not take that dish!" her mother ordered. "My lady, I insist that you at least try my tea. After all the trouble I took to make it on your behalf."

"I am mindful of the effort, my lady, but I am unable to drink the tea."

"And why are you unable to drink tea with milk, my lady?"

"Di, it is of no importance why Lady Salt cannot drink tea with milk," Sir Antony said on a sigh of exasperation. "That her ladyship does not wish it should suffice. Merry, take the tea dish back to the trolley forthwith."

"No, Merry, do not touch that dish," her mother enunciated. "Lady Salt will do me the courtesy of drinking the tea."

The little girl hesitated, halfway between her mother and the Countess, not knowing which way to turn. Wanting to take the tea dish from the Countess yet afraid of her mother's wrath if she did. Ron saw his sister's distress and went toward her, but Sir Antony, exchanging a look of exasperation with Lady Caroline, stayed his nephew with a hand on his shoulder and came to his niece's rescue.

"What a lot of bother over a trifle! Let Merry take the dish and be done with it."

"Don't interfere! This is none of your concern! Lady Salt *will* drink the tea Merry so graciously gave her. It would be the height of bad manners not to do so. Would it not, my lady?"

Jane suppressed her own exasperation and reasoned that if one sip of milky tea would put an end to all the fuss and make Merry comfortable again, then she would do her best to oblige Diana St. John. Surely she could conquer her nausea for a matter of mere moments. But just the thought of milk made her queasy. Perhaps if she held her breath…

Arthur Ellis, who was silently perched on a corner of the sofa, his presence forgotten, now rose up, intent on rescuing the Countess from the misery of being forced to drink a substance that clearly even the thought of which was making her wilt. Merry still stood in the middle of the room her distress evident though she felt a huge relief when the Countess lifted the dish from its saucer.

Jane tried her best to bring the dish up to her mouth but the curl of steam that rose from the milky liquid and assailed her nose made her pull back, return the dish to its saucer and close her eyes. It was too much for Arthur Ellis, and for Sir Antony, who both stepped forward as one and almost collided, the secretary stepping back to allow Sir Antony to play knight-errant.

Such was his annoyance with his sister's pigheadedness that Sir Antony inadvertently snatched the tea dish and saucer from Jane's hand. In so doing, the tea dish toppled and its hot milky contents splashed across the front of his exquisite silver-threaded velvet waistcoat. What was not soaked up by the plush velvet dripped onto his highly polished shoes with their enormous silver buckles and into his left shoe, soaking his stockinged foot.

Diana St. John was on her feet in furious disbelief. She stared at the tea-soaked front of her brother's ruined waistcoat and then down at his shoes. "You idiot! You *fool*," she seethed. "I could *kill* you! All that effort. It was the *perfect* opportunity! You have no idea, no idea at all, what you've just done!"

"But *I* do," the Earl announced from the doorway, and strolled further into his wife's pretty sitting room crowded with his relatives, and immediately dominated the space.

EIGHTEEN

"WELL, ARTHUR, WHAT PART OF *escort Lady St. John to my bookroom at once* did you not understand? It doesn't matter now," Salt said dismissively to his secretary's red-faced and incomprehensible garbled apology. "Take a breath and sit down before you lose consciousness." He placed two folded parchments, one with a freshly broken seal, upon the mantel shelf between several propped-up cards of invitation then turned to stare Sir Antony up and down. "Dear me, Tony. A waist-coat ruined. But for the greater good, I assure you." Over his shoulder he sensed Diana St. John had taken a step toward him. "Sit down," he snarled. "At once." Then turned a bright smile on his godchildren. "Merry. Ron. Be so good as to follow me."

Jane watched her husband move away from the fireplace to stand by the narrow door hidden in the patterned chinoiserie wall-paper of peonies that provided access to the servant passageway and stairs that led to the nursery above. She found it difficult to believe he had ever suffered a collapse in his life, and just hours ago on the tennis court. If not for the clench to his square jaw, he appeared at ease, and as strong and as healthy as ever. His brown eyes were alert and there was a healthy color in his clean-shaven cheeks, which made her breathe a sigh of relief. But that clench bothered her. It was a sign she had come to read very well indeed. He might appear to the world to be untroubled, but in truth he was doing his best to keep his emotions well and truly under control. She did not envy him the task that lay ahead. And she was just as anxious for him, and the children.

That Tom had followed Salt into the sitting room gave her some comfort. Yet Tom looked as worried as the Earl appeared unruffled. Her stepbrother was not good at hiding his feelings. As soon he saw Jane, he ignored the room full of people and went straight over to bow over her hand. It was only when he was seated beside her in the window seat that he nodded to the assembled company before looking to the Earl for direction.

Salt told Ron and Merry to bring with them the Countess's furry four-legged fiend, and waited while they scooped up Viscount Fourpaws, who did not want to be unsettled from the warmth to be had curled up on Lady Caroline's lap. When Diana St. John half rose out of the wingchair in expectation of following her children across the room, one word from the Earl reluctantly sat her down again. Sir Antony, Lady Caroline and Arthur Ellis, who was red-faced and still on his feet, remained silent. A quiet word from Jane and the secretary slowly sank back down onto the corner of the sofa. Like everyone else in the room, his gaze remained fixed on the Earl.

Salt went down on his haunches before his godchildren.

"I need you both to do me a great favor," he said very quietly so only the twins could hear him. He looked from Ron to Merry and back to the pale-faced boy with his sunken wary eyes. "I know you were promised afternoon tea with her ladyship and me. But a matter of great importance has arisen that requires my immediate attention. So I need you to do me this favor: To spend a few hours in the nursery. I know that is not what you wanted and your disappointment is understandable, but it will help me enormously. I hate to break my promise at any time but most particularly to you both. I don't do so lightly. Can you understand that?"

Merry was the first to nod and say with a smile, "If it is important to you, Uncle Salt, then we understand. Don't we, Ron?"

Salt gently cupped her cheek. "Thank you, Merry. Ron?"

Ron nodded, though his disappointment was evident. "Of course."

"Good man. I've sent for your clothes and favorite things from

South Audley Street because I have decided you will be staying here. So you will be able to take supper tonight in the Yellow Saloon and we may even have time for a round of charades before bedtime. Is that fair compensation for spending a few hours cooped up in the nursery, do you think?

"Very fair! Are we truly to stay with you here?" Merry asked breathlessly and when the Earl nodded, couldn't suppress her excitement by jumping up and down on the spot. But she had a sudden awful thought. "Clary and Taylor aren't coming here, too?"

Salt smiled at Merry's look of wide-eyed dread. The dour governess and the cold-fish tutor were repellent beings that had no place caring for children; his stables of horses received better care.

"No. You need never see those two again."

"No Clary and Taylor, Ron! Did you hear that?"

Ron wasn't so demonstrative, and when he glanced fearfully across at his mother, the Earl gently squeezed his thin arm, an encouraging smile at Merry, who was beaming with happiness and holding tightly to the kitten.

"I gave your father my word that I would take good care of you, Ron, and I promise you that I mean to take better care of you from this day forward. You and Merry both."

"But you do take very good care of us, Uncle Salt," Merry assured him and gently nudged her brother. "Doesn't he, Ron?"

"Yes. Always! I don't need you to tell him for me," Ron complained, acknowledging his sister's prompting by nudging her in return. He frowned at the Earl, another quick, furtive glance at his mother, and said hesitantly, "You do mean it, don't you, Uncle Salt, about staying here with you?" His voice dropped to a whisper. "You won't—you won't send me—send us—back? Last night you promised I'd never have to take Mamma's medicine ever again. You did mean it? I don't *want* to be ill. I don't *like* being ill. I won't have to take it again, will I?"

Salt held the boy's haunted gaze, so reminiscent of his father St. John that he felt a tightening in his throat and chest. He wanted to hug the boy and reassure him that he would never allow harm to come to him again, yet he refrained from doing so because he knew Ron would be embarrassed by such demonstrative behavior in public. Instead, he held out his hand.

"Last night we shook hands on it, Ron," he said quietly. "But I will gladly shake hands with you again if it will convince you that I mean it."

Again, Ron looked warily over at his mother before turning his gaze on the Countess. She was smiling at him. He liked her smile. It was sweet and understanding and so full of comfort. He would never tell his sister this, but secretly the Countess was just as he imagined a fairy to be, if fairies really did live at the bottom of gardens. Unconsciously, his thin shoulders sagged with relief and he let out a small sigh. Finally, he thrust out his hand to the Earl and when it was taken, allowed himself to be drawn into his godfather's embrace. Overcome, he buried his face in the soft velvet of the Earl's frock coat. Merry put a comforting hand to her brother's shaking back, saying in a confidential whisper to her uncle,

"He's tired or he wouldn't be like this."

"You are quite right, Merry," Salt agreed when he had mastered his emotions, the boy still clinging tightly to him. He lightly brushed her cheek with one finger. "Tomorrow he will be more himself. We all will."

Sensing a presence loomed over them, he swiveled on a flat heel with Ron still in his arms, and found petticoats of gold watered-silk brushing up against his leg. It was Diana. Before Salt could disentangle himself and stand up, she lunged for Merry, frightening Viscount Fourpaws, who hissed and swiped his paw across the back of her hand. She shrieked and let out an expletive and tried to pull the kitten by the scruff of the neck up out of her daughter's arms, but Merry would not let go. She held on tightly to Viscount Fourpaws, who meowed his protests at such rough treatment, and pulled away from her mother, the frightened kitten trying to scramble out of her arms to safety.

"Give me that disgusting little ferret, Magna!" Diana St. John hissed, making another lunge for the kitten. "It should've been drowned at birth! It will be drowned."

"No! No, Mamma! You can't!" Merry implored, big brown eyes staring up at her mother. Her bottom lip quivered and tears pricked her eyelids. "You frightened him. You can't drown him!

Uncle Salt won't let you! He belongs to Aunt Jane. He's just a baby cat!"

"Babies are offensive, vile creations!" Diana St. John spat out before she could stop herself. "No one deserves to have his babies. *She* doesn't deserve to have his babies. She mustn't. She won't. *She* isn't worthy. I won't allow it! Mamma will be miserable. You don't want Mamma to be miserable, do you, Magna? Now give me that odious creature!"

Salt caught her wrist before she could grab again for the kitten and her daughter. He had sprung to his feet, as had everyone in the room, and quickly put Ron behind him. Merry darted to join her brother, the kitten meowing in protest as he was hugged tightly to her silk bodice. Both children huddled against the Earl's broad back, little fingers grabbing on tightly to the silver trimmed short skirts of his frock coat, their faces hidden in the soft cloth, eyes tightly shut, not daring to peer at their seething mother.

Diana St. John swirled about, wild-eyed and panting, to stare up at the Earl, who was ashen-faced and thin-lipped, before looking about her uncomprehendingly at the still silent faces gathered around the tea trolley. When she wondered aloud why the Earl had her by the wrist, it was evident she was oblivious to the fact her rage had driven her to reveal her innermost thoughts, thoughts that appalled everyone in the room. Nor could she comprehend their horror or the effect her words had had on the Earl and Countess.

"Let that be your last defiant act, Madam. Had you come to my bookroom as requested, your brother would have been spared the humiliation of having his sister's contemptible and reprehensible behavior aired in public. Apologies, Antony, but now I don't care. Sit," he ordered and let go of her wrist with a little push and an opening of his hand, as if he did not want the touch of her. "Caroline, be so good as to come here. The rest of you, sit down. You too, my lady," he added gently when Jane took a step towards him.

He dared to allow his gaze to focus on his wife for the first time since coming into her sitting room, and he wished he had had the will power to refrain from doing so. Jane had been halfway across

the room, brow furrowed in concern for the twins, who still clung
to either side of his short skirts. It was only when he addressed her
that she brought herself up short and her blue-eyed gaze flickered up
to his brown eyes. A mix of emotions crossed her beautiful face and
it took all his self-control to turn away and pray that she did as she
was told. His overwhelming desire was to scoop her up in his arms
and twirl her round and round and cover her face with kisses for
making him the happiest man alive. Instead, he opened the servant
door and went into the narrow passage where he gently disentangled
Ron and Merry from his frock coat, then spoke to someone out of
view. Soothing words and hugs of reassurance and he let the twins
go, returned to the sitting room to stand in the open doorway. He
beckoned Lady Caroline to him and kissed her hand.

"I want you to go up to the nursery and keep an eye on them.
They shouldn't be left with servants as their only company at this
time. I'll explain later. I can't do that now. You will have to trust
me, Caro. Please. Do this for me."

Lady Caroline pouted and opened her mouth to protest about
being treated as a child and sent away when anything of interest
occurred, but something in the Earl's brown eyes, in the set of his
mouth and the tiredness in his face forestalled her. She nodded,
obedient and remarkably composed for her seventeen and a half
years of age.

"Yes, of course. Will you—will you be all right? Will everything be all right?"

He kissed her forehead and smiled down at her. "Yes. Before
the day is out everything will be set to rights. That I promise you."

Lady Caroline nodded, curtsied to the room, and was gone.

Salt closed the door on her back and joined the rest of the
silent group, all eyes upon him in mute expectation.

Recovered from her extraordinary outburst, Diana St. John
had resumed her place in front of the tea trolley and was languidly
fanning herself and looking for the world as if nothing was amiss.
To everyone's amazement, she even went so far as to order Arthur
Ellis to fetch the Countess's dolt of a maid to go in search of the
butler. The teapot needed replenishing and she couldn't understand why Jenkins wasn't in attendance on them for afternoon tea.
Completely oblivious to the heavy air of tension in the light-filled

sitting room, she began rearranging the tea dishes in anticipation of pouring out more tea when it arrived.

Still in shock, no one bothered to reply, not even Jane. She was preoccupied with watching her husband, whose inscrutable gaze remained fixed on Diana St. John. It was only when Tom squeezed her fingers that Jane reluctantly tore her gaze from the Earl. When Tom winked conspiratorially and smiled warmly she wondered why and what he knew, though his seeming buoyancy helped ease her mind, but it did not dissipate the crescendo of anticipation that something of significance was about to occur here in her sitting room.

The silence was broken by Sir Antony taking snuff.

It was the spur Arthur Ellis needed to come to life, and he shot to his feet, unable to take another moment of the suspense and silent forced restraint. Diana St. John thought he had done so at her command, to fetch the Countess's maid and looked up at the Earl expectantly.

"Shall you take a dish of tea when it comes, Salt?" she asked pleasantly. "Or would you prefer claret? You look tired unto death. Hardly surprising, is it, when we spent another all-night vigil at Ron's bedside. Did you manage to get a few hours sleep? Ellis, when you find that insipid creature, have her get Jenkins to fetch up a bottle of claret for his lordship."

The secretary, instead of doing her bidding, looked to his employer and then at the Countess, seeking direction, completely at a loss to know what he should do, or what he should say.

The Earl came to his rescue.

He was staring at Diana St. John but thinking about the day he had met Jane Despard. He thought about the hollowness of his existence these past four years without her. With his hopes of marrying her so cruelly dashed, and caught up in the political machinations of Westminster, the social events of Polite Society and the running of his estates, he had convinced himself that domesticity was unimportant to him, all because of his malaise of the heart. Yet, since marrying Jane he had come to regard his domestic arrangements as vital to his health and happiness. Tom's astonishing revelations had provided him with proof of his ability to father a child with Jane, but such welcome news had come at a heart-breaking cost; the loss of a much-wanted child, maliciously destroyed, and that brought him back to Diana St. John and her interference in his life. The more he had ruminated, the more he realized St. John's wife had meddled in his life more years then he cared to contemplate. That she had interfered where it mattered most to him, with Jane and her happiness and wellbeing, made him livid.

"I had hoped to make this as painless as possible, and without an audience," he said with great forbearance, standing by the fire-place. "Never mind. Perhaps this way is for the best. If one is to humbly atone, then it is appropriate that those who matter most should bear witness. But I'm afraid, Arthur, that you must leave us. It is not that I do not trust you. I do, implicitly. It is for the sake of her ladyship and my need to have you run a number of important errands without delay that you cannot remain. I have left instructions on my desk for what I need from you. There are also letters that require immediate delivery: One to Rockingham, one to Bute. A third is addressed to His Majesty. Deliver them yourself and do so at once. There are copies of my correspondence, which you are welcome to read and digest. If you then decide to reconsider your present employment, and what ambitious man would not, I will understand and recommend you with a glowing reference."

Arthur Ellis gave a start, looked swiftly at his friend Tom, who smiled at him, before composing himself and bowing to his lord-ship. "Yes, of course, my lord. I will see to matters at once," he replied obediently and deposited his dish and saucer on the silver tray. He hesitated, then crossed to Jane to make her a deep bow. "I am, my lady, your humble and most obedient servant, always."

"Thank you, Mr. Ellis. Your loyalty means a great deal to me, and," Jane added with a smile at the Earl, "to my husband."

What her husband said next truly surprised her.

"Oh, and Arthur," added the Earl, "send her ladyship's maid to the nursery. Mr. Willis will join her there shortly. I presume Miss Anne Springer is lurking in some nether room?"

"Listening at the keyhole, if the truth be told," Diana St. John grumbled.

As the secretary departed, he left the door ajar, allowing Jane a glimpse into the passageway. To her astonishment and consternation there lingered just outside her sitting room what appeared to be a battalion of liveried footmen, kicking their heels in wait, and with them were Mr. Jenkins and Rufus Willis. The butler closing over the door and Lady St. John's exuberance brought her gaze back into the room, where the woman was holding court.

"So! It's finally come. You are to be First Lord of the Treasury at last! When do you kiss hands?" Diana St. John asked excitedly, gazing adoringly up at the Earl. "All our hard work has paid off. I knew it would! How could it not? You will make a brilliant first minister. When does Bute resign? Tomorrow? Today? Is it not exciting, Antony? Perhaps Salt will find you a place in his cabinet? What think you, Salt? Is my little brother to have the Foreign Department? Have you decided on the rest of your ministry? Naturally, Rockingham must be given something, Newcastle too. If only those two would cooperate more with one another. No matter. You will keep them both in line. Now, let me see, who else is deserving of your notice—"

"I have declined His Majesty's offer to form government," Salt answered matter-of-factly, taking one of the sheets of parchment from the mantel where he had placed them. From his waistcoat pocket he produced his gold-rimmed spectacles. "In fact," he continued calmly, deftly sitting his eyeglasses on the end of his nose with the paper still in his hand, "I have informed His Majesty that I have decided to rusticate for the foreseeable future. I have also vacated my chair on the Privy Council, effective immediately."

"*Wh-what?*" Lady St. John demanded, up out of the wingchair. She was so incredulous that it subdued her enough to ask quietly, "How can you throw away the opportunity of a lifetime? We have spent years working towards this goal. You cannot resign your posts! You cannot vacate the Privy Council. You certainly can't waste your talents rusticating in a Wiltshire backwater! His Majesty won't allow it. *I* won't allow it! I don't understand."

"You have never understood and you never will," Salt replied evenly. "My own house must be in good order before I can possibly contemplate running the kingdom. To do that, I must be true to myself; a gentleman and a family man, the Earl of Salt Hendon a paltry third."

Sir Antony smiled, completely attune to the Earl's feelings. "Bravo for you, Salt," he said quietly, all admiration for his friend's decision. "Bravo."

"Don't be an ass, Antony!" Diana St. John said dismissively and peered keenly at the Earl. "You're not well. It's the strain of the past few months. The corridor machinations over Bute's possible resignation and the Peace negotiations have taken their toll. You're wearing your eyeglasses. You must be suffering megrims. A few days at Strawberry Hill with Walpole to lift your spirits and you will see that you cannot possibly rusticate. You are needed to lead your country."

Salt opened out the letter and turned to Lady St. John to stare at her over the rims of his spectacles. "I have made my decision. Sit down, Diana."

But Lady St. John remained standing. She was too disbelieving to do as commanded. She shut her fan with a snap and put up her chin. "You are in *jest*. This is a *cruel* joke. You know very well that a few years, one year, playing sheep farmer on your estate is a-a lifetime in the political wilderness. You may never again have the opportunity to form government. You truly *can't* be serious!"

"I have never been more so." Salt held up the parchment. "This letter bears my seal, but I did not write it. It is a forgery, and not a very good copy of my handwriting. It is a letter you wrote in my name, Diana," he drawled, an ugly pull to his mouth. "No doubt you were confident that the recipient would presume I had written it in haste and with some emotion, and that this would explain the lack of consistency in the forming of my letters. Or perhaps you rightly predicted that my betrothed would be in such a state of emotional duress upon reading this breach of promise note that she would be unlikely to think beyond the letter's deplorable content?"

Jane let out an involuntary gasp, a shaking hand to her mouth, and looked from her husband to Lady St. John and then to her stepbrother. "How did Salt recover—"

"From me, Jane. Uncle Jacob left the letter to me in his will,"

Tom explained gently. He smiled and kissed the back of her hand. "I thought the time had come to hand it over."

"My betrothed would hardly worry about the authenticity of the writing, given her deeply distressed state," the Earl said, gaze remaining on Lady St. John. "Well, Madam. Do you have anything to add?"

Diana St. John's response was unemotional, but her confidence had slipped to be so coldly addressed by the Earl. She sensed an impenetrable wall of ice was forming between them and yet years of self-delusion convinced her that she was in the right and he must see that she was in the right. After all, everything she had done, no matter how unpleasant or demeaning, had been done for his benefit and his alone. She loved him unconditionally, but with that love came sacrifices, sacrifices he had to be willing to make if she was to help him become First Lord of the Treasury. She would make him understand. She met the Earl's brown eyes with an air of confidence.

"I am not about to deny it. Why should I? What I did, my actions in all things, have always been governed by my ambition for you. You are destined for political greatness. Everyone says so, from Holland to Rockingham to Bute. All sides of the political pen agree on that, even if they cannot agree on anything else. You have done so much for your country already, and will do more in the future. Sinclairs have been serving king and country since the Plantagenets. I could not allow you to throw away your future and your happiness on some lust-driven whim taken in the summer-house. I was merely protecting you from yourself."

"*Future? Happiness?*" The Earl's self-control unraveled. He ripped off his eyeglasses. "What the bloody hell would you know about my-my *feelings?*" He thrust out his velvet arm in Jane's direction. "She—*Jane* is my future. *Jane* is my happiness. Even in her despair, when under the power of a religious lunatic, Jane never gave up hope in me. Jane loves me—*me*, not because one day I will be First Lord of the Treasury or of this or of that or of any-bloody-thing else! Does that penetrate your skull, Madam? Jane loves *me.*"

Diana St. John's laugh was one of outraged skepticism.

"Good God, Salt! I do despair of you at times," she said with a sad shake of her perfectly coiffured head as she took a turn from the wing chair by the fireplace to the sofa and back again to stand before the Earl with her chin up. She patted the silver-threaded narrow lapel of his frock coat. "You are a brilliant political strategist, to be sure, but the instant you allow the blood to pool between your tree-trunk thighs your mind is reduced to that of a jellyfish! Ah, such are the minds of warm-blooded vigorous men of intellect when they allow lust to override sense. But that's what I am here for. To ensure you don't come completely unstuck." She turned with a swish of her layered gown to address the Countess. "Lord! You didn't even have the wit or skill to keep your legs closed until you were up before a parson," she taunted with a menacing wave of her fan. "You're so pathetically naïve you even allowed him to impreg—"

The Earl dropped his spectacles and had her by the throat.

"*Murderess*," he hissed in her face, fingers under her jaw to keep her mouth shut. It took all his self-control not to squeeze the life out of her. "If not for *you*, my wife would not have suffered the *shame* of being banished from her own home; of being *shunned* by her own father who wrongly accused her of being a whore. If not for *you*, she would not have been *forced* to accept Jacob Allenby's protection, and whose obsession with redemption made her life a *misery*. If not for *you*, I would not have considered her beneath my contempt for tossing me over so lightly. If not for *you*, I would not have spent *four years* wondering what my life could have been.

"You had it within your power to set matters to rights with Sir Felix. You knew the truth and you *concealed* it. Worse. You willfully *fabricated* the truth to suit your own selfish ends. I put it to *you* that you read and destroyed the note concealed in the secret compartment of the Sinclair locket. A note, if it had reached me would have saved Jane and our—and our—" He swallowed and dug deep in a frock coat pocket and drew out a leather pouch. This he held out to Jane. "*Take it. Open it.* Anne and Rufus found it under her pillow."

But Jane could not move. She did not trust her legs to carry her across the room. Tom retrieved the pouch for her and at her request spilled the contents into his hand. He held up a diamond-encrusted gold chain that had at its center a large sapphire. It was the genuine Sinclair locket, and for Jane its recovery was bitter-sweet. She did not open the secret compartment; she knew she would find only emptiness. She laid the locket on the window seat cushion and blinked away tears.

"Jane. Tell me what you wrote," Salt commanded gently.

She shook her head, hand to her mouth to stop a sob. Tom put a comforting arm around her and she leaned into his shoulder. Sir Antony and Salt waited. Jane finally straightened and looked at her husband and said just three words. They were devastatingly heartbreaking.

"*Enceinte.* Please come."

The Earl bowed his head, but just for a moment, before lifting his chin to stare hard at Lady St. John, whose jaw he still held closed, fingers cupped menacingly about her throat.

"By destroying that note and forging my writing on a breach of promise document, you made my darling girl believe me to be a licentious monster capable of cruelly using and abusing her for my own wanton satisfaction. Those who sought to cover up what you had turned into a scandal, who conspired to assist Sir Felix to avert the shame of his daughter giving birth to a bastard of indeterminate lineage, were ignorant of the truth, and you *kept* them in ignorance. They had no idea I was the-the—*father* of her child.

"You could have averted tragedy and yet you *promoted* it," he added, rummaging again in his frock coat pocket to pull free a small blue bottle. This he held up between thumb and forefinger before Diana St. John's unblinking gaze. "Worse. You procured a medicinal from an unscrupulous apothecary, Syrup of Artemisia —*poison*—and gave it to Sir Felix to administer to his daughter to *kill* the child growing in her womb."

"*What*? No! No! *No*! Not *that*! I can't—I don't believe it!" The anguished outburst came from Sir Antony, who could no longer listen in silence to the litany of horrendous crimes perpetrated by his sister. "My God, Salt, not *that*. Not the murder of your *child*..."

He glanced at Jane, saw the anguish in her face, and then at Tom, whose eyes were full of sadness, and he had his answer. He went numb. When the Earl directed him to take down off the mantel shelf and read the second parchment, he did so, at first without seeing what he was reading. It was a list, a long list of names, names of women known to him and there was an address in the Strand of an apothecary's place of business. He looked at the Earl and then at his sister and he knew he was crying.

"Consign it to the flames, Tony," Salt told him gently and turned back to expend his rage on his cousin, fingers tightening about her throat when she dared to move her head. "I gave your brother permission to turn that document to ash because it is a damning piece of evidence that would see you hang. I cannot have your foul deeds made public, your children branded the offspring of a murderess, and your brother's diplomatic career ruined. That document was evidence that you are a terminating midwife and a procuress of murderous substances. Over the course of many years, you have supplied Syrup of Artemisia to noblewomen with unwanted pregnancies; many of these women were my lovers at one time or another. I do not judge them. They have to reconcile their actions with their consciences and with their Maker, but to dispense your evil concoction on the innocent and unsuspecting, to menace and coerce my wife's maid to administer a known abortifacient in her ladyship's tea... To then try and do so yourself, just now...

"How will you ever reconcile with *your* conscience what you have done? Ruining our happiness, debasing the woman I love... At every turn, you have done your utmost to cause us heartache and misery. Your wickedness knows no bounds... Stooping so low as to risk the health and wellbeing of your son. Forcing that little boy to suffer—Merry to suffer to see her brother in pain. Putting them through *hell*... Making us live a nightmare of your devising... And to think while I was comforting your children for the tragic loss of their father, whom I loved as a brother, you were aiding and abetting the *torment* of the woman I love and the *murder* of our child... What shape of-of—*monster* are you?"

"*Magnus.* Please. Don't do this," Jane said gently but firmly, standing at her husband's elbow, a hand on his velvet sleeve. She glanced anxiously at Sir Antony, whose desolate face was as white as chalk, and then at Tom, who was wearing a brave face of understanding, and added firmly, looking up at the Earl's strong profile, "Choking the life out of her will give you temporary satisfaction, but I do not want any more unhappiness. Think of Ron and Merry. Think of *our* future. *I love you.* Please. She's ill. Her mind— it isn't well. She needs help."

"When I think of the wanton suffering she inflicted on her small son, all to gain my singular attention, it makes me—*me* ill," Salt uttered, throat dry and raw with despair. "What you have endured… I can never—*ever*—make amends."

"Yes. Yes you can," Jane argued calmly. "When all is said and done, four years is not such a long time to be apart. A seaman's wife can wait many years for word that her husband is safe. Sons go off wandering the Continent on the Grand Tour for just as many years while their families wait uneasy at home for their return. We have each other and a long future together. Ron and Merry are now out of harm's way and they will learn to be happy, carefree children again. Please, Magnus. I do not want to dwell in the past. I want to go forward with you and the children into the future, together as a family."

Slowly, Salt's grip about Diana St. John's throat slackened and with her release came unbridled relief. He tossed the small blue bottle amongst the clutter on the tea trolley and turned to gather Jane into his embrace. He buried his face in the abundance of her shiny black hair, and when she put her arms up about his neck and went on tiptoe to murmur soothing words of comfort, a deep breath escaped him and he shuddered with a mixture of a dozen emotions.

And as the couple found relief and tenderness in their embraces, Sir Antony stepped forward and caught his sister as she staggered back, coughing, and spluttering, a hand to her burning throat which wore the imprints of the Earl's fingers. But for all her distress, she would not have the touch of her brother and kept her gaze firmly fixed on the Earl and Countess. Her mouth twisted up with loathing to see him so happy and his life full of promise, when all she had ever done, all she had ever strived for, was to make the Sinclair name synonymous with power and this handsome nobleman the most influential politician in the kingdom. She would show him. She would make them both pay. He would live to regret this day for the rest of his life.

She snatched up the blue bottle he had tossed amongst the tea things, uncorked it and in one last defiant act threw the contents down her dry throat and swallowed. It was done. She had poisoned herself, and when she was dead, he would realize just how much she had meant to him.

"*No! Di! Don't!*" Sir Antony shouted and grabbed for the blue bottle. But he was too late and all he managed to do was wrest the empty vessel from her fingers and fling it away from him.

"My little apothecary on the Strand tells me that if too much is administered, death will follow quite quickly. That's good to know. But it will be painful, *agonizing* in fact. *You* will appreciate that," she said with a sneering smile at Jane. "And you," she added, blinking up at the Earl, who frowned down at her, his arm about his wife's waist and holding her close, "you shall have my death on your conscience for the rest of your long illustrious life. You'll regret the loss of me once I'm gone. Only then will you realize my true worth."

"Leave her to me," Sir Antony demanded, a hand on the back of the wing chair where his sister sat in state. Tearfully, he stared at Tom and then at the Earl and Countess, who bravely met his gaze with a sad smile. "I'll take care of her. She's still my sister whatever mad demons possess her. It's the least I can do for Ron and Merry, and for you, Salt. Now go. This isn't the place for your wife, or you. Take her up to the nursery. Caroline and the children are waiting."

"Your loyalty is to be admired, Tony, and one day it will be duly rewarded," the Earl responded calmly, a nod to Tom to open the door that led out onto the passageway. Four burly footmen, the butler and Willis, followed by two dour-faced gentlemen in plain frock coats silently filled the room. "Your sister doesn't deserve you, nor does she deserve to have a melodramatic exit."

Jane looked from Sir Antony to her stepbrother and then up at her husband. They were all unbelievably calm given Diana St. John had just downed a vial of poison.

"*Please*. Magnus, call a physician. She must be given something to bring up the poison." She glanced at the two men in plain frock coats who now stepped forward. "Are these men physicians? Are they here to help her?"

"Yes. They are here to help, but not in the way you think," Salt answered and kissed Jane's forehead. "My darling, do you honestly believe I'd have left poison in that bottle? It was flushed out long ago. Nothing more harmful than a lemon cordial went down her throat."

"*What?*" Diana St. John demanded, half out of the wing chair. Sir Antony held her in check, a firm hand to her shoulder. "How *dare* you! How dare you deprive me!" she snarled, defeated. "Why is that sniveling servant here? Who are these men? *Unhand* me at once, Antony! Do they have any idea who *I am?*"

"They know precisely who you are and what you have done, and they will be amply compensated for taking on the care of you," the Earl advised, a nod to the two plainly-dressed gentlemen who stepped forward to either side of Diana St. John's chair and bowed to him. "I suggest you do as you are told. If you do not… These gentlemen are well versed in the care of lunatics. Tony, you may wish to accompany her to the courtyard to say your farewells. The coach is leaving at once."

WHEN THE SITTING ROOM was again tranquil and deserted of attending physicians and the Lady St. John, who did not go quietly but screaming and kicking and heaping curses upon all and sundry as the butler closed the door, Tom asked what Jane wanted to know. "Where are you sending the Lady St. John, my lord?"

"Where she can do no harm. And yes, she will be well cared for and all her needs accommodated," he assured Jane with a smile and a chuff under the chin. "But she will be pressed for company. I won't tell you the precise location in the Welsh mountains, but the views from the castle keep, so I am told, are spectacular." He saw Jane's glance of concern at Willis, who was issuing last minute instructions to the four burly footmen accompanying the coach as outriders. "Rufus is coming to live with us in Wiltshire. He is the new steward of Salt Hall. He will marry Anne and settle in the gatehouse lodge, where they will no doubt produce half a dozen brats, some of whom will make up the Salt Hall cricket team." He grinned. "The rest of the team I have promised to supply."

Jane gasped and took her gaze from the under-butler, blushing furiously. "Magnus! You made no such promise to Willis!"

"Didn't I? I gave the man my word. Now come along, wife," he added, effortlessly scooping Jane up into his arms and striding out of the pretty sitting room without looking back. "You too, Tom. I'm really rather ravenous."

"I'm not surprised," Tom added in the servant passage. "It's not every day the Earl of Salt Hendon is beaten at his own game."

Jane struggled to sit up in her husband's arms, blue eyes wide with disbelief. "Tom beat you at tennis! Magnus?"

The Earl refused to look at either of them. He stretched his neck in its intricately tied cravat. "I'm not entirely infallible."

"Thus spoke the noble nostrils," Tom muttered disrespectfully.

"I beg your pardon, Tom Allenby?"

Jane sighed and pretended to be exasperated. "It's that dreaded pedestal, again. It comes with the nostrils, I'm afraid."

Salt stopped at the base of the stairs that led up to the nursery and let Jane stand on her own feet.

"The pedestal has been consigned to the fire," he murmured, brushing the tip of his nose against hers, then looking over her head at Tom, who was grinning like a sentimental idiot. He raised his eyebrows in mock hauteur. "But, if you don't mind, I shall keep my noble nostrils. They are useful for quelling recalcitrant servants and very small children, and self-satisfied brothers-in-law."

Jane giggled and then was suddenly shy. She glanced at Tom, who understood at once that he should make himself scarce and with a smile excused himself. Salt watched him go up to the nursery two steps at a time. Not a minute later a door banged against a wall above their heads and Tom's voice could be heard booming out a boisterous welcome to which there was a crescendo of footfall followed by squeals of delight before the door closed on the playful cacophony.

"I like your brother. He's a good man."

"Yes. Will you confide in him about Caroline? They are first cousins after all."

"I suspect he may already know…"

"That bothers you?"

Salt shook his head and smiled down at her. "What bothered me was Caroline marrying Tony and seeing them with a brood of brats with no prospect of my good self becoming a father." He grinned. "Mind you, not from want of trying."

Jane laughed. "Magnus! You voice the most shocking thoughts."

"I've had a surfeit of Magnuses today. Dear me, my lady. Stop or I shall come to expect to hear my Christian name on your beautiful lips out from under the bedsheets."

"Well, you can banish thoughts of the wrong order of things," she said quietly, smoothing down an imaginary crease in the lapel of his velvet frock coat. "You've no need to fear Antony becoming a father before you."

Salt tried to keep his features perfectly composed, despite the boyish excitement welling up within him. In exposing Diana St. John's unforgivable wickedness, Rufus Willis had been forced to confide what his betrothed Anne had revealed to him—that the Countess was three months with child. It was such badly-wanted news, confirmation of what Jane had always believed, that they were capable of having a family. He dared not accept the happy reality until he heard it from his wife. Thus he found it hard to contain his enthusiasm and joy, despite his best efforts to look suitably grave.

"Why need I not fear Tony beating me to fatherhood, Lady Salt?" he asked gently, and made her look up at him.

"Tell me first that you truly do want to rusticate. What of your ambitions and dreams to make this little kingdom an empire to be reckoned with, your promise to the nation that the mistakes of the war will not be repeated? You cannot make me believe you will be wholly satisfied farming sheep in Wiltshire."

He pinched her chin. "So you have been following my Parliamentary proclamations from the newssheets."

"I may not know the first thing about politics, nor what constitutes good government, but I do know you," Jane stated with quiet dignity. "I cannot imagine you could walk away from your duty to your country nor from those people who rely on your patronage for their livelihoods, anymore than Tom could abandon his factory workers for a life of leisure as a country squire."

"My dear Lady Salt, your husband is looking forward to farming sheep, albeit from the comfort of that grand pile of

Jacobean stone, and within the bosom of his family, for the fore-seeable future. But who knows what the next couple of years will bring? Ministries come and go. But while I rusticate in style, no one will go hungry; no one will lose his post. I will still maintain an interest and influence in what goes on in the capital, but from a distance. I will just have to develop very long arms of influence, that's all."

"Well, at least you won't have any trouble focusing at a distance," Jane quipped.

He gave a shout of laughter. "If it will make you happy, I shall abandon my ridiculous vanity and wear those wretched eyeglasses at the breakfast table. But be warned: A bespectacled Lord Salt perusing the newssheets is a sight almost as quelling as a flare of the noble nostrils."

Jane smiled cheekily. "What an irresistible combination. My knees are trembling with anticipation already!"

"Baggage!" He brushed a stray wisp of hair from her flushed cheek and smiled down at her lovingly. "You have yet to quell my fears…"

She placed the palm of his large hand on the delicately embroidered hem of her satin bodice where it covered her belly and smiled up at him. "My dear Lord Salt, you are to become a father. Our baby is due with the fall of the first autumn leaves." When he visibly gulped, all her shyness evaporated and she laughed and touched his cheek. "I did warn you I had a surprise for you and that you should have it sitting down. But somehow, telling you about our baby on the nursery stairs is more fitting, isn't it?"

He stared down into her radiantly beautiful face. "Yes, much more fitting… Have I told you how much I love you, Lady Salt?"

Jane dimpled. "You did admit to it on the tennis court. And you told me you loved me when we were naked in the carriage coming home from the Richmond Ball. But I would dearly love to hear you say it here, in the mundane surroundings of a narrow stairwell."

"I love you, Jane," he stated. "I have loved you since you were seventeen years old. There was a time, those few glorious hours we spent alone in the summerhouse, when I, too, believed anything was possible, even miracles. The past four years without you have felt like fifty. Events, people, both conspired to keep us apart, but never again... *Never*, Jane." He grinned. "Later, when we are out of these wretched clothes, I will show you just how much I love you."

Jane peered through her dark lashes as she went up on tiptoe to put her arms about his strong neck to the riband that secured his hair. "Oh, if you are going to show me how much, then I will need a great deal of convincing."

He bent to kiss her mouth. "Oh, yes," he murmured huskily, "a very great deal of convincing."

BEHIND-THE-SCENES

Explore the places, objects, and history in *Salt Bride* on Pinterest.

www.pinterest.com/lucindabrant

The story continues in…

Salt Redux

Jane and Salt — four years of Happily Ever After
Sir Antony Templestowe — four years of Exile
Lady Caroline — four years of Heartache
Diana St. John — four years plotting Revenge

The time has come…

EVERY MONTH, THE GUARDIAN OF THE UNNAMED PERSON OF interest detained at Castle Harlech in remote north Wales sent a report to the Earl of Salt Hendon. A messenger delivered the report, always at night, into the hands of Mr. Rufus Willis, steward of the Earl's estate in Wiltshire. Mr. Willis then gave the report to his lordship when his employer was alone in the vastness of his library, and when there was no expectation of the Countess being present.

Mr. Willis caught the anguish on his lordship's face every time he handed over these reports. Upon one occasion, Mr. Willis offered to read the report to spare the Earl, but his noble employer declined saying it was his duty, however distasteful and difficult the task. Mr. Willis knew the Earl was punishing himself. The Earl believed the punishment justified. The monthly reports were a painful reminder that the unnamed person of interest had brought untold suffering on her own children and was a murderer of innocents. She had also caused the death of the Earl and Countess of Salt Hendon's first child while still in the womb. However, some comfort came from the reports. While his prisoner remained locked up, her children were safe, and so, too, were his. Although he did not need reminding of his good fortune, the Earl knew he was the luckiest of men and that nothing and no one was more important to him than his wife and family.

The guardian of the unnamed person of interest wrote much the same report every month. His "guest" was the model prisoner, afforded every comfort such a remote location could provide. The prisoner had maids to help her into velvet and satin petticoats and bodices, who dressed her waist-length auburn hair in the latest styles as remembered from her life in London, and who helped her choose what pieces of jewelry went best with each outfit. As befitting her exalted rank, she insisted on changing her gown three times a day. Servants waited on her at table as if she were queen of her own dominion and came swiftly in answer to the constant tinkling of her little hand bell. Her guardian accompanied her on walks about the parapets and courtyards of the castle, dined with her when invited, and over coffee and cake listened to her witty recollections about politicians and the esteemed persons of Polite Society, all known to her personally.

The unnamed person of interest spent most days reading the latest issues of *The Gentleman's Magazine*, particularly the reports of Parliamentary sittings, and wrote at her escritoire in her prettily-furnished drawing room, with its view of the sea. Her letters were sent but never delivered, and thus she never received a reply. These letters were sometimes ten pages in length and most were addressed to the Earl of Salt Hendon. Her guardian read these letters as part of his duties and found them full of advice for his lordship on all manner of topics political and domestic. The letters were then burned. While the guardian informed the Earl in general terms about these letters, he did not report what was most vital, though such information surely confirmed that the woman was indeed insane. Every letter was signed Diana, Countess of Salt Hendon.

She had one correspondent who wrote regularly and who did receive her letters of reply. There was a brother, a diplomat, who lived abroad. He wrote from St. Petersburg, long, detailed letters about the growing Russian capital and its environs, its people, and how he occupied his days as an assistant to the Ambassador. He often enclosed small gifts—a fan, a lace-bordered handkerchief, a pair of silk stockings, and for one of her birthdays he sent an embroidered silk shawl. His letters were also full of the latest Court gossip and palace intrigues, and sometimes he included clippings from months-old English newssheets dispatched to him in Russia.

The guardian knew this because his prisoner took great delight in reading these letters aloud. He soon realized that this brother was an astute gentleman because he never mentioned the Earl of Salt Hendon or any member of his family. What the brother knew from his sister's correspondence that the Earl and his family did not, and he, too, kept to himself, was that his sister signed her letters to him as if she was indeed the wife of the Earl of Salt Hendon.

After three years of incarceration, the unnamed person of interest no longer answered to her own name. Nor did she recognize the person she had once been when this person was described to her. She was the Countess of Salt Hendon, and Magnus Sinclair, the Earl of Salt Hendon was her dear husband. There was no persuading her otherwise. The guardian saw no harm in humoring her. After all, she was never to be released.

And so by her fourth year of imprisonment, the unnamed person of interest was in every way treated as if she were indeed the Countess of Salt Hendon. Her guardian, her apothecary, her personal maid, and her servants all addressed her by that title. So, too, did the local townspeople.

For her good behavior, and under strict supervision, she was eventually permitted visitors. Prominent members of the local town came to pay their respects and to see with their own eyes the beautiful noblewoman rumor said had been locked up by a brutish husband. The unnamed person of interest proved to be a gracious hostess, full of charm and grace, and possessing a noble bearing. It was an easy thing for the outsiders to believe they were indeed in the presence of English nobility. She was majestic in velvet and silks, with rubies about her throat and wrists. Her witty conversation was peppered with anecdotes of prominent politicians, exalted noblemen and their relatives, faraway marble palaces, and sleepless cities the local townspeople could only dream about. Soon her ladyship was holding court once a week to a room full of eager listeners.

This, too, the guardian withheld from his reports to his noble employer. Again, he reasoned there was little harm in his prisoner receiving a bunch of ignorant yokels to afternoon tea, who knew no one and were going nowhere. It kept her ladyship pacified, entertained and occupied, her thoughts on trivialities—a far cry from her disposition when first brought to the castle as a venomous abhorrent monster, whose every hate-filled word dripped vengeance and who vowed escape.

What the guardian failed to appreciate, what he could not know and never discovered, was that he was in the presence of a far superior and utterly malevolent intellect. In his confident conceit, that in four years he had tamed a monster and beaten down a beast, he remained ignorant, almost until the last breath left his body. He failed to grasp that just under the surface of her beautiful façade, the perfumed silks, the witty conversation, and the charming manners, the monster still lurked, biding its time, awaiting the perfect opportunity to escape and unleash its vengeance.

The horror of realization came the day the guardian was racked with stomach cramp and fell into a fever. The local apothecary thought it food poisoning and prescribed an emetic. A great favorite with her ladyship, whom he had treated for megrim for some months, the apothecary left the guardian in her capable hands. He advised he would return the following day. By nightfall, the guardian was dead. In his last conscious moments, he was blind and incapable of speech, but he could still hear. Her ladyship whispered at his ear as she gently tucked up his coverlet. The servants thought it a touching scene, an indication of her lady-ship's high regard for her guardian.

In truth, she gleefully whispered she had poisoned him. Every speck of megrim powder the apothecary had prescribed she had carefully stored up until she had harvested enough to administer a lethal dose. She loathed him and she hoped he was in agony. Her greatest hatred she kept stored for the woman she believed falsely paraded about society as the wife and Countess of the Earl of Salt

Hendon. She had spent four years devising her scheme for retribution and now, with freedom, she would put her plan into effect.

Upon the guardian's death, the unknown person of interest did not immediately flee. She mourned his passing, wearing dove gray petticoats and inviting the local townspeople to a dinner in his honor. Then, after the guardian's burial, a courier arrived in the dead of night. It was so late the horse's hooves on the cobblestones did not wake the servants. However, a restless maid heard voices echoing in the courtyard and was up, pressing her nose to the windowpane in time to see her ladyship in her nightgown and slippers, taper in hand, scurry under the arch and enter by the big oak door. She held a sealed packet.

The late-night letter was from the Earl begging her to return to him. He had been bewitched by a whore of a mistress, and with her death, so died her influence over him. To his shame, he now recognized his great wrongdoing in sending his devoted wife into exile. Could she forgive him? Would she come back to him? He could not wait to be reconciled and would ride to meet her at the Welsh border. She was to hurry with all speed.

The servants, the apothecary and, indeed, those prominent townspeople who counted themselves friends of the Countess of Salt Hendon, all knew word for word the contents of the Earl's letter, for she joyfully announced the news to them and showed them the letter. The apothecary did not doubt the seal and hand-writing belonged to the illustrious Earl of Salt Hendon. There was much rejoicing, and the townspeople held a celebratory dinner to honor Lady Salt and wish her well, to which she wore her most magnificent gown and jewelry.

Holland covers draped furniture, and trunks and portman-teaux were packed to bursting. A splendid carriage pulled by four high-spirited grays took up Lady Salt and her personal maid, and her ladyship was farewelled with much fanfare. She was never seen again.

Two days following her departure a letter arrived. It was from Sir Antony Templestowe, and it had traveled all the way from St. Petersburg.

The apothecary, who had stayed on at the castle to settle her ladyship's small pile of accounts with money the dead guardian had for that purpose, did not know what was to be done with the letter. It was addressed to a Diana, Lady St. John, a person unknown to the apothecary, and yet the direction was correct.

Perhaps the correspondent did not personally know Lady Salt.

He had correctly identified her Christian name, but then become confused when writing her title. It was a mystery to the apothecary. Still, he would do his duty by her ladyship, and so he redirected the unopened letter to the Earl of Salt Hendon's estate, Salt Hall in Wiltshire, which he had heard Lady Salt talk of so many times he felt he had visited the grand Jacobean mansion and its spacious parkland.

As Sir Antony had provided his direction in St. Petersburg, the apothecary wrote him a civil letter. He explained what he had done with his letter and, presuming he knew Lady Salt because he had used her Christian name, he took the liberty of giving Sir Antony the good news: Her ladyship had departed Harlech Castle and was on her way to be reunited with her noble lord the Earl of Salt Hendon.

A month later, Sir Antony received the apothecary's letter. Upon reading it, he promptly threw up.

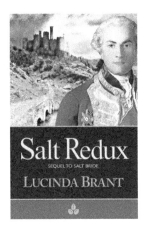